CREATED BY
DANIEL WARREN JOHNSON

DANIEL WARREN JOHNSON
CREATOR, WRITER, ARTIST

MIKE SPICER
COLORIST

RUS WOOTON
LETTERER

ARIELLE BASICH
ASSOCIATE EDITOR

SEAN MACKIEWICZ
EDITOR

DANIEL WARREN JOHNSON & MIKE SPICER
COVER

For Rachel. Thank you for fighting for me.

FOR SKYBOUND ENTERTAINMENT

Robert Kirkman *Chairman*
David Alpert *CEO*
Sean Mackiewicz *SVP, Editor-in-Chief*
Shawn Kirkham *SVP, Business Development*
Brian Huntington *Online Editorial Director*
June Alian *Publicity Director*
Andres Juarez *Art Director*
Jon Moisan *Editor*
Arielle Basich *Associate Editor*
Carina Taylor *Production Artist*
Paul Shin *Business Development Coordinator*
Johnny O'Dell *Social Media Manager*
Sally Jacka *Skybound Retailer Relations*
Dan Petersen *Director of Operations & Events*
Nick Palmer *Operations Coordinator*

International Inquiries: ag@sequentialrights.com
Licensing Inquiries: contact@skybound.com
WWW.SKYBOUND.COM

IMAGE COMICS, INC.

Robert Kirkman—Chief Operating Officer
Erik Larsen—Chief Financial Officer
Todd McFarlane—President
Marc Silvestri—Chief Executive Officer
Jim Valentino—Vice President

Eric Stephenson—Publisher / Chief Creative Officer
Corey Hart—Director of Sales
Jeff Boison—Director of Publishing Planning & Book Trade Sales
Chris Ross—Director of Digital Sales
Jeff Stang—Director of Specialty Sales
Kat Salazar—Director of PR & Marketing
Drew Gill—Art Director
Heather Doornink—Production Director
Nicole Lapalme—Controller

IMAGECOMICS.COM

EXTREMITY VOLUME 2: WARRIOR. FIRST PRINTING. May 2018. Published by Image Comics, Inc. Office of publication: 2701 NW Vaughn St., Ste. 780, Portland, OR 97210. Originally published in single magazine form as EXTREMITY #7-12.

For information regarding the CPSIA on this printed material call: 203-595-3636 and provide reference # RICH – 785831. ISBN: 978-1-5343-0649-3

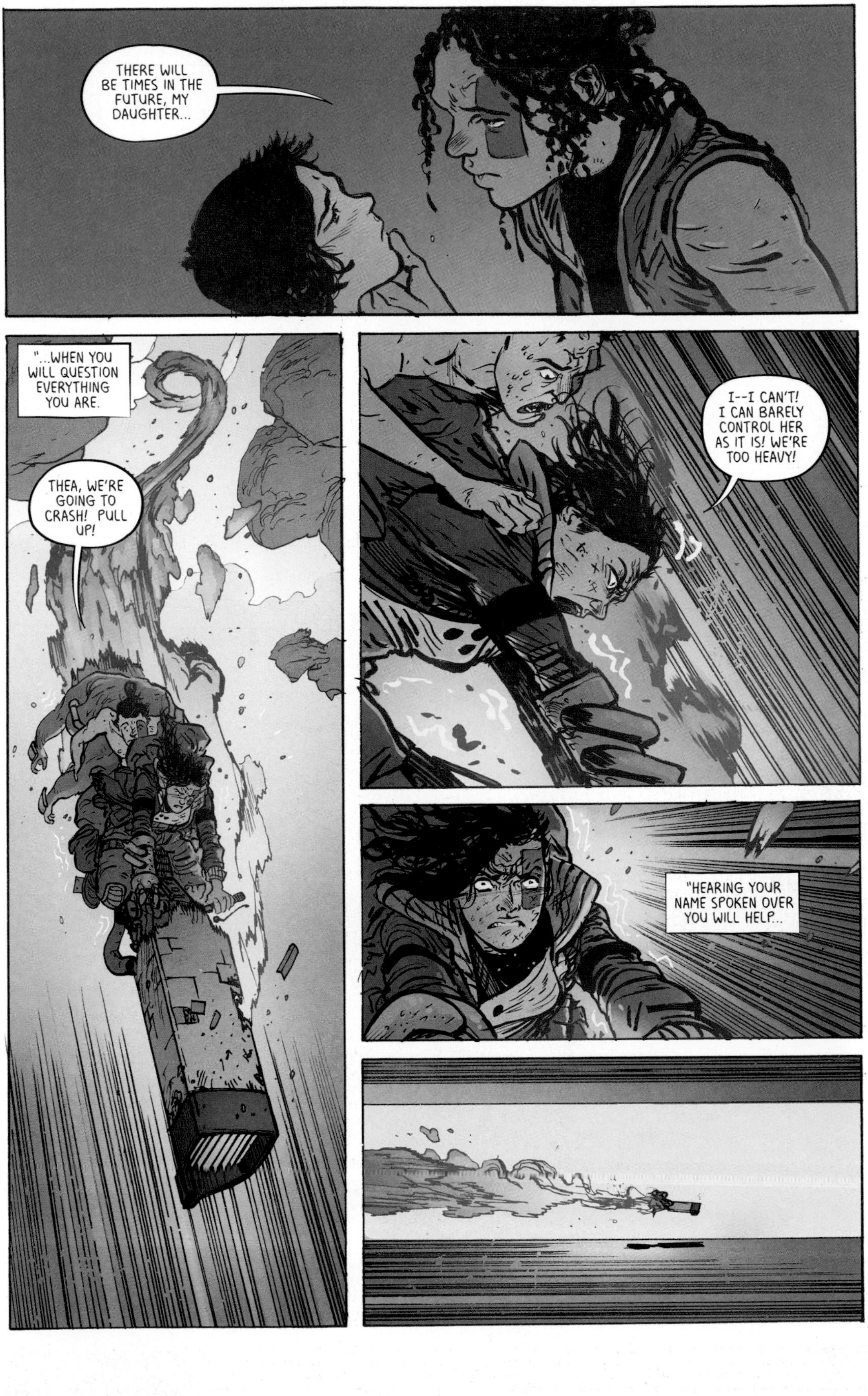
THERE WILL BE TIMES IN THE FUTURE, MY DAUGHTER...
"...WHEN YOU WILL QUESTION EVERYTHING YOU ARE.
THEA, WE'RE GOING TO CRASH! PULL UP!
I--I CAN'T! I CAN BARELY CONTROL HER AS IT IS! WE'RE TOO HEAVY!
"HEARING YOUR NAME SPOKEN OVER YOU WILL HELP...

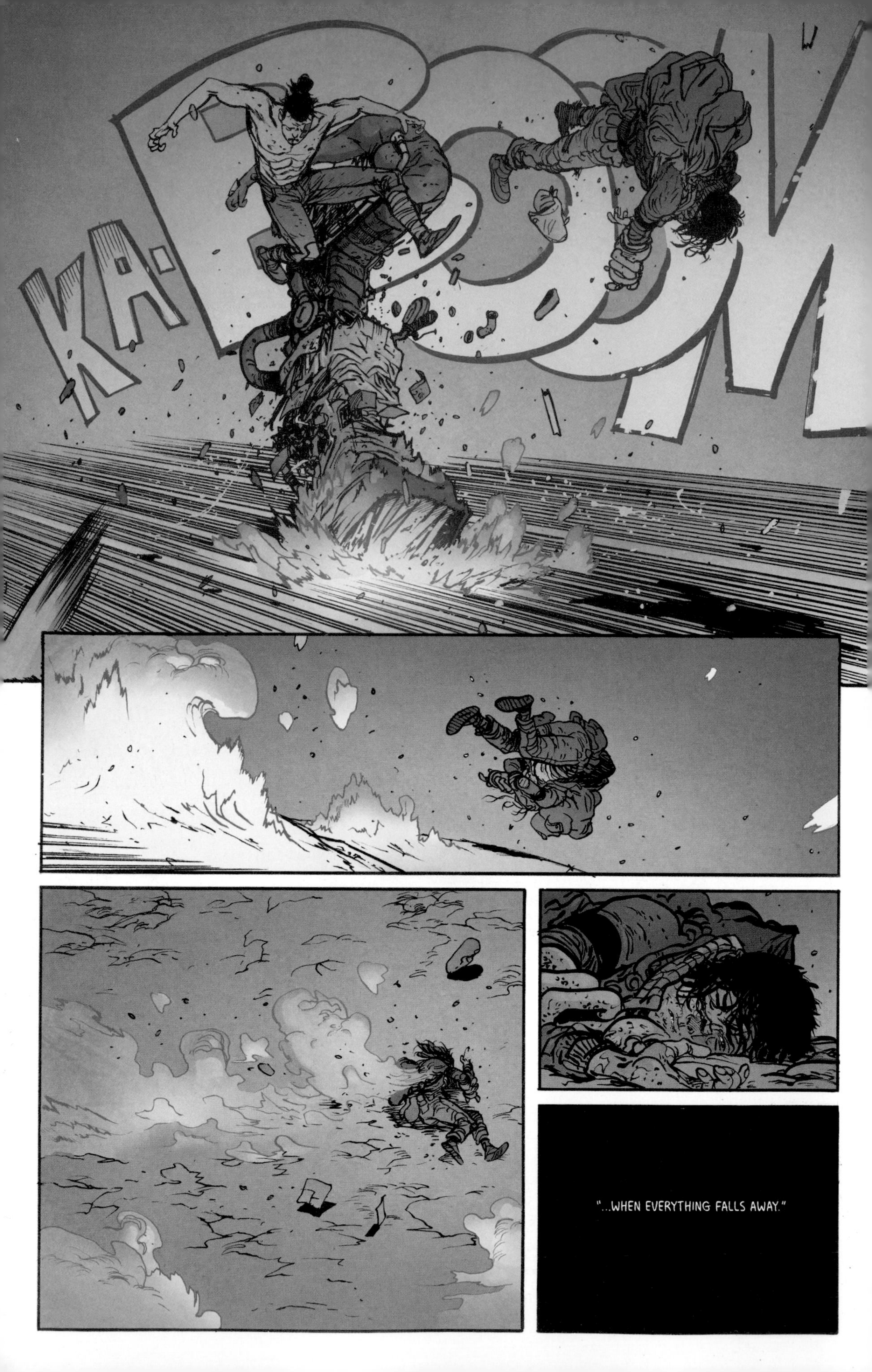
KA-BOOM
"...WHEN EVERYTHING FALLS AWAY."

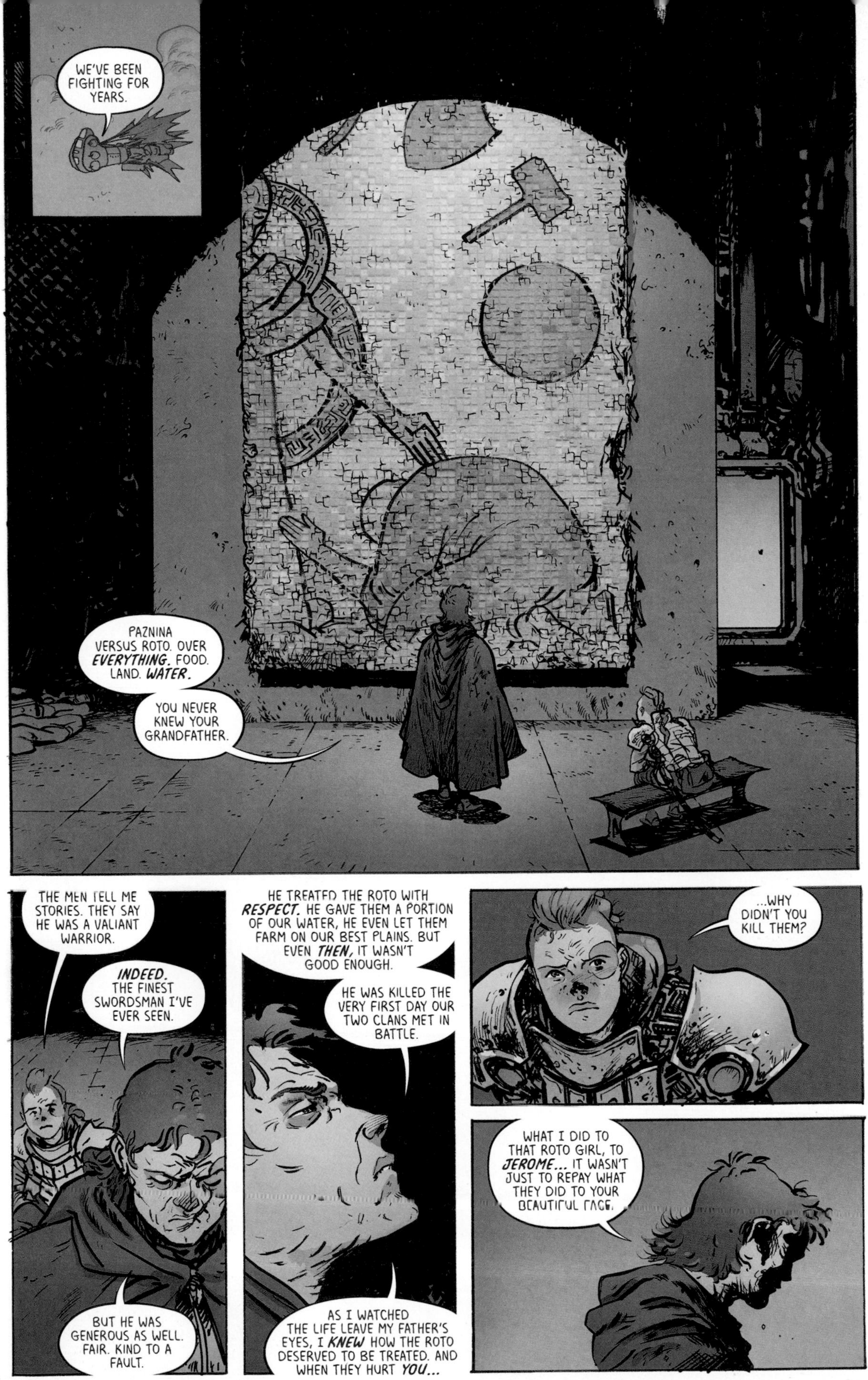
WE'VE BEEN FIGHTING FOR YEARS.
PAZNINA VERSUS ROTO. OVER *EVERYTHING.* FOOD. LAND. *WATER.*
YOU NEVER KNEW YOUR GRANDFATHER.
THE MEN TELL ME STORIES. THEY SAY HE WAS A VALIANT WARRIOR.
INDEED. THE FINEST SWORDSMAN I'VE EVER SEEN.
BUT HE WAS GENEROUS AS WELL. FAIR. KIND TO A FAULT.
HE TREATED THE ROTO WITH *RESPECT.* HE GAVE THEM A PORTION OF OUR WATER, HE EVEN LET THEM FARM ON OUR BEST PLAINS. BUT EVEN *THEN,* IT WASN'T GOOD ENOUGH.
HE WAS KILLED THE VERY FIRST DAY OUR TWO CLANS MET IN BATTLE.
AS I WATCHED THE LIFE LEAVE MY FATHER'S EYES, I *KNEW* HOW THE ROTO DESERVED TO BE TREATED. AND WHEN THEY HURT *YOU...*
...WHY DIDN'T YOU KILL THEM?
WHAT I DID TO THAT ROTO GIRL, TO *JEROME...* IT WASN'T JUST TO REPAY WHAT THEY DID TO YOUR BEAUTIFUL FACE.

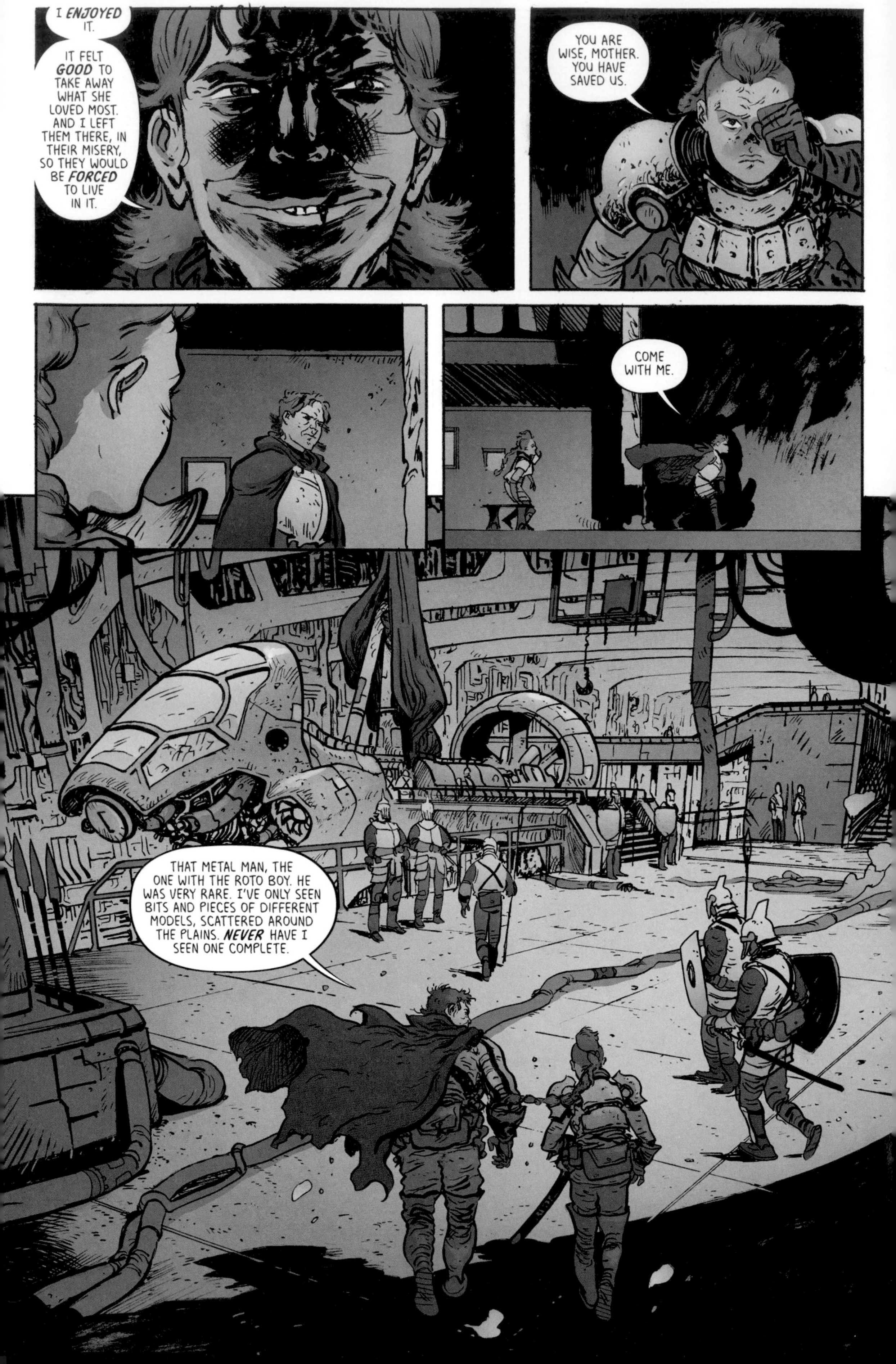
I ENJOYED IT.
IT FELT GOOD TO TAKE AWAY WHAT SHE LOVED MOST. AND I LEFT THEM THERE, IN THEIR MISERY, SO THEY WOULD BE FORCED TO LIVE IN IT.
YOU ARE WISE, MOTHER. YOU HAVE SAVED US.
COME WITH ME.
THAT METAL MAN, THE ONE WITH THE ROTO BOY. HE WAS VERY RARE. I'VE ONLY SEEN BITS AND PIECES OF DIFFERENT MODELS, SCATTERED AROUND THE PLAINS. NEVER HAVE I SEEN ONE COMPLETE.

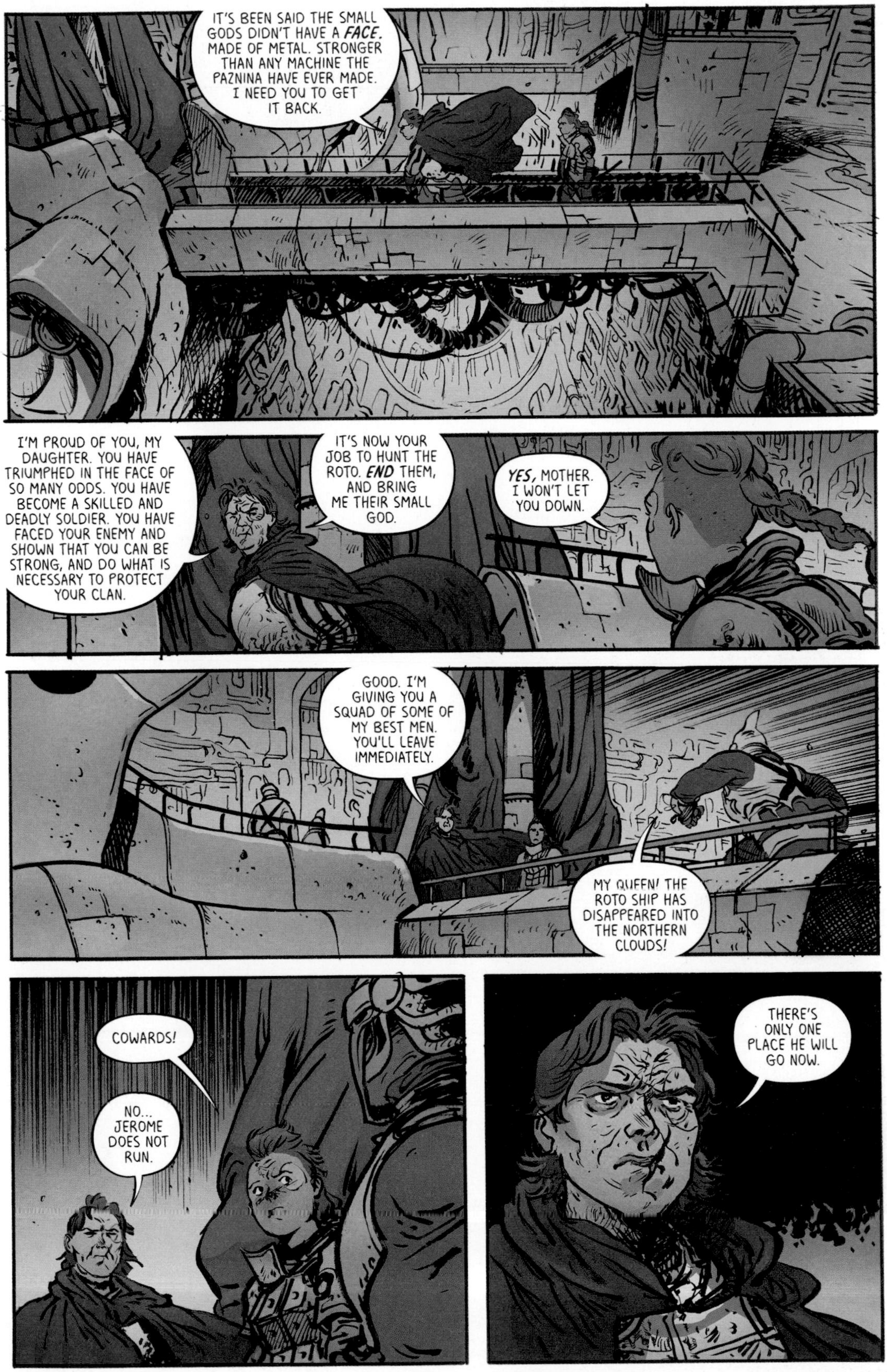
IT'S BEEN SAID THE SMALL GODS DIDN'T HAVE A FACE. MADE OF METAL. STRONGER THAN ANY MACHINE THE PAZNINA HAVE EVER MADE. I NEED YOU TO GET IT BACK.
I'M PROUD OF YOU, MY DAUGHTER. YOU HAVE TRIUMPHED IN THE FACE OF SO MANY ODDS. YOU HAVE BECOME A SKILLED AND DEADLY SOLDIER. YOU HAVE FACED YOUR ENEMY AND SHOWN THAT YOU CAN BE STRONG, AND DO WHAT IS NECESSARY TO PROTECT YOUR CLAN.
IT'S NOW YOUR JOB TO HUNT THE ROTO. END THEM, AND BRING ME THEIR SMALL GOD.
YES, MOTHER. I WON'T LET YOU DOWN.
GOOD. I'M GIVING YOU A SQUAD OF SOME OF MY BEST MEN. YOU'LL LEAVE IMMEDIATELY.
MY QUEEN! THE ROTO SHIP HAS DISAPPEARED INTO THE NORTHERN CLOUDS!
COWARDS!
NO... JEROME DOES NOT RUN.
THERE'S ONLY ONE PLACE HE WILL GO NOW.

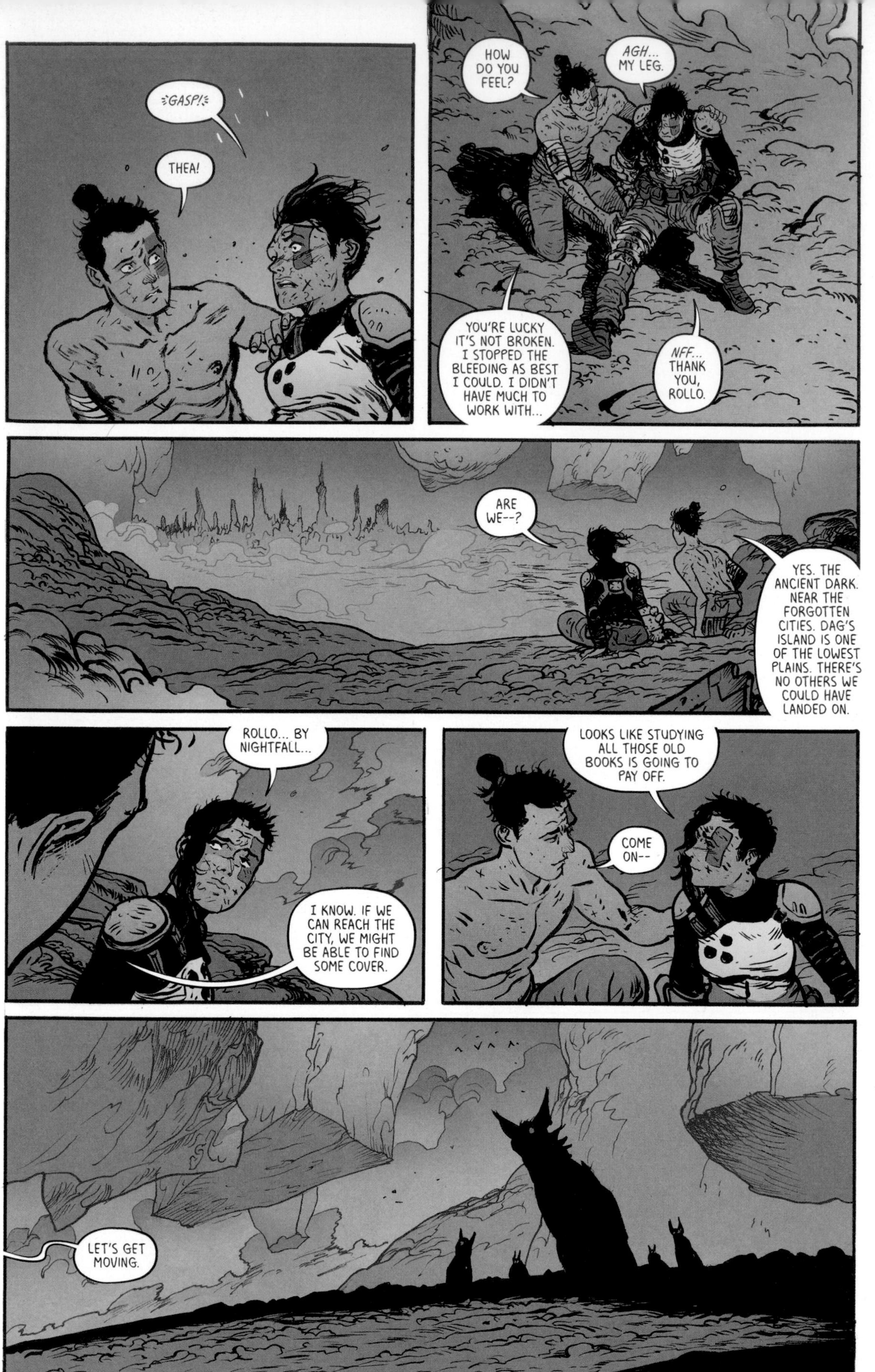
GASP!
THEA!
HOW DO YOU FEEL?
AGH... MY LEG.
YOU'RE LUCKY IT'S NOT BROKEN. I STOPPED THE BLEEDING AS BEST I COULD. I DIDN'T HAVE MUCH TO WORK WITH...
NFF... THANK YOU, ROLLO.
ARE WE--?
YES. THE ANCIENT DARK. NEAR THE FORGOTTEN CITIES. DAG'S ISLAND IS ONE OF THE LOWEST PLAINS. THERE'S NO OTHERS WE COULD HAVE LANDED ON.
ROLLO... BY NIGHTFALL...
I KNOW. IF WE CAN REACH THE CITY, WE MIGHT BE ABLE TO FIND SOME COVER.
LOOKS LIKE STUDYING ALL THOSE OLD BOOKS IS GOING TO PAY OFF.
COME ON--
LET'S GET MOVING.

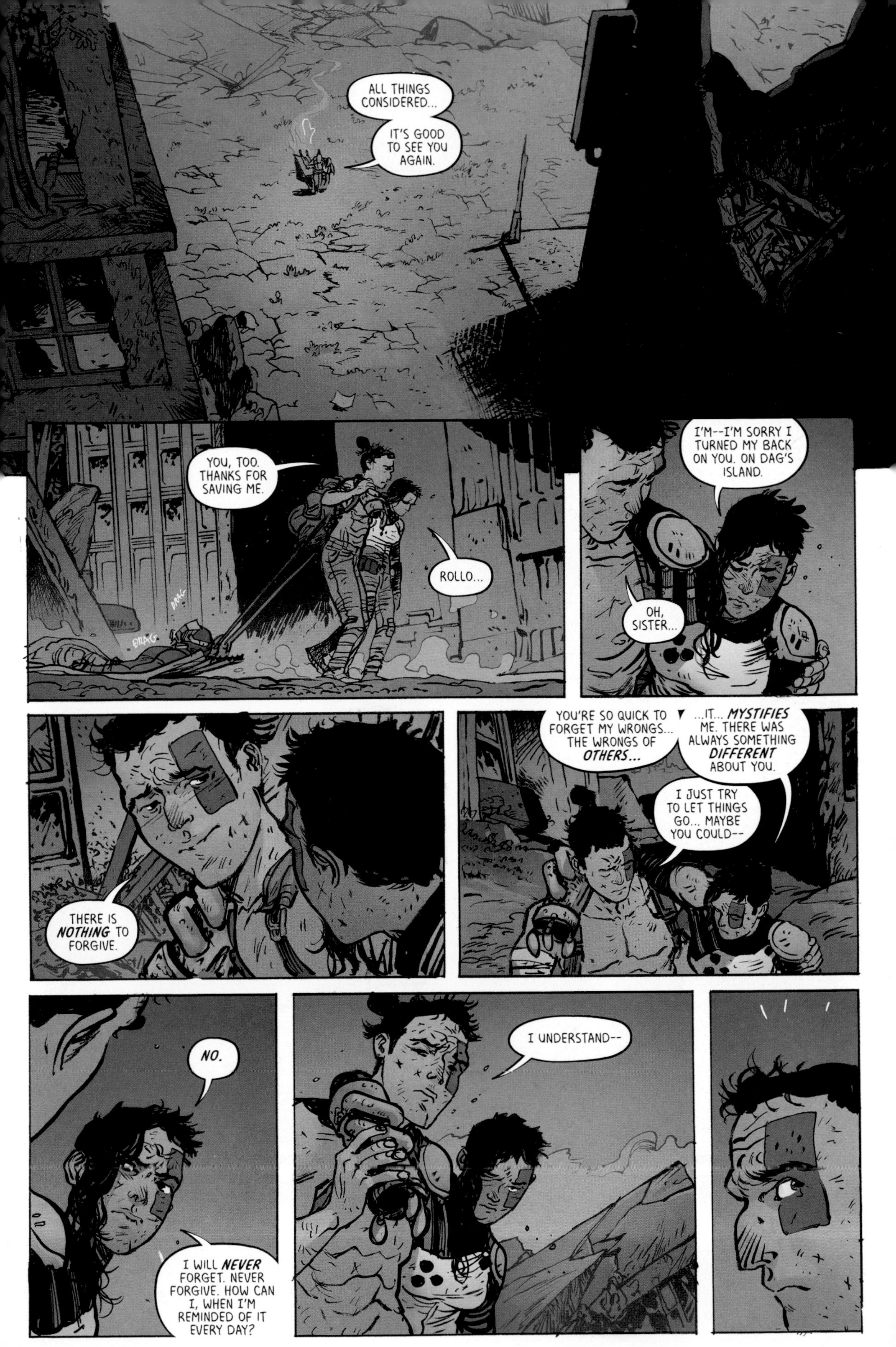
ALL THINGS CONSIDERED...
IT'S GOOD TO SEE YOU AGAIN.
YOU, TOO. THANKS FOR SAVING ME.
ROLLO...
DRAG
DRAG
I'M--I'M SORRY I TURNED MY BACK ON YOU. ON DAG'S ISLAND.
OH, SISTER...
THERE IS *NOTHING* TO FORGIVE.
YOU'RE SO QUICK TO FORGET MY WRONGS... THE WRONGS OF *OTHERS...*
...IT... *MYSTIFIES* ME. THERE WAS ALWAYS SOMETHING *DIFFERENT* ABOUT YOU.
I JUST TRY TO LET THINGS GO... MAYBE YOU COULD--
NO.
I WILL *NEVER* FORGET. NEVER FORGIVE. HOW CAN I, WHEN I'M REMINDED OF IT EVERY DAY?
I UNDERSTAND--

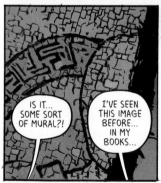

IS IT... SOME SORT OF MURAL?!

I'VE SEEN THIS IMAGE BEFORE... IN MY BOOKS...

IT'S OF THE OLD GOD, DESIDEN. AFTER WATCHING THE WORLD BE DESTROYED BY WAR.

...I WONDER WHAT THESE MARKINGS STAND FOR...?

ROLLO...

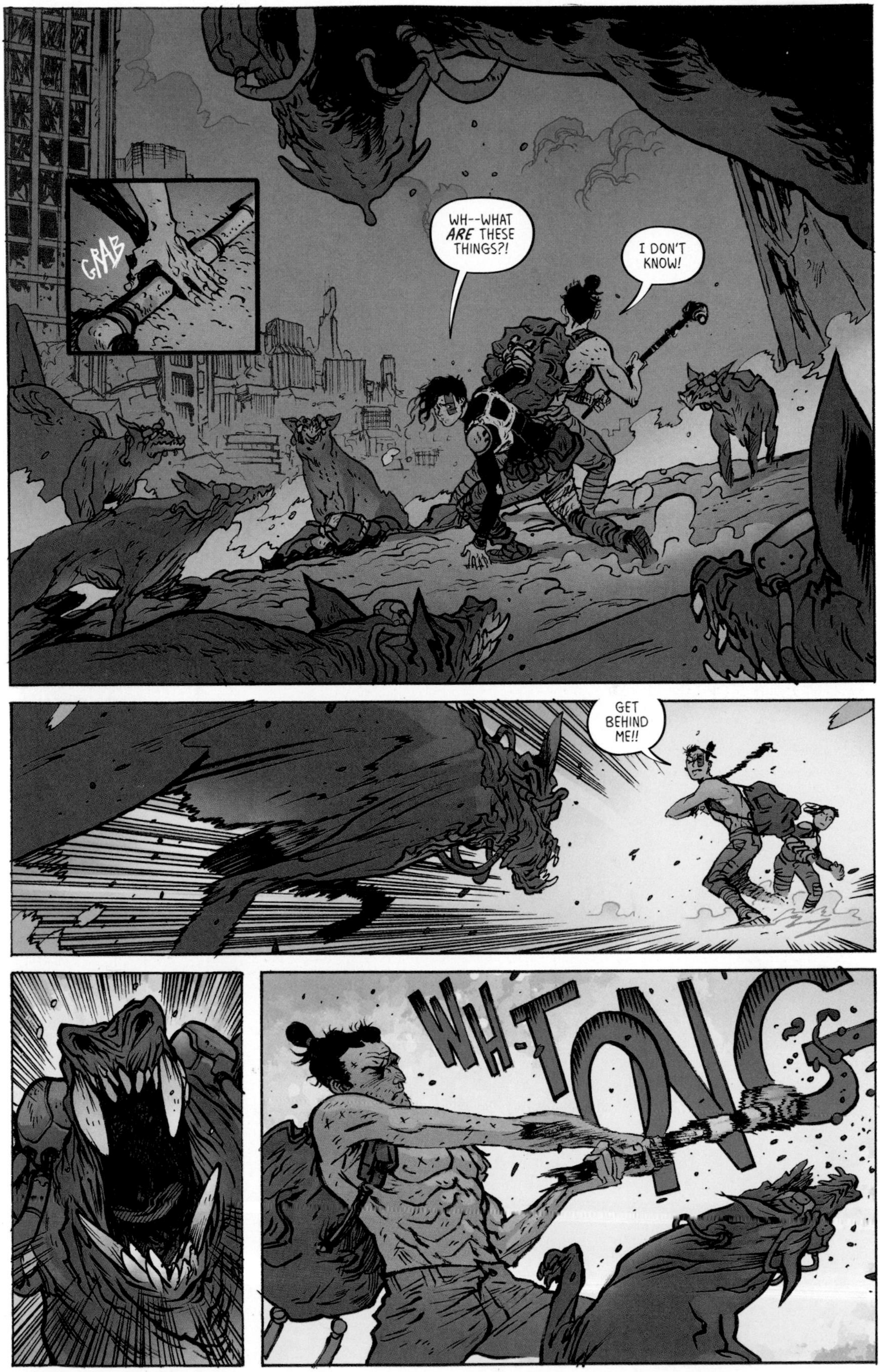
GRAB
WH--WHAT ARE THESE THINGS?!
I DON'T KNOW!
GET BEHIND ME!!
WH-TONG

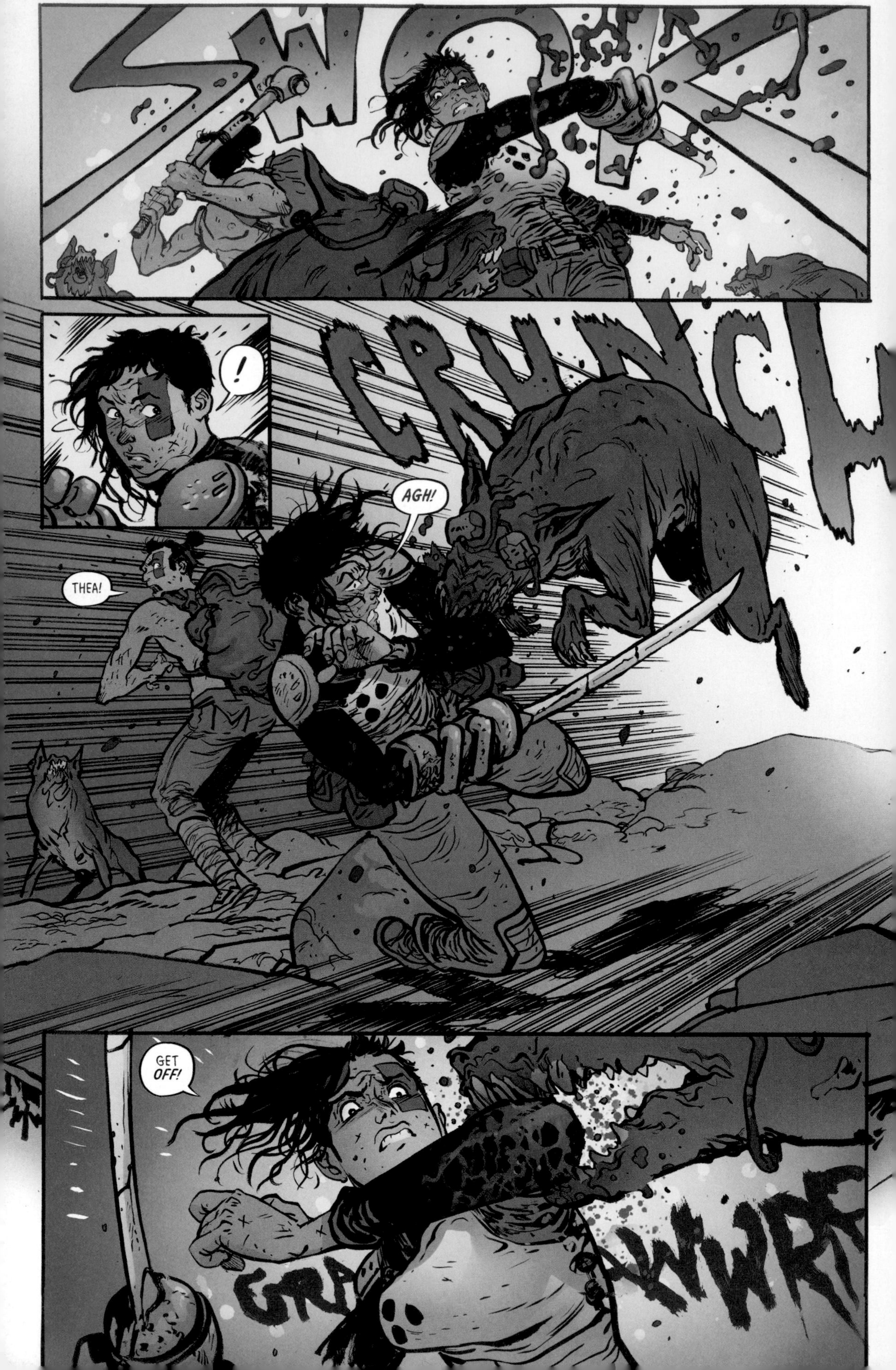
SWOK
!
CRUNCH
AGH!
THEA!
GET OFF!
GRAWWRF

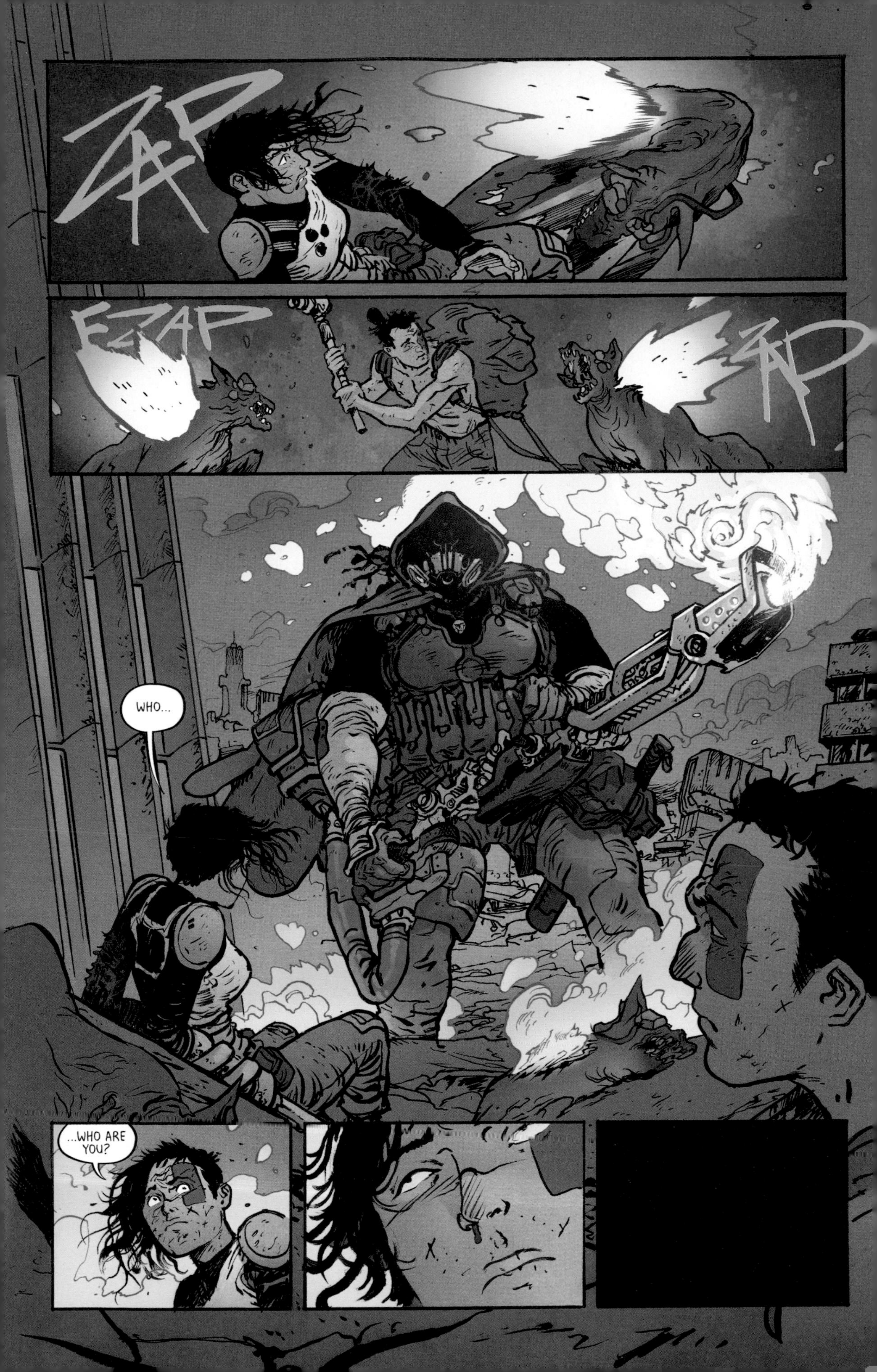
ZAP
FZZAP
ZAP
WHO...
...WHO ARE YOU?

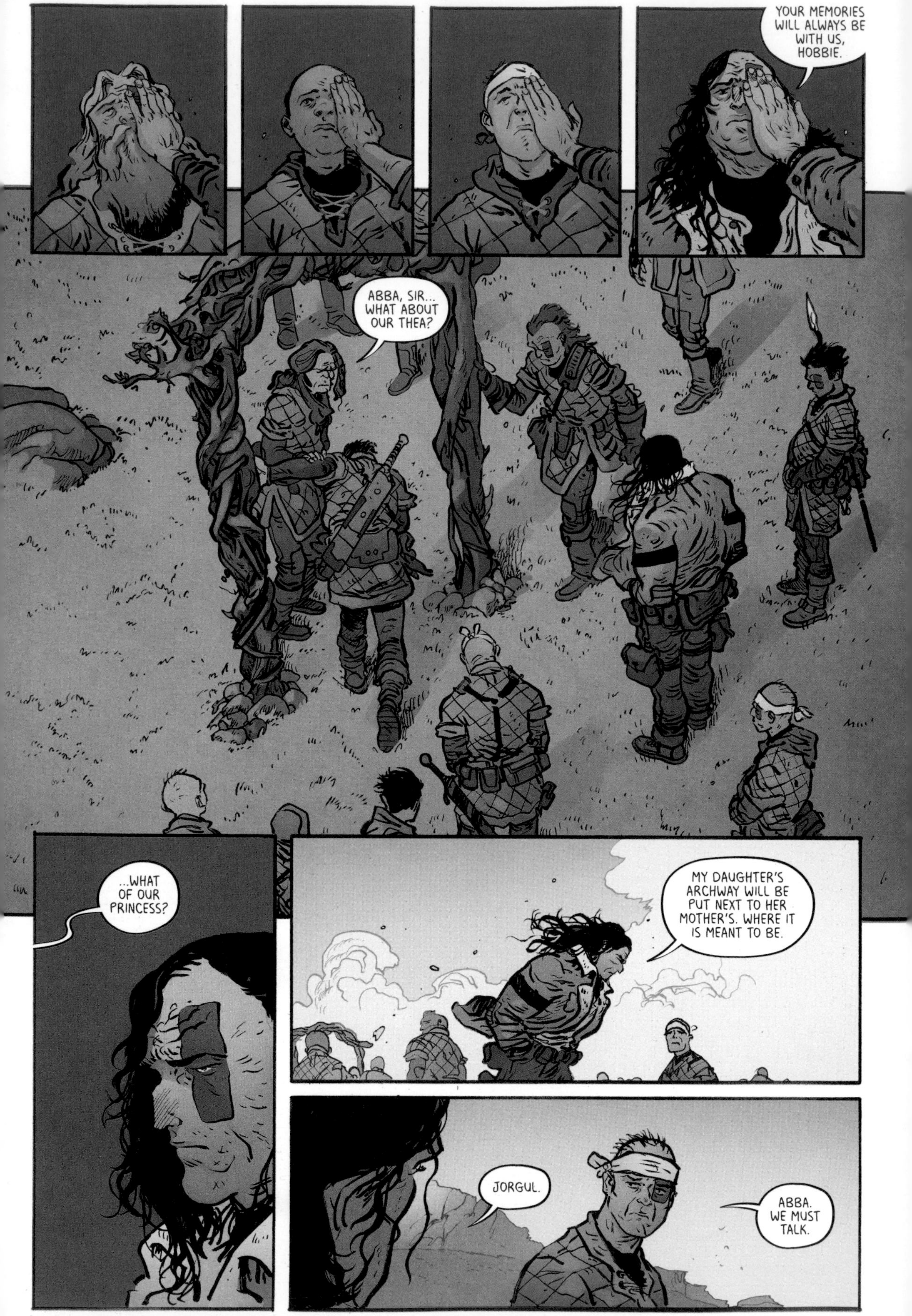
YOUR MEMORIES WILL ALWAYS BE WITH US, HOBBIE.
ABBA, SIR... WHAT ABOUT OUR THEA?
...WHAT OF OUR PRINCESS?
MY DAUGHTER'S ARCHWAY WILL BE PUT NEXT TO HER MOTHER'S. WHERE IT IS MEANT TO BE.
JORGUL.
ABBA. WE MUST TALK.

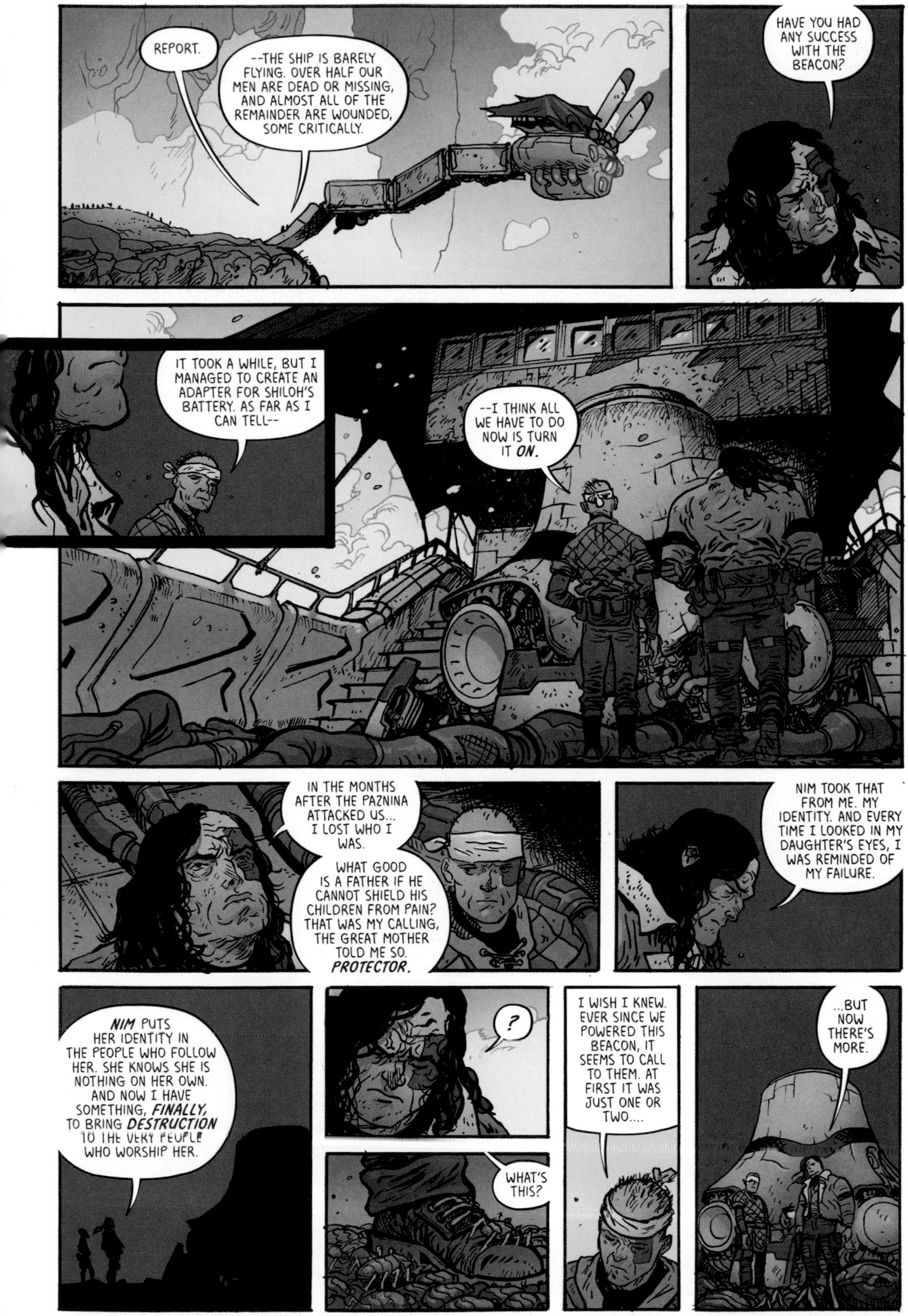
REPORT.
--THE SHIP IS BARELY FLYING. OVER HALF OUR MEN ARE DEAD OR MISSING, AND ALMOST ALL OF THE REMAINDER ARE WOUNDED, SOME CRITICALLY.
HAVE YOU HAD ANY SUCCESS WITH THE BEACON?
IT TOOK A WHILE, BUT I MANAGED TO CREATE AN ADAPTER FOR SHILOH'S BATTERY. AS FAR AS I CAN TELL--
--I THINK ALL WE HAVE TO DO NOW IS TURN IT ON.
IN THE MONTHS AFTER THE PAZNINA ATTACKED US... I LOST WHO I WAS.
WHAT GOOD IS A FATHER IF HE CANNOT SHIELD HIS CHILDREN FROM PAIN? THAT WAS MY CALLING, THE GREAT MOTHER TOLD ME SO. PROTECTOR.
NIM TOOK THAT FROM ME. MY IDENTITY. AND EVERY TIME I LOOKED IN MY DAUGHTER'S EYES, I WAS REMINDED OF MY FAILURE.
NIM PUTS HER IDENTITY IN THE PEOPLE WHO FOLLOW HER. SHE KNOWS SHE IS NOTHING ON HER OWN. AND NOW I HAVE SOMETHING, FINALLY, TO BRING DESTRUCTION TO THE VERY PEOPLE WHO WORSHIP HER.
?
WHAT'S THIS?
I WISH I KNEW. EVER SINCE WE POWERED THIS BEACON, IT SEEMS TO CALL TO THEM. AT FIRST IT WAS JUST ONE OR TWO....
...BUT NOW THERE'S MORE.

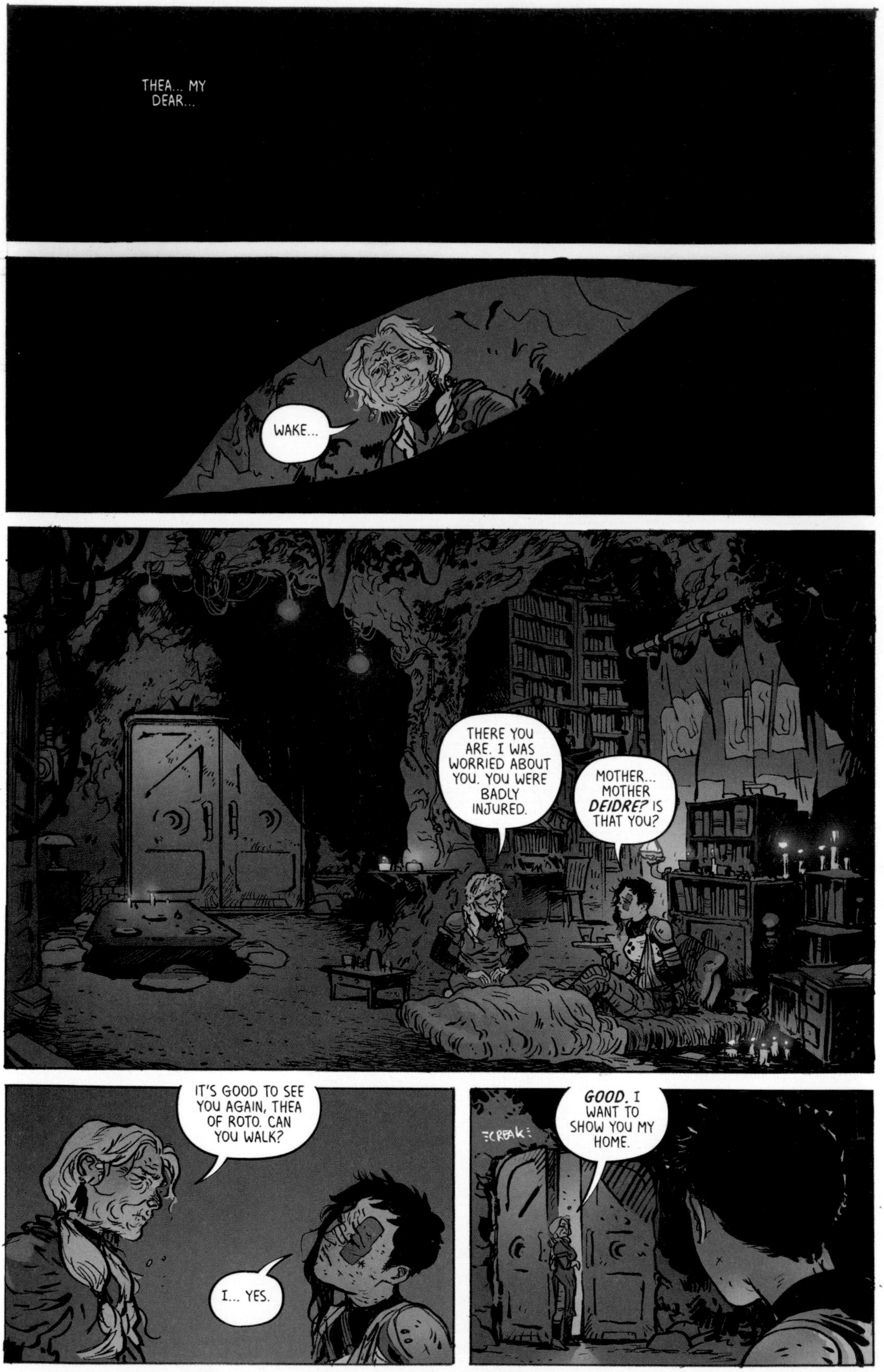
THEA... MY DEAR...
WAKE...
THERE YOU ARE. I WAS WORRIED ABOUT YOU. YOU WERE BADLY INJURED.
MOTHER... MOTHER *DEIDRE?* IS THAT YOU?
IT'S GOOD TO SEE YOU AGAIN, THEA OF ROTO. CAN YOU WALK?
I... YES.
CREAK
GOOD. I WANT TO SHOW YOU MY HOME.

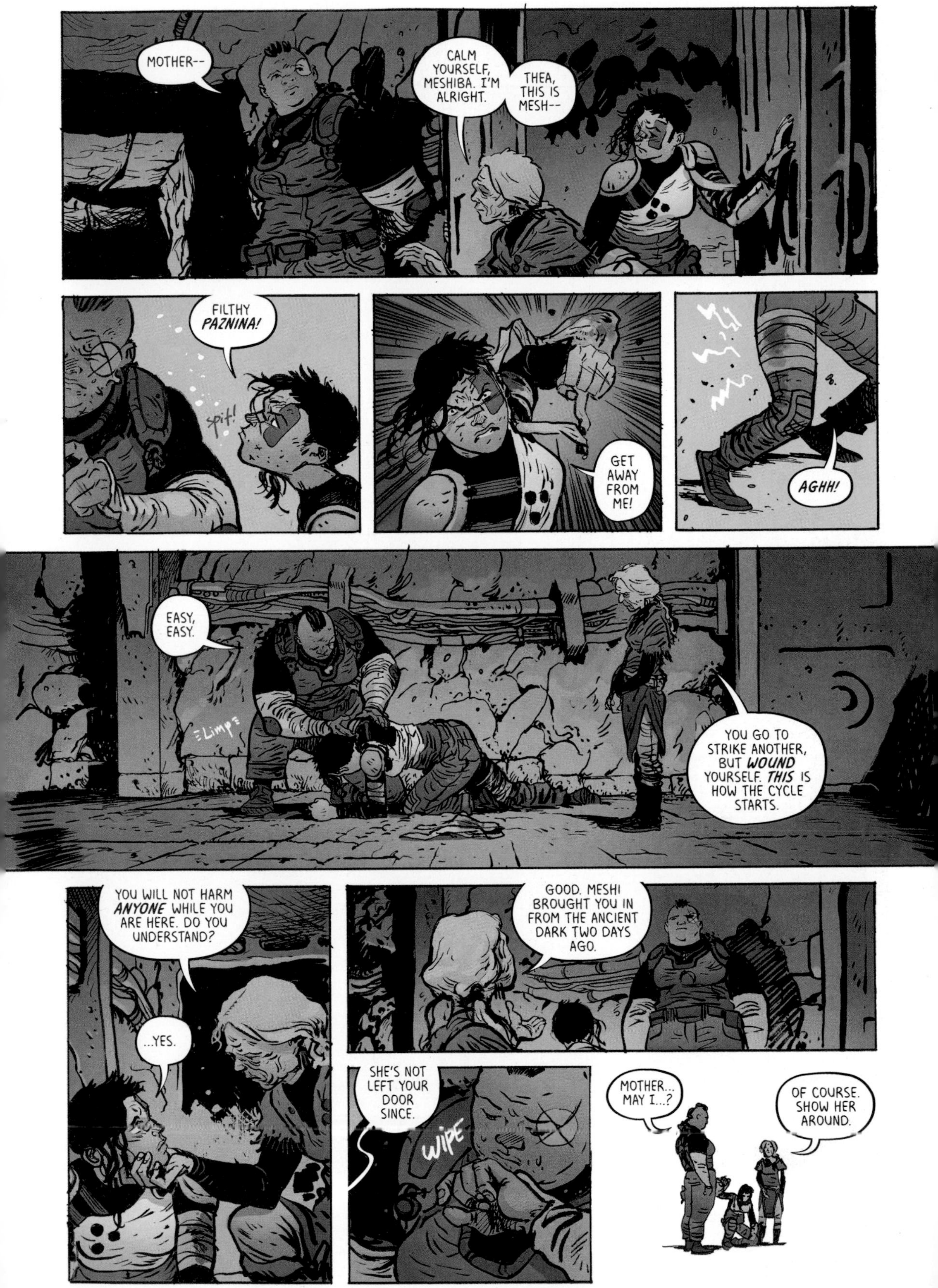
MOTHER--
CALM YOURSELF, MESHIBA. I'M ALRIGHT.
THEA, THIS IS MESH--
FILTHY PAZNINA!
spit!
GET AWAY FROM ME!
AGHH!
EASY, EASY.
LIMP
YOU GO TO STRIKE ANOTHER, BUT WOUND YOURSELF. THIS IS HOW THE CYCLE STARTS.
YOU WILL NOT HARM ANYONE WHILE YOU ARE HERE. DO YOU UNDERSTAND?
...YES.
GOOD. MESHI BROUGHT YOU IN FROM THE ANCIENT DARK TWO DAYS AGO.
SHE'S NOT LEFT YOUR DOOR SINCE.
WIPE
MOTHER... MAY I...?
OF COURSE. SHOW HER AROUND.

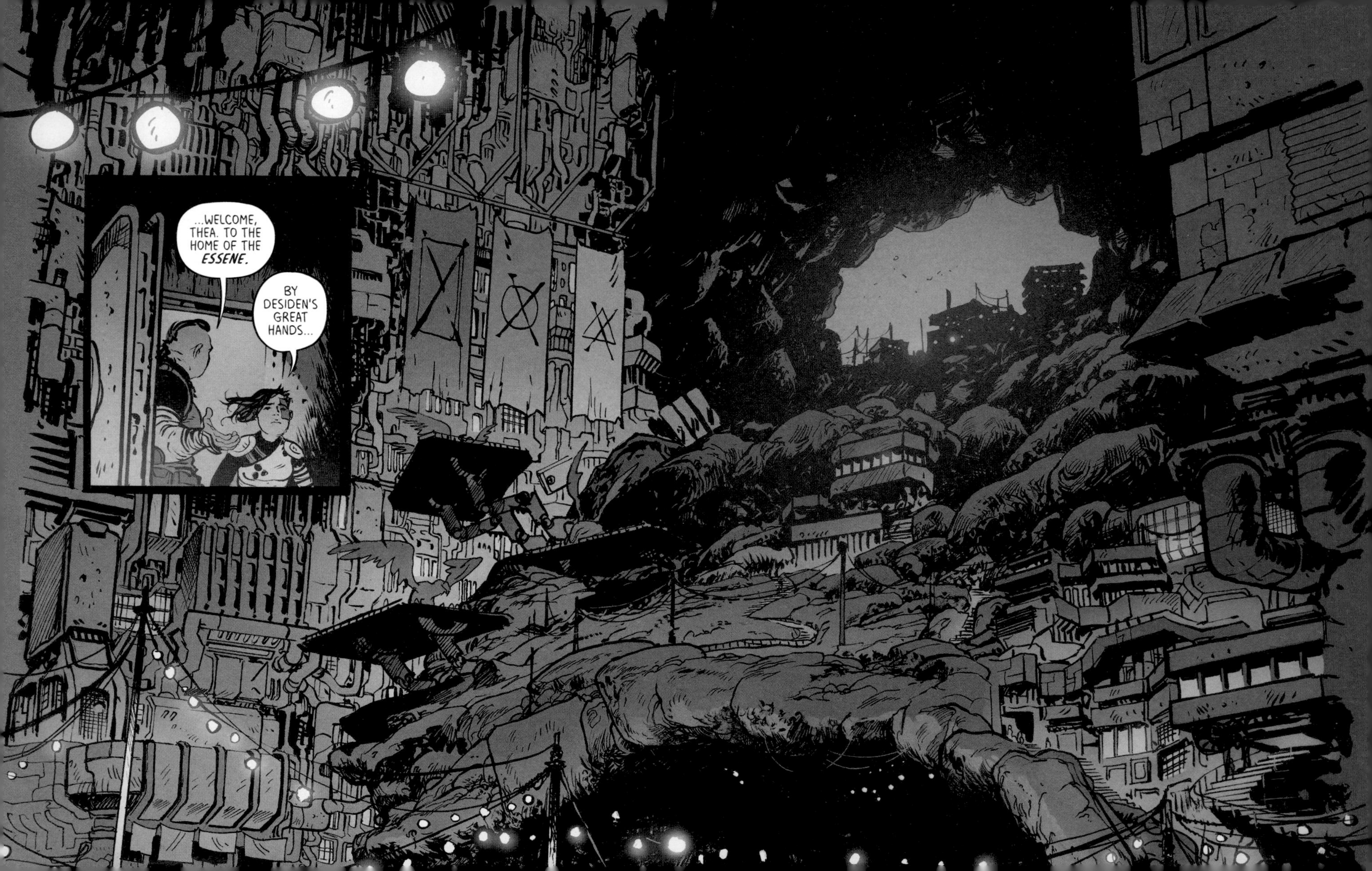
...WELCOME, THEA. TO THE HOME OF THE ESSENE.
BY DESIDEN'S GREAT HANDS...

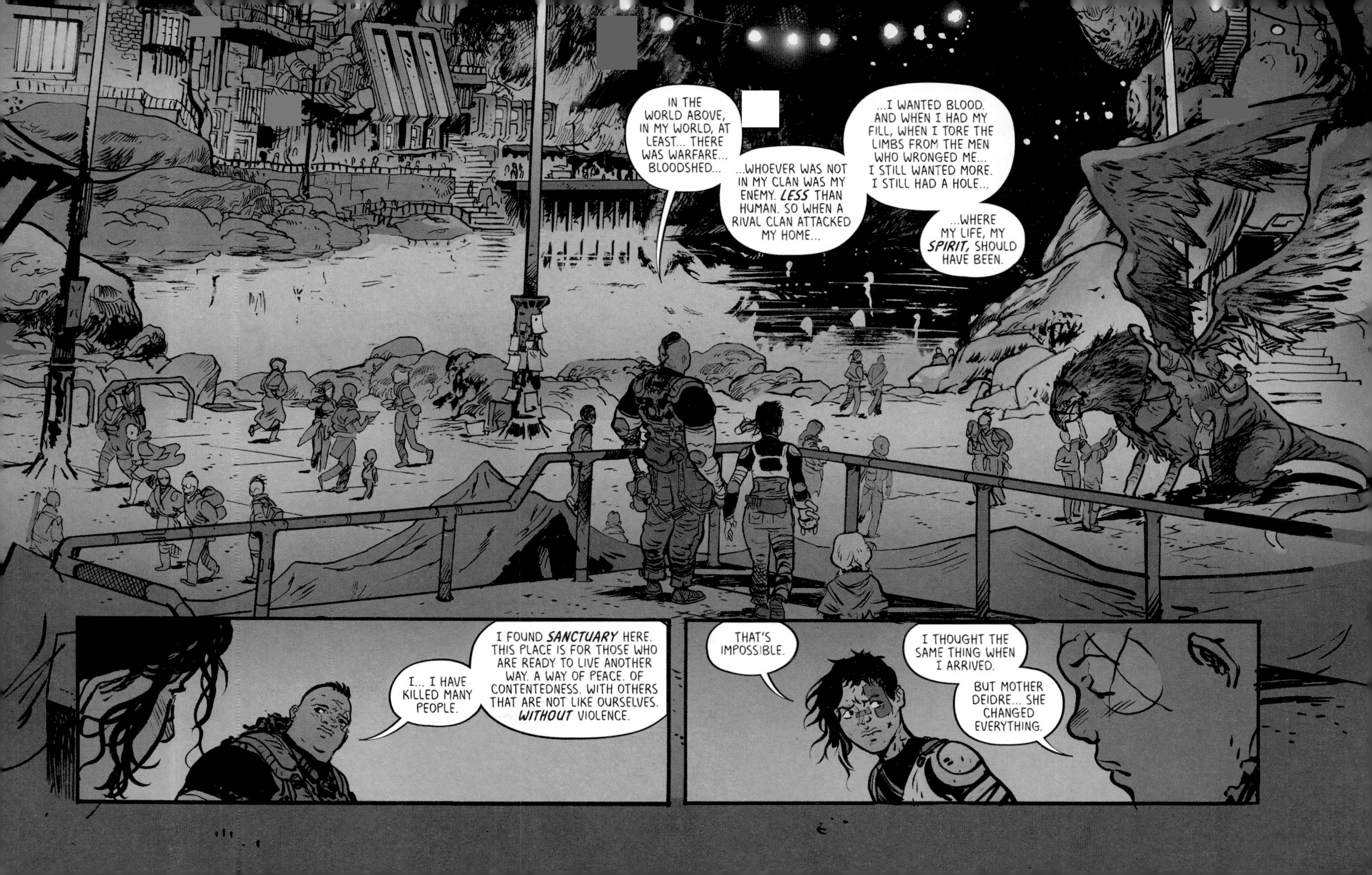
IN THE WORLD ABOVE, IN MY WORLD, AT LEAST... THERE WAS WARFARE... BLOODSHED...
...WHOEVER WAS NOT IN MY CLAN WAS MY ENEMY. *LESS* THAN HUMAN. SO WHEN A RIVAL CLAN ATTACKED MY HOME...
...I WANTED BLOOD. AND WHEN I HAD MY FILL, WHEN I TORE THE LIMBS FROM THE MEN WHO WRONGED ME... I STILL WANTED MORE. I STILL HAD A HOLE...
...WHERE MY LIFE, MY *SPIRIT,* SHOULD HAVE BEEN.
I FOUND *SANCTUARY* HERE. THIS PLACE IS FOR THOSE WHO ARE READY TO LIVE ANOTHER WAY. A WAY OF PEACE. OF CONTENTEDNESS. WITH OTHERS THAT ARE NOT LIKE OURSELVES. *WITHOUT* VIOLENCE.
I... I HAVE KILLED MANY PEOPLE.
THAT'S IMPOSSIBLE.
I THOUGHT THE SAME THING WHEN I ARRIVED.
BUT MOTHER DEIDRE... SHE CHANGED EVERYTHING.

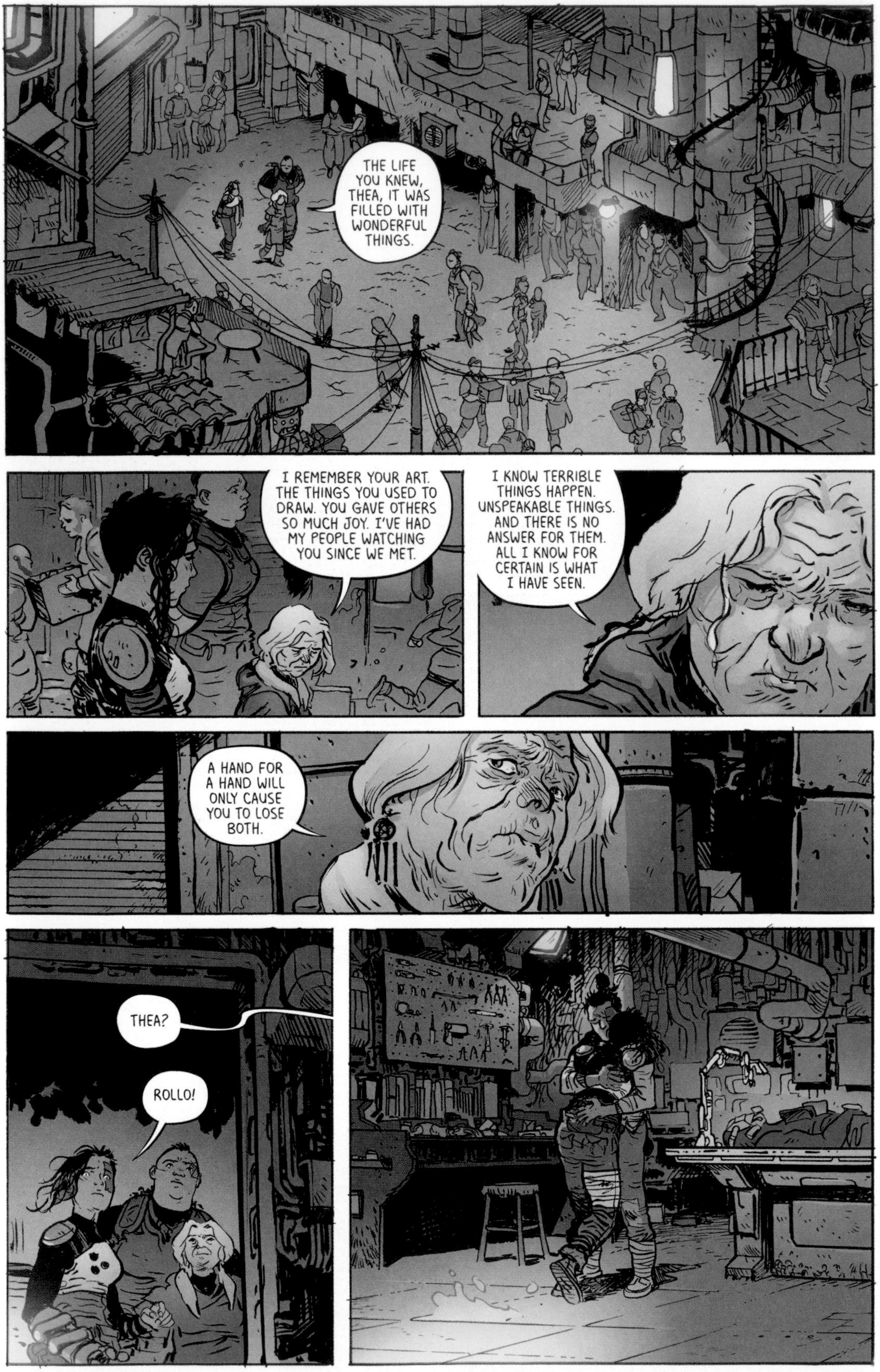
THE LIFE YOU KNEW, THEA, IT WAS FILLED WITH WONDERFUL THINGS.
I REMEMBER YOUR ART. THE THINGS YOU USED TO DRAW. YOU GAVE OTHERS SO MUCH JOY. I'VE HAD MY PEOPLE WATCHING YOU SINCE WE MET.
I KNOW TERRIBLE THINGS HAPPEN. UNSPEAKABLE THINGS. AND THERE IS NO ANSWER FOR THEM. ALL I KNOW FOR CERTAIN IS WHAT I HAVE SEEN.
A HAND FOR A HAND WILL ONLY CAUSE YOU TO LOSE BOTH.
THEA?
ROLLO!

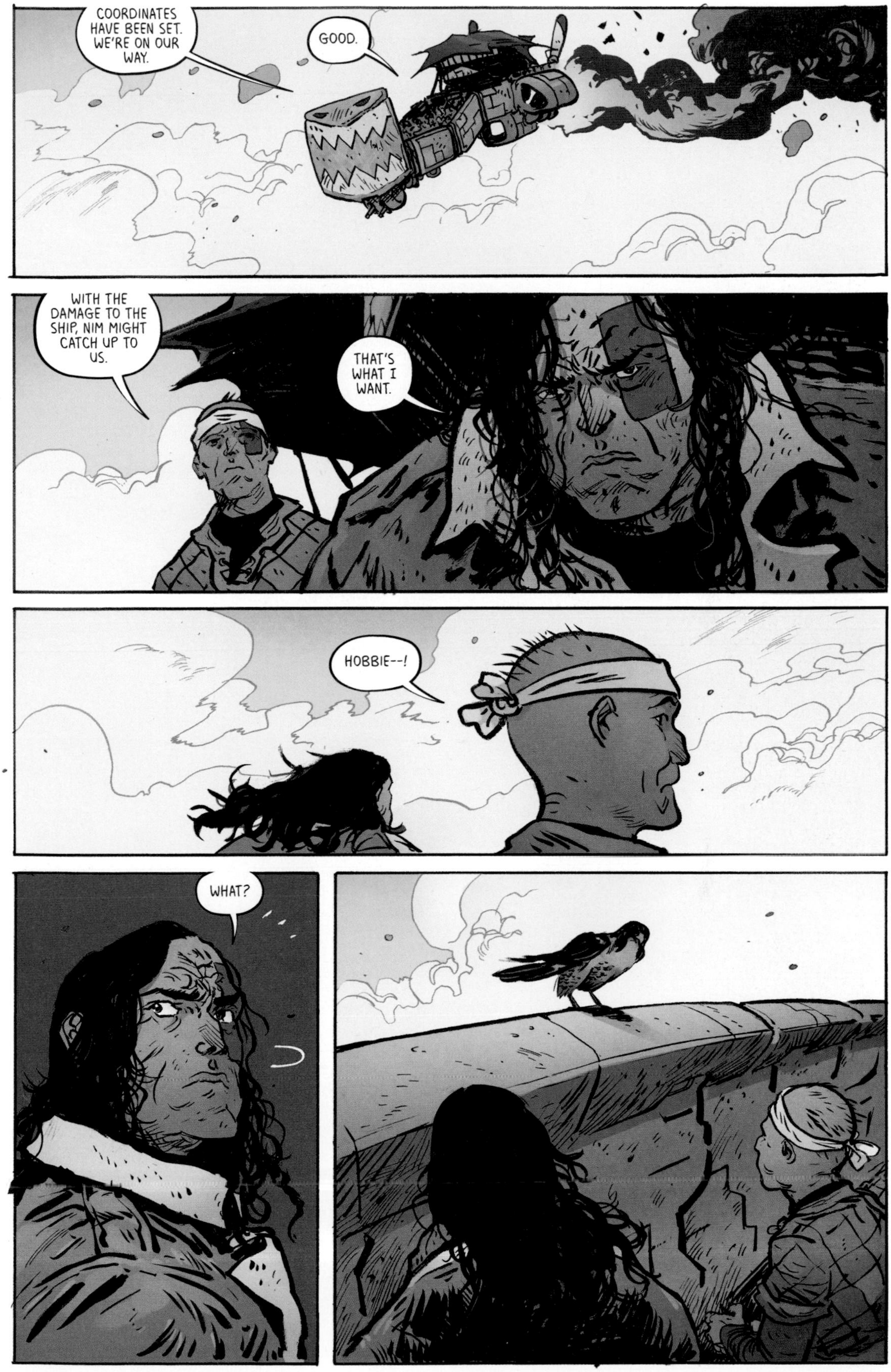

COORDINATES HAVE BEEN SET. WE'RE ON OUR WAY.
GOOD.
WITH THE DAMAGE TO THE SHIP, NIM MIGHT CATCH UP TO US.
THAT'S WHAT I WANT.
HOBBIE--!
WHAT?

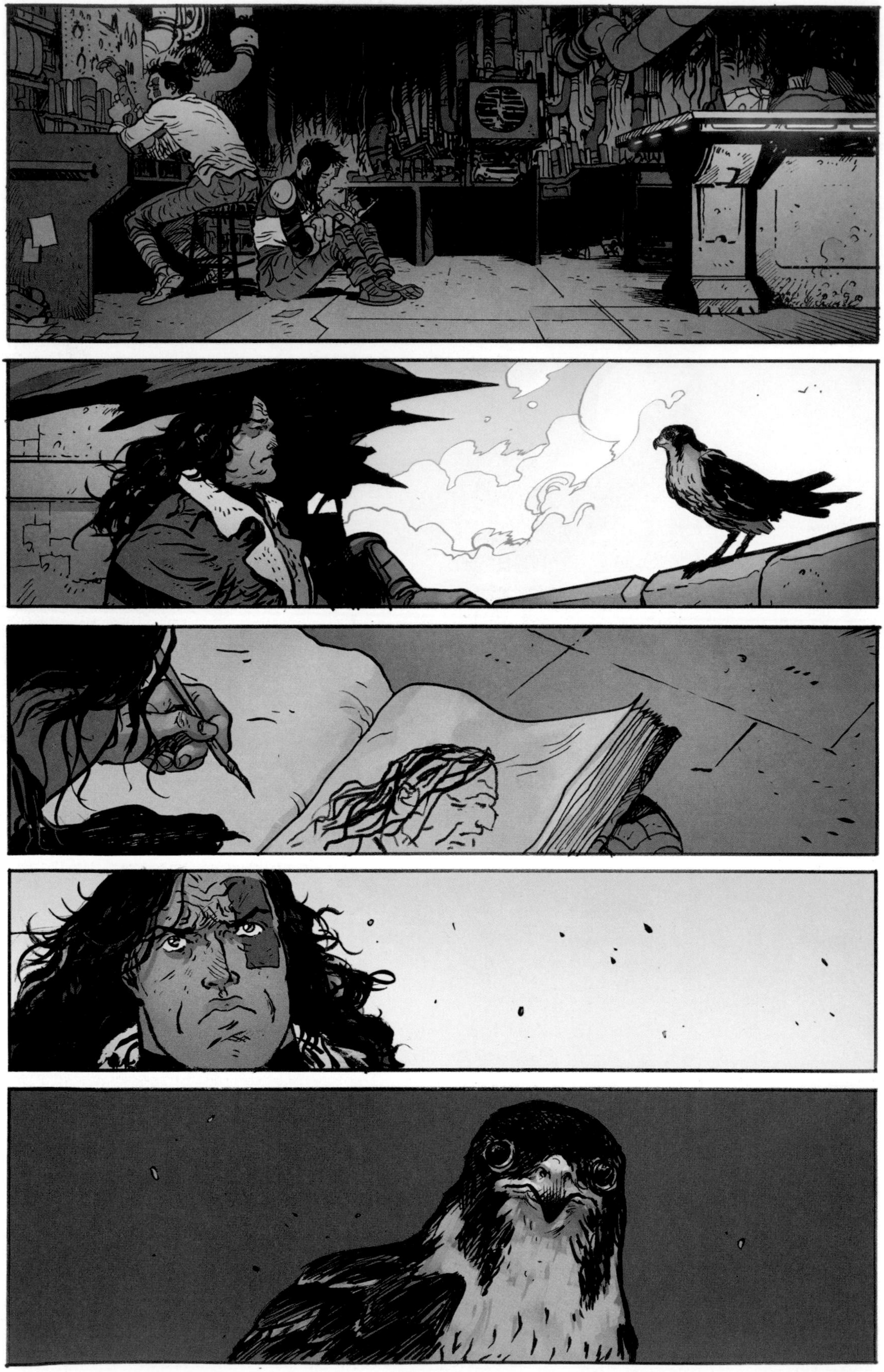

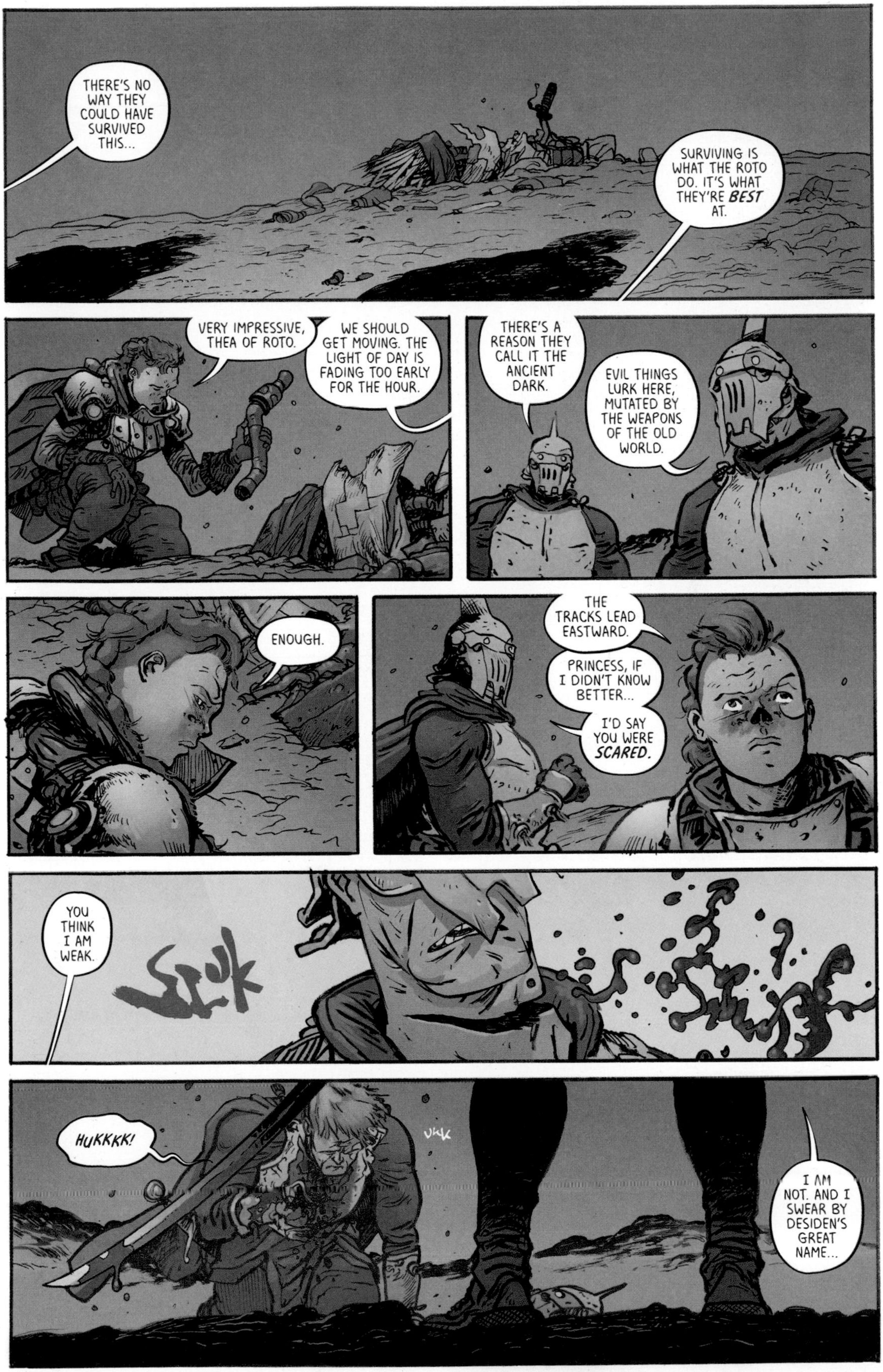
THERE'S NO WAY THEY COULD HAVE SURVIVED THIS...
SURVIVING IS WHAT THE ROTO DO. IT'S WHAT THEY'RE BEST AT.
VERY IMPRESSIVE, THEA OF ROTO.
WE SHOULD GET MOVING. THE LIGHT OF DAY IS FADING TOO EARLY FOR THE HOUR.
THERE'S A REASON THEY CALL IT THE ANCIENT DARK.
EVIL THINGS LURK HERE, MUTATED BY THE WEAPONS OF THE OLD WORLD.
ENOUGH.
THE TRACKS LEAD EASTWARD.
PRINCESS, IF I DIDN'T KNOW BETTER...
I'D SAY YOU WERE SCARED.
YOU THINK I AM WEAK.
SPLUK
HUKKKK!
UKK
I AM NOT. AND I SWEAR BY DESIDEN'S GREAT NAME...

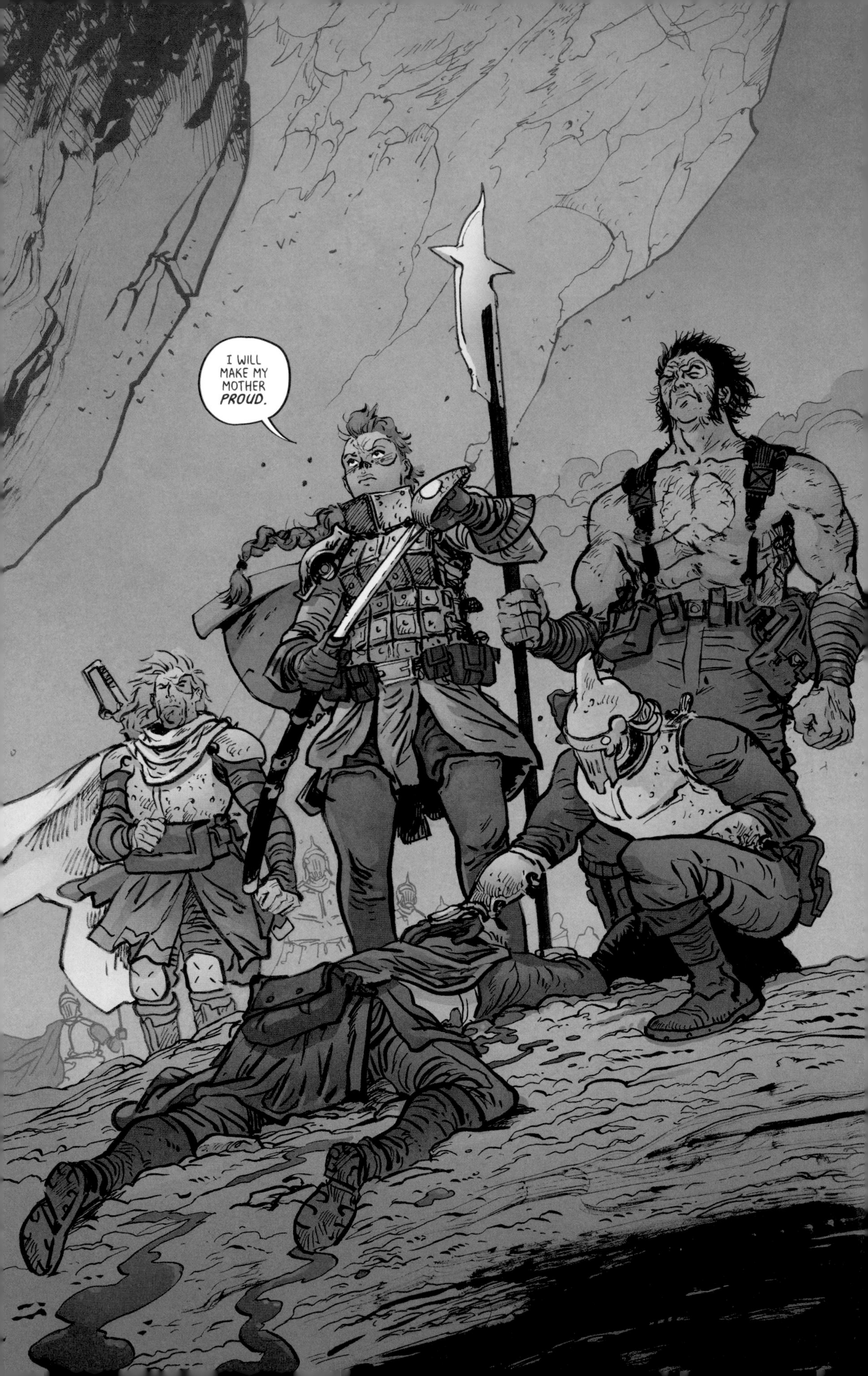
I WILL MAKE MY MOTHER *PROUD*.

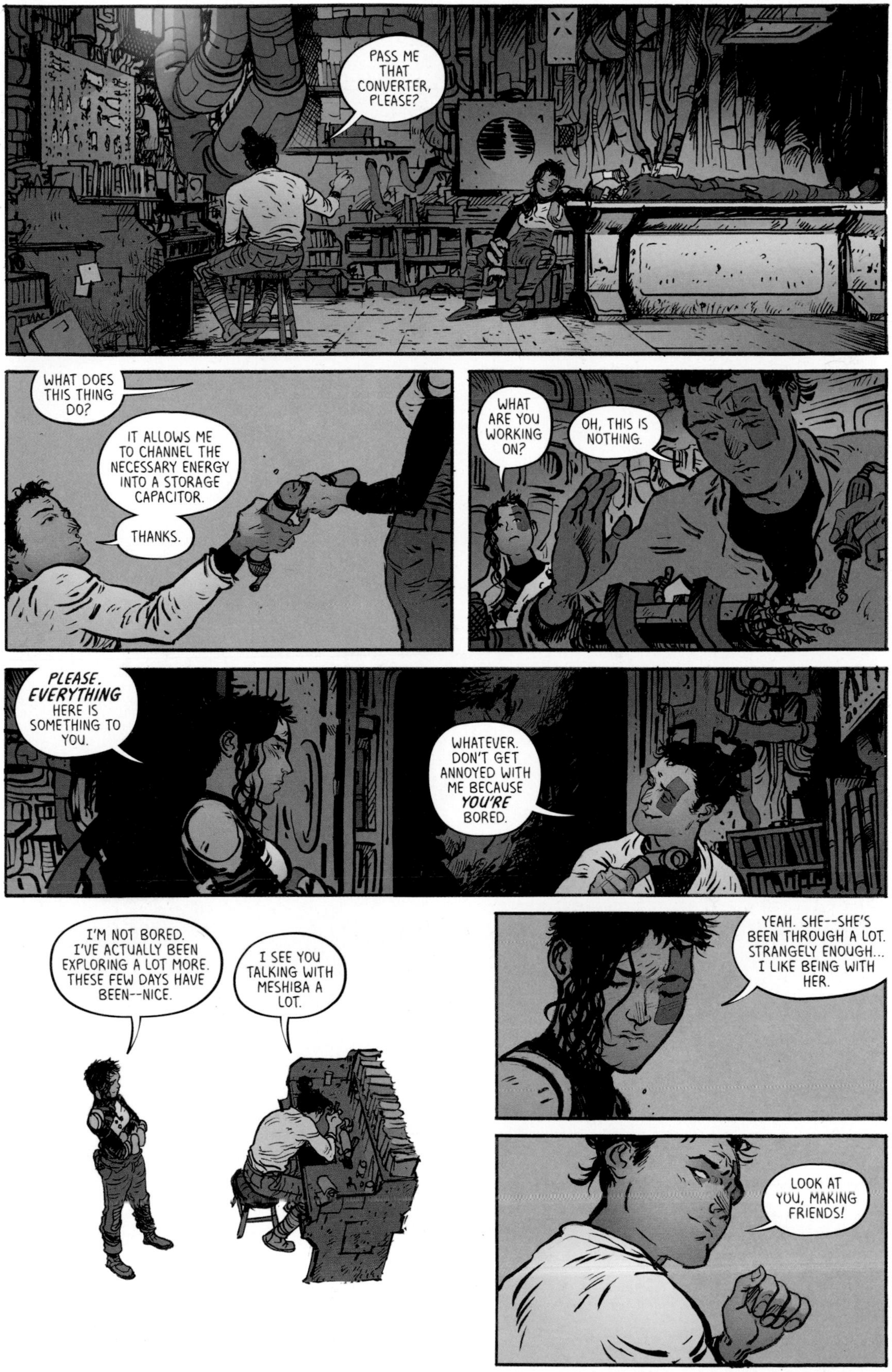
PASS ME THAT CONVERTER, PLEASE?
WHAT DOES THIS THING DO?
IT ALLOWS ME TO CHANNEL THE NECESSARY ENERGY INTO A STORAGE CAPACITOR.
THANKS.
WHAT ARE YOU WORKING ON?
OH, THIS IS NOTHING.
PLEASE. ***EVERYTHING*** HERE IS SOMETHING TO YOU.
WHATEVER. DON'T GET ANNOYED WITH ME BECAUSE *YOU'RE* BORED.
I'M NOT BORED. I'VE ACTUALLY BEEN EXPLORING A LOT MORE. THESE FEW DAYS HAVE BEEN--NICE.
I SEE YOU TALKING WITH MESHIBA A LOT.
YEAH. SHE--SHE'S BEEN THROUGH A LOT. STRANGELY ENOUGH... I LIKE BEING WITH HER.
LOOK AT YOU, MAKING FRIENDS!

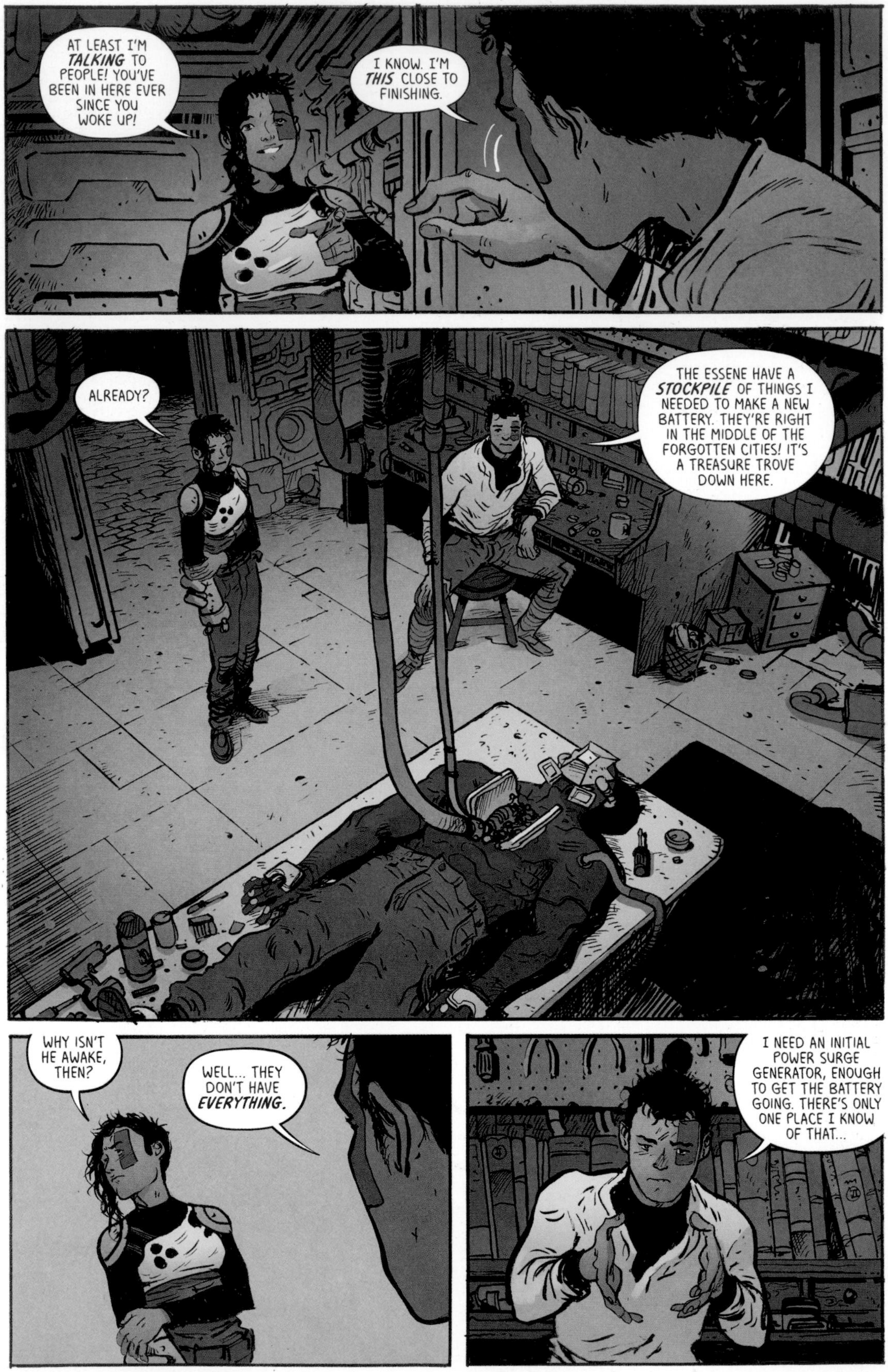
AT LEAST I'M TALKING TO PEOPLE! YOU'VE BEEN IN HERE EVER SINCE YOU WOKE UP!
I KNOW. I'M THIS CLOSE TO FINISHING.
ALREADY?
THE ESSENE HAVE A STOCKPILE OF THINGS I NEEDED TO MAKE A NEW BATTERY. THEY'RE RIGHT IN THE MIDDLE OF THE FORGOTTEN CITIES! IT'S A TREASURE TROVE DOWN HERE.
WHY ISN'T HE AWAKE, THEN?
WELL... THEY DON'T HAVE EVERYTHING.
I NEED AN INITIAL POWER SURGE GENERATOR, ENOUGH TO GET THE BATTERY GOING. THERE'S ONLY ONE PLACE I KNOW OF THAT...

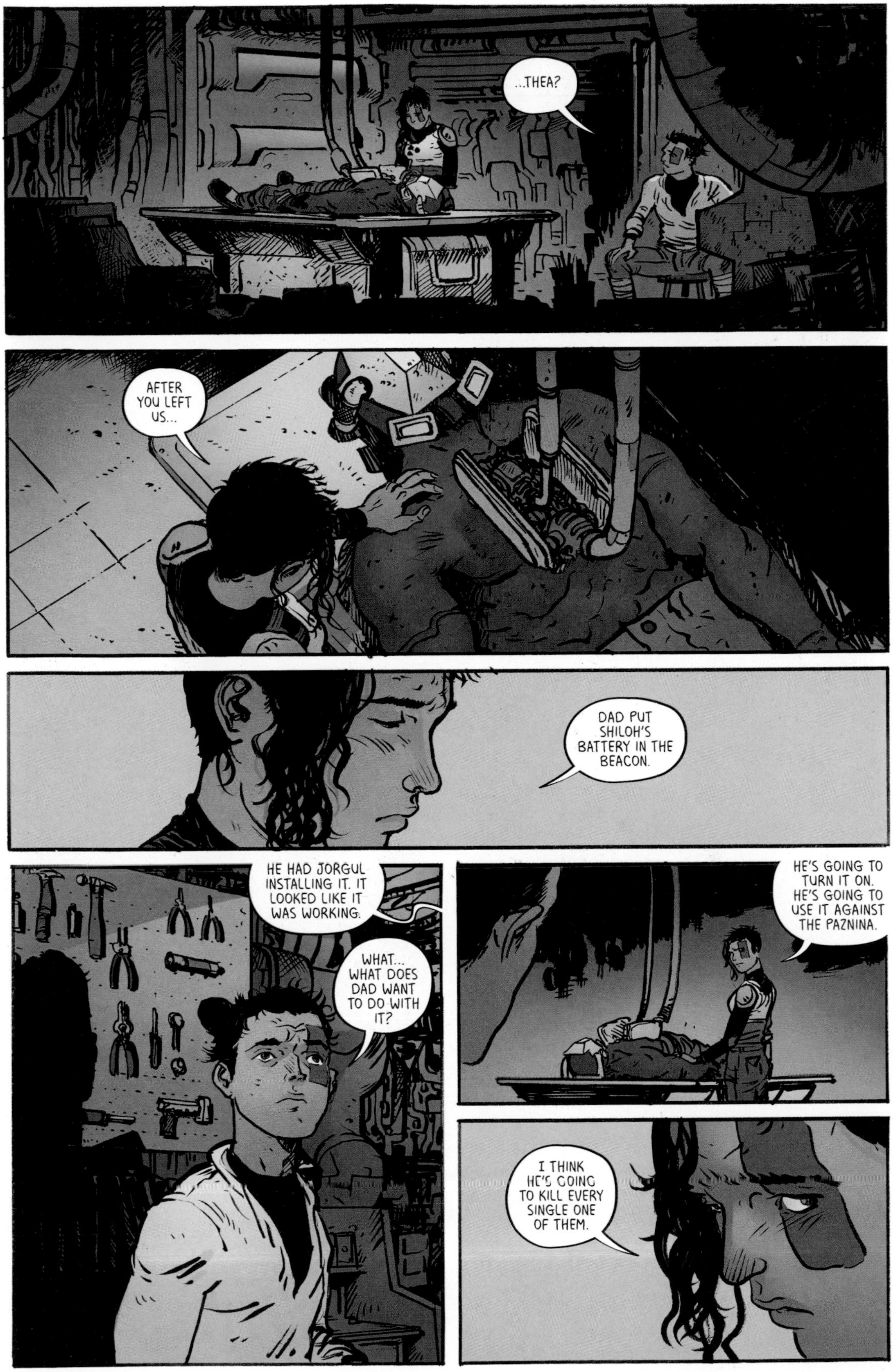
...THEA?
AFTER YOU LEFT US...
DAD PUT SHILOH'S BATTERY IN THE BEACON.
HE HAD JORGUL INSTALLING IT. IT LOOKED LIKE IT WAS WORKING.
WHAT... WHAT DOES DAD WANT TO DO WITH IT?
HE'S GOING TO TURN IT ON. HE'S GOING TO USE IT AGAINST THE PAZNINA.
I THINK HE'S GOING TO KILL EVERY SINGLE ONE OF THEM.

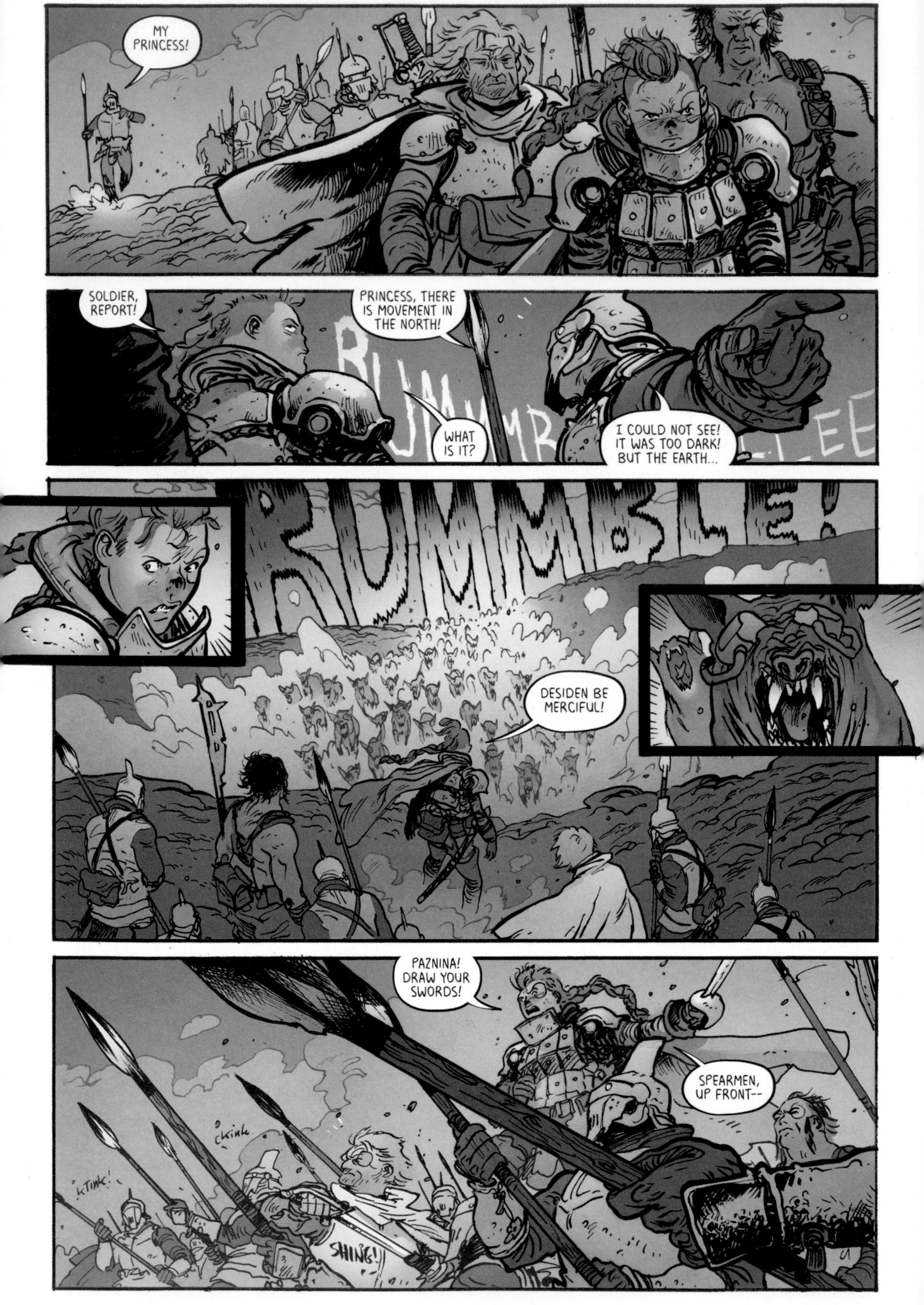
MY PRINCESS!
SOLDIER, REPORT!
PRINCESS, THERE IS MOVEMENT IN THE NORTH!
WHAT IS IT?
I COULD NOT SEE! IT WAS TOO DARK! BUT THE EARTH...
RUMMBLE!
DESIDEN BE MERCIFUL!
PAZNINA! DRAW YOUR SWORDS!
SPEARMEN, UP FRONT--
SHING!

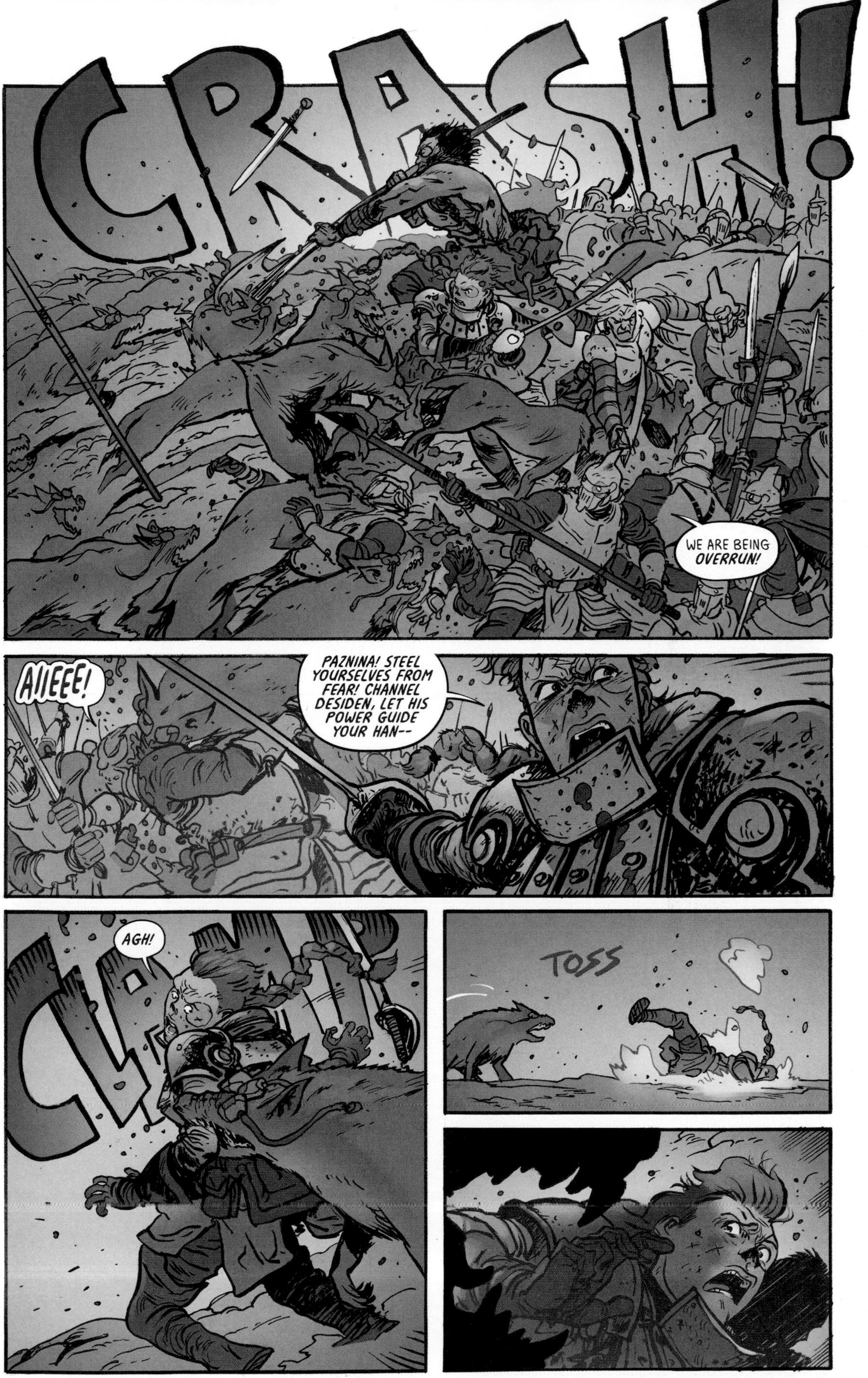
CRASH!
WE ARE BEING OVERRUN!
AIIEEE!
PAZNINA! STEEL YOURSELVES FROM FEAR! CHANNEL DESIDEN, LET HIS POWER GUIDE YOUR HAN--
AGH!
TOSS

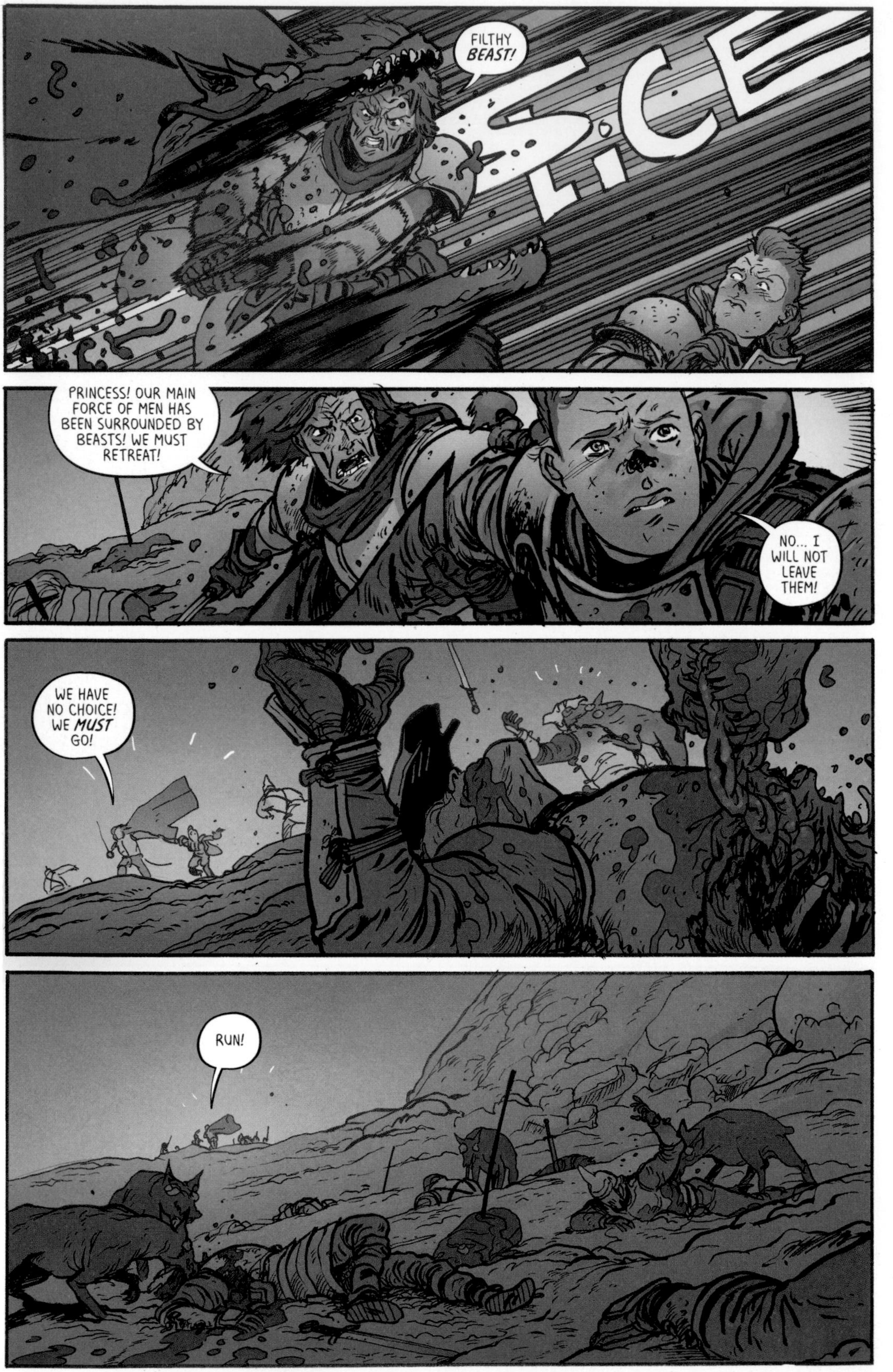
FILTHY *BEAST!*
SLICE
PRINCESS! OUR MAIN FORCE OF MEN HAS BEEN SURROUNDED BY BEASTS! WE MUST RETREAT!
NO... I WILL NOT LEAVE THEM!
WE HAVE NO CHOICE! WE *MUST* GO!
RUN!

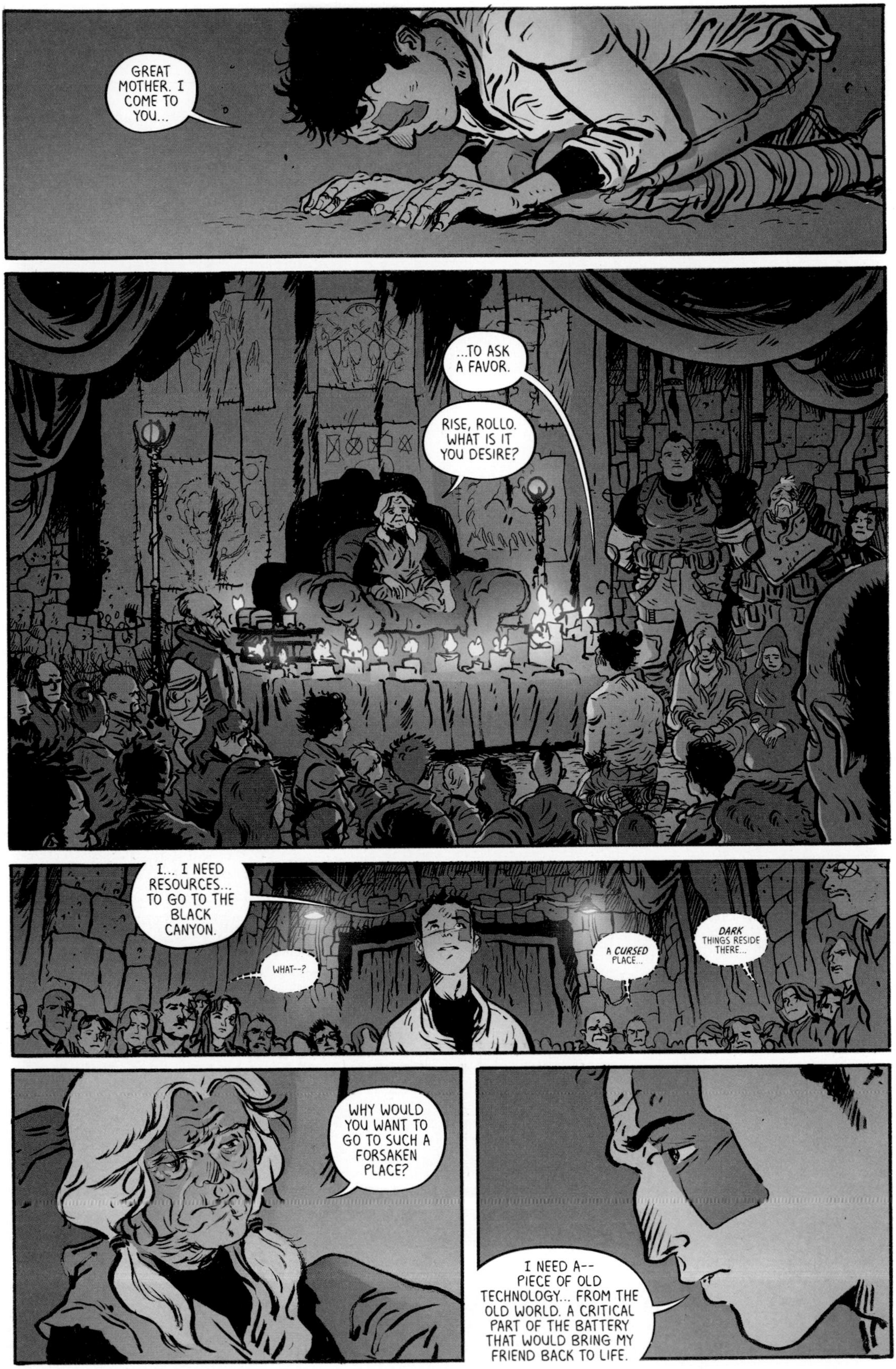
GREAT MOTHER. I COME TO YOU...
...TO ASK A FAVOR.
RISE, ROLLO. WHAT IS IT YOU DESIRE?
I... I NEED RESOURCES... TO GO TO THE BLACK CANYON.
WHAT--?
A CURSED PLACE...
DARK THINGS RESIDE THERE...
WHY WOULD YOU WANT TO GO TO SUCH A FORSAKEN PLACE?
I NEED A-- PIECE OF OLD TECHNOLOGY... FROM THE OLD WORLD. A CRITICAL PART OF THE BATTERY THAT WOULD BRING MY FRIEND BACK TO LIFE.

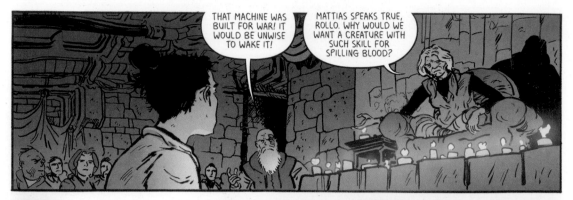

THAT MACHINE WAS BUILT FOR WAR! IT WOULD BE UNWISE TO WAKE IT!

MATTIAS SPEAKS TRUE, ROLLO. WHY WOULD WE WANT A CREATURE WITH SUCH SKILL FOR SPILLING BLOOD?

MOTHER DEIDRE, I REALIZE THE CONCERN. BUT THIS MACHINE, THIS PERSON, HAS NO HEART FOR WAR. WHATEVER WAS PROGRAMMED IN HIM HAS FADED. HE DESIRES PEACE AS MUCH AS YOU AND I. SO MUCH SO THAT HE GAVE HIS LIFE TO PROTECT IT. THIS IS A WARRIOR SO SKILLED AND POWERFUL, HE COULD INCAPACITATE THE ONES WHO MIGHT HUNT YOU...

WITHOUT KILLING THEM.

VERY WELL, ROLLO. WE WILL HELP YOU.

WHAT?! BUT--

MATTIAS. I FEAR WHAT YOU FEAR.

BUT I TRUST ROLLO AND HIS SISTER.

OUR WALLS HAVE GROWN WEAK. MORE CREATURES ARE COMING FROM THE DEEP EVERY DAY. WE NEED PROTECTION... I WILL NOT LOSE WHAT SO MANY HAVE SACRIFICED TO GAIN.

AND THIS... *SHILOH*... COULD HELP US.

I SEE THE FAITH YOU HAVE IN THESE TWO, MESHIBA, AND I WILL TRUST THAT. TAKE ROLLO AND THEA TO THE BLACK CANYON, ALONG WITH OUR BEST WARRIORS. I HOPE YOU FIND WHAT YOU NEED, ROLLO.

FOR THE GOOD OF ALL OF US.

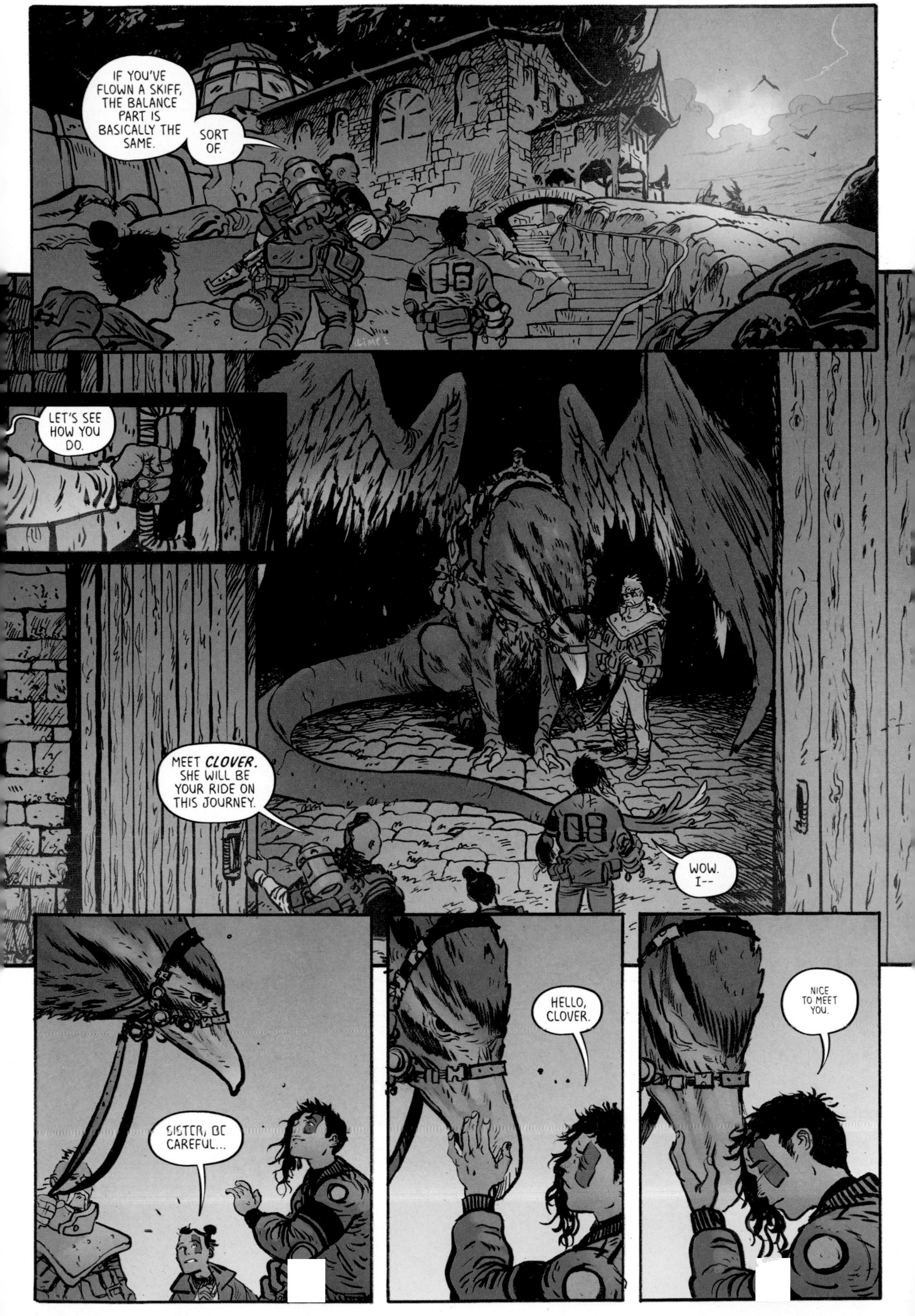
IF YOU'VE FLOWN A SKIFF, THE BALANCE PART IS BASICALLY THE SAME.
SORT OF.
LET'S SEE HOW YOU DO.
MEET CLOVER. SHE WILL BE YOUR RIDE ON THIS JOURNEY.
WOW. I--
SISTER, BE CAREFUL...
HELLO, CLOVER.
NICE TO MEET YOU.

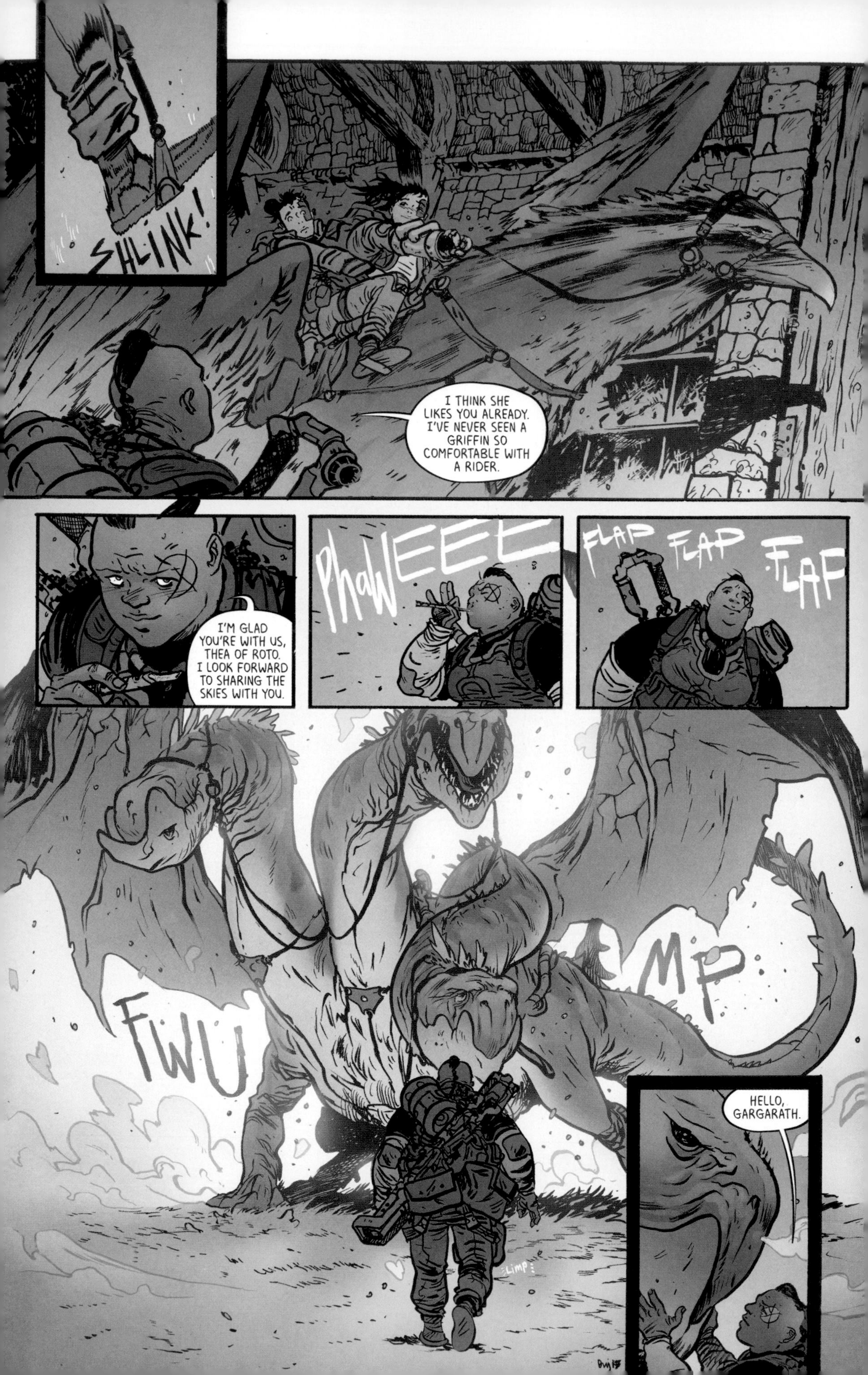
SHLINK!
I THINK SHE LIKES YOU ALREADY. I'VE NEVER SEEN A GRIFFIN SO COMFORTABLE WITH A RIDER.
I'M GLAD YOU'RE WITH US, THEA OF ROTO. I LOOK FORWARD TO SHARING THE SKIES WITH YOU.
PhaWEEET
FLAP FLAP FLAP
FWUMP
Limp
HELLO, GARGARATH.

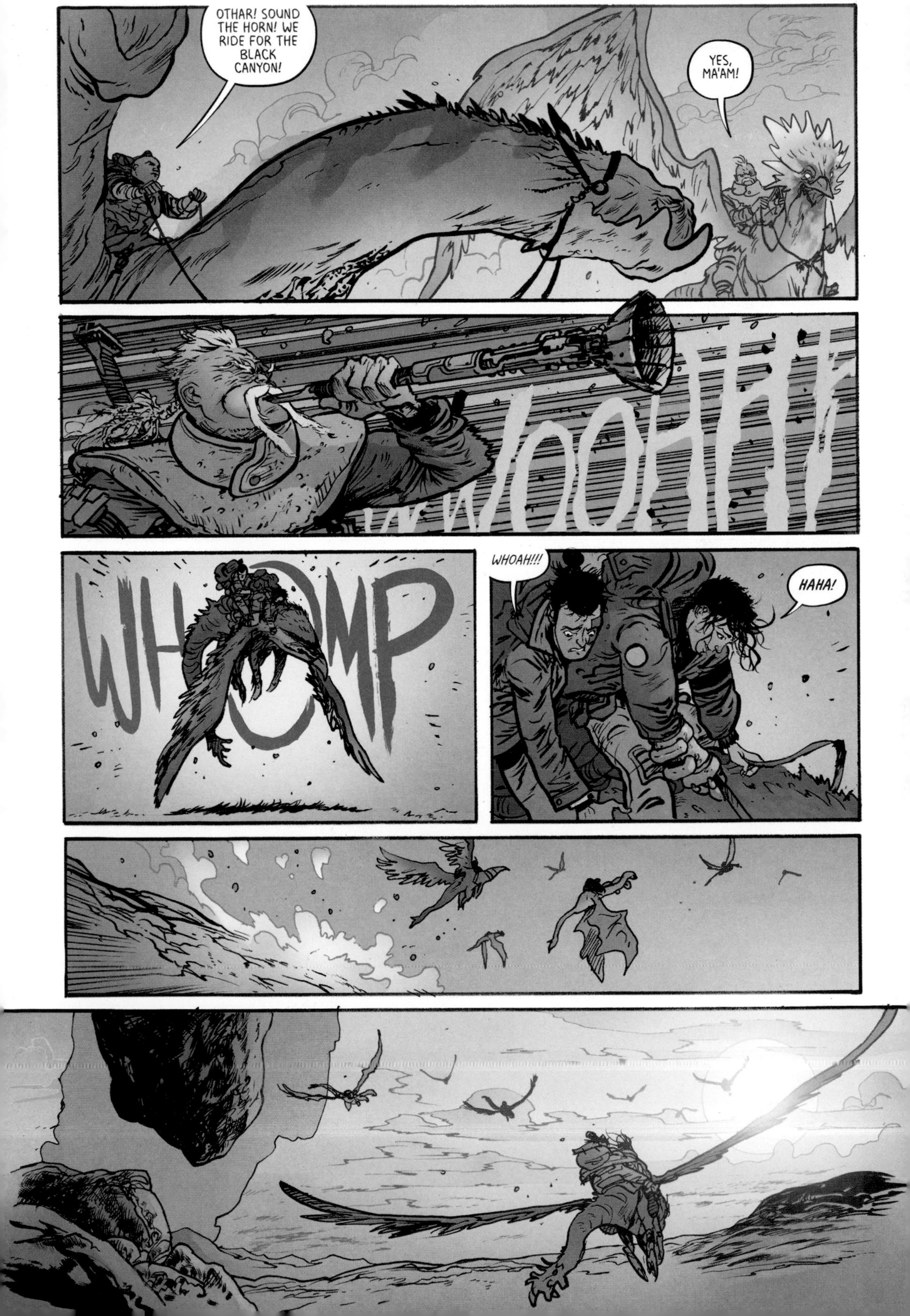
OTHAR! SOUND THE HORN! WE RIDE FOR THE BLACK CANYON!
YES, MA'AM!
WOOHH
WHOMP
WHOAH!!!
HAHA!

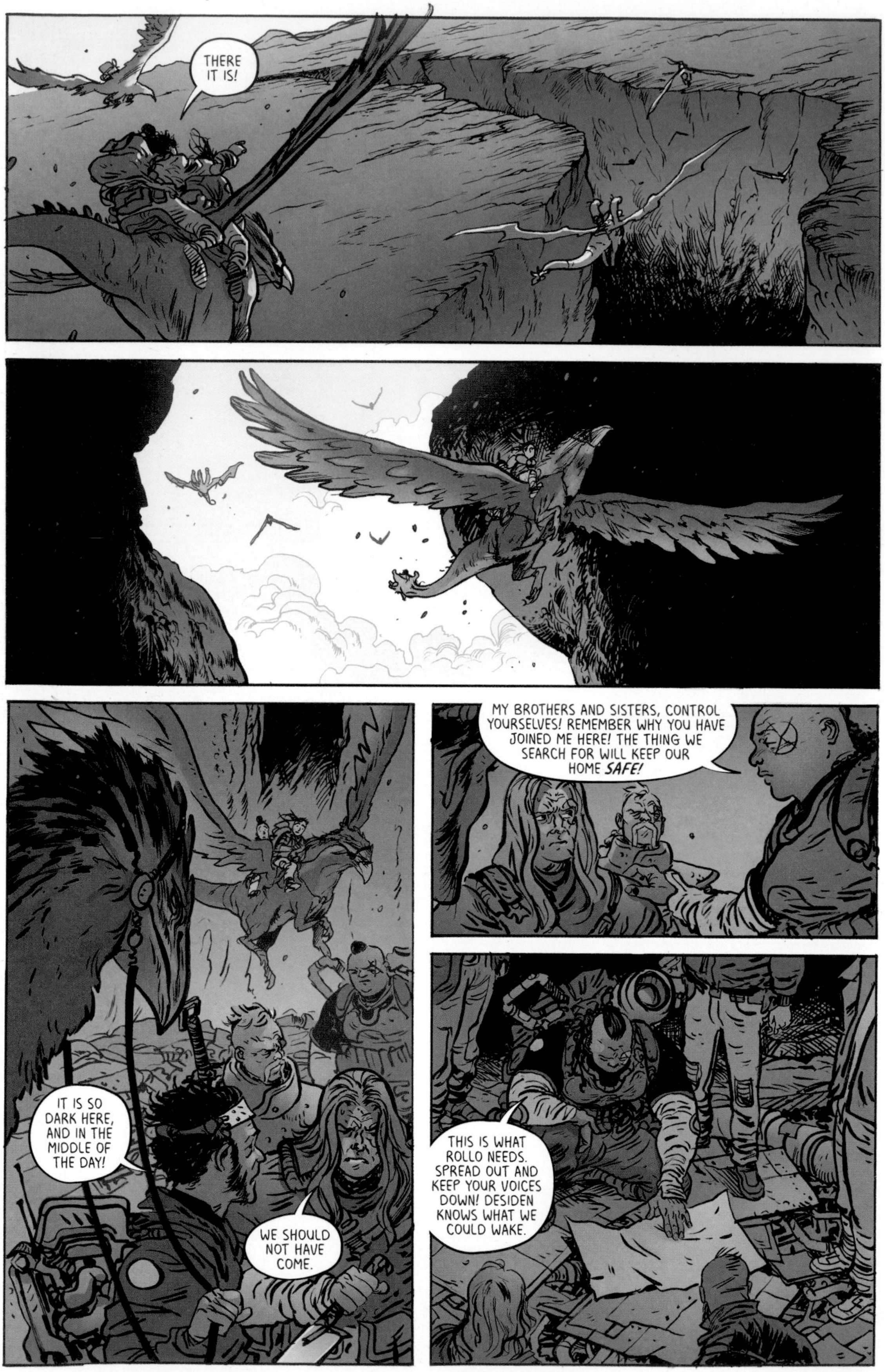
THERE IT IS!
IT IS SO DARK HERE, AND IN THE MIDDLE OF THE DAY!
WE SHOULD NOT HAVE COME.
MY BROTHERS AND SISTERS, CONTROL YOURSELVES! REMEMBER WHY YOU HAVE JOINED ME HERE! THE THING WE SEARCH FOR WILL KEEP OUR HOME SAFE!
THIS IS WHAT ROLLO NEEDS. SPREAD OUT AND KEEP YOUR VOICES DOWN! DESIDEN KNOWS WHAT WE COULD WAKE.

ROLLO! IS THIS--?

NOPE. SORRY.

DAMN.

I DON'T LIKE IT HERE. THESE HUSKS... WHAT CREATURE MADE THEM?

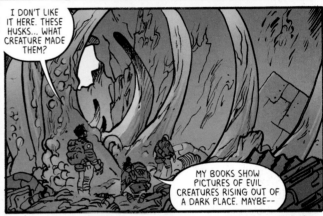

MY BOOKS SHOW PICTURES OF EVIL CREATURES RISING OUT OF A DARK PLACE. MAYBE--

WHAT... WHAT IS THIS?

HEY! I FOUND IT!

I FOUND I--

THOOOM

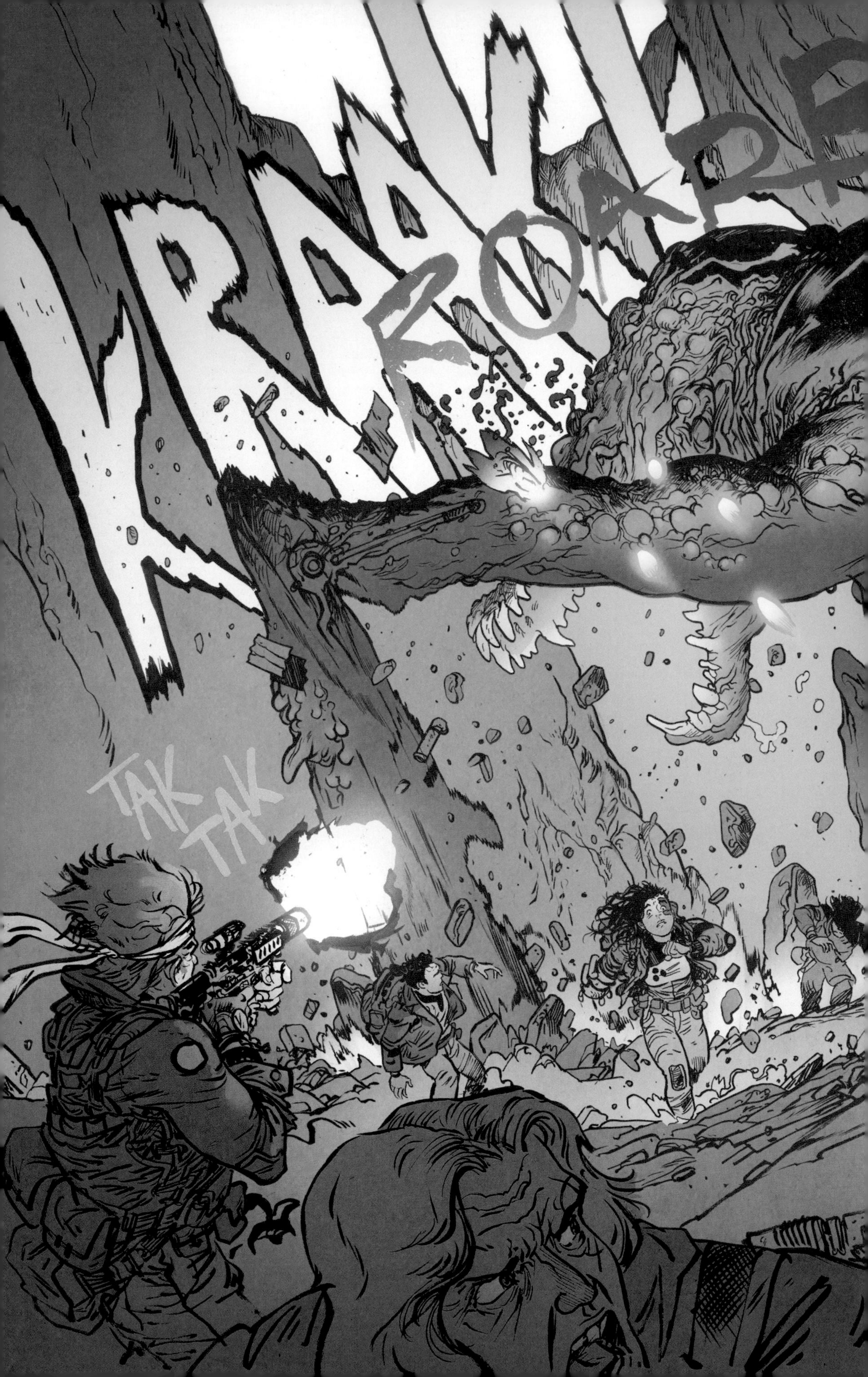
TAK TAK

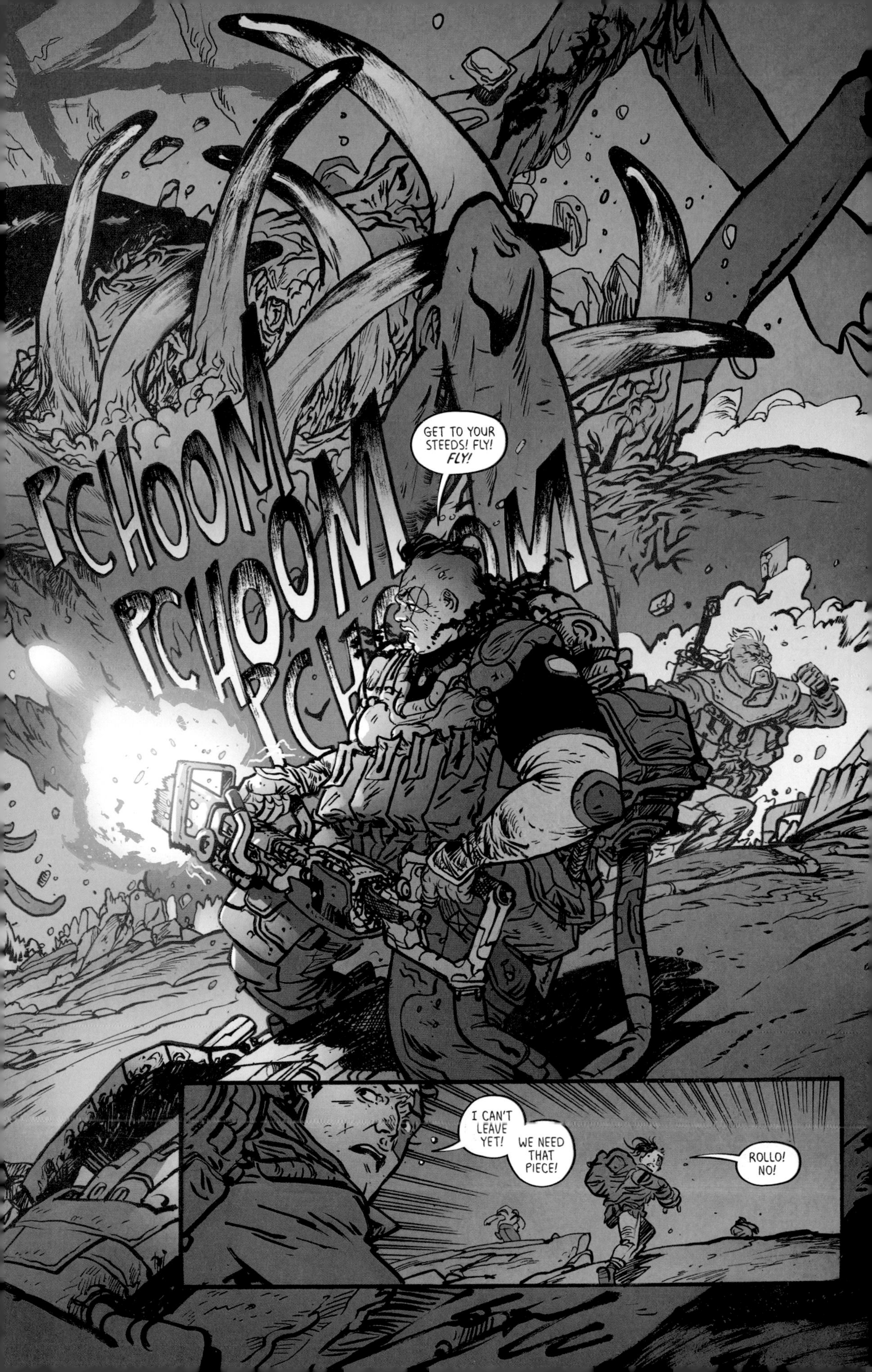
PCHOOM
PCHOOM
PCHOOM
GET TO YOUR STEEDS! FLY! *FLY!*
I CAN'T LEAVE YET!
WE NEED THAT PIECE!
ROLLO! NO!

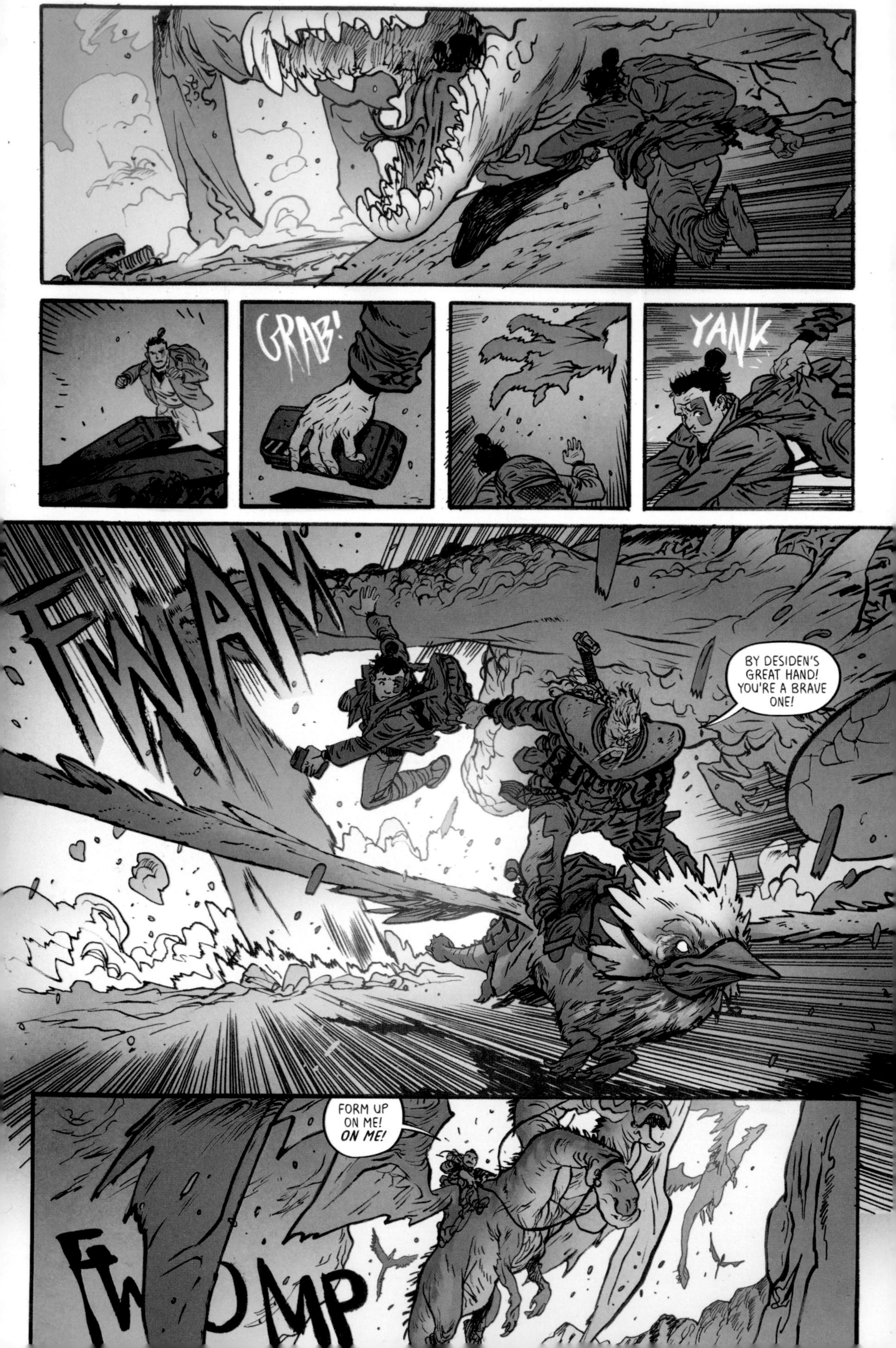
GRAB!
YANK
FWAM
BY DESIDEN'S GREAT HAND! YOU'RE A BRAVE ONE!
FORM UP ON ME! *ON ME!*
FWOMP

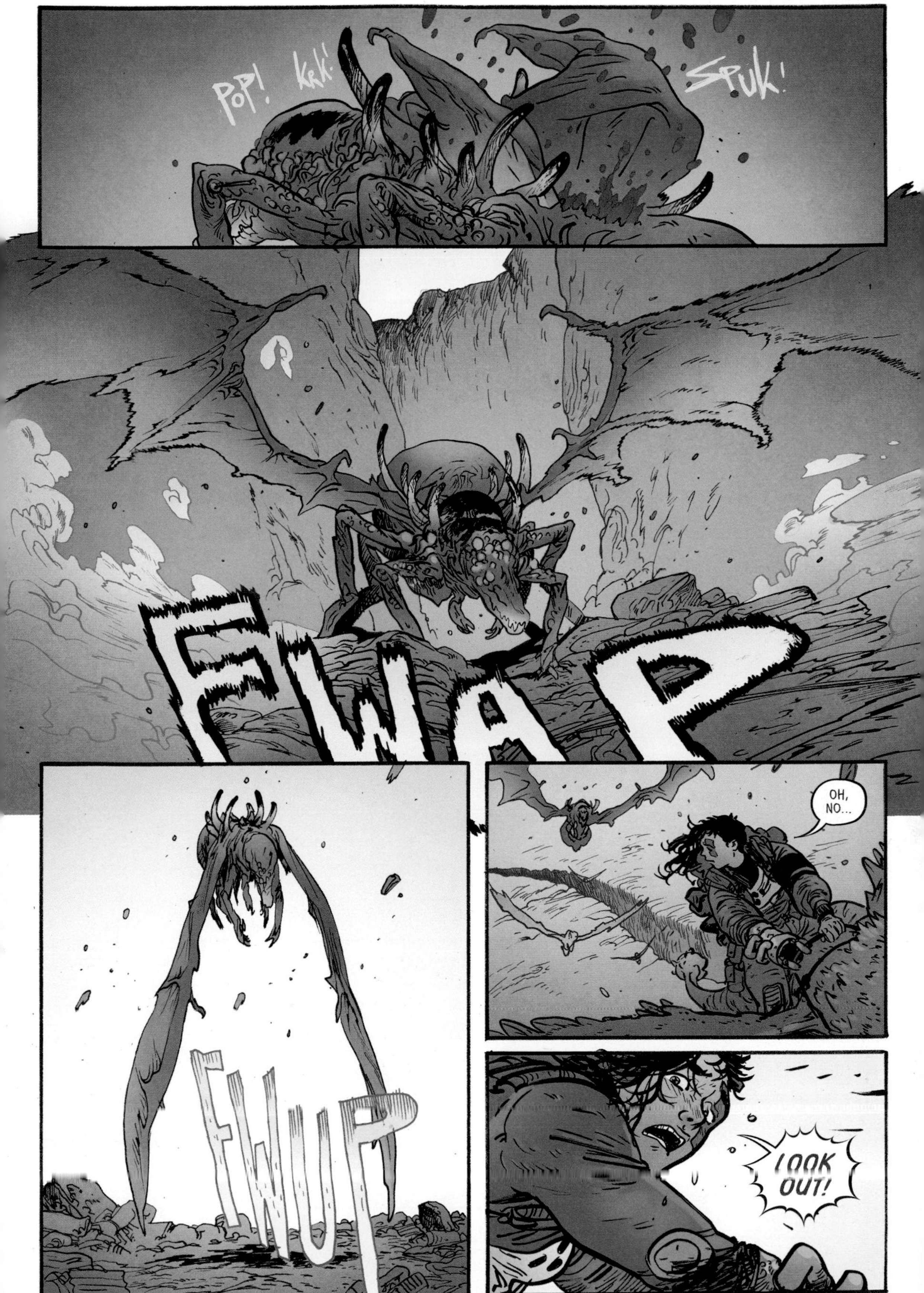
POP!
KRK!
SPUK!
FWAP
FWUP
OH, NO...
LOOK OUT!

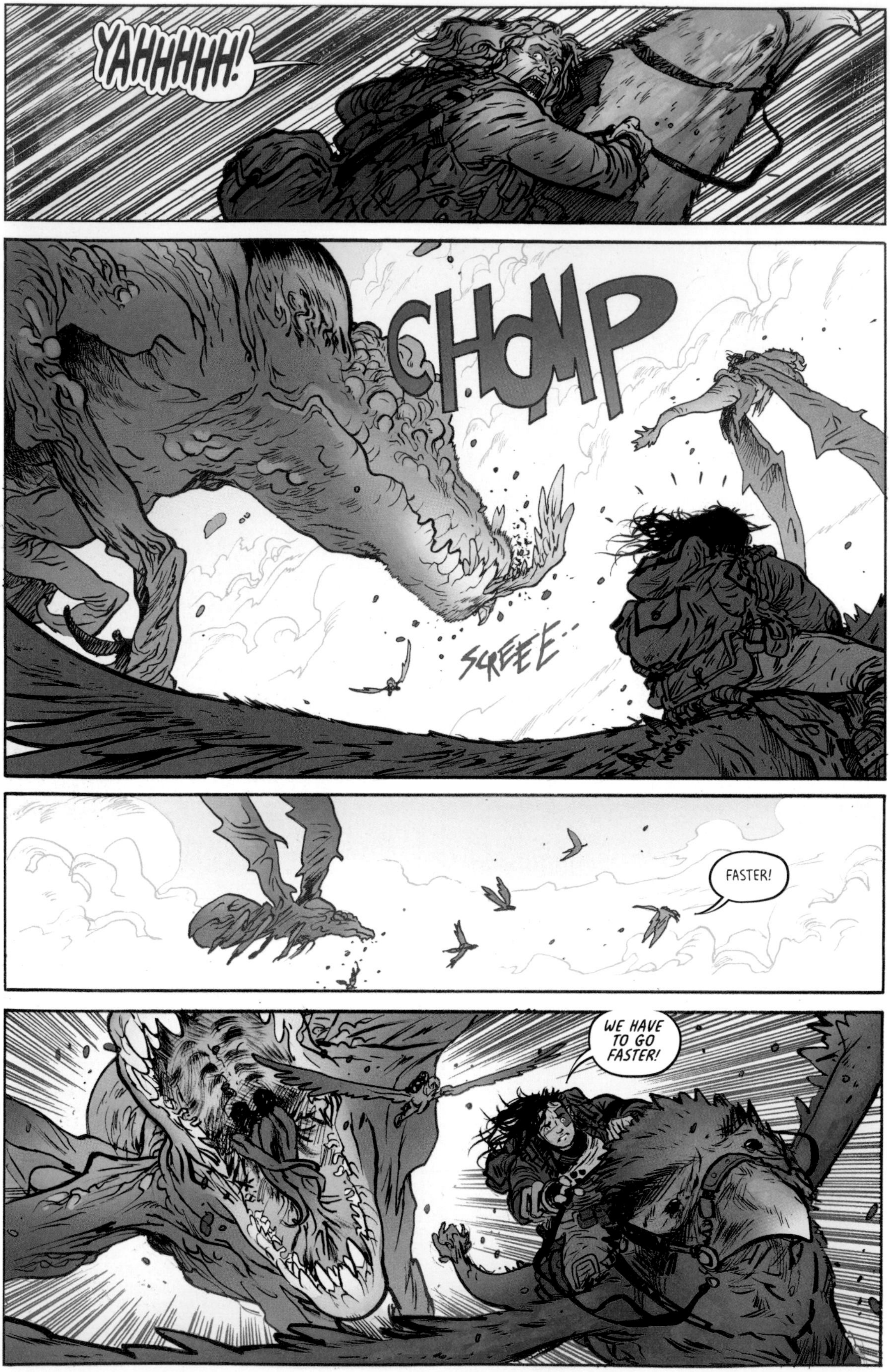
YAHHHHH!
CHOMP
SCREEE...
FASTER!
WE HAVE TO GO FASTER!

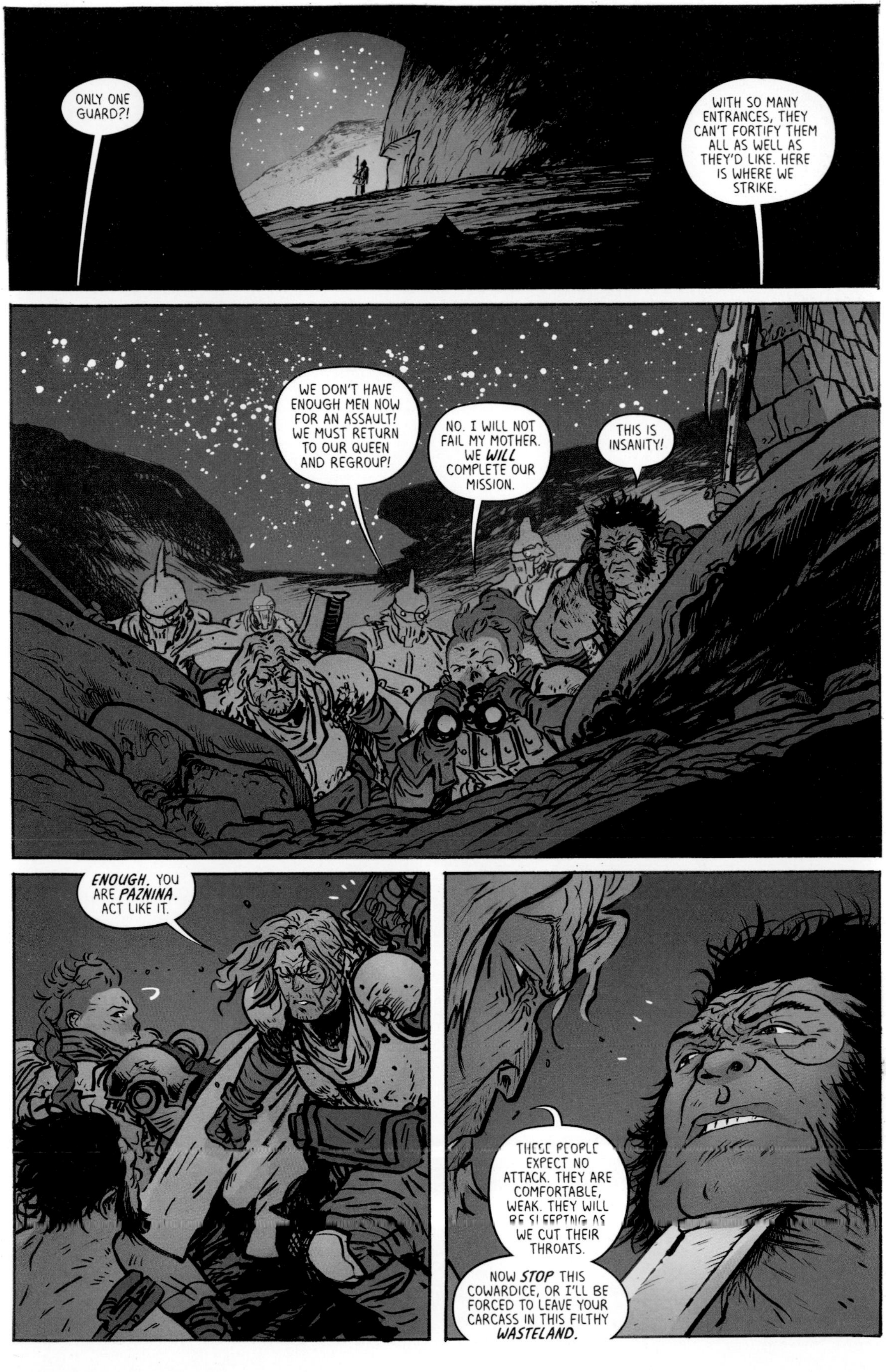
ONLY ONE GUARD?!
WITH SO MANY ENTRANCES, THEY CAN'T FORTIFY THEM ALL AS WELL AS THEY'D LIKE. HERE IS WHERE WE STRIKE.
WE DON'T HAVE ENOUGH MEN NOW FOR AN ASSAULT! WE MUST RETURN TO OUR QUEEN AND REGROUP!
NO. I WILL NOT FAIL MY MOTHER. WE WILL COMPLETE OUR MISSION.
THIS IS INSANITY!
ENOUGH. YOU ARE PAZNINA. ACT LIKE IT.
THESE PEOPLE EXPECT NO ATTACK. THEY ARE COMFORTABLE, WEAK. THEY WILL BE SLEEPING AS WE CUT THEIR THROATS.
NOW STOP THIS COWARDICE, OR I'LL BE FORCED TO LEAVE YOUR CARCASS IN THIS FILTHY WASTELAND.

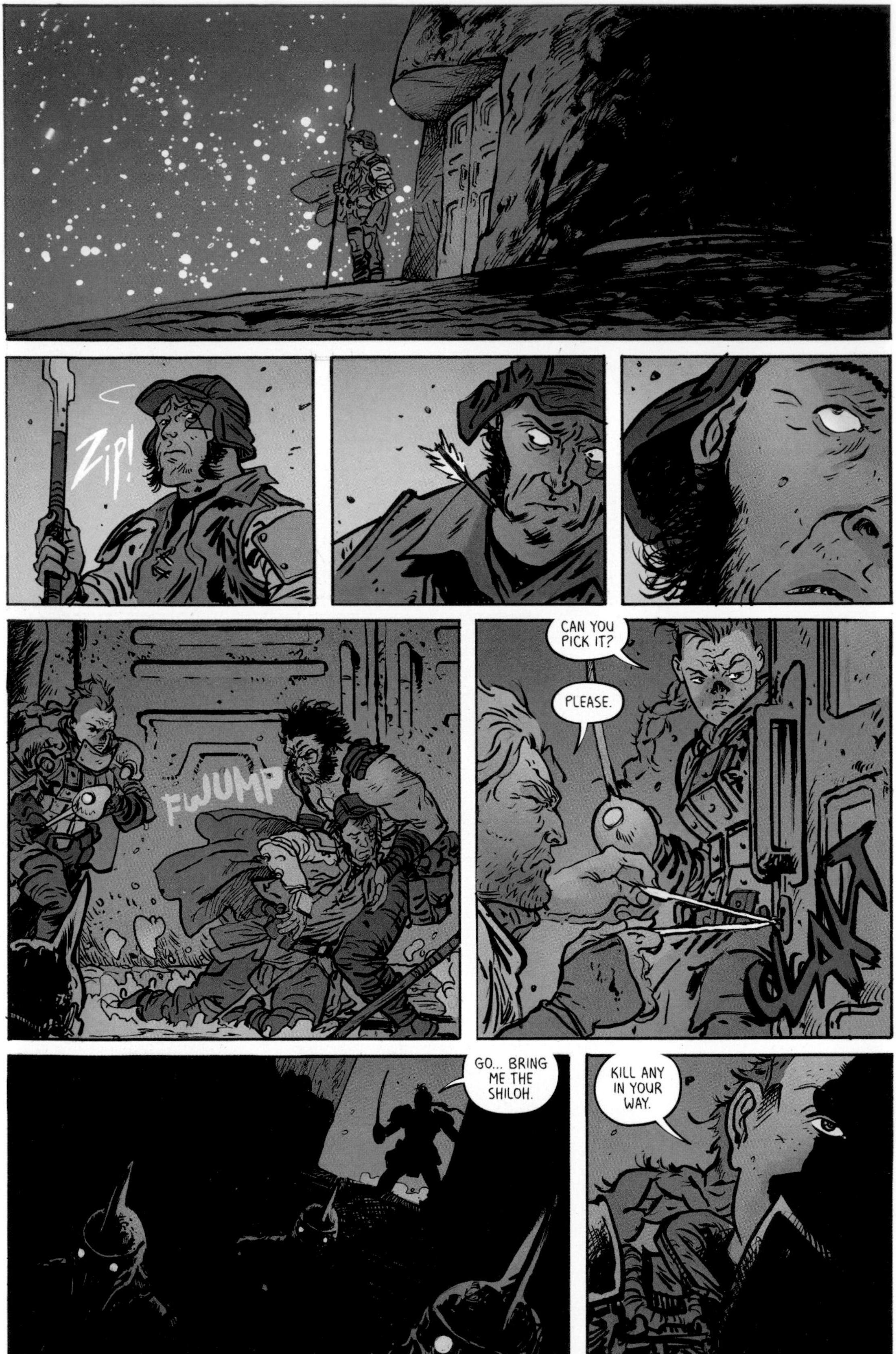
ZIP!
FWUMP
CAN YOU PICK IT?
PLEASE.
GO... BRING ME THE SHILOH.
KILL ANY IN YOUR WAY.

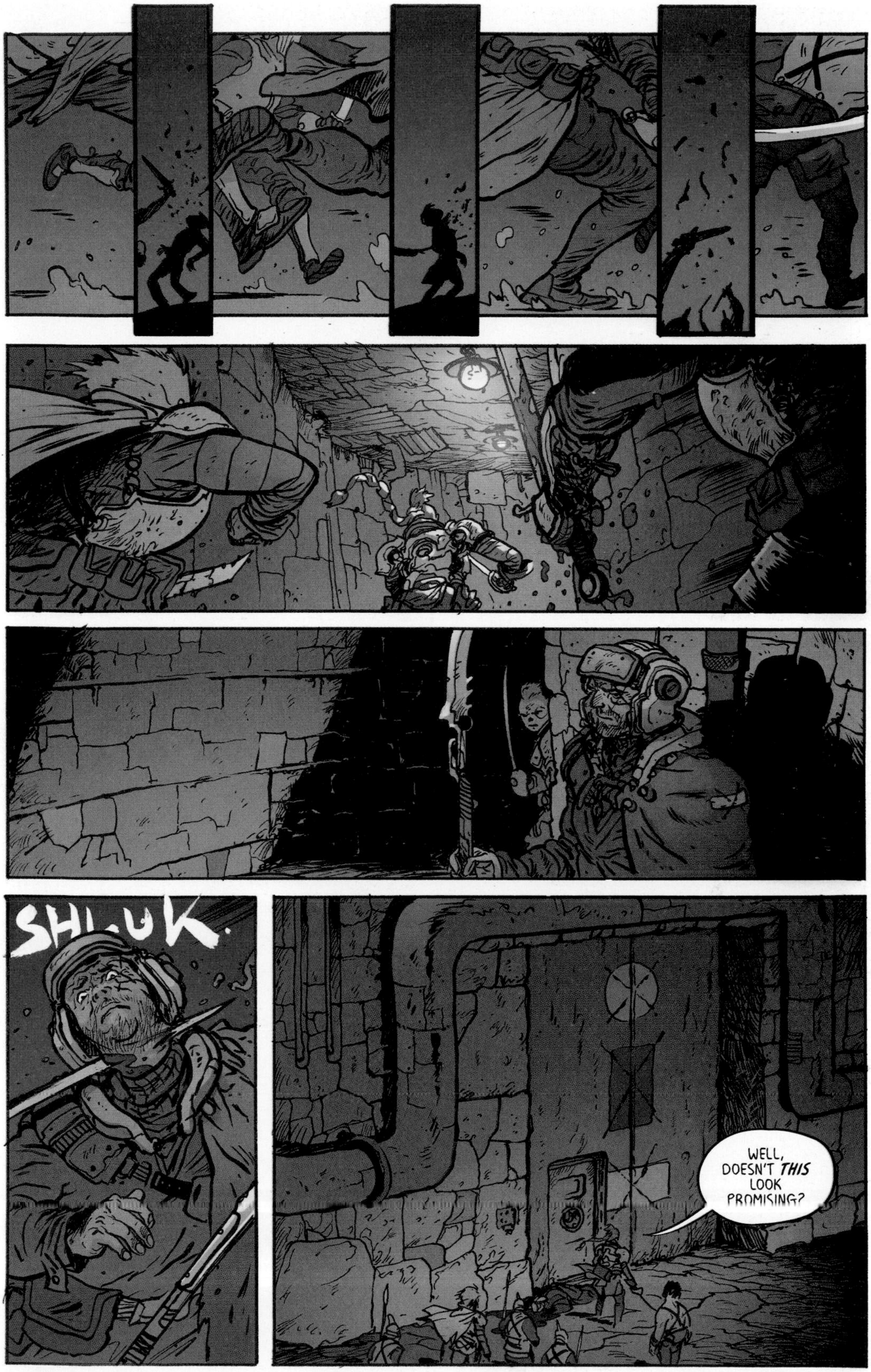
SHLUK.
WELL, DOESN'T THIS LOOK PROMISING?

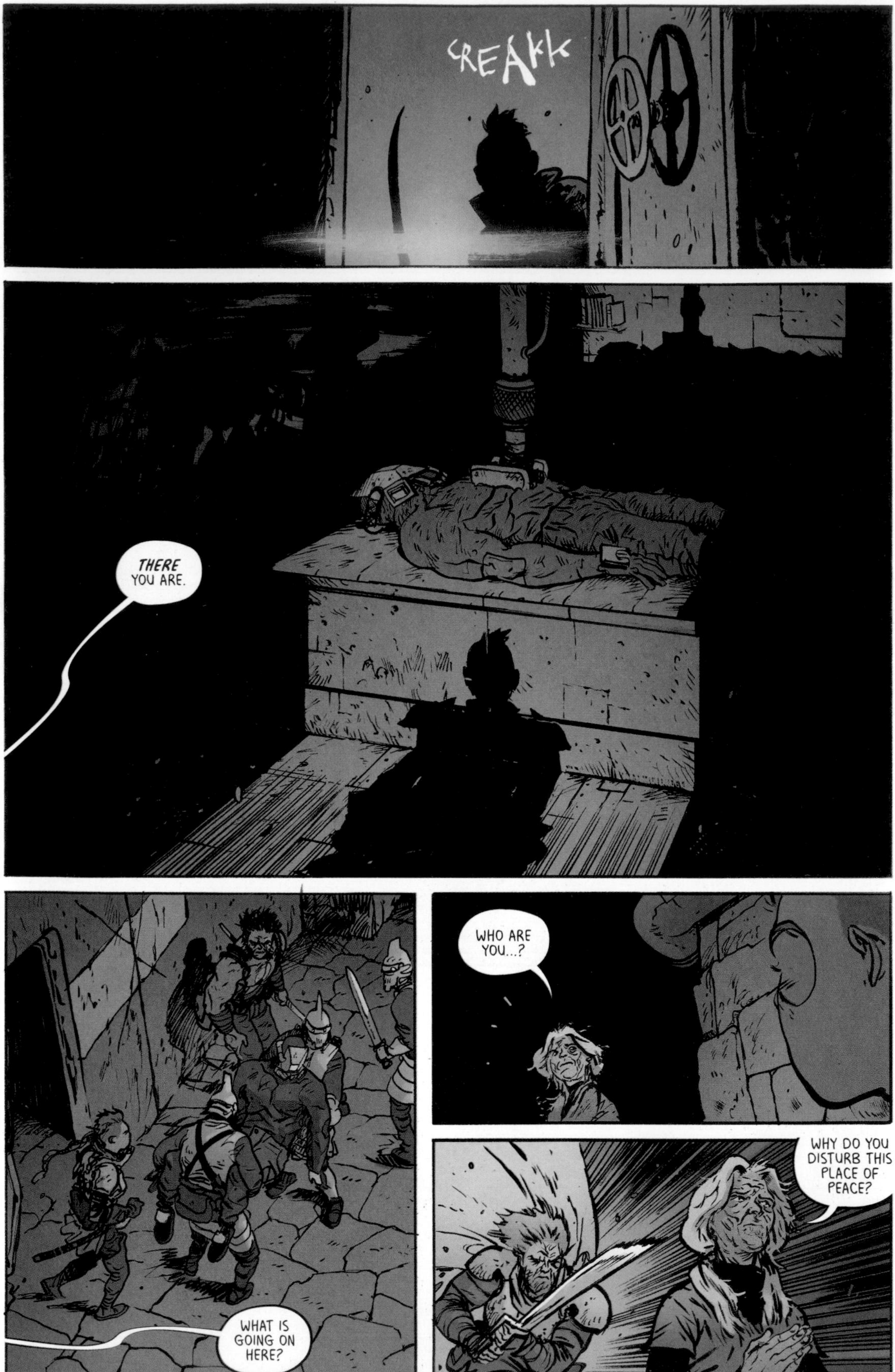
CREAKK
THERE YOU ARE.
WHAT IS GOING ON HERE?
WHO ARE YOU...?
WHY DO YOU DISTURB THIS PLACE OF PEACE?

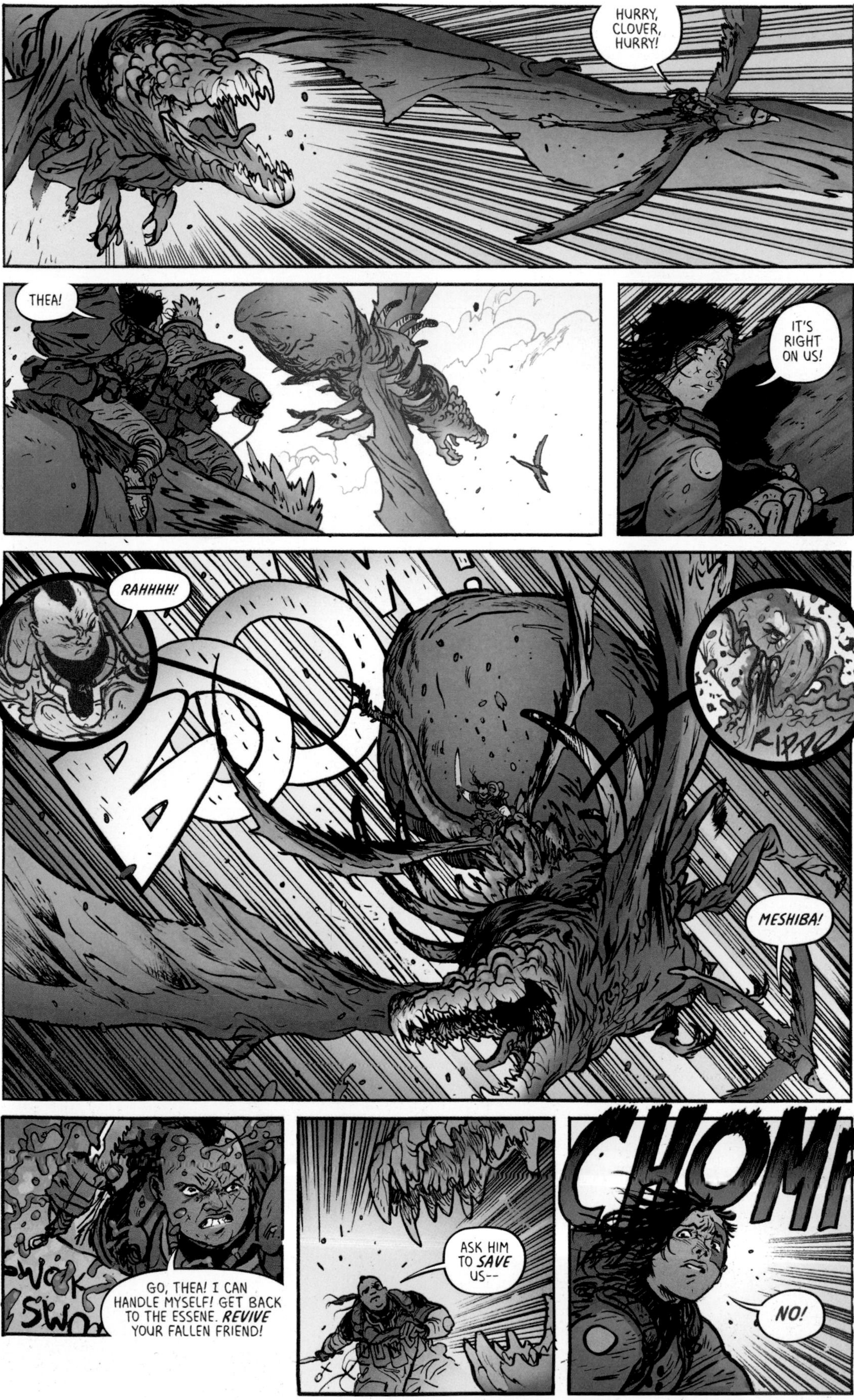
HURRY, CLOVER, HURRY!
THEA!
IT'S RIGHT ON US!
RAHHHH!
BOOM
RIPPP
MESHIBA!
SWOK
SWO
GO, THEA! I CAN HANDLE MYSELF! GET BACK TO THE ESSENE. *REVIVE* YOUR FALLEN FRIEND!
ASK HIM TO *SAVE* US--
CHOMP
NO!

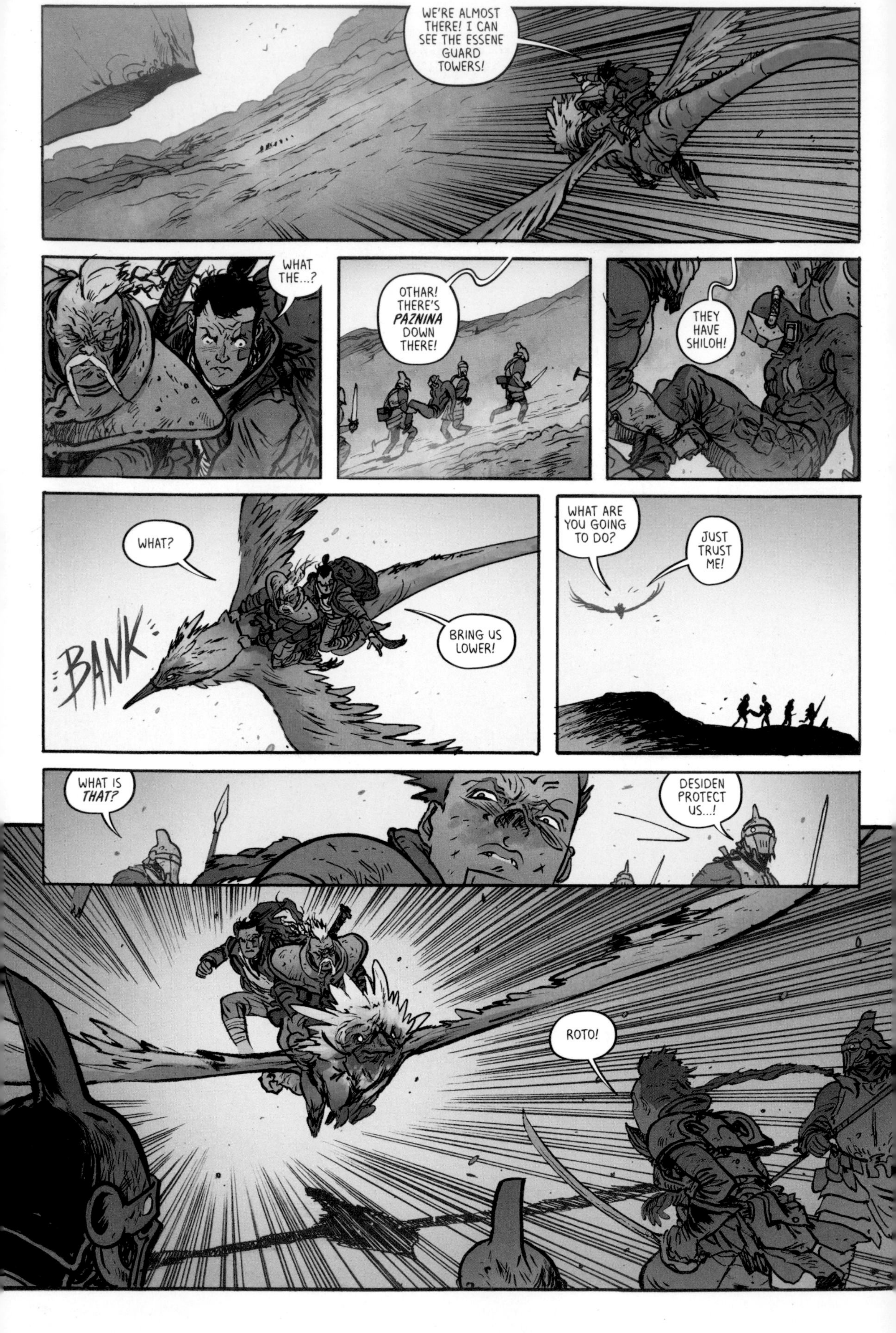
WE'RE ALMOST THERE! I CAN SEE THE ESSENE GUARD TOWERS!
WHAT THE...?
OTHAR! THERE'S PAZNINA DOWN THERE!
THEY HAVE SHILOH!
WHAT?
BANK
BRING US LOWER!
WHAT ARE YOU GOING TO DO?
JUST TRUST ME!
WHAT IS THAT?
DESIDEN PROTECT US...!
ROTO!

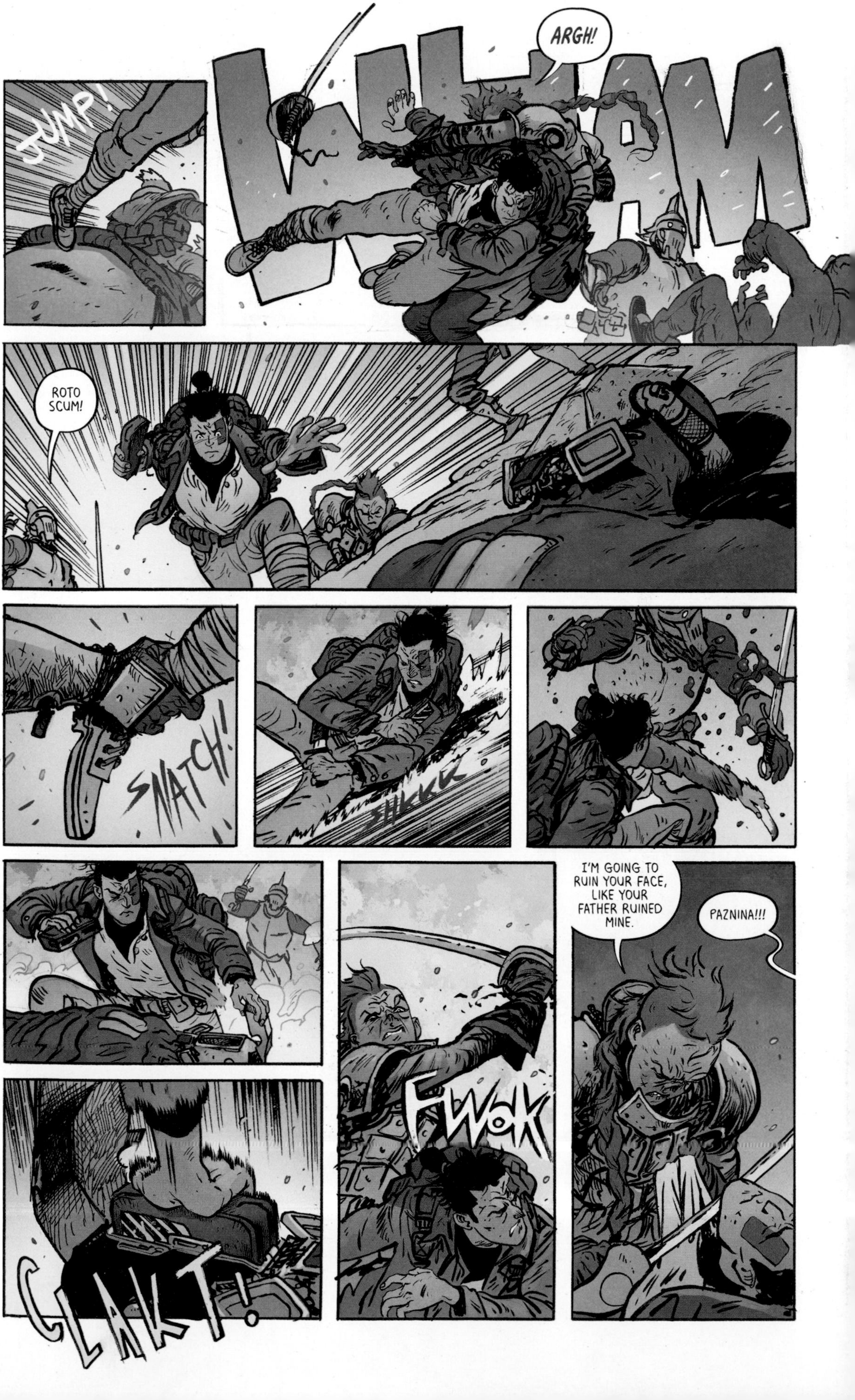
JUMP!
ARGH!
WHAM
ROTO SCUM!
SNATCH!
SHKKK
I'M GOING TO RUIN YOUR FACE, LIKE YOUR FATHER RUINED MINE.
PAZNINA!!!
FWOK
CLAKT!

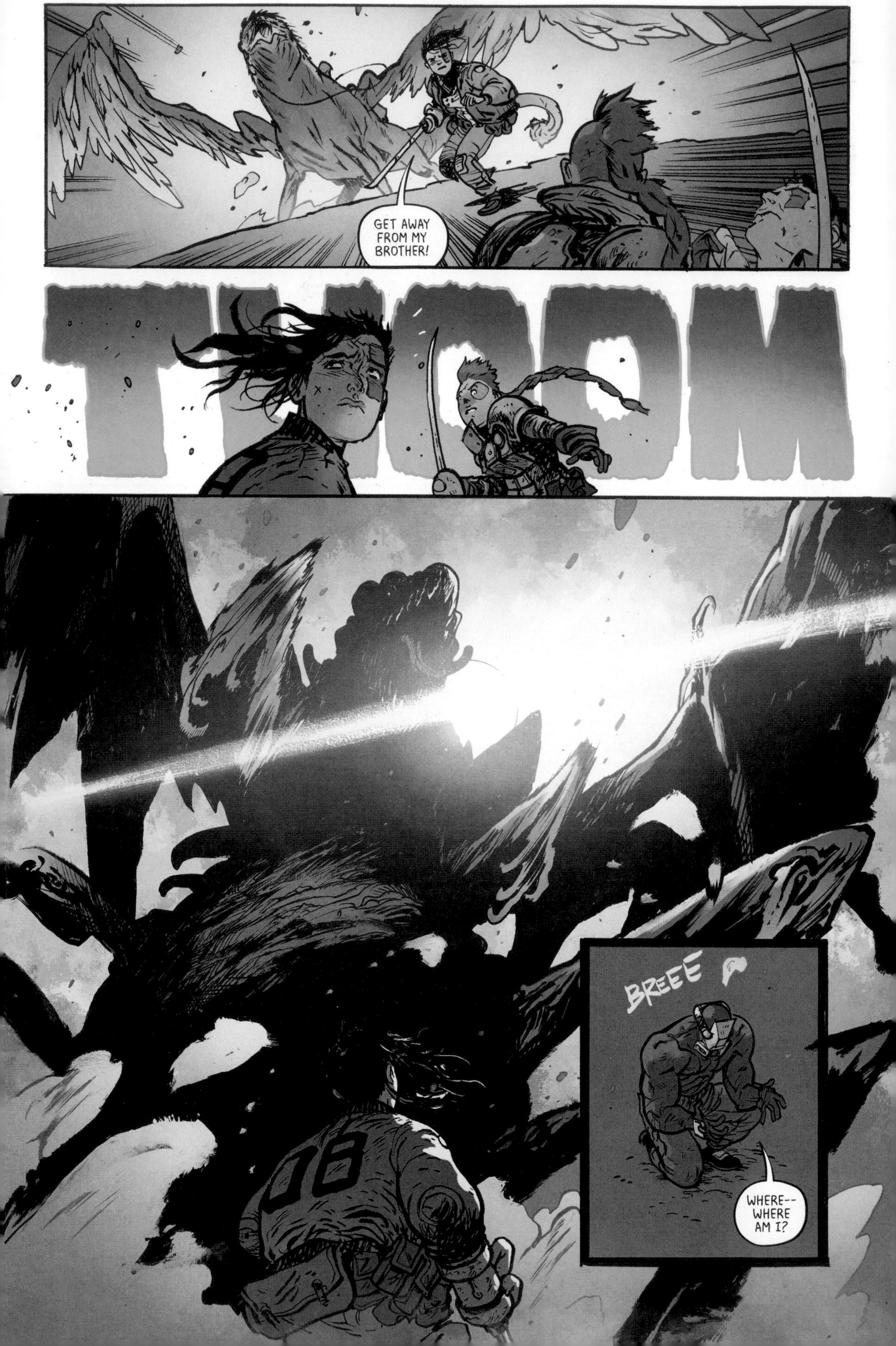
GET AWAY FROM MY BROTHER!
THOOM
BREEE
WHERE-- WHERE AM I?

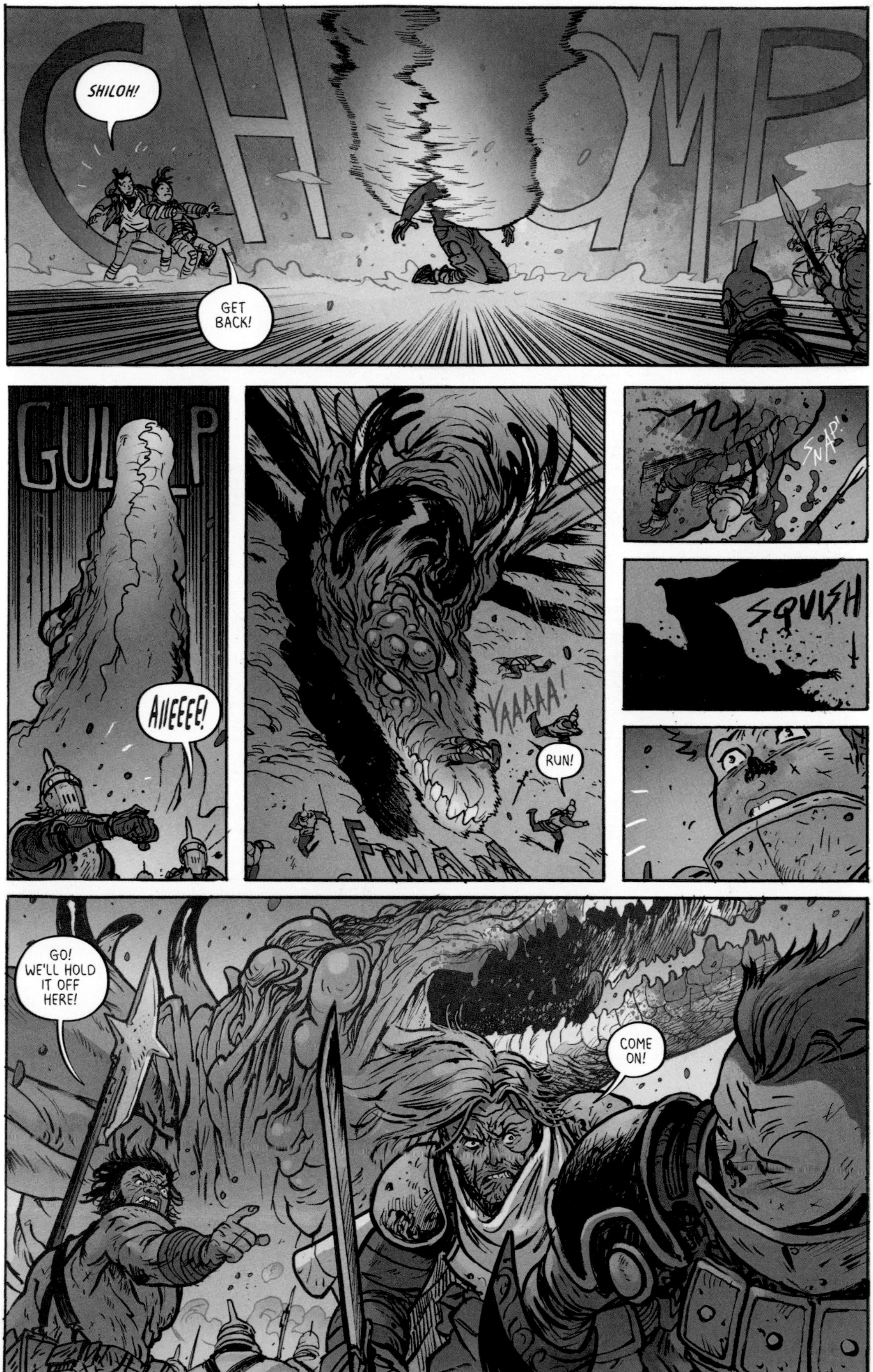
CH
SHILOH!
MP
GET BACK!
GUL P
AIEEEE!
YAAAAA!
RUN!
SNAP!
SQUISH
GO! WE'LL HOLD IT OFF HERE!
COME ON!

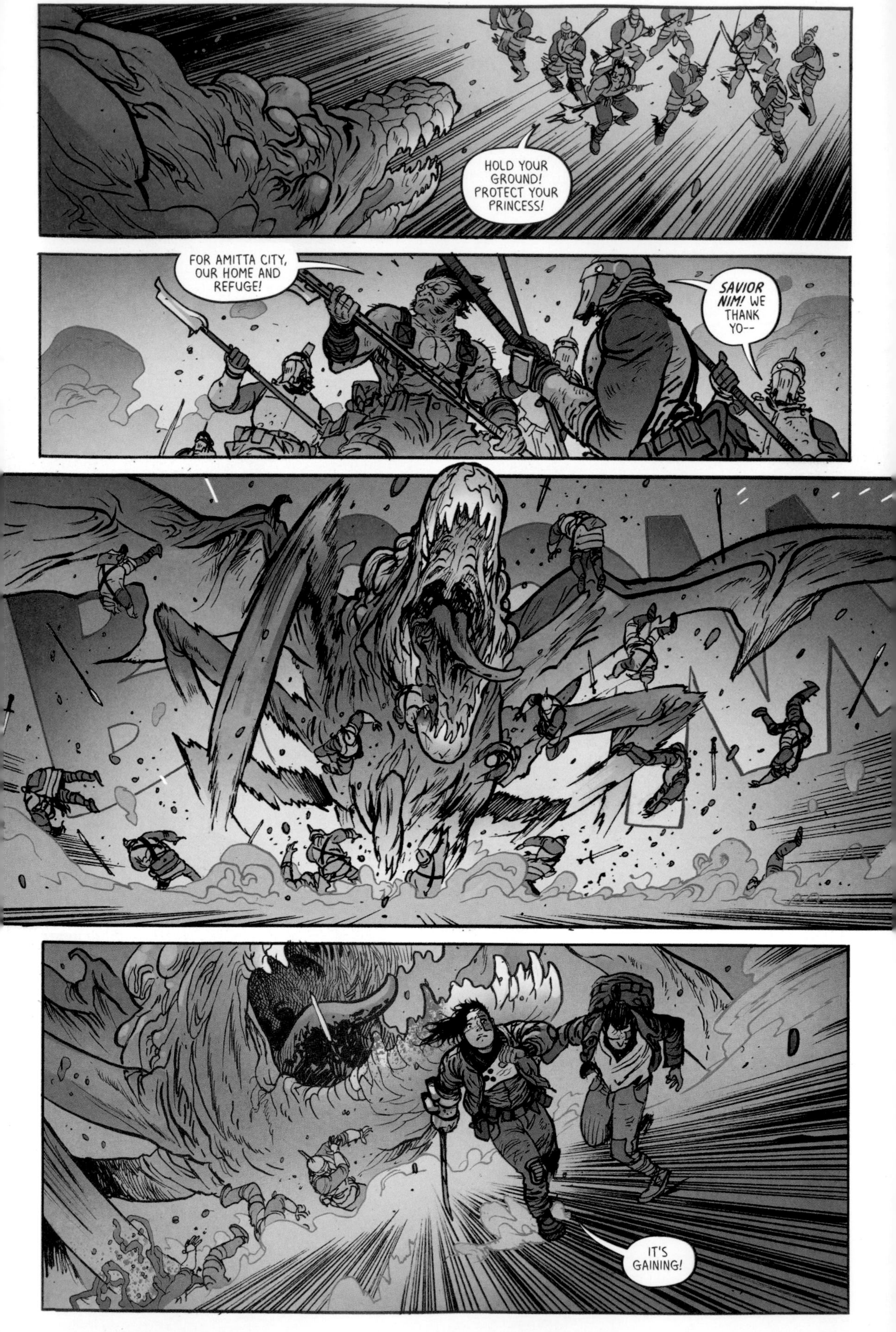

HOLD YOUR GROUND! PROTECT YOUR PRINCESS!
FOR AMITTA CITY, OUR HOME AND REFUGE!
SAVIOR NIM! WE THANK YO--
IT'S GAINING!

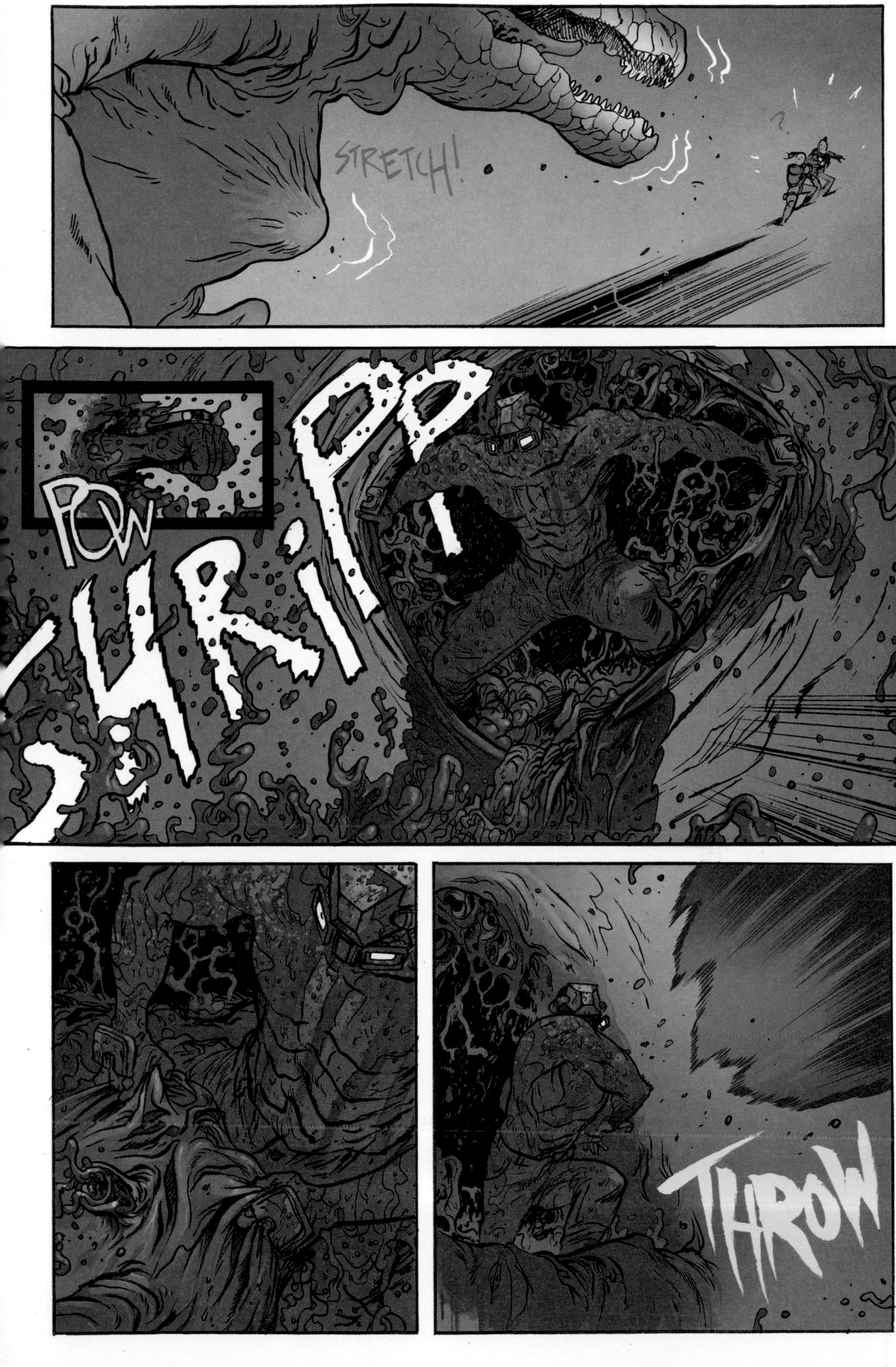

STRETCH!
?
POW
SHRIPP
THROW

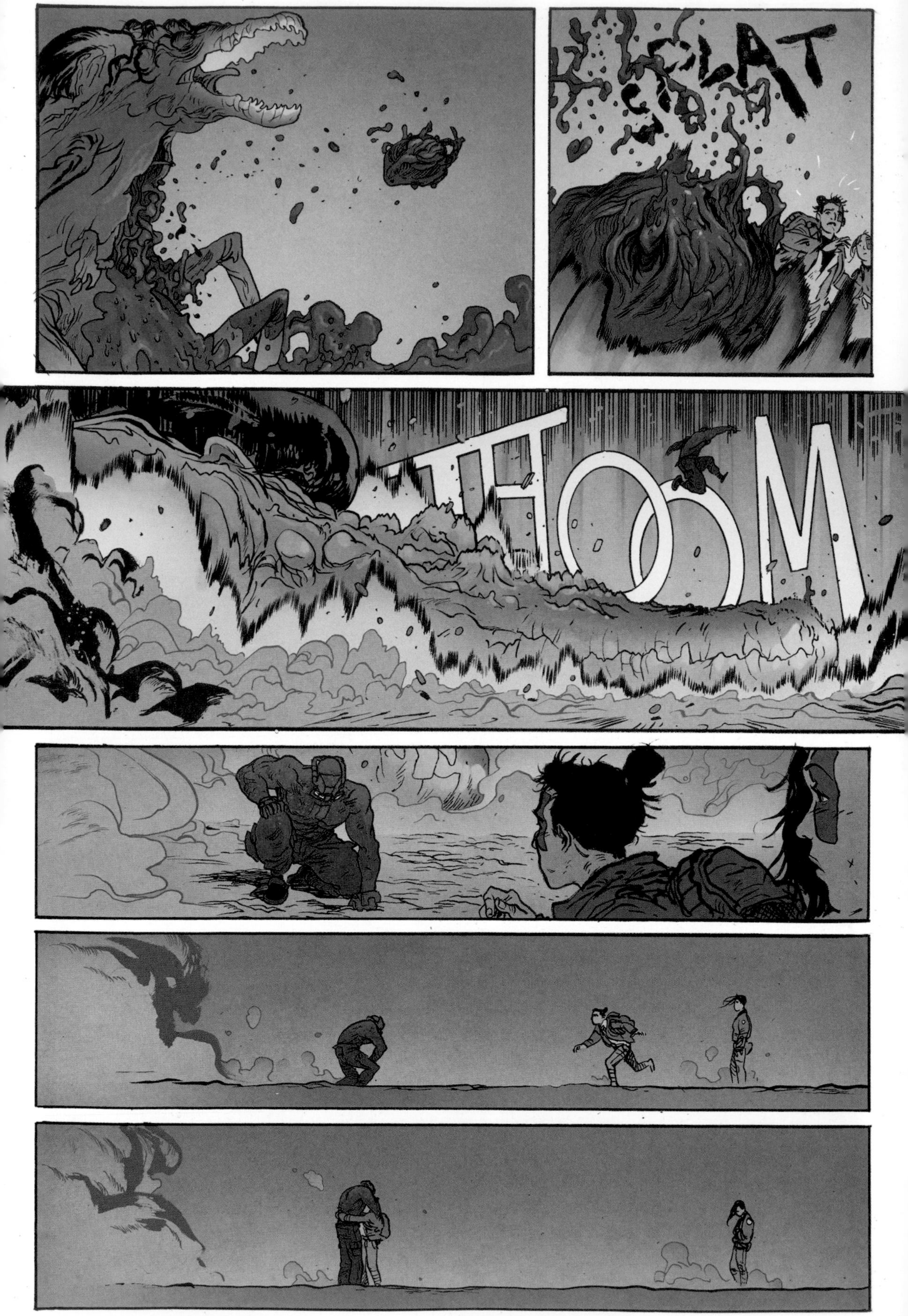
SPLAT
THOOM

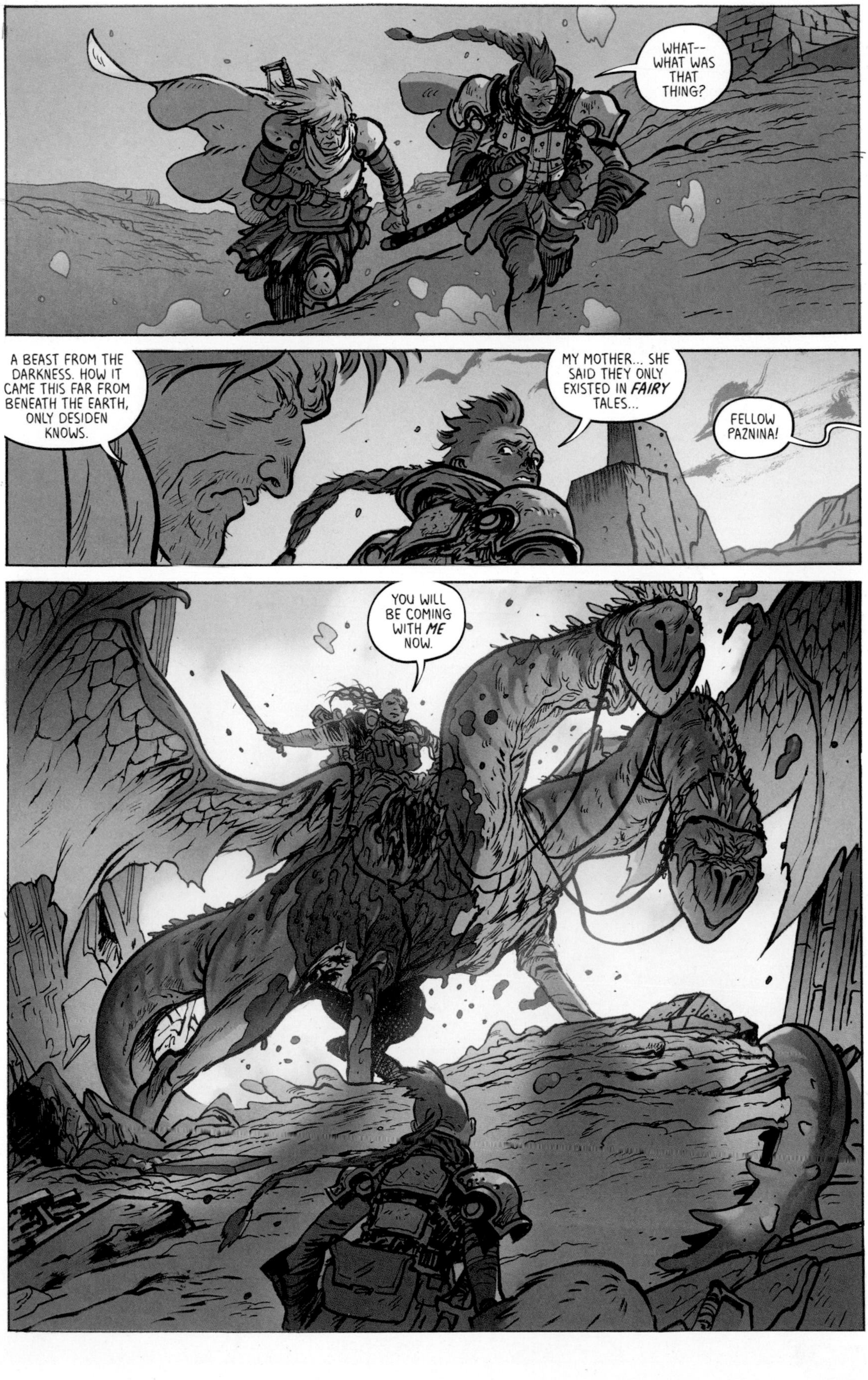
WHAT-- WHAT WAS THAT THING?
A BEAST FROM THE DARKNESS. HOW IT CAME THIS FAR FROM BENEATH THE EARTH, ONLY DESIDEN KNOWS.
MY MOTHER... SHE SAID THEY ONLY EXISTED IN *FAIRY* TALES...
FELLOW PAZNINA!
YOU WILL BE COMING WITH *ME* NOW.

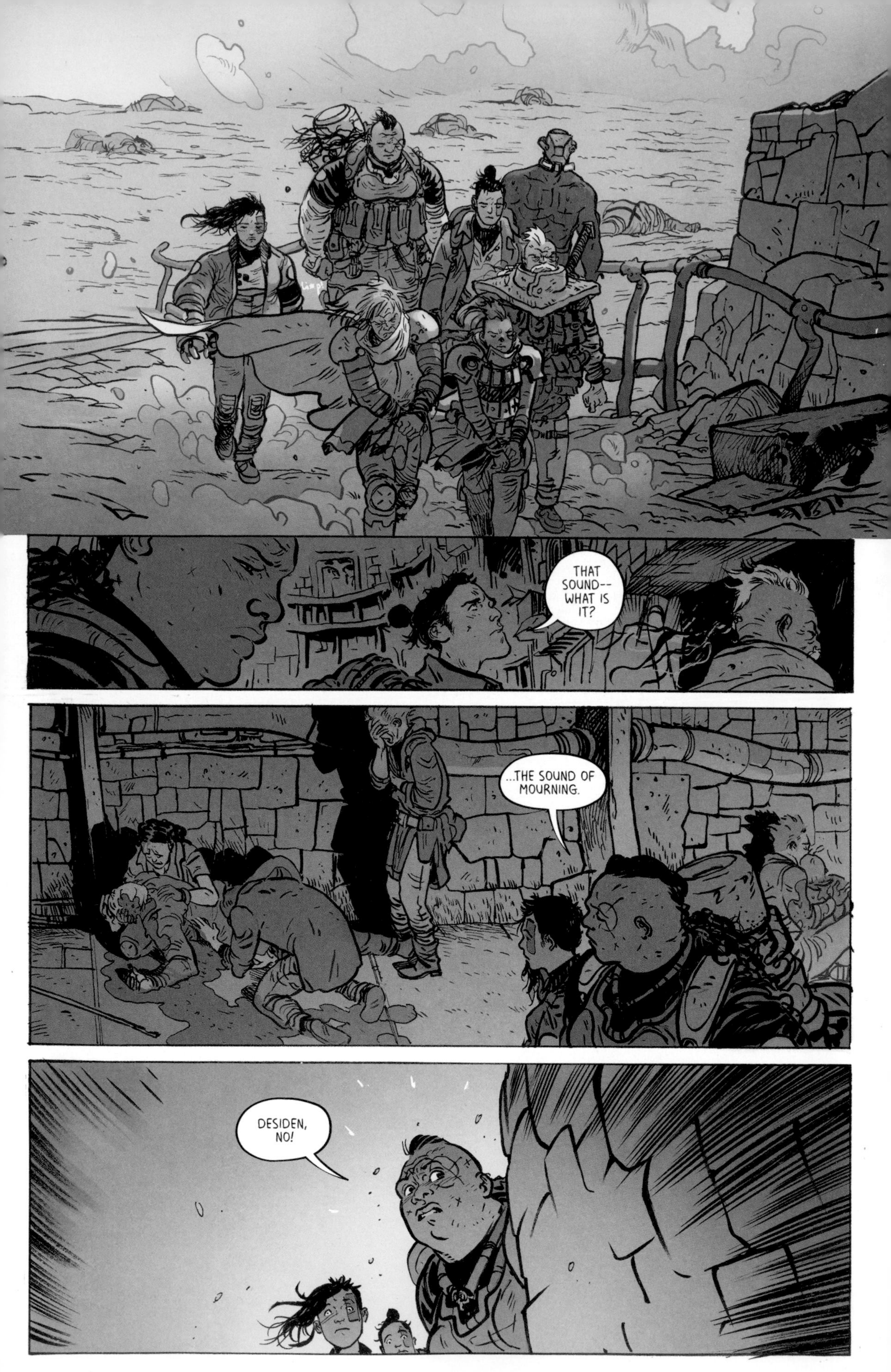
THAT SOUND-- WHAT IS IT?
...THE SOUND OF MOURNING.
DESIDEN, NO!

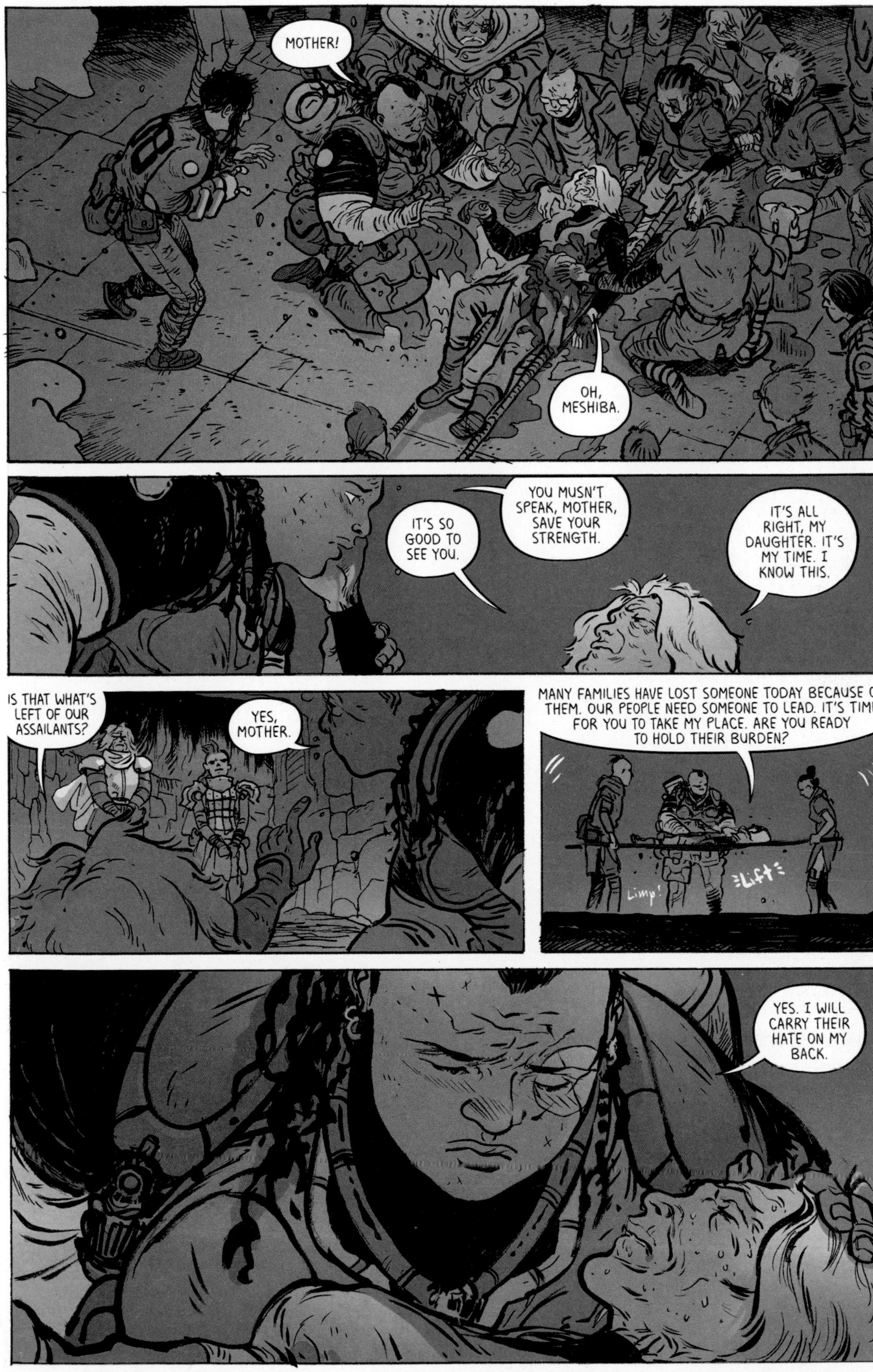
MOTHER!
OH, MESHIBA.
IT'S SO GOOD TO SEE YOU.
YOU MUSN'T SPEAK, MOTHER, SAVE YOUR STRENGTH.
IT'S ALL RIGHT, MY DAUGHTER. IT'S MY TIME. I KNOW THIS.
IS THAT WHAT'S LEFT OF OUR ASSAILANTS?
YES, MOTHER.
MANY FAMILIES HAVE LOST SOMEONE TODAY BECAUSE OF THEM. OUR PEOPLE NEED SOMEONE TO LEAD. IT'S TIME FOR YOU TO TAKE MY PLACE. ARE YOU READY TO HOLD THEIR BURDEN?
Limp!
Lift
YES. I WILL CARRY THEIR HATE ON MY BACK.

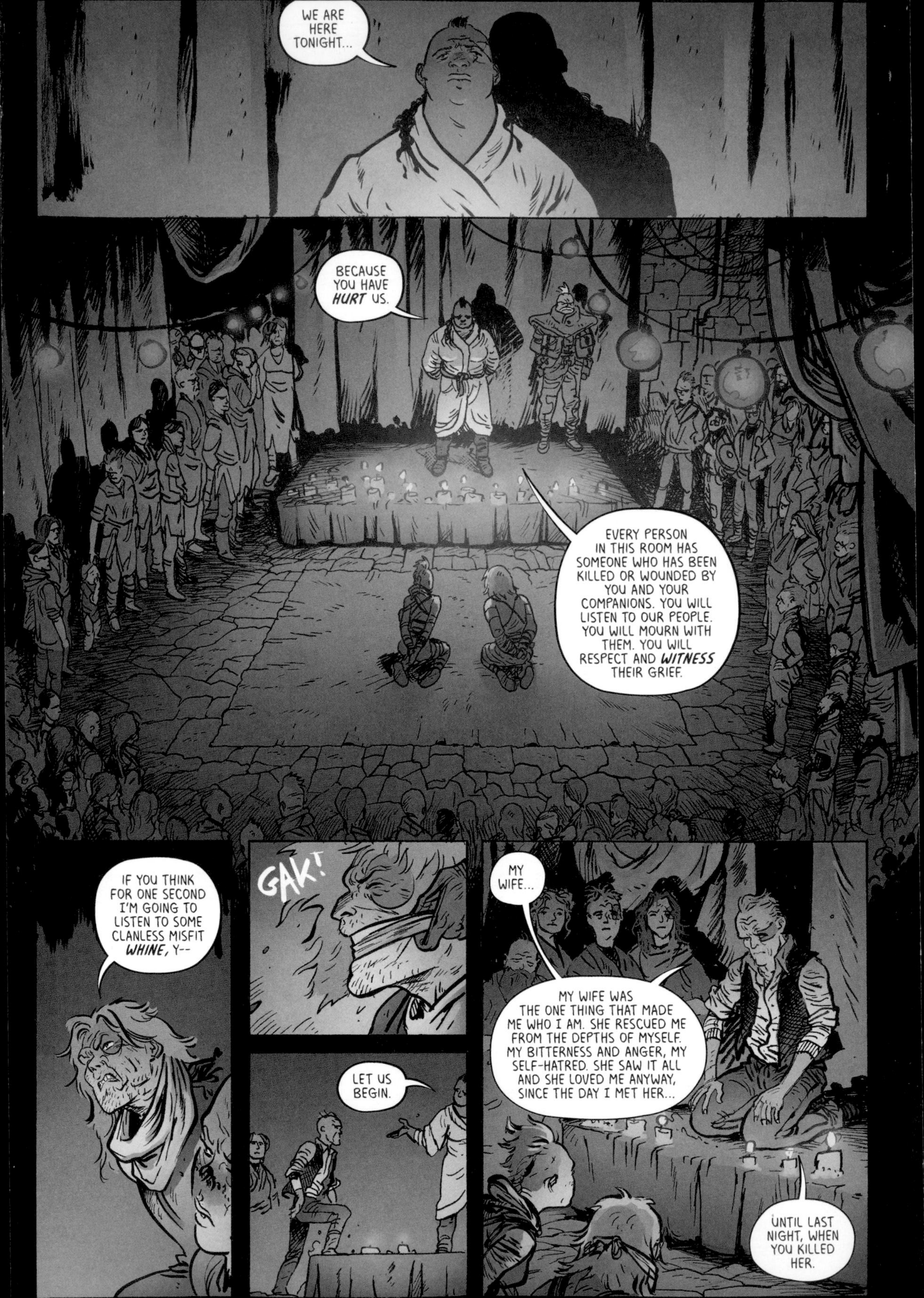

WE ARE HERE TONIGHT...
BECAUSE YOU HAVE *HURT* US.
EVERY PERSON IN THIS ROOM HAS SOMEONE WHO HAS BEEN KILLED OR WOUNDED BY YOU AND YOUR COMPANIONS. YOU WILL LISTEN TO OUR PEOPLE. YOU WILL MOURN WITH THEM. YOU WILL RESPECT AND *WITNESS* THEIR GRIEF.
IF YOU THINK FOR ONE SECOND I'M GOING TO LISTEN TO SOME CLANLESS MISFIT *WHINE*, Y--
GAK!
LET US BEGIN.
MY WIFE...
MY WIFE WAS THE ONE THING THAT MADE ME WHO I AM. SHE RESCUED ME FROM THE DEPTHS OF MYSELF. MY BITTERNESS AND ANGER, MY SELF-HATRED. SHE SAW IT ALL AND SHE LOVED ME ANYWAY, SINCE THE DAY I MET HER...
UNTIL LAST NIGHT, WHEN YOU KILLED HER.

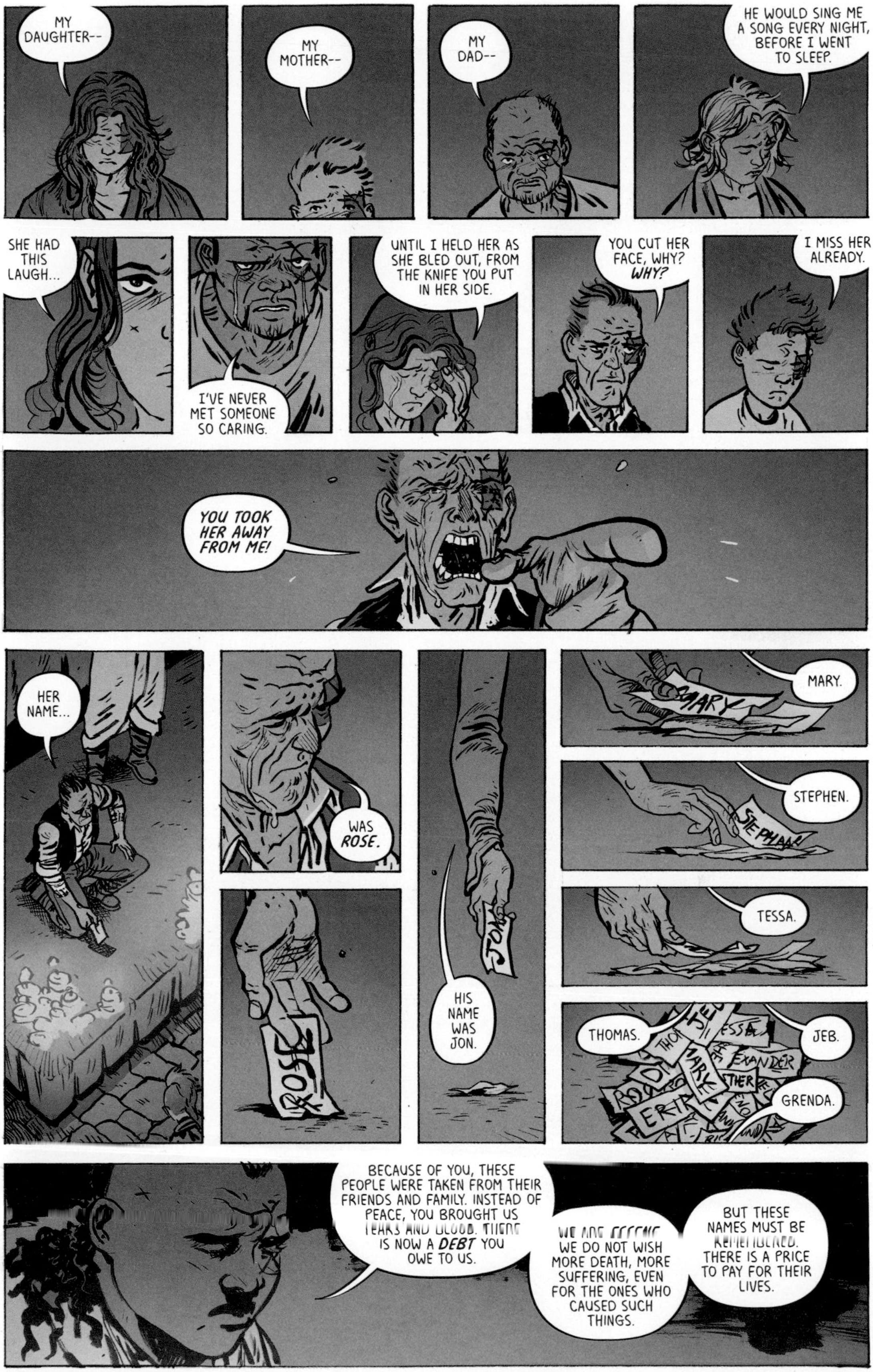
MY DAUGHTER--
MY MOTHER--
MY DAD--
HE WOULD SING ME A SONG EVERY NIGHT, BEFORE I WENT TO SLEEP.
SHE HAD THIS LAUGH...
I'VE NEVER MET SOMEONE SO CARING.
UNTIL I HELD HER AS SHE BLED OUT, FROM THE KNIFE YOU PUT IN HER SIDE.
YOU CUT HER FACE, WHY? *WHY?*
I MISS HER ALREADY.
YOU TOOK HER AWAY FROM ME!
HER NAME...
WAS *ROSE.*
ROSE
JON
HIS NAME WAS JON.
MARY
MARY.
STEPHAN
STEPHEN.
TESSA.
THOMAS.
JEB.
GRENDA.
BECAUSE OF YOU, THESE PEOPLE WERE TAKEN FROM THEIR FRIENDS AND FAMILY. INSTEAD OF PEACE, YOU BROUGHT US TEARS AND BLOOD. THERE IS NOW A *DEBT* YOU OWE TO US.
WE DO NOT WISH MORE DEATH, MORE SUFFERING, EVEN FOR THE ONES WHO CAUSED SUCH THINGS.
BUT THESE NAMES MUST BE REMEMBERED. THERE IS A PRICE TO PAY FOR THEIR LIVES.

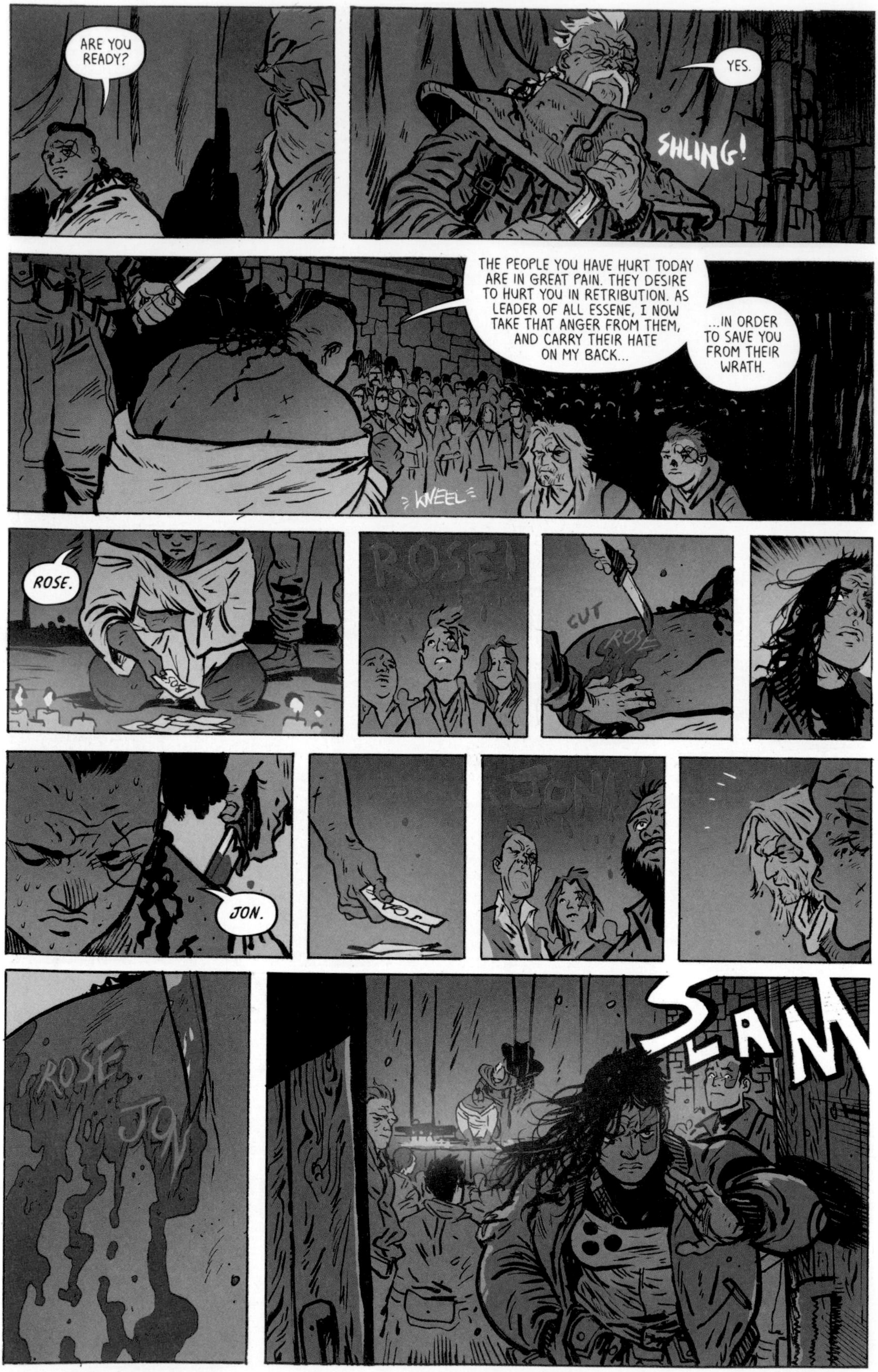
ARE YOU READY?
YES.
SHLING!
THE PEOPLE YOU HAVE HURT TODAY ARE IN GREAT PAIN. THEY DESIRE TO HURT YOU IN RETRIBUTION. AS LEADER OF ALL ESSENE, I NOW TAKE THAT ANGER FROM THEM, AND CARRY THEIR HATE ON MY BACK...
...IN ORDER TO SAVE YOU FROM THEIR WRATH.
KNEEL
ROSE.
ROSE
CUT
JON.
JON
SLAM

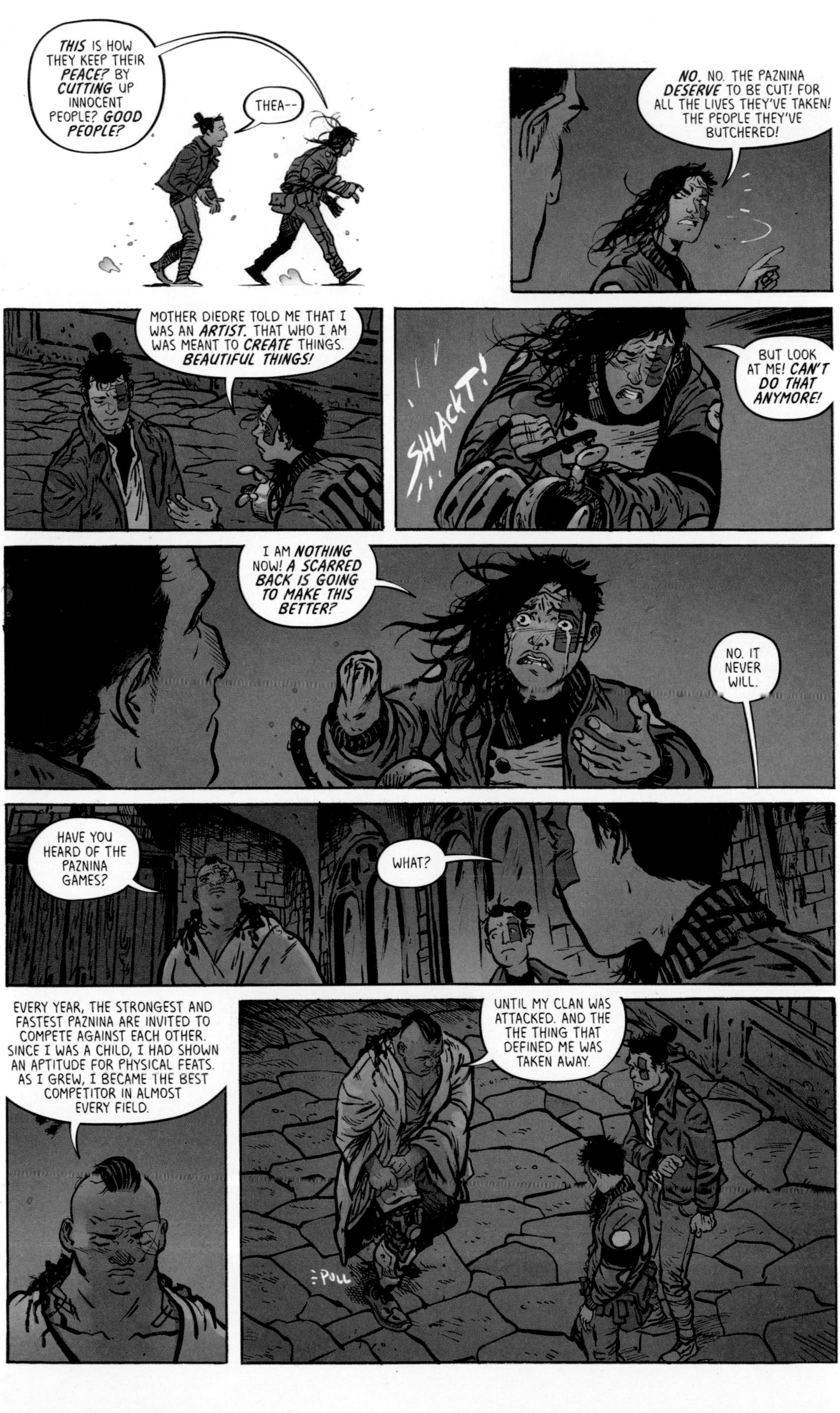
THIS IS HOW THEY KEEP THEIR PEACE? BY CUTTING UP INNOCENT PEOPLE? GOOD PEOPLE?
THEA--
NO. NO. THE PAZNINA DESERVE TO BE CUT! FOR ALL THE LIVES THEY'VE TAKEN! THE PEOPLE THEY'VE BUTCHERED!
MOTHER DIEDRE TOLD ME THAT I WAS AN ARTIST. THAT WHO I AM WAS MEANT TO CREATE THINGS. BEAUTIFUL THINGS!
SHLACKT!
BUT LOOK AT ME! CAN'T DO THAT ANYMORE!
I AM NOTHING NOW! A SCARRED BACK IS GOING TO MAKE THIS BETTER?
NO. IT NEVER WILL.
HAVE YOU HEARD OF THE PAZNINA GAMES?
WHAT?
EVERY YEAR, THE STRONGEST AND FASTEST PAZNINA ARE INVITED TO COMPETE AGAINST EACH OTHER. SINCE I WAS A CHILD, I HAD SHOWN AN APTITUDE FOR PHYSICAL FEATS. AS I GREW, I BECAME THE BEST COMPETITOR IN ALMOST EVERY FIELD.
UNTIL MY CLAN WAS ATTACKED. AND THE THE THING THAT DEFINED ME WAS TAKEN AWAY.
PULL

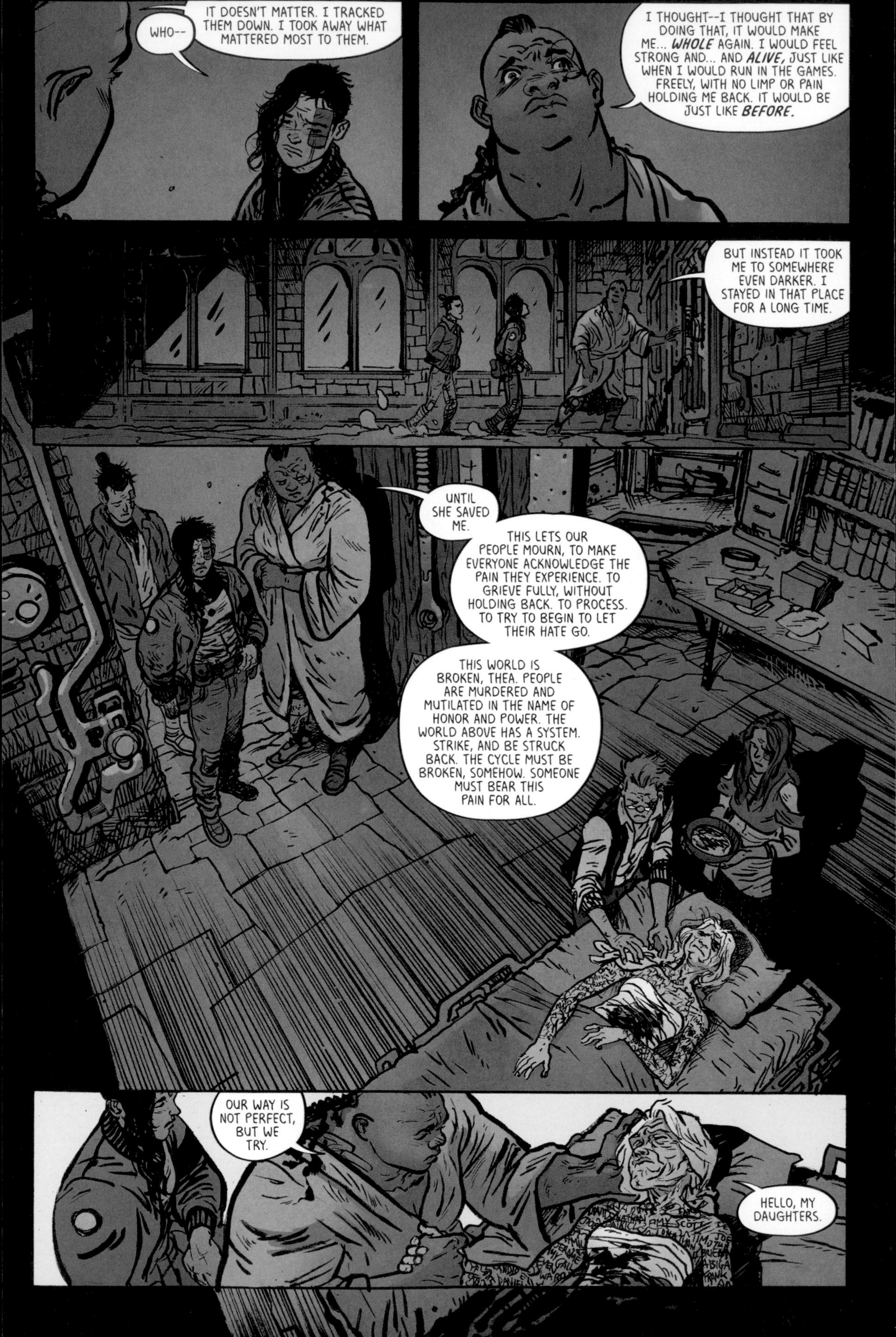
WHO--
IT DOESN'T MATTER. I TRACKED THEM DOWN. I TOOK AWAY WHAT MATTERED MOST TO THEM.
I THOUGHT--I THOUGHT THAT BY DOING THAT, IT WOULD MAKE ME... WHOLE AGAIN. I WOULD FEEL STRONG AND... AND ALIVE, JUST LIKE WHEN I WOULD RUN IN THE GAMES. FREELY, WITH NO LIMP OR PAIN HOLDING ME BACK. IT WOULD BE JUST LIKE BEFORE.
BUT INSTEAD IT TOOK ME TO SOMEWHERE EVEN DARKER. I STAYED IN THAT PLACE FOR A LONG TIME.
UNTIL SHE SAVED ME.
THIS LETS OUR PEOPLE MOURN, TO MAKE EVERYONE ACKNOWLEDGE THE PAIN THEY EXPERIENCE. TO GRIEVE FULLY, WITHOUT HOLDING BACK. TO PROCESS. TO TRY TO BEGIN TO LET THEIR HATE GO.
THIS WORLD IS BROKEN, THEA. PEOPLE ARE MURDERED AND MUTILATED IN THE NAME OF HONOR AND POWER. THE WORLD ABOVE HAS A SYSTEM. STRIKE, AND BE STRUCK BACK. THE CYCLE MUST BE BROKEN, SOMEHOW. SOMEONE MUST BEAR THIS PAIN FOR ALL.
OUR WAY IS NOT PERFECT, BUT WE TRY.
HELLO, MY DAUGHTERS.

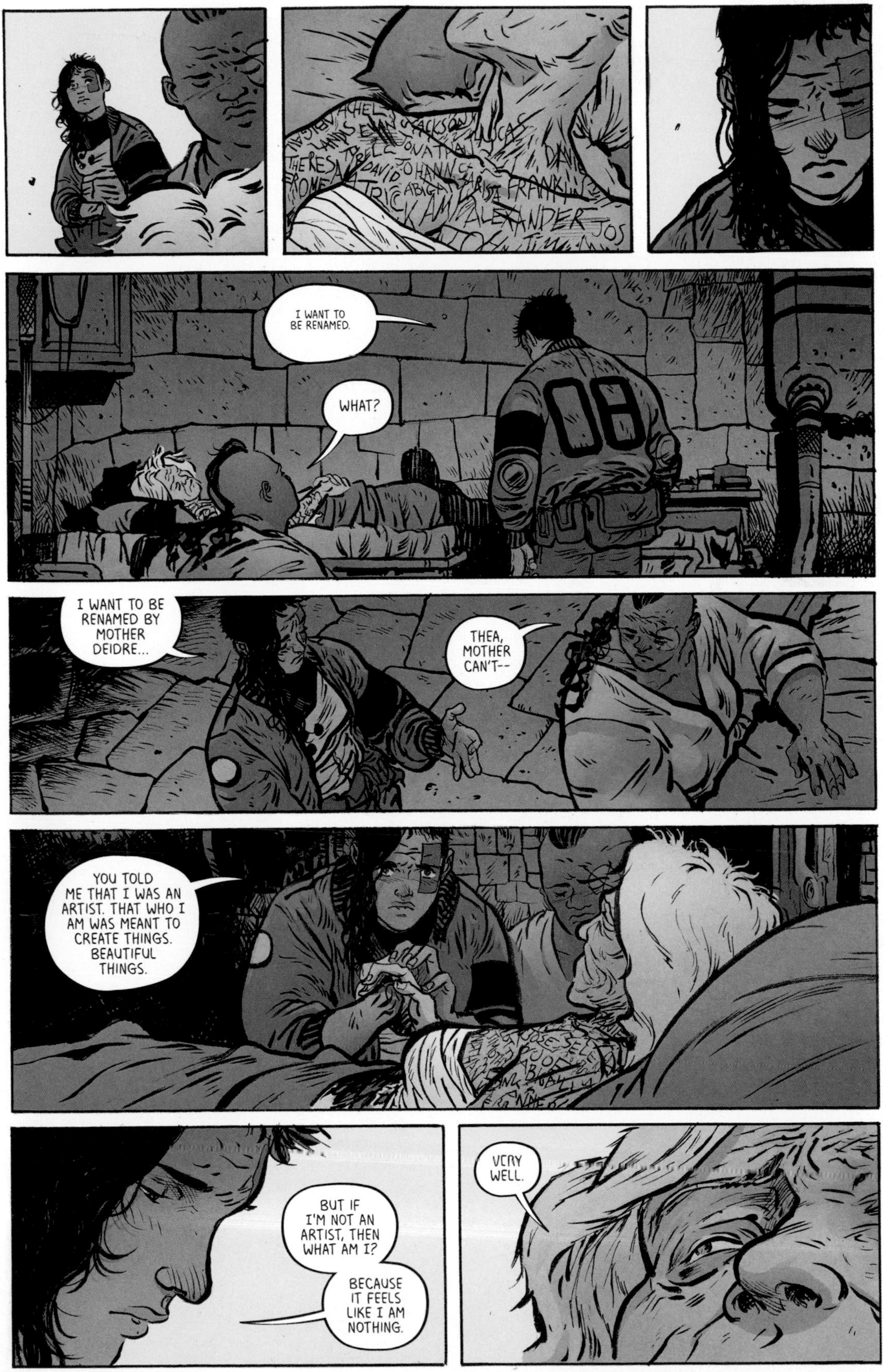
I WANT TO BE RENAMED.
WHAT?
I WANT TO BE RENAMED BY MOTHER DEIDRE...
THEA, MOTHER CAN'T--
YOU TOLD ME THAT I WAS AN ARTIST. THAT WHO I AM WAS MEANT TO CREATE THINGS. BEAUTIFUL THINGS.
BUT IF I'M NOT AN ARTIST, THEN WHAT AM I?
BECAUSE IT FEELS LIKE I AM NOTHING.
VERY WELL.

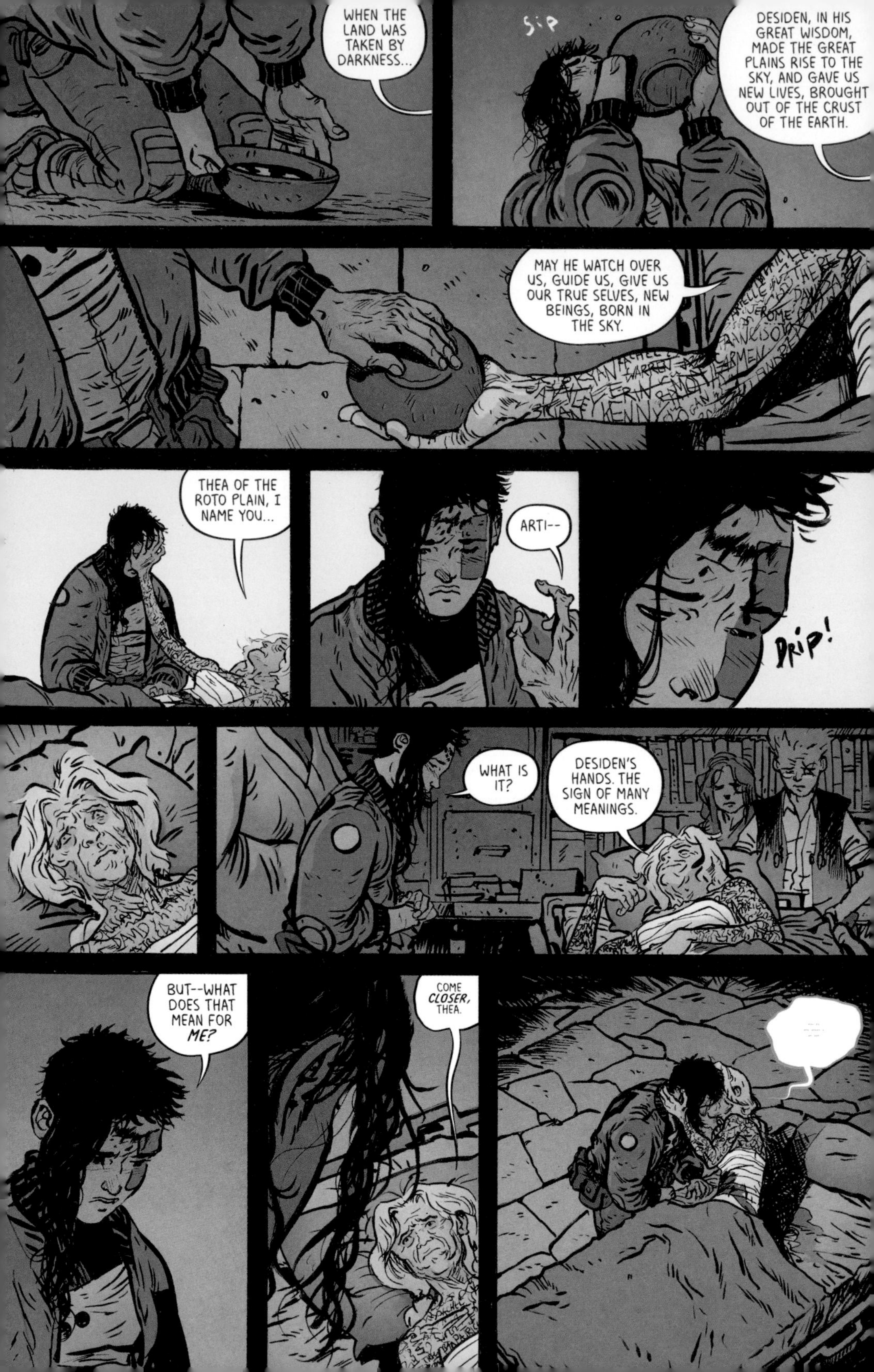
WHEN THE LAND WAS TAKEN BY DARKNESS...
SIP
DESIDEN, IN HIS GREAT WISDOM, MADE THE GREAT PLAINS RISE TO THE SKY, AND GAVE US NEW LIVES, BROUGHT OUT OF THE CRUST OF THE EARTH.
MAY HE WATCH OVER US, GUIDE US, GIVE US OUR TRUE SELVES, NEW BEINGS, BORN IN THE SKY.
THEA OF THE ROTO PLAIN, I NAME YOU...
ARTI--
DRIP!
WHAT IS IT?
DESIDEN'S HANDS. THE SIGN OF MANY MEANINGS.
BUT--WHAT DOES THAT MEAN FOR ME?
COME CLOSER, THEA.

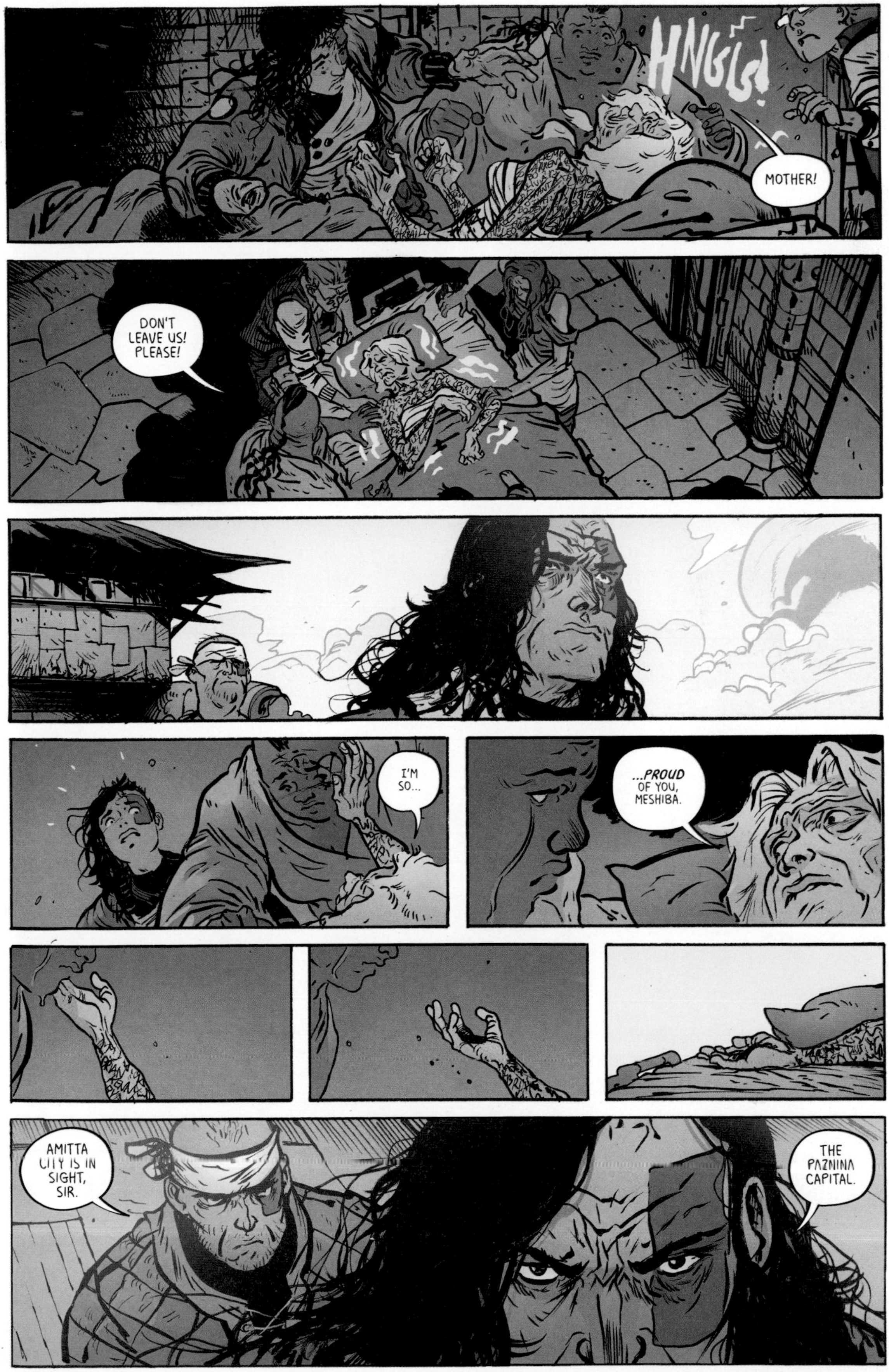
HNGLS!
MOTHER!
DON'T LEAVE US! PLEASE!
I'M SO...
...PROUD OF YOU, MESHIBA.
AMITTA CITY IS IN SIGHT, SIR.
THE PAZNINA CAPITAL.

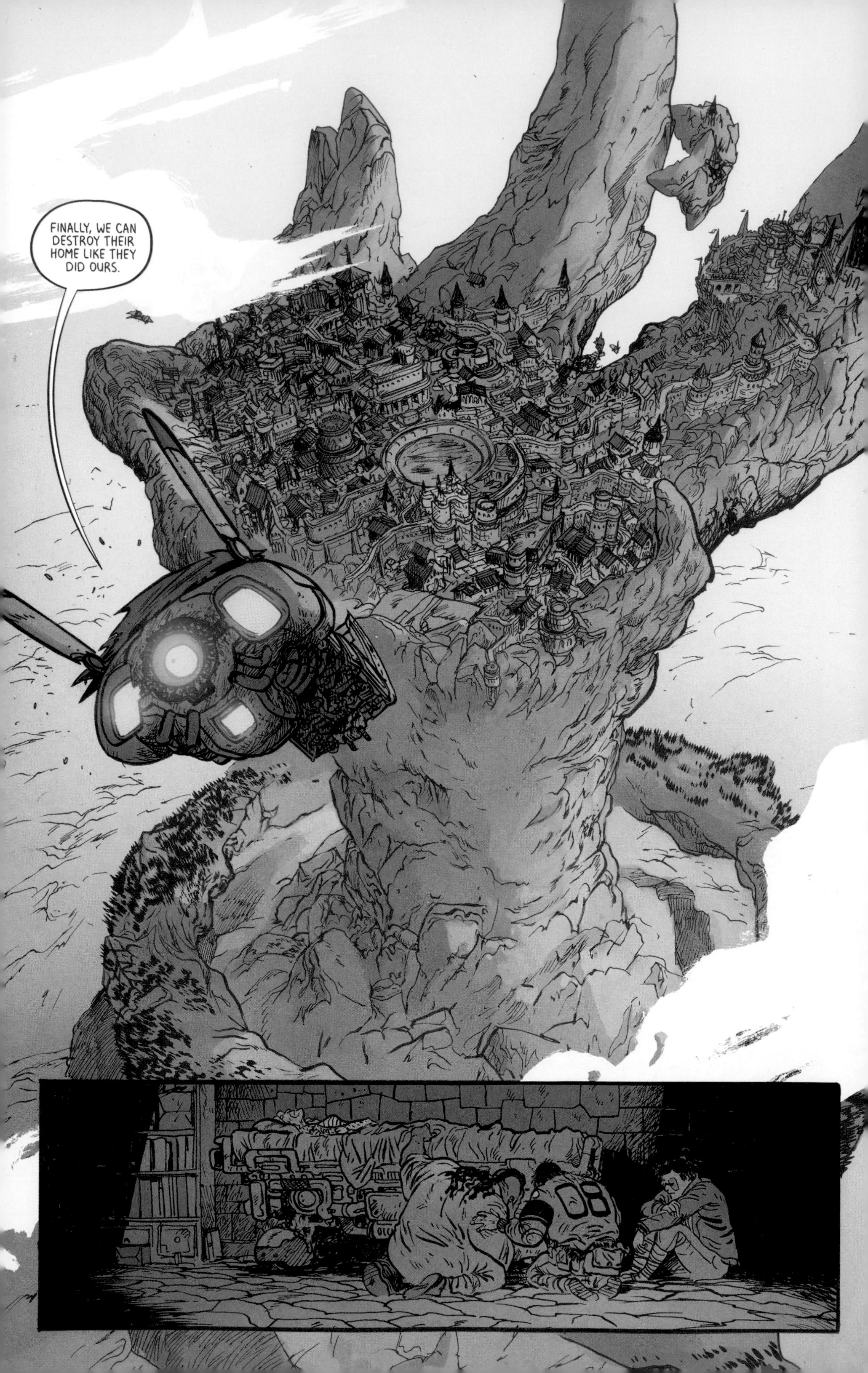
FINALLY, WE CAN DESTROY THEIR HOME LIKE THEY DID OURS.

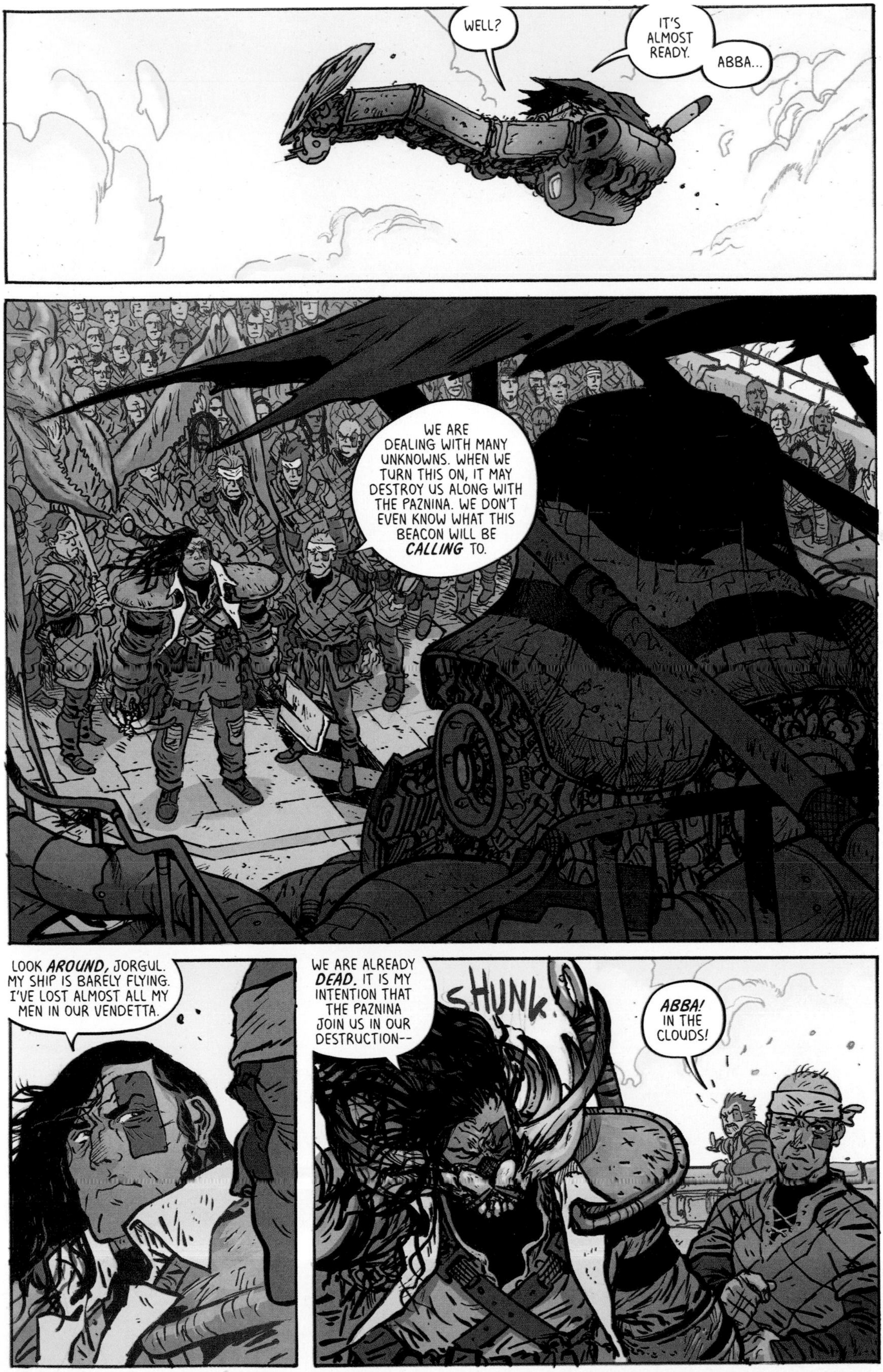
WELL?
IT'S ALMOST READY.
ABBA...
WE ARE DEALING WITH MANY UNKNOWNS. WHEN WE TURN THIS ON, IT MAY DESTROY US ALONG WITH THE PAZNINA. WE DON'T EVEN KNOW WHAT THIS BEACON WILL BE *CALLING* TO.
LOOK *AROUND,* JORGUL. MY SHIP IS BARELY FLYING. I'VE LOST ALMOST ALL MY MEN IN OUR VENDETTA.
WE ARE ALREADY *DEAD.* IT IS MY INTENTION THAT THE PAZNINA JOIN US IN OUR DESTRUCTION--
SHUNK
ABBA! IN THE CLOUDS!

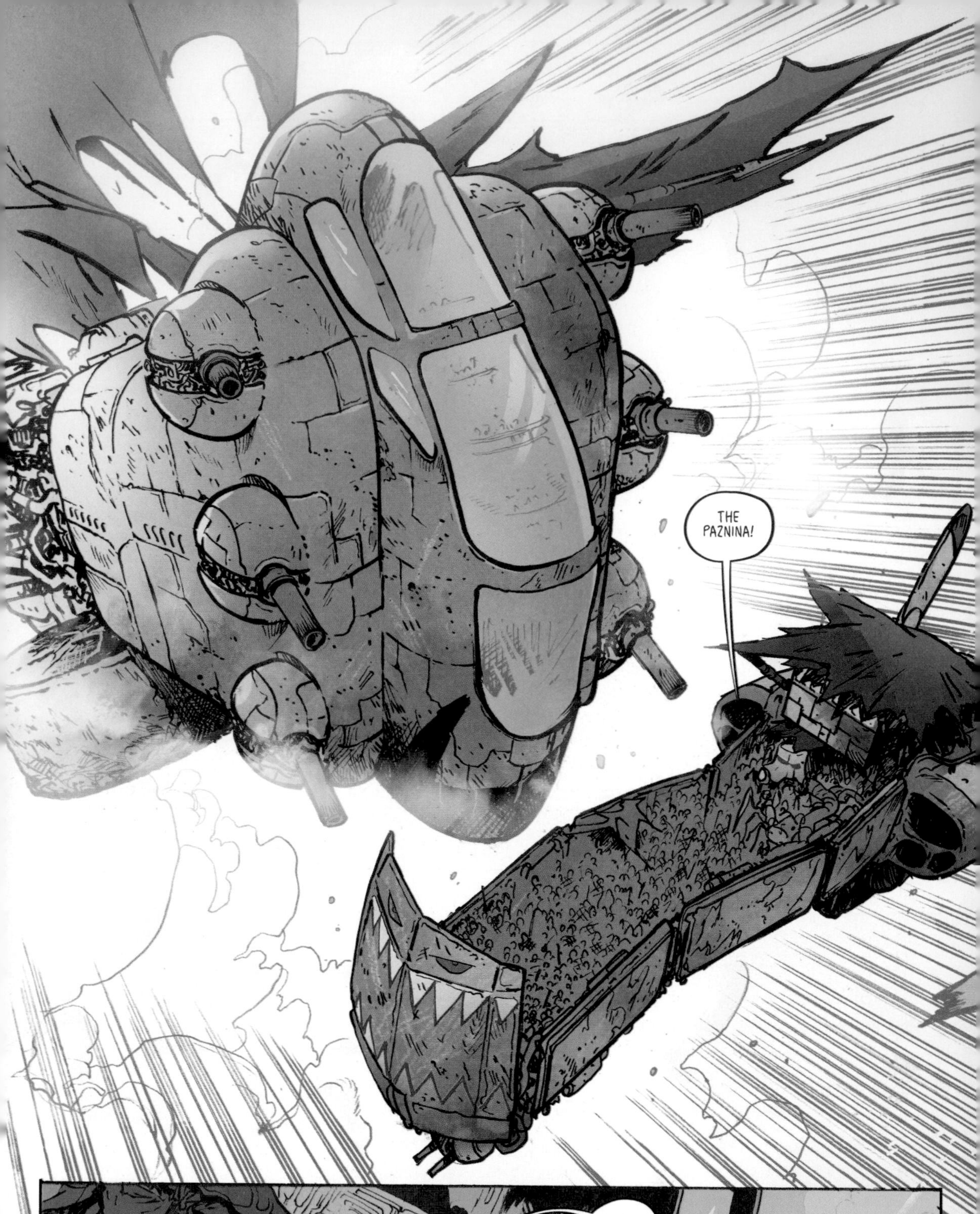
THE PAZNINA!
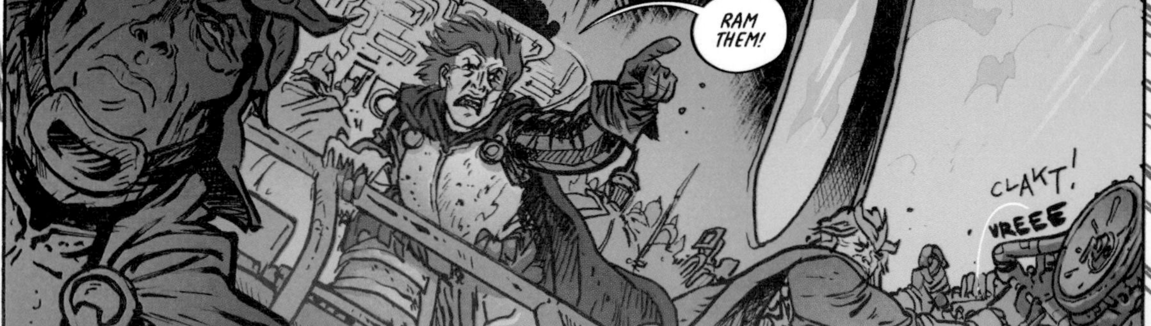
RAM THEM!
CLAKT!
VREEE

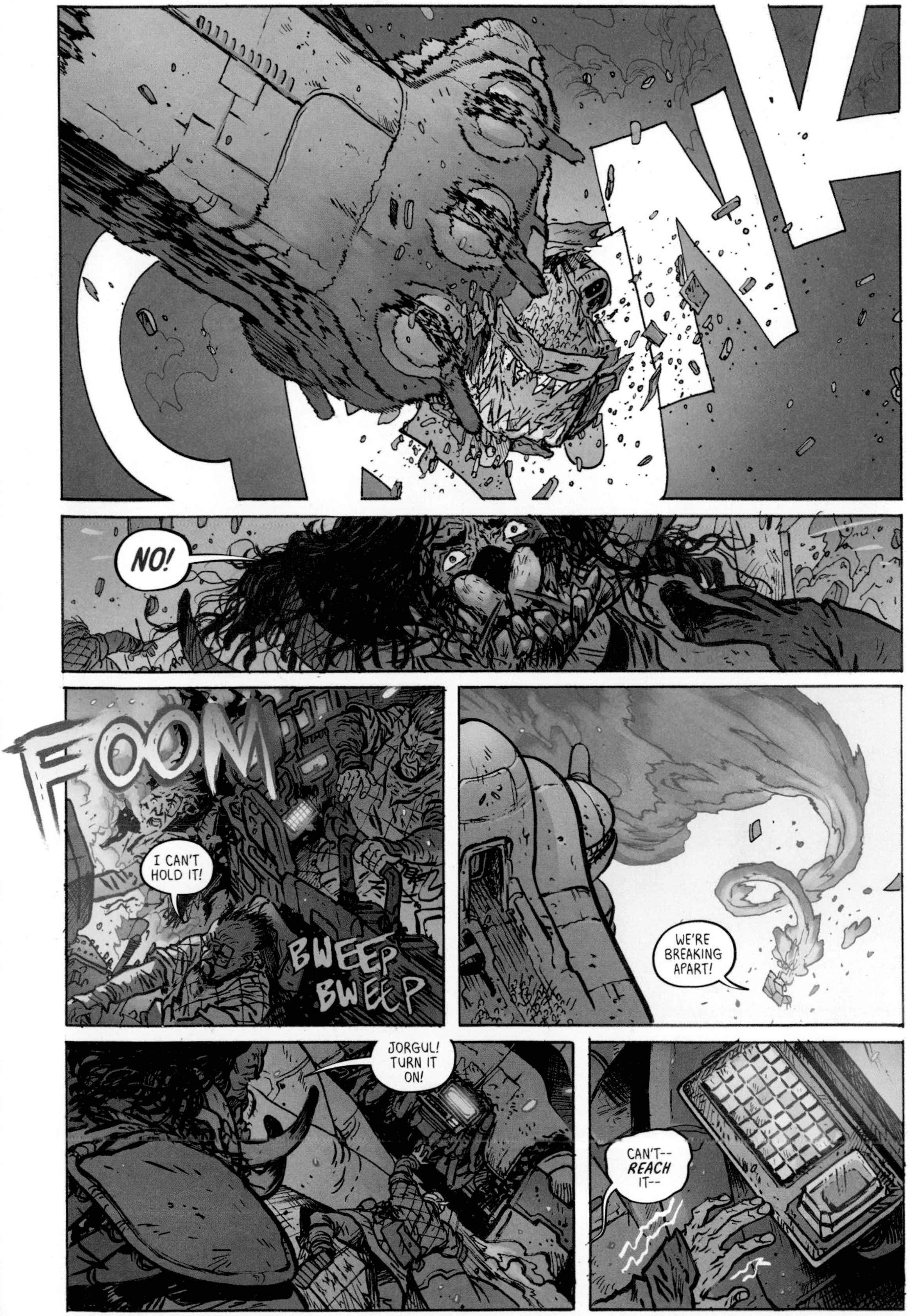
NO!
FOOM
I CAN'T HOLD IT!
BWEEP BWEEP
WE'RE BREAKING APART!
JORGUL! TURN IT ON!
CAN'T-- *REACH* IT--

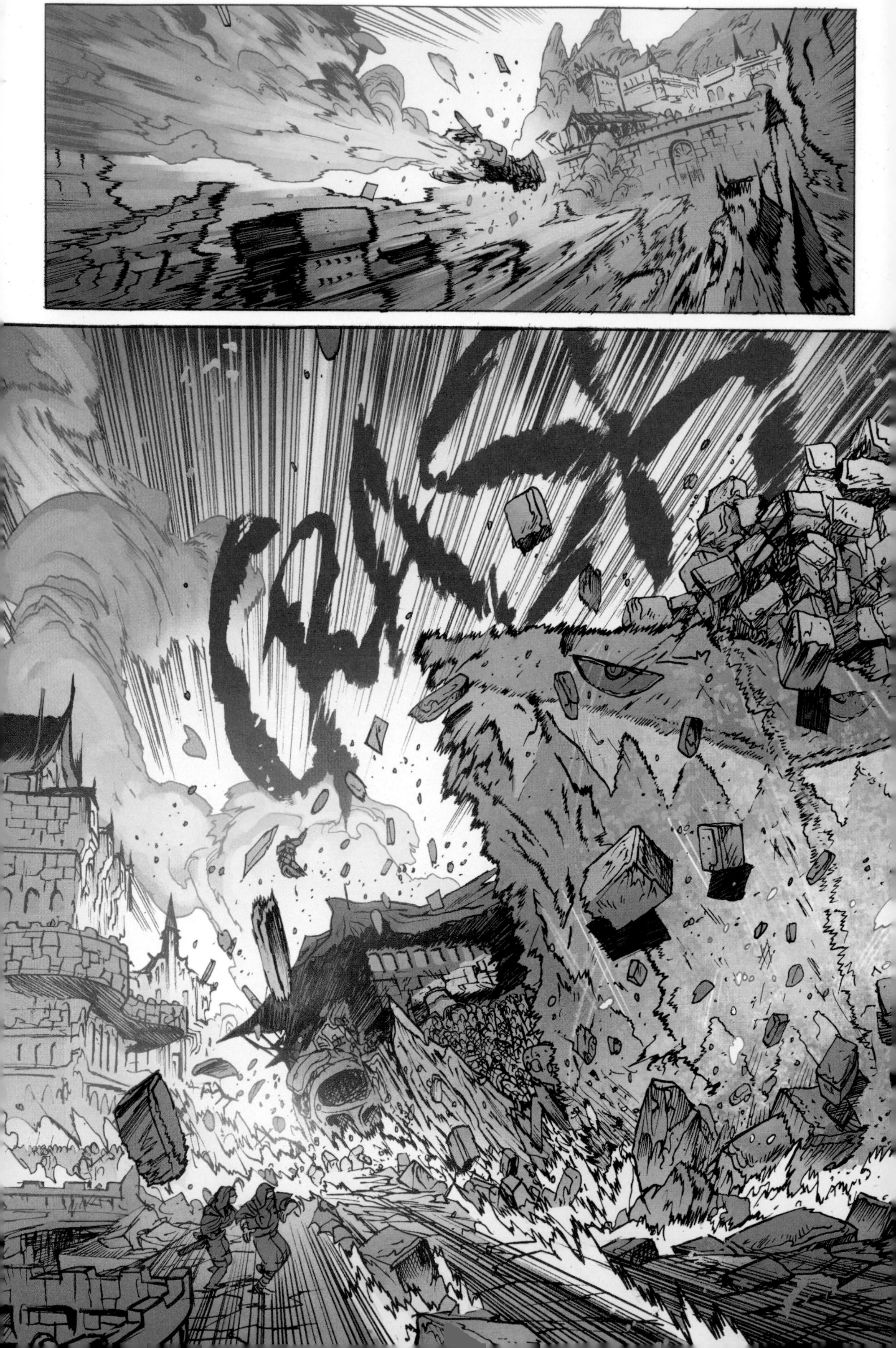

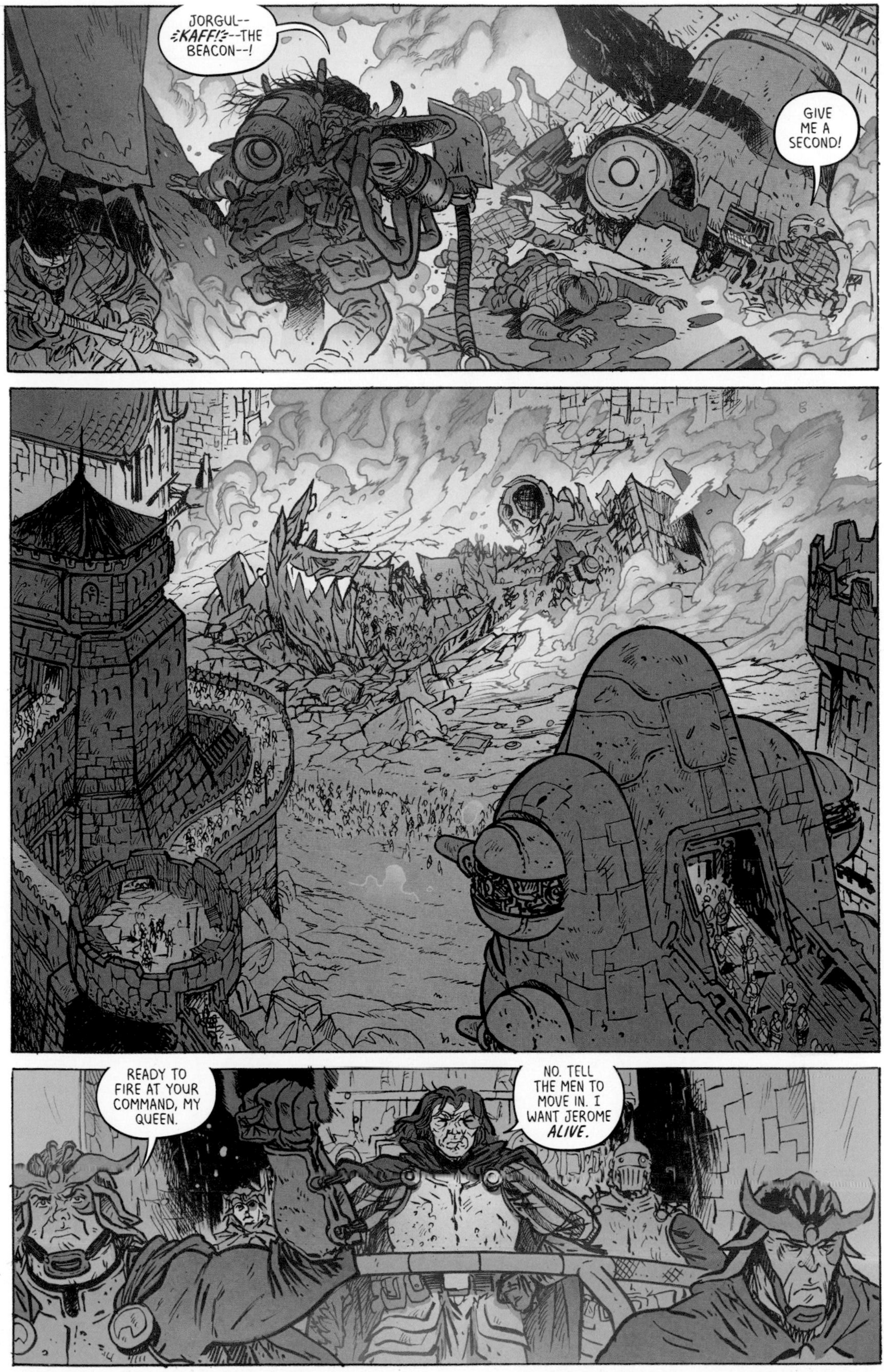
JORGUL-- KAFF!--THE BEACON--!
GIVE ME A SECOND!
READY TO FIRE AT YOUR COMMAND, MY QUEEN.
NO. TELL THE MEN TO MOVE IN. I WANT JEROME ALIVE.

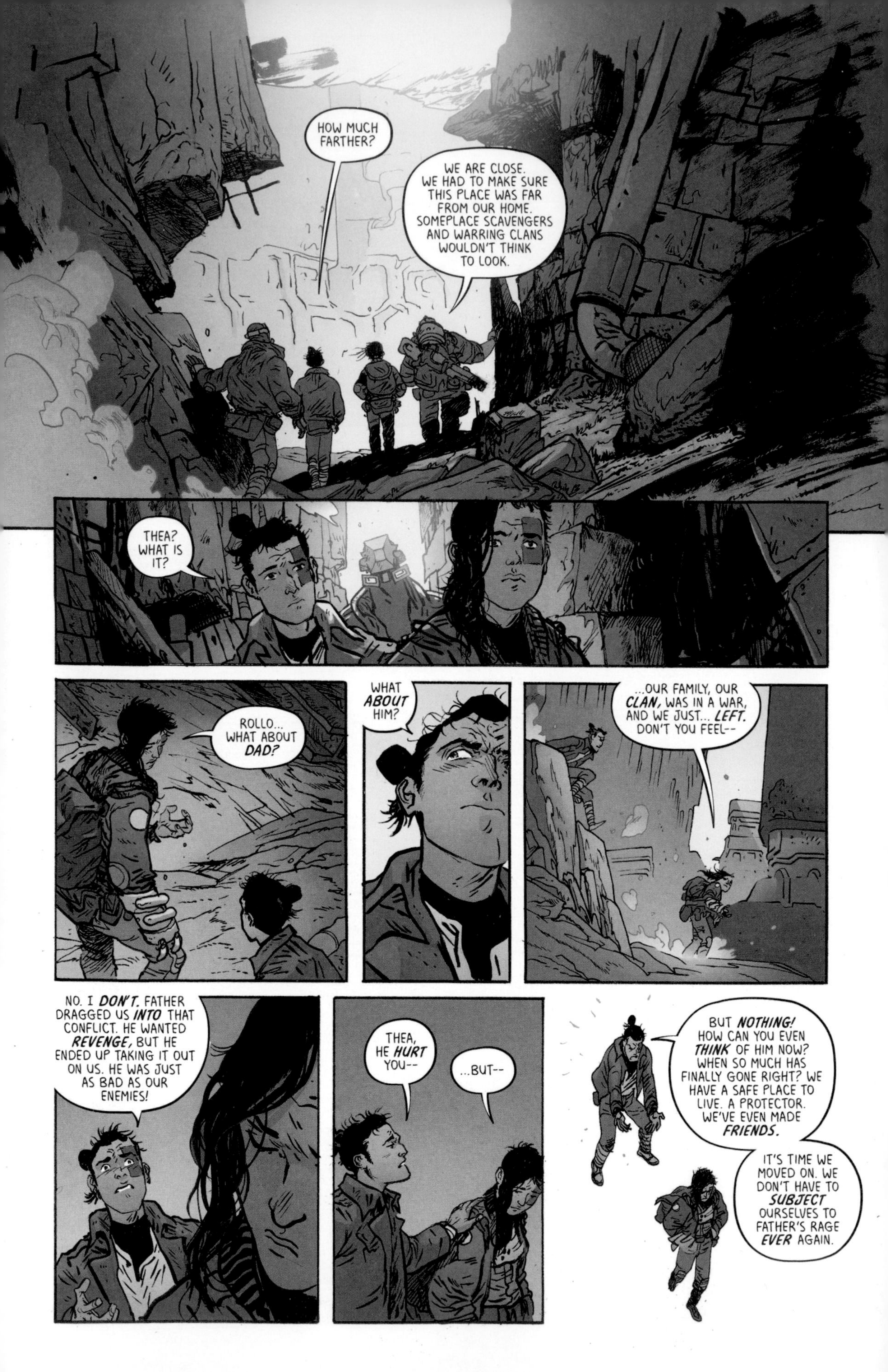
HOW MUCH FARTHER?
WE ARE CLOSE. WE HAD TO MAKE SURE THIS PLACE WAS FAR FROM OUR HOME. SOMEPLACE SCAVENGERS AND WARRING CLANS WOULDN'T THINK TO LOOK.
THEA? WHAT IS IT?
ROLLO... WHAT ABOUT DAD?
WHAT ABOUT HIM?
...OUR FAMILY, OUR CLAN, WAS IN A WAR, AND WE JUST... LEFT. DON'T YOU FEEL--
NO. I DON'T. FATHER DRAGGED US INTO THAT CONFLICT. HE WANTED REVENGE, BUT HE ENDED UP TAKING IT OUT ON US. HE WAS JUST AS BAD AS OUR ENEMIES!
THEA, HE HURT YOU--
...BUT--
BUT NOTHING! HOW CAN YOU EVEN THINK OF HIM NOW? WHEN SO MUCH HAS FINALLY GONE RIGHT? WE HAVE A SAFE PLACE TO LIVE. A PROTECTOR. WE'VE EVEN MADE FRIENDS.
IT'S TIME WE MOVED ON. WE DON'T HAVE TO SUBJECT OURSELVES TO FATHER'S RAGE EVER AGAIN.

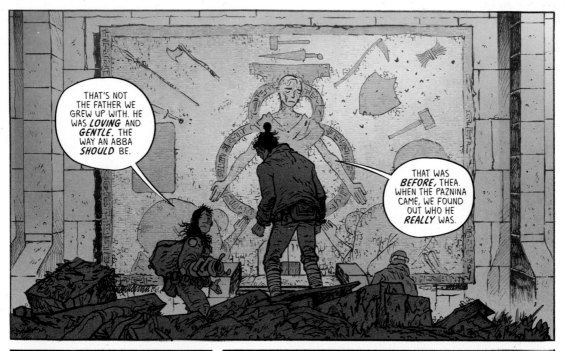

THAT'S NOT THE FATHER WE GREW UP WITH. HE WAS *LOVING* AND *GENTLE*. THE WAY AN ABBA *SHOULD* BE.

THAT WAS *BEFORE*, THEA. WHEN THE PAZNINA CAME, WE FOUND OUT WHO HE *REALLY* WAS.

HE'S CHANGED, YES, BUT THE *GOOD* PARTS OF HIM ARE STILL THERE! HE'S JUST--HE'S *LOST* HIMSELF IN HIS OWN HATRED.

NOT FOR THE PAZNINA, BUT FOR *HIMSELF.*

HE'S OUR *FATHER*, ROLLO.

CAN WE JUST *STAY* HERE AND DO NOTHING?

IF YOU FEEL SO STRONGLY ABOUT IT, GO AHEAD. *LEAVE.*

BUT I'M *STAYING.*

WITH PEOPLE THAT *CARE* ABOUT ME.

COME... WE'VE ARRIVED.

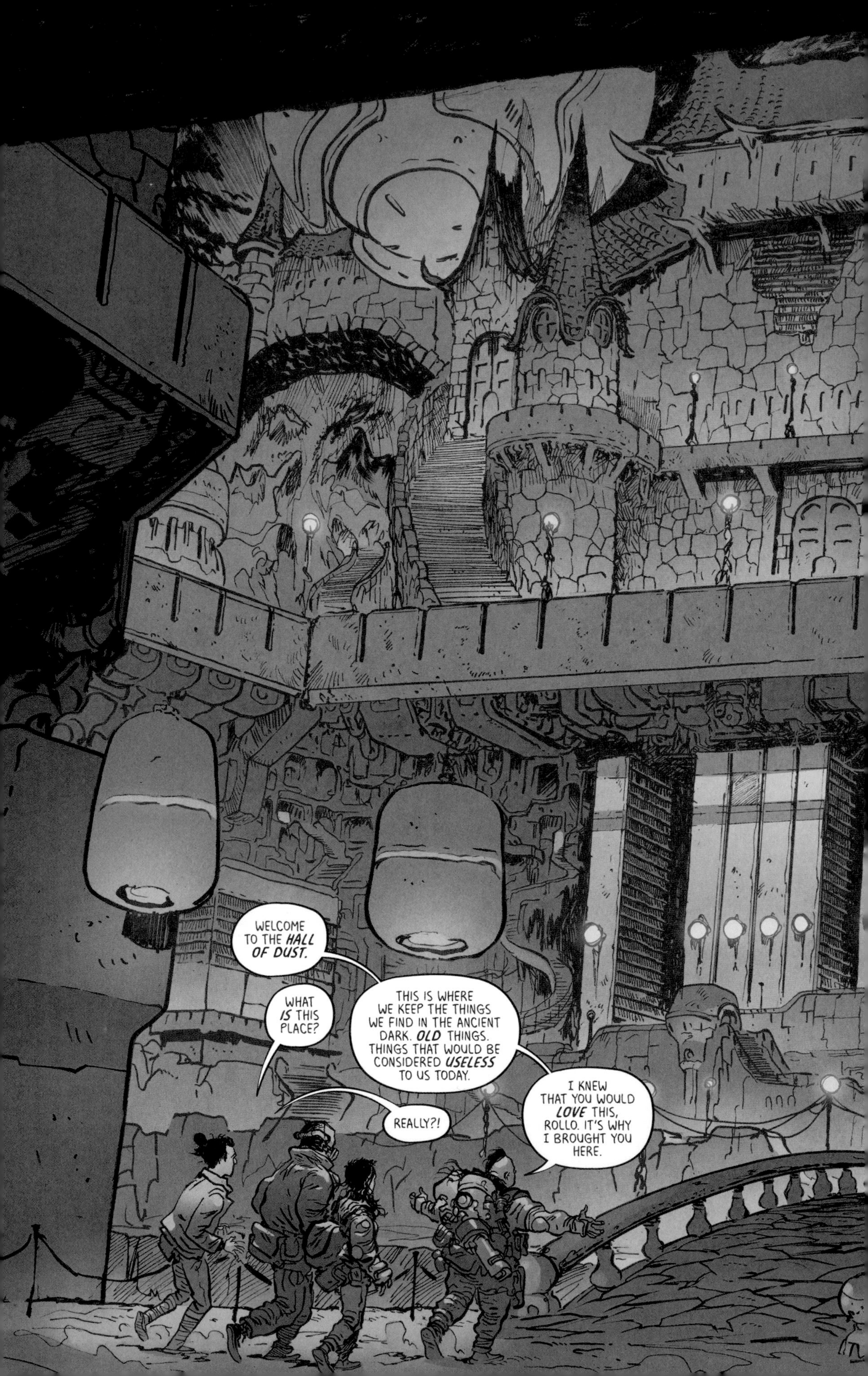
WELCOME TO THE HALL OF DUST.
WHAT IS THIS PLACE?
THIS IS WHERE WE KEEP THE THINGS WE FIND IN THE ANCIENT DARK. OLD THINGS. THINGS THAT WOULD BE CONSIDERED USELESS TO US TODAY.
REALLY?!
I KNEW THAT YOU WOULD LOVE THIS, ROLLO. IT'S WHY I BROUGHT YOU HERE.

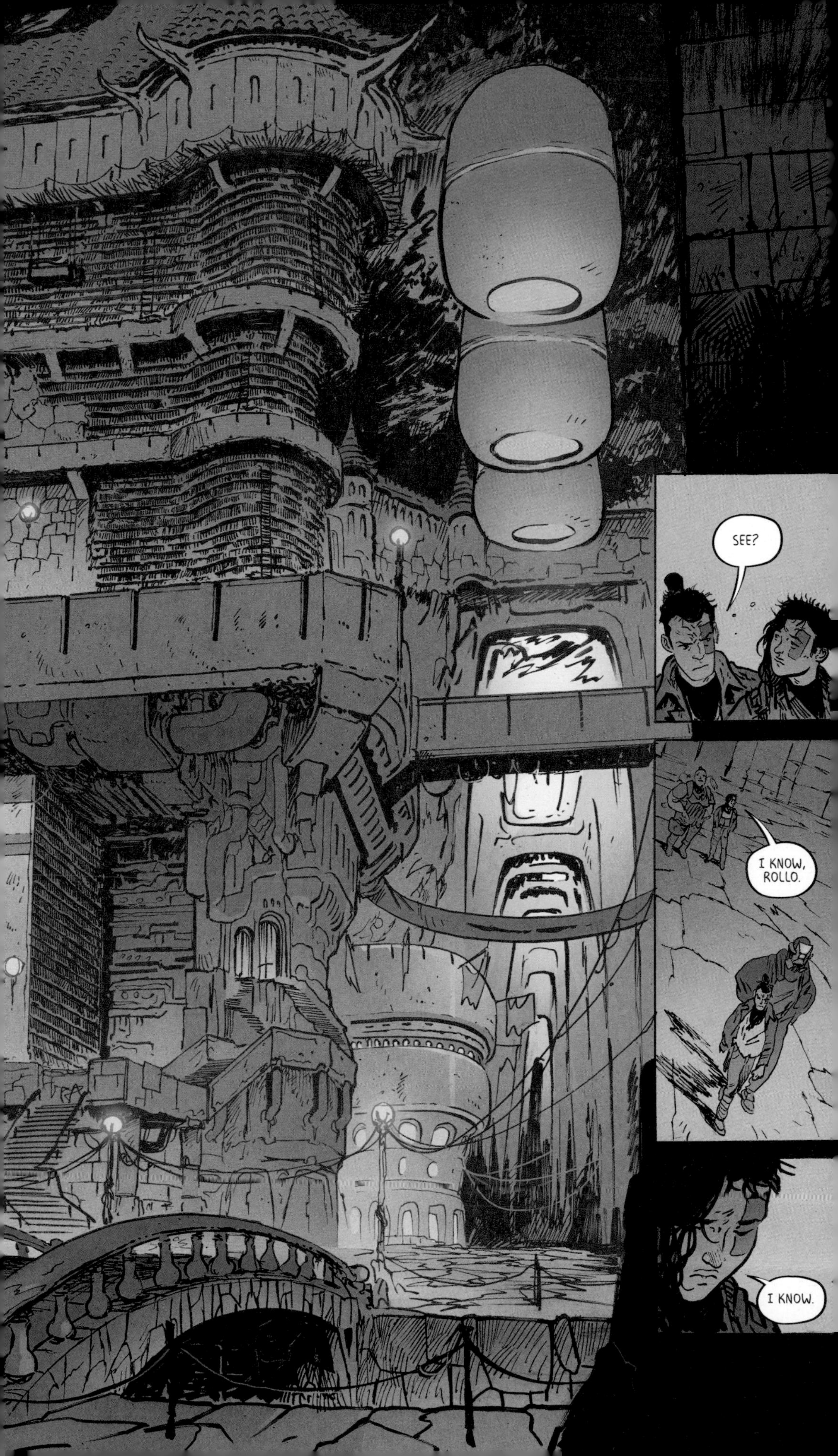
SEE?
I KNOW, ROLLO.
I KNOW.

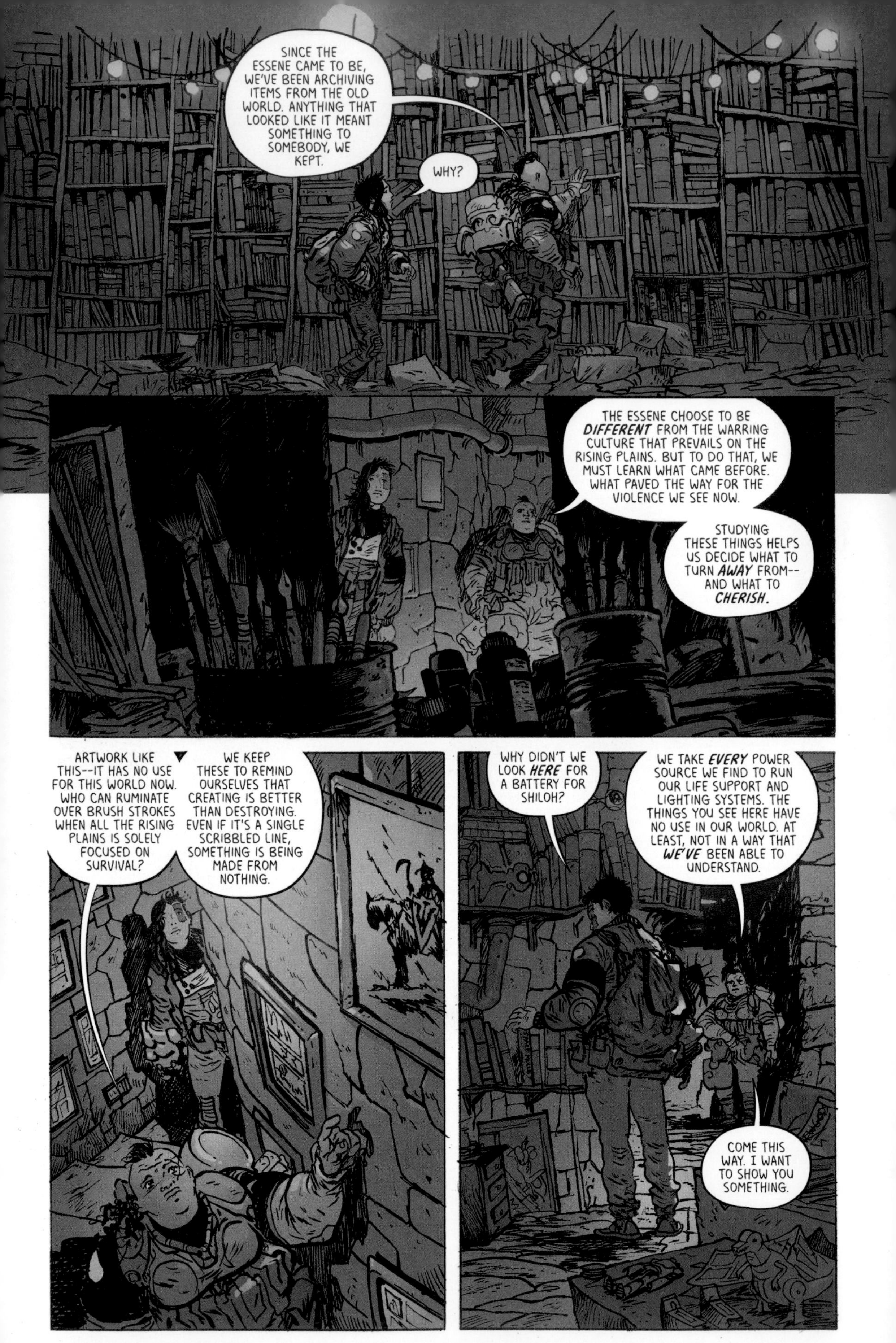
SINCE THE ESSENE CAME TO BE, WE'VE BEEN ARCHIVING ITEMS FROM THE OLD WORLD. ANYTHING THAT LOOKED LIKE IT MEANT SOMETHING TO SOMEBODY, WE KEPT.
WHY?
THE ESSENE CHOOSE TO BE DIFFERENT FROM THE WARRING CULTURE THAT PREVAILS ON THE RISING PLAINS. BUT TO DO THAT, WE MUST LEARN WHAT CAME BEFORE. WHAT PAVED THE WAY FOR THE VIOLENCE WE SEE NOW.
STUDYING THESE THINGS HELPS US DECIDE WHAT TO TURN AWAY FROM-- AND WHAT TO CHERISH.
ARTWORK LIKE THIS--IT HAS NO USE FOR THIS WORLD NOW. WHO CAN RUMINATE OVER BRUSH STROKES WHEN ALL THE RISING PLAINS IS SOLELY FOCUSED ON SURVIVAL?
WE KEEP THESE TO REMIND OURSELVES THAT CREATING IS BETTER THAN DESTROYING. EVEN IF IT'S A SINGLE SCRIBBLED LINE, SOMETHING IS BEING MADE FROM NOTHING.
WHY DIDN'T WE LOOK HERE FOR A BATTERY FOR SHILOH?
WE TAKE EVERY POWER SOURCE WE FIND TO RUN OUR LIFE SUPPORT AND LIGHTING SYSTEMS. THE THINGS YOU SEE HERE HAVE NO USE IN OUR WORLD. AT LEAST, NOT IN A WAY THAT WE'VE BEEN ABLE TO UNDERSTAND.
COME THIS WAY. I WANT TO SHOW YOU SOMETHING.

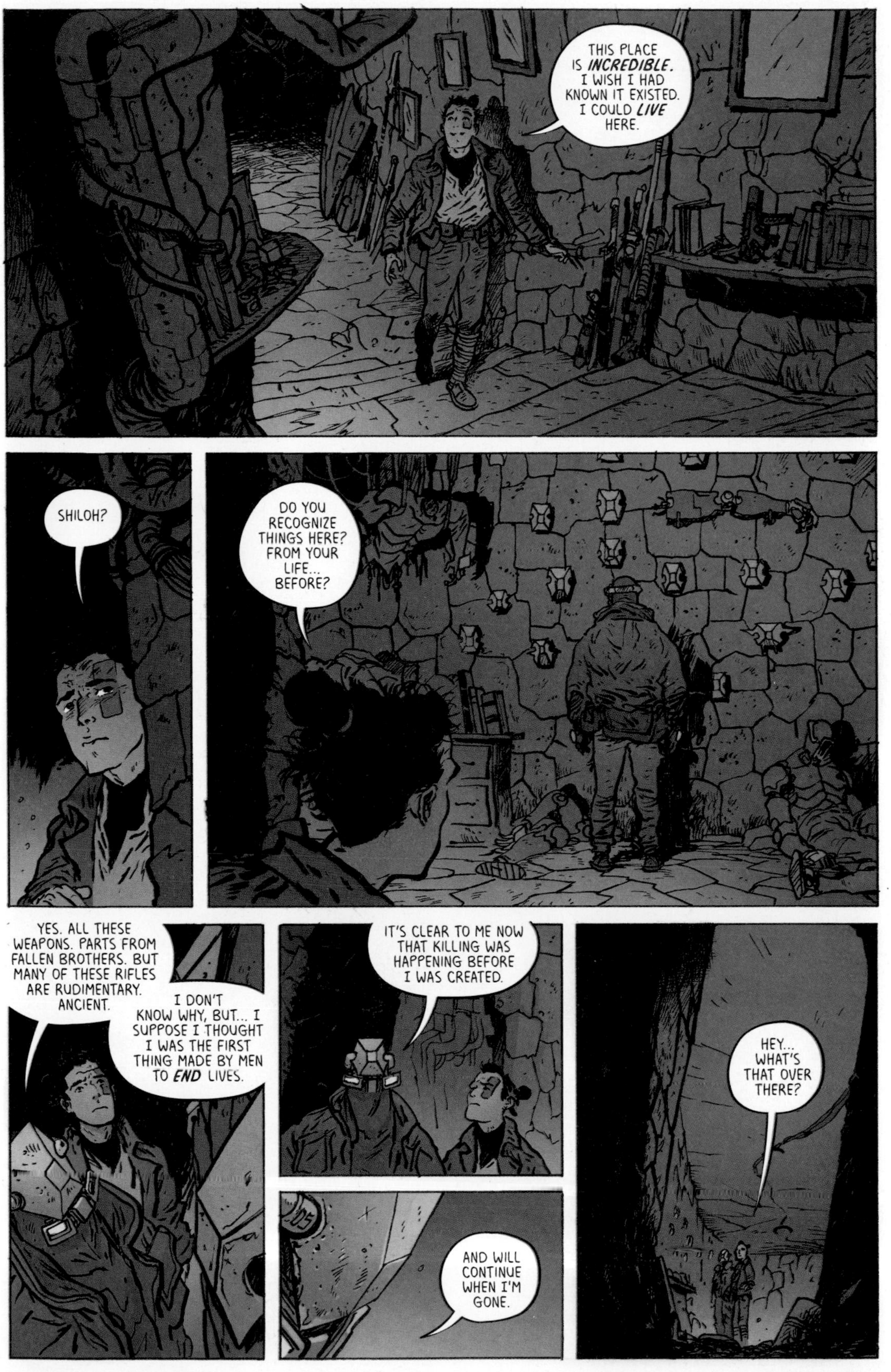
THIS PLACE IS INCREDIBLE. I WISH I HAD KNOWN IT EXISTED. I COULD LIVE HERE.
SHILOH?
DO YOU RECOGNIZE THINGS HERE? FROM YOUR LIFE... BEFORE?
YES. ALL THESE WEAPONS. PARTS FROM FALLEN BROTHERS. BUT MANY OF THESE RIFLES ARE RUDIMENTARY. ANCIENT.
I DON'T KNOW WHY, BUT... I SUPPOSE I THOUGHT I WAS THE FIRST THING MADE BY MEN TO END LIVES.
IT'S CLEAR TO ME NOW THAT KILLING WAS HAPPENING BEFORE I WAS CREATED.
AND WILL CONTINUE WHEN I'M GONE.
HEY... WHAT'S THAT OVER THERE?

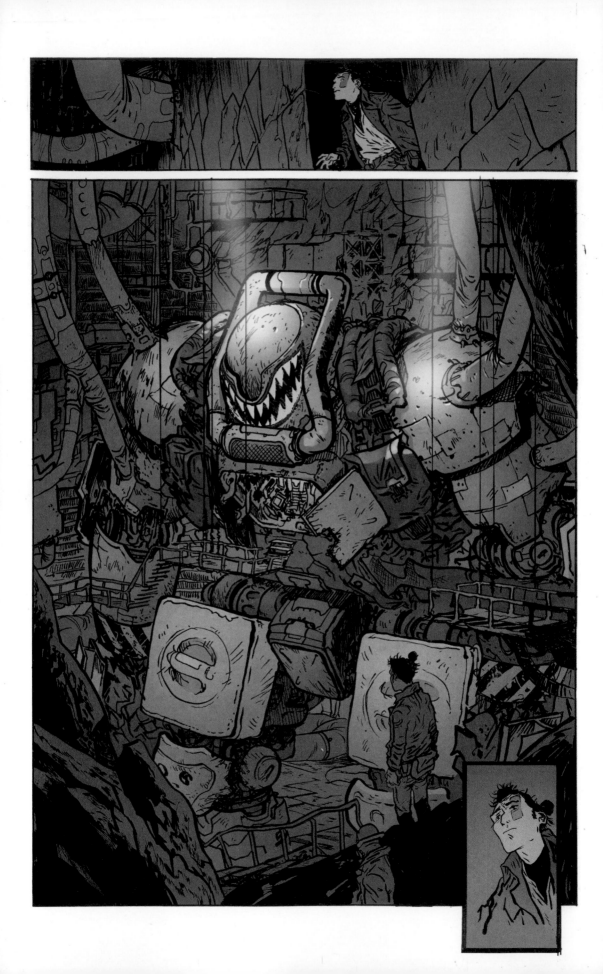

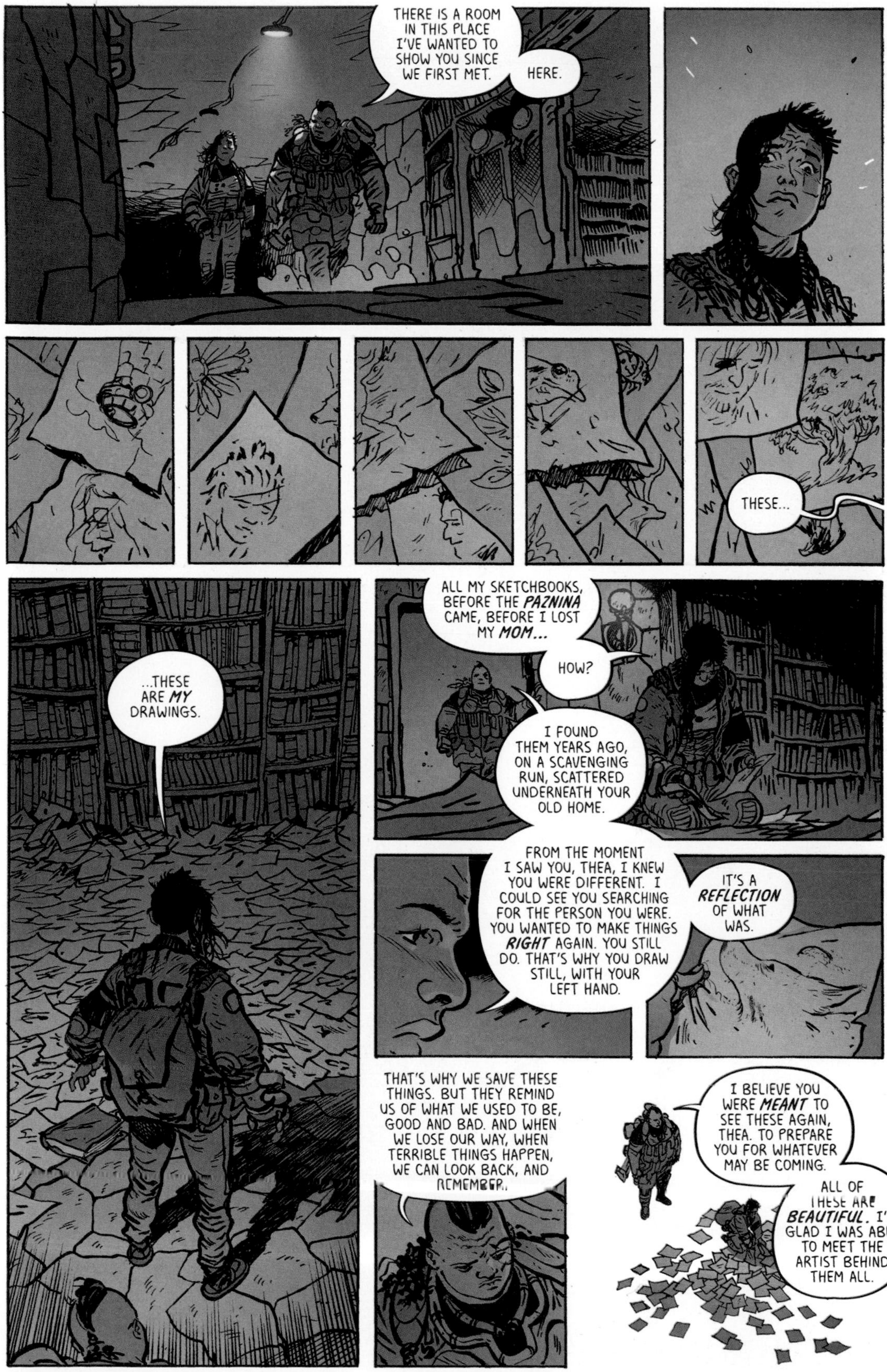
THERE IS A ROOM IN THIS PLACE I'VE WANTED TO SHOW YOU SINCE WE FIRST MET.
HERE.
THESE...
...THESE ARE MY DRAWINGS.
ALL MY SKETCHBOOKS, BEFORE THE PAZNINA CAME, BEFORE I LOST MY MOM...
HOW?
I FOUND THEM YEARS AGO, ON A SCAVENGING RUN, SCATTERED UNDERNEATH YOUR OLD HOME.
FROM THE MOMENT I SAW YOU, THEA, I KNEW YOU WERE DIFFERENT. I COULD SEE YOU SEARCHING FOR THE PERSON YOU WERE. YOU WANTED TO MAKE THINGS RIGHT AGAIN. YOU STILL DO. THAT'S WHY YOU DRAW STILL, WITH YOUR LEFT HAND.
IT'S A REFLECTION OF WHAT WAS.
THAT'S WHY WE SAVE THESE THINGS. BUT THEY REMIND US OF WHAT WE USED TO BE, GOOD AND BAD. AND WHEN WE LOSE OUR WAY, WHEN TERRIBLE THINGS HAPPEN, WE CAN LOOK BACK, AND REMEMBER.
I BELIEVE YOU WERE MEANT TO SEE THESE AGAIN, THEA. TO PREPARE YOU FOR WHATEVER MAY BE COMING.
ALL OF THESE ARE BEAUTIFUL. I'M GLAD I WAS ABLE TO MEET THE ARTIST BEHIND THEM ALL.

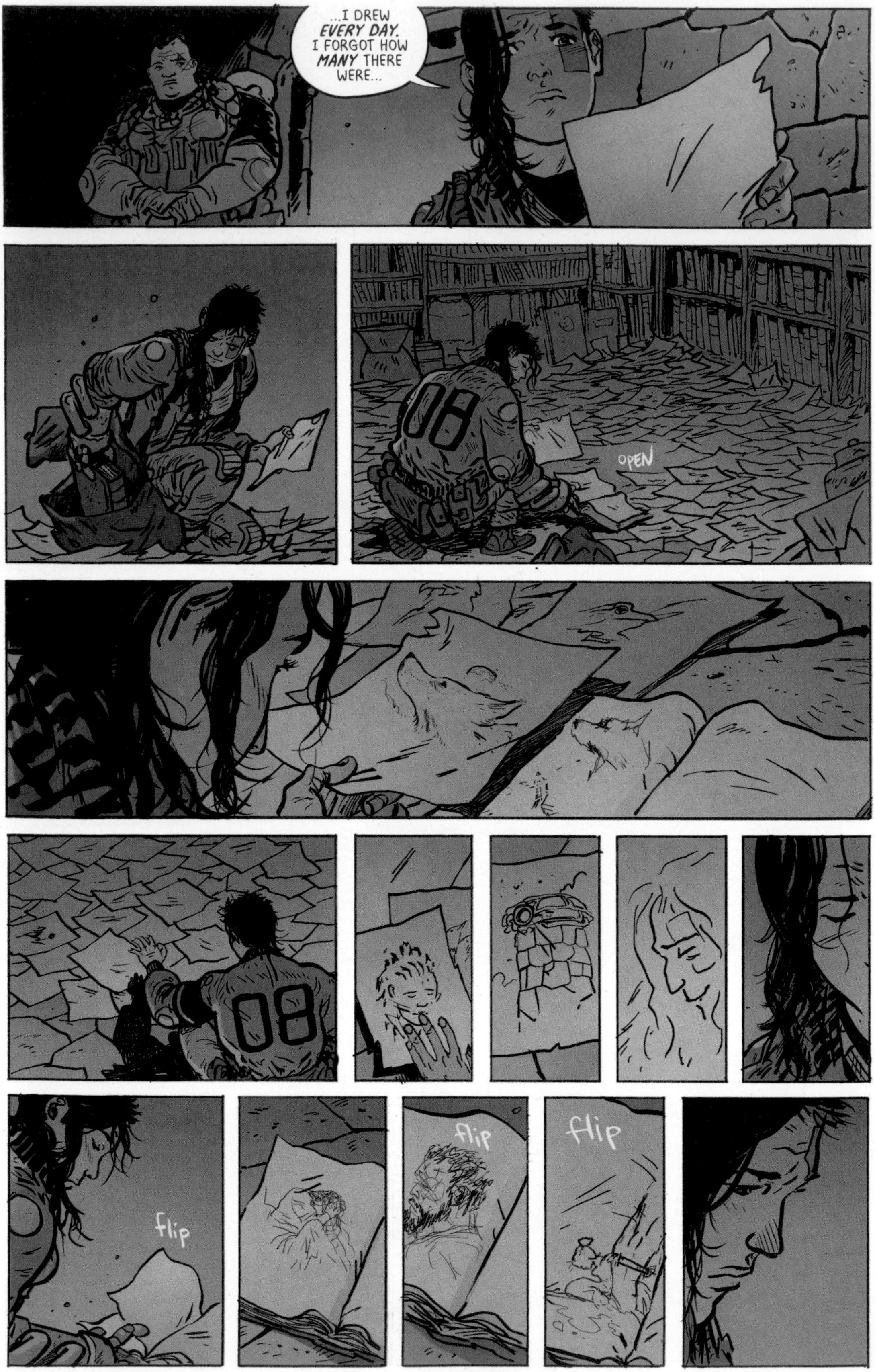
...I DREW
EVERY DAY.
I FORGOT HOW
MANY THERE
WERE...
OPEN
flip
flip
flip

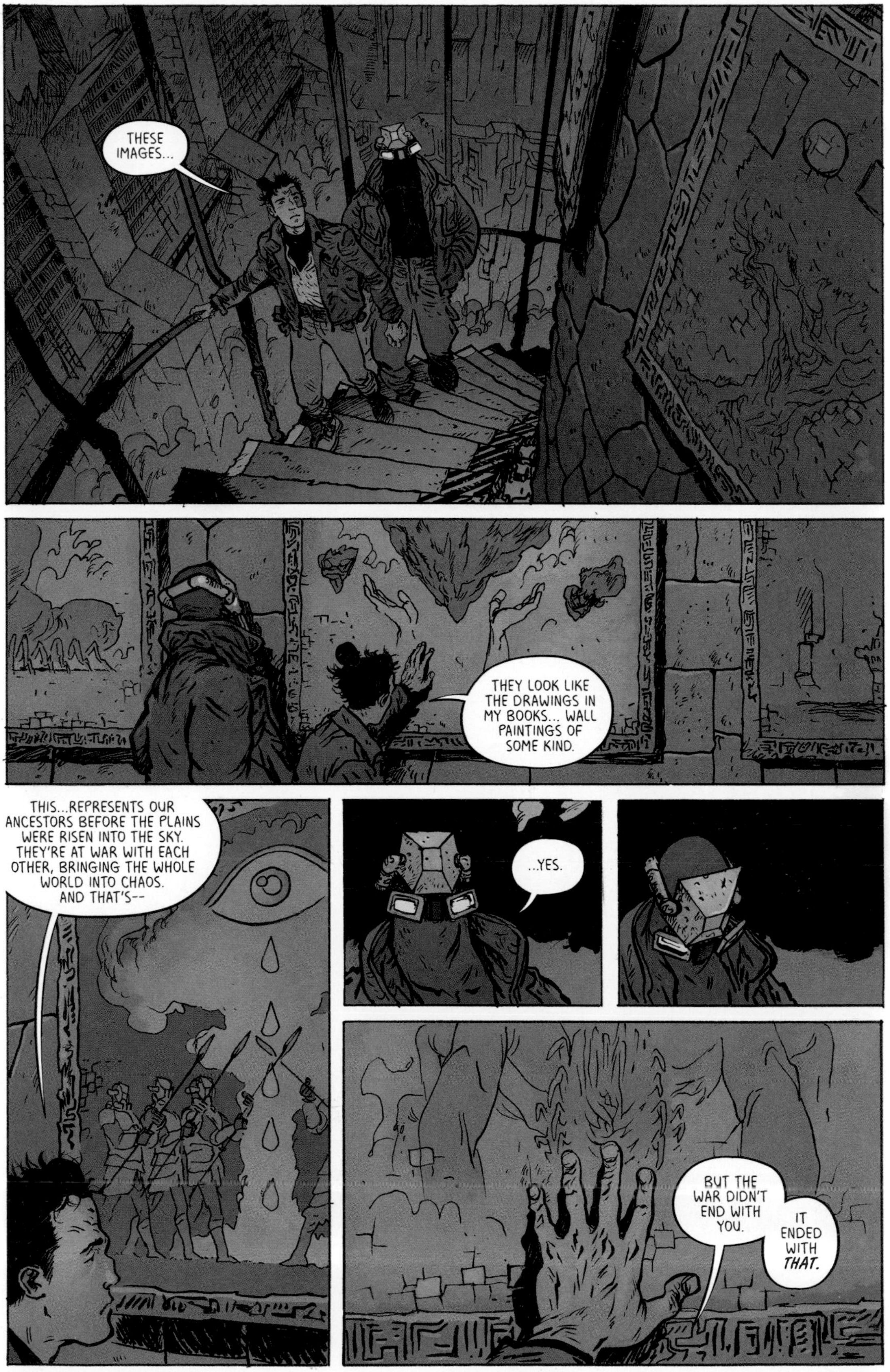
THESE IMAGES...
THEY LOOK LIKE THE DRAWINGS IN MY BOOKS... WALL PAINTINGS OF SOME KIND.
THIS...REPRESENTS OUR ANCESTORS BEFORE THE PLAINS WERE RISEN INTO THE SKY. THEY'RE AT WAR WITH EACH OTHER, BRINGING THE WHOLE WORLD INTO CHAOS. AND THAT'S--
...YES.
BUT THE WAR DIDN'T END WITH YOU.
IT ENDED WITH *THAT.*

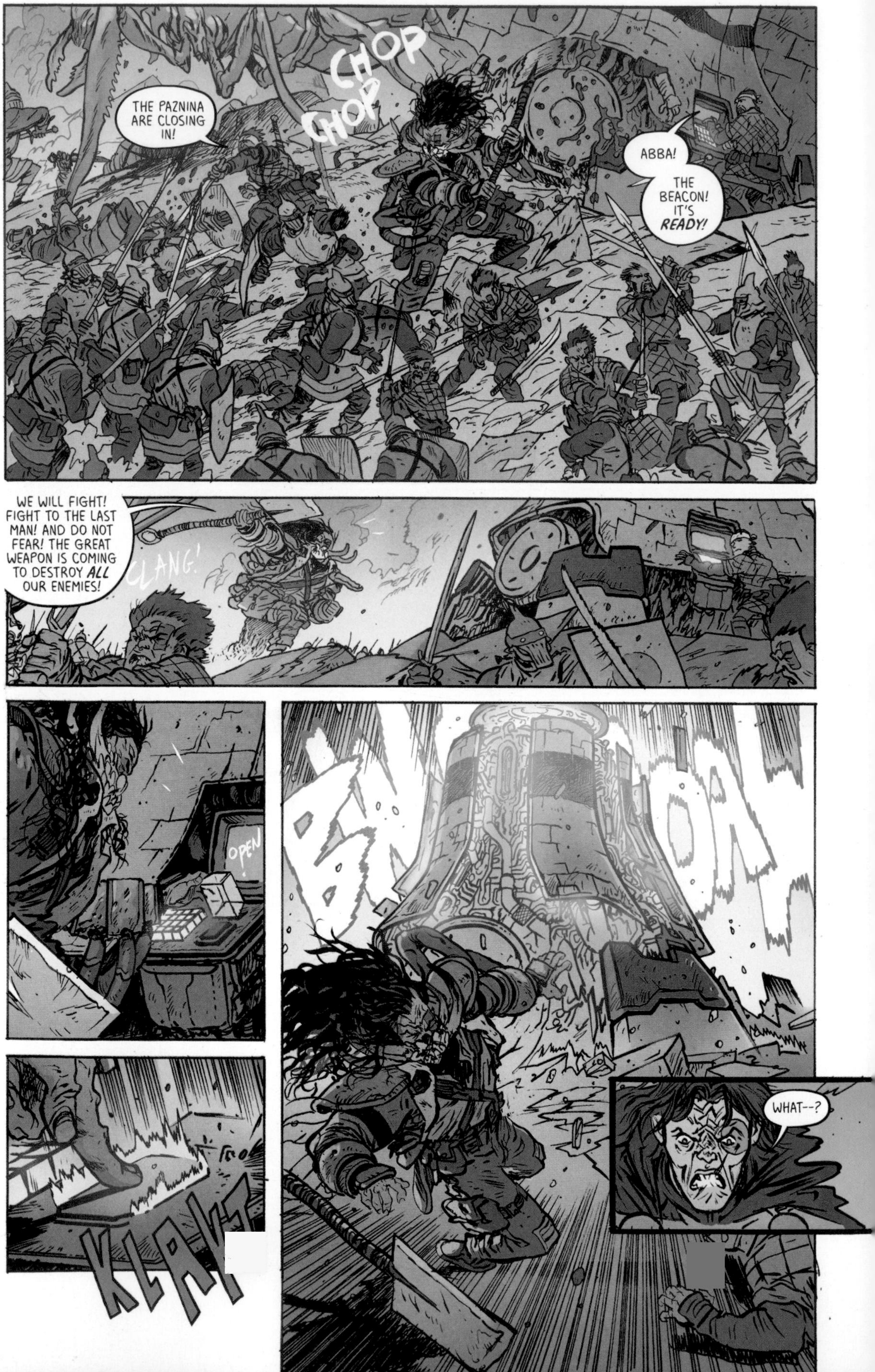
CHOP
CHOP
THE PAZNINA ARE CLOSING IN!
ABBA!
THE BEACON! IT'S *READY!*
WE WILL FIGHT! FIGHT TO THE LAST MAN! AND DO NOT FEAR! THE GREAT WEAPON IS COMING TO DESTROY *ALL* OUR ENEMIES!
CLANG!
OPEN
KLAK!
WHAT--?

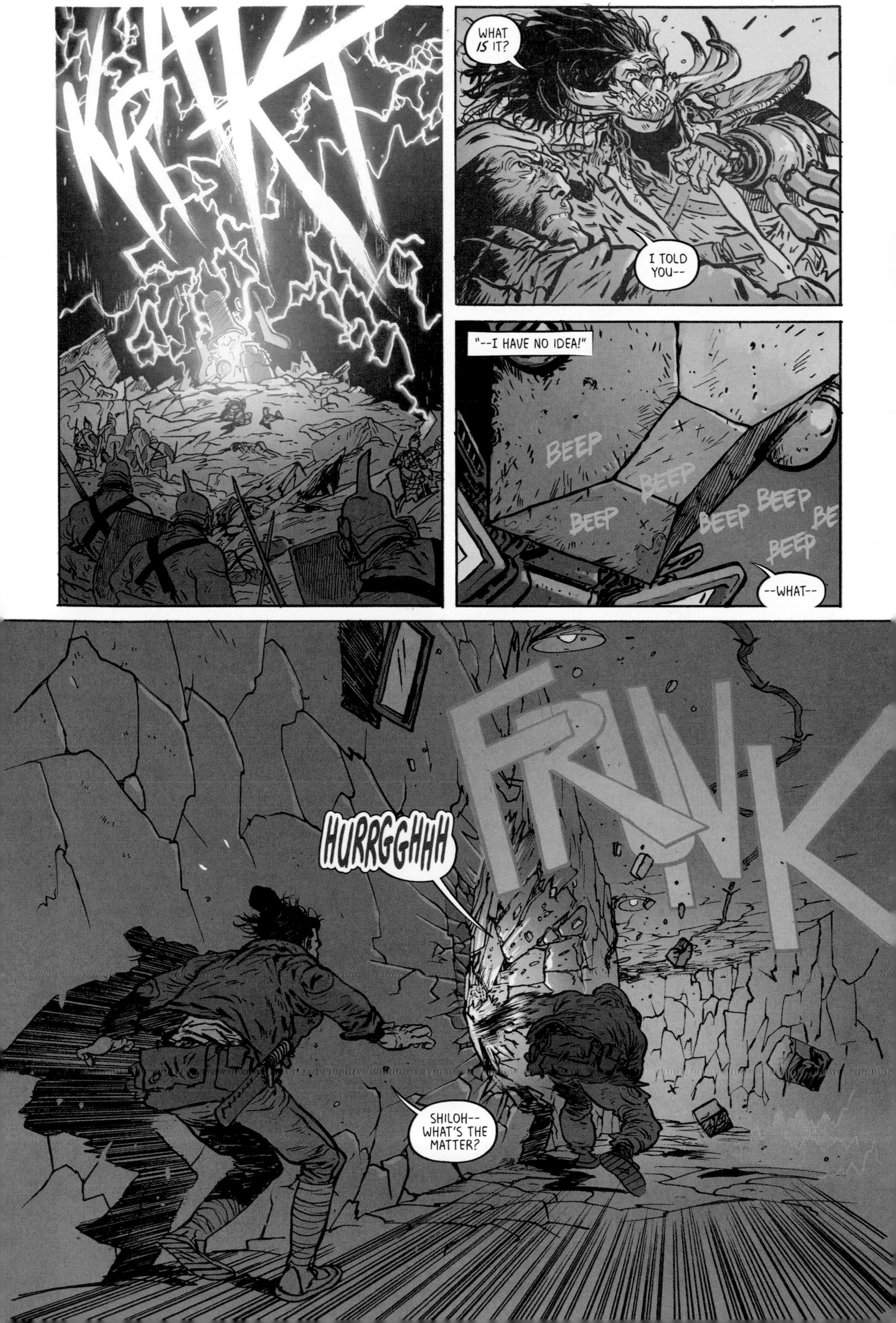

KRAKT
WHAT IS IT?
I TOLD YOU--
"--I HAVE NO IDEA!"
BEEP
BEEP
BEEP
BEEP BEEP
BEEP
--WHAT--
FRUNK
HURRGGHHH
SHILOH-- WHAT'S THE MATTER?

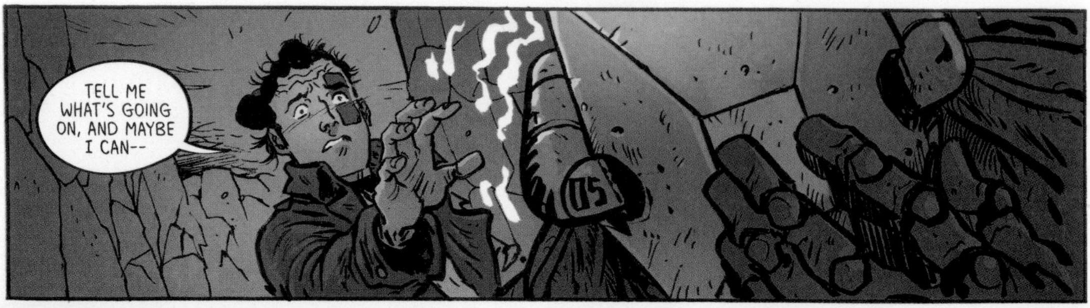
TELL ME WHAT'S GOING ON, AND MAYBE I CAN--

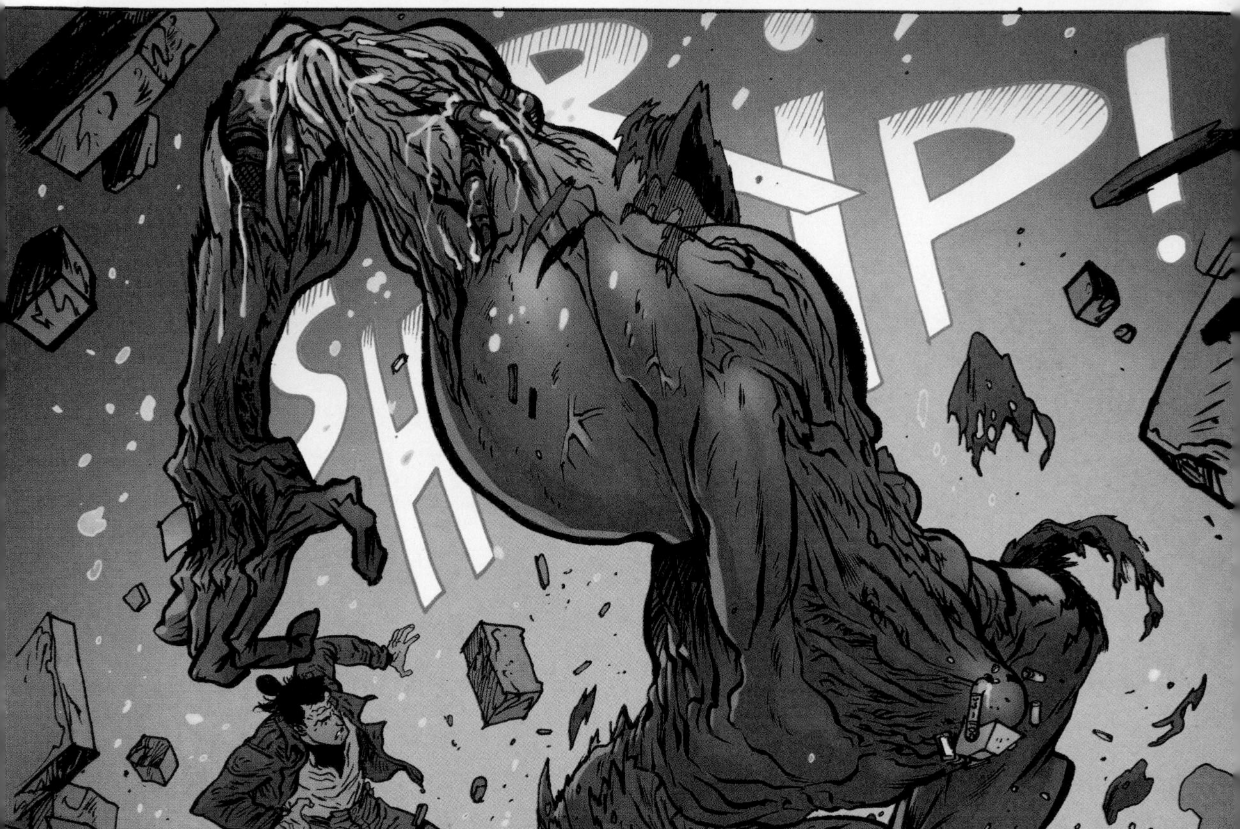
SHRIP!
SHILOH!!!

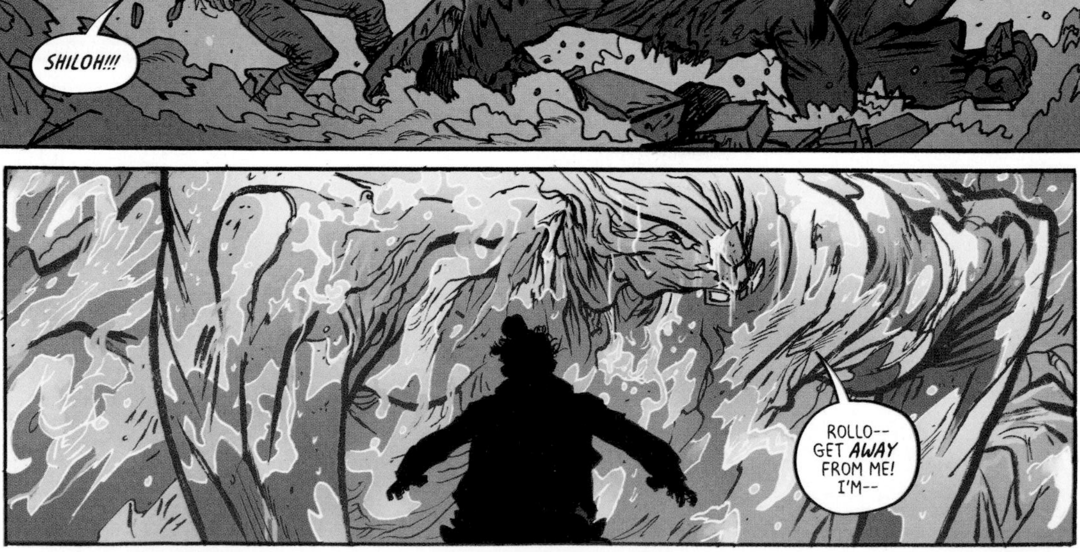
ROLLO-- GET *AWAY* FROM ME! I'M--

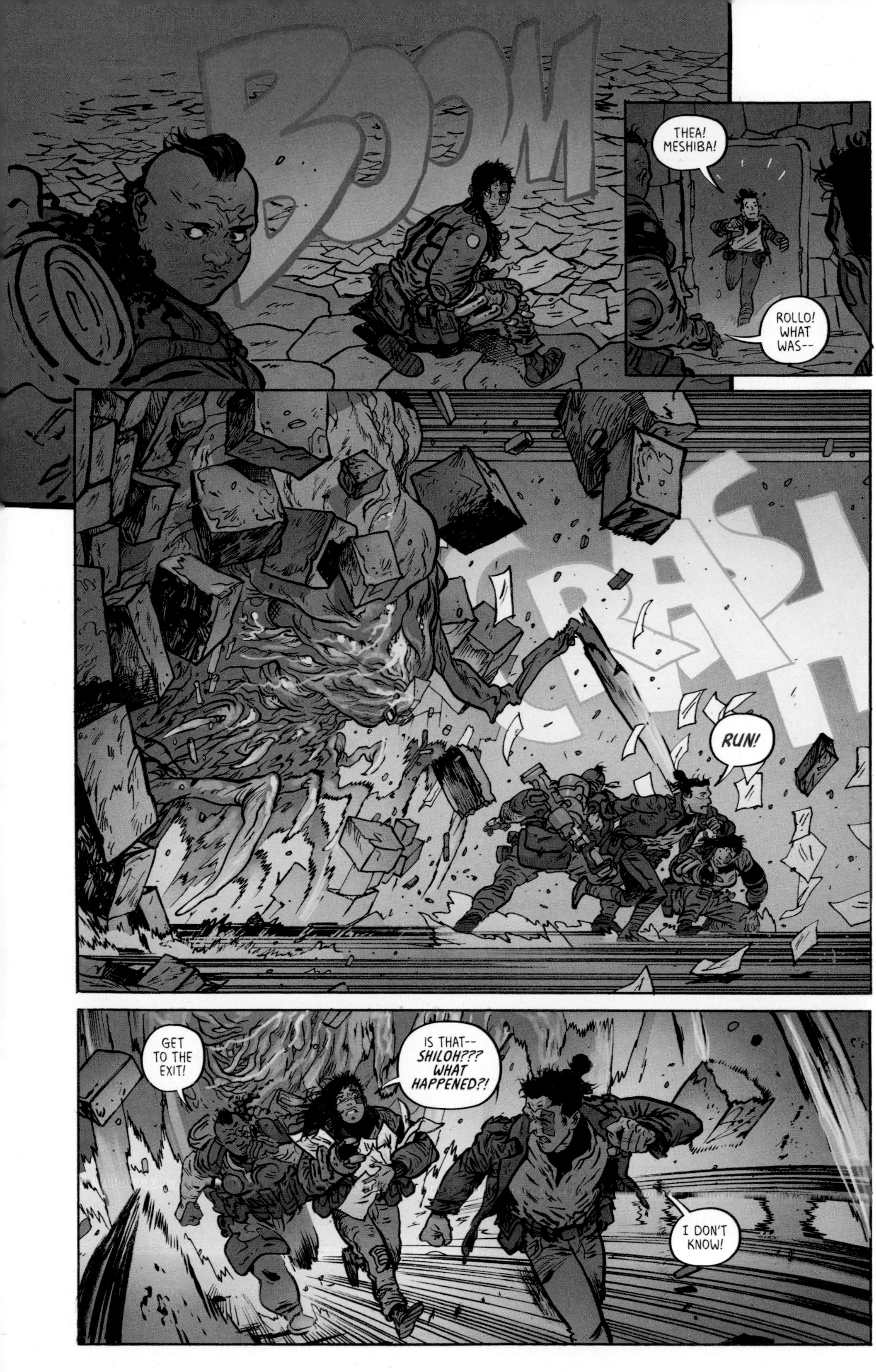
BOOM
THEA! MESHIBA!
ROLLO! WHAT WAS--
CRASH
RUN!
GET TO THE EXIT!
IS THAT-- SHILOH??? WHAT HAPPENED?!
I DON'T KNOW!

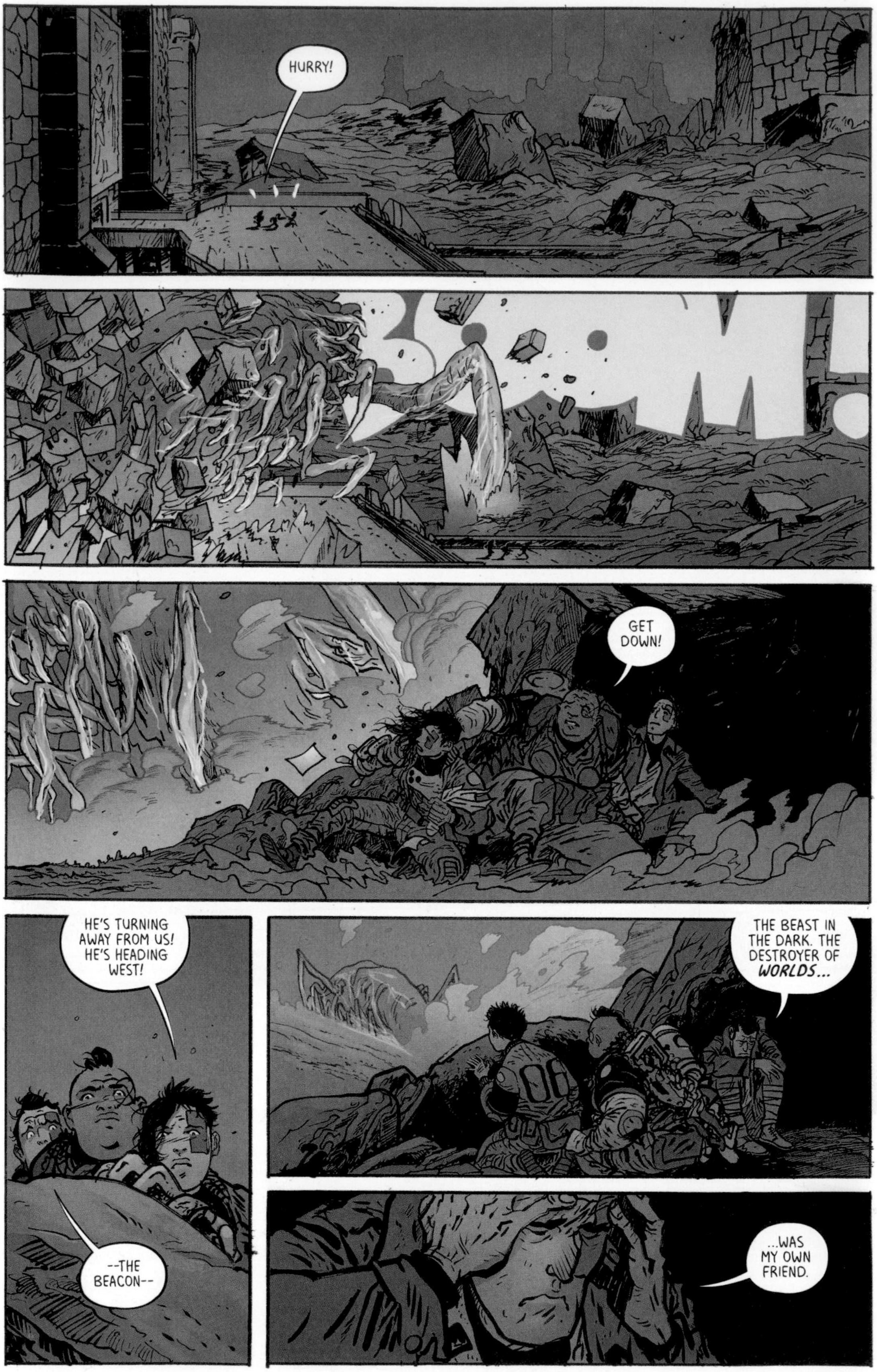
HURRY!
BOOM!
GET DOWN!
HE'S TURNING AWAY FROM US! HE'S HEADING WEST!
--THE BEACON--
THE BEAST IN THE DARK. THE DESTROYER OF *WORLDS*...
...WAS MY OWN FRIEND.

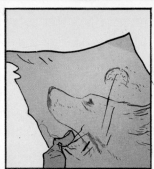

SHILOH IS GOING TO HURT MANY PAZNINA.

I THOUGHT THAT'S WHAT I WANTED-- BUT--

I HAVE TO STOP HIM.

I HAVE TO STOP MY ABBA.

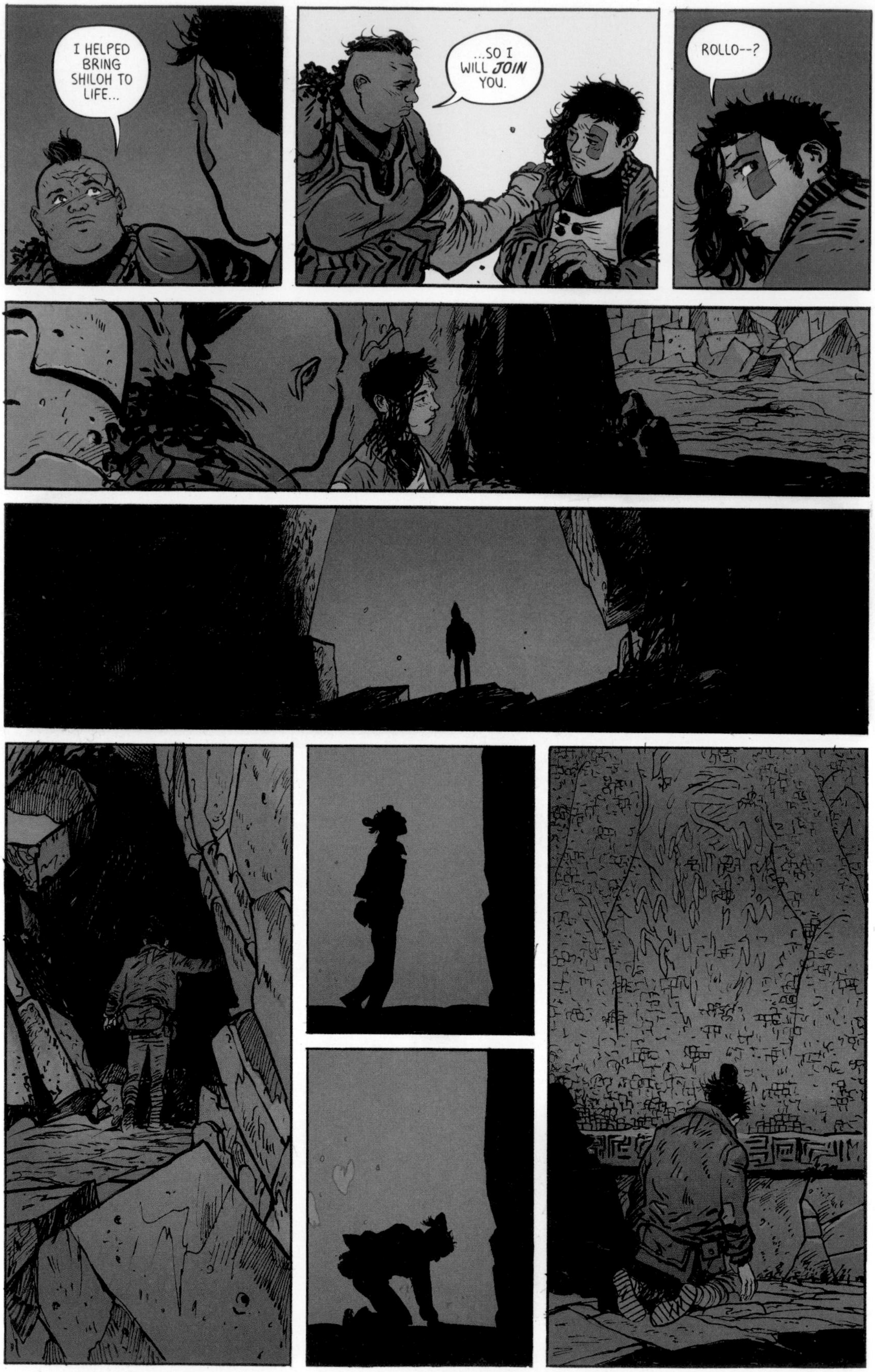
I HELPED BRING SHILOH TO LIFE...
...SO I WILL JOIN YOU.
ROLLO--?

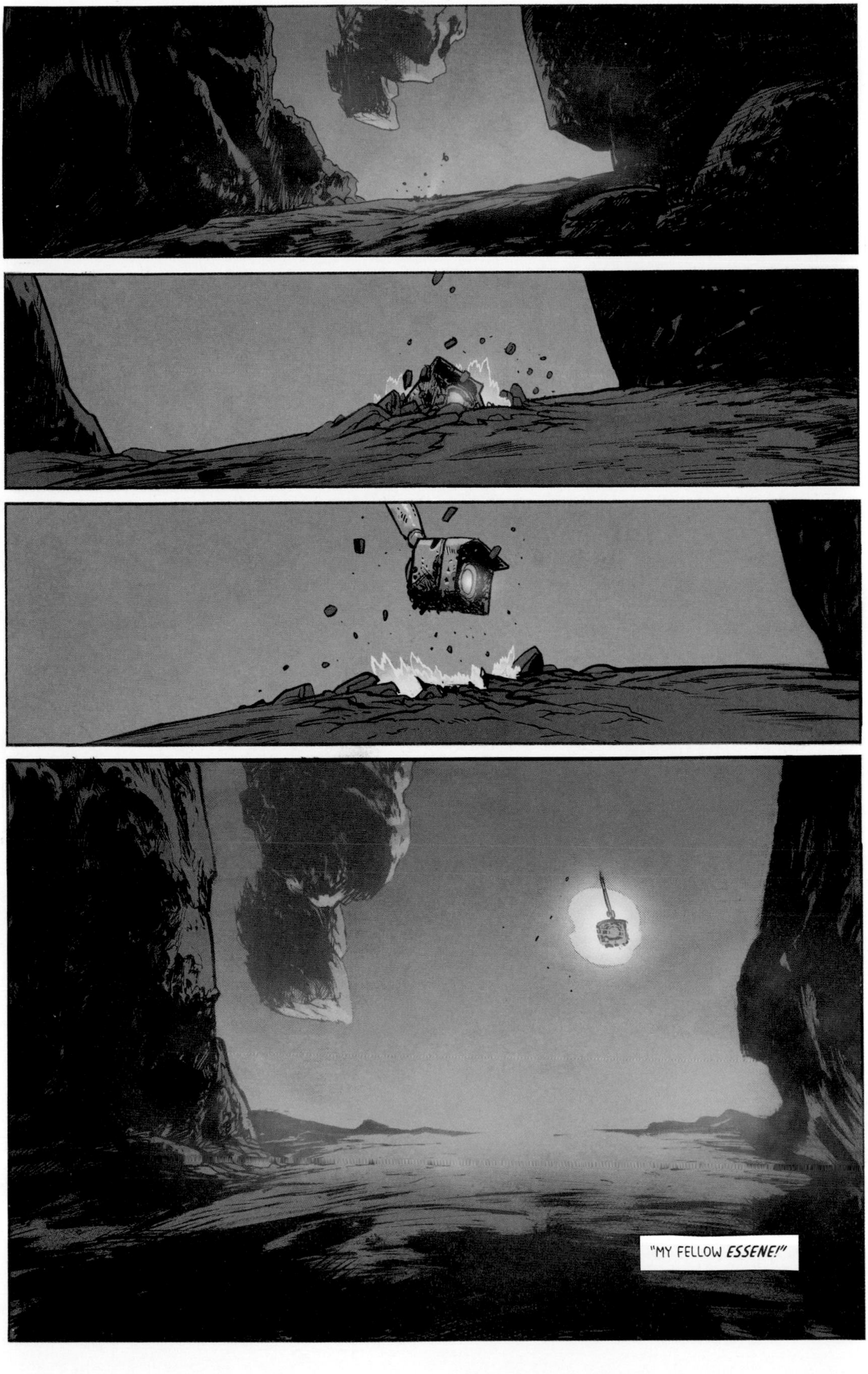
"MY FELLOW ESSENE!"

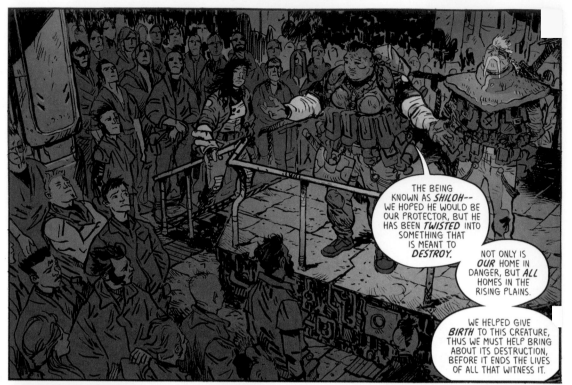

THE BEING KNOWN AS *SHILOH*-- WE HOPED HE WOULD BE OUR PROTECTOR, BUT HE HAS BEEN *TWISTED* INTO SOMETHING THAT IS MEANT TO *DESTROY.*

NOT ONLY IS *OUR* HOME IN DANGER, BUT *ALL* HOMES IN THE RISING PLAINS.

WE HELPED GIVE *BIRTH* TO THIS CREATURE, THUS WE MUST HELP BRING ABOUT ITS DESTRUCTION, BEFORE IT ENDS THE LIVES OF ALL THAT WITNESS IT.

I KNOW WHAT I ASK OF YOU IS *DIFFICULT,* MY CHILDREN, BUT--

GREAT MOTHER, PLEASE.

YOU ARE NOW OUR LEADER. WE WILL FOLLOW YOU INTO ANY BATTLE, INTO ANY PLACE, NO MATTER HOW DARK. WE TRUST YOUR WISDOM.

WE ARE *WITH* YOU.

THEA, WHAT OF ROLLO?

I DON'T KNOW...

"...HE WON'T COME OUT OF THE HALL OF DUST."

OH! I WONDERED WHEN YOU'D FIND ME.

YOU'VE ARRIVED JUST IN TIME.

SMASH

I'M SORRY, MY FRIEND.

I NEED WHAT'S INSIDE YOU FOR SOMETHING BIGGER.

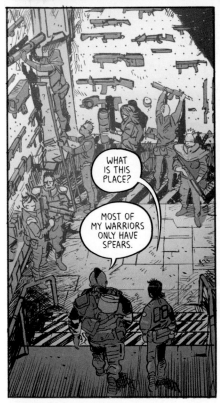

WHAT IS THIS PLACE?

MOST OF MY WARRIORS ONLY HAVE SPEARS.

TODAY, WE USE THE WEAPONS OF THE OLD WORLD.

GRAB!

I'M READY.

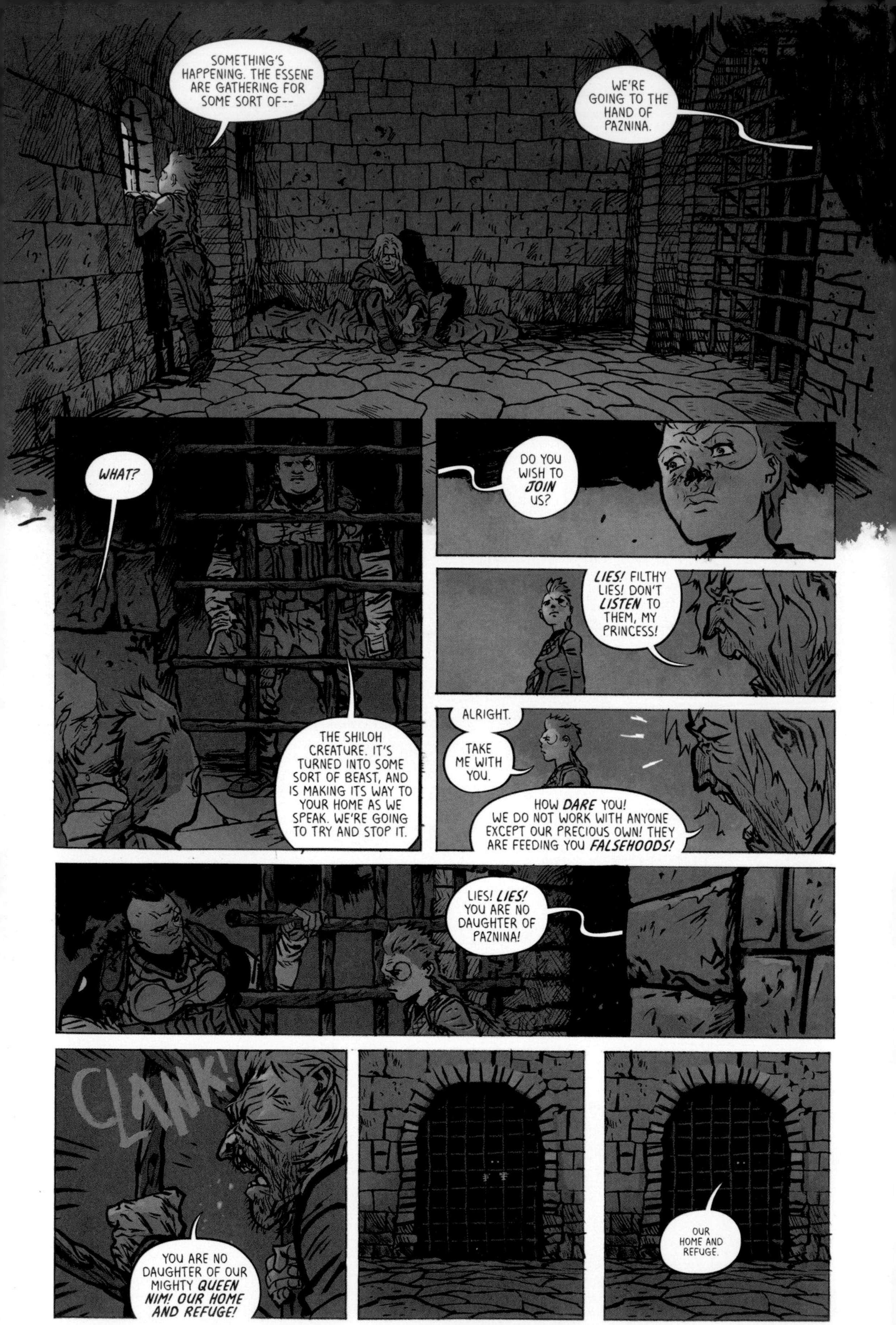

SOMETHING'S HAPPENING. THE ESSENE ARE GATHERING FOR SOME SORT OF--
WE'RE GOING TO THE HAND OF PAZNINA.
WHAT?
THE SHILOH CREATURE. IT'S TURNED INTO SOME SORT OF BEAST, AND IS MAKING ITS WAY TO YOUR HOME AS WE SPEAK. WE'RE GOING TO TRY AND STOP IT.
DO YOU WISH TO JOIN US?
LIES! FILTHY LIES! DON'T LISTEN TO THEM, MY PRINCESS!
ALRIGHT.
TAKE ME WITH YOU.
HOW DARE YOU! WE DO NOT WORK WITH ANYONE EXCEPT OUR PRECIOUS OWN! THEY ARE FEEDING YOU FALSEHOODS!
LIES! LIES! YOU ARE NO DAUGHTER OF PAZNINA!
CLANK!
YOU ARE NO DAUGHTER OF OUR MIGHTY QUEEN NIM! OUR HOME AND REFUGE!
OUR HOME AND REFUGE.

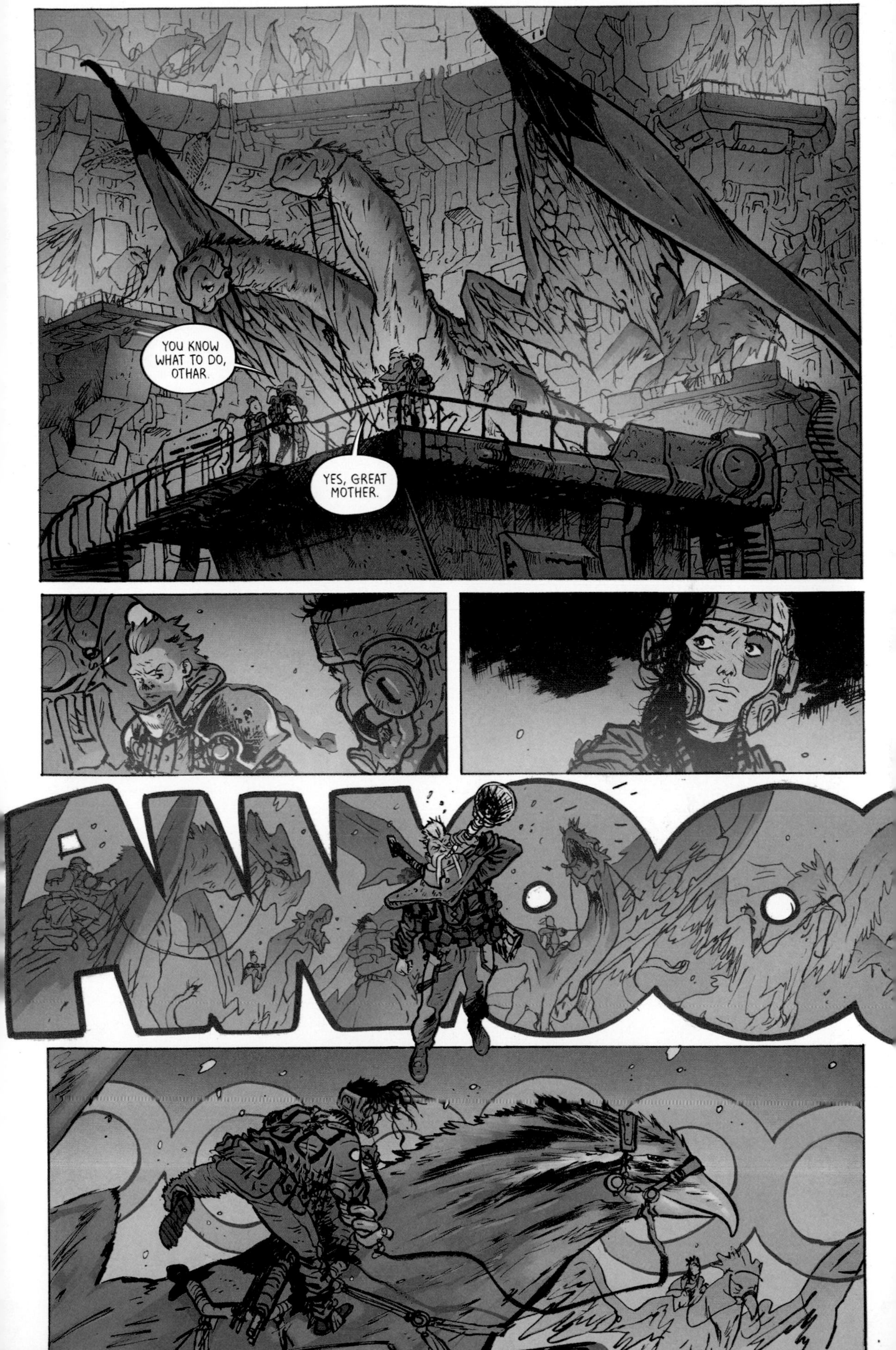
YOU KNOW WHAT TO DO, OTHAR.
YES, GREAT MOTHER.
AWOOO

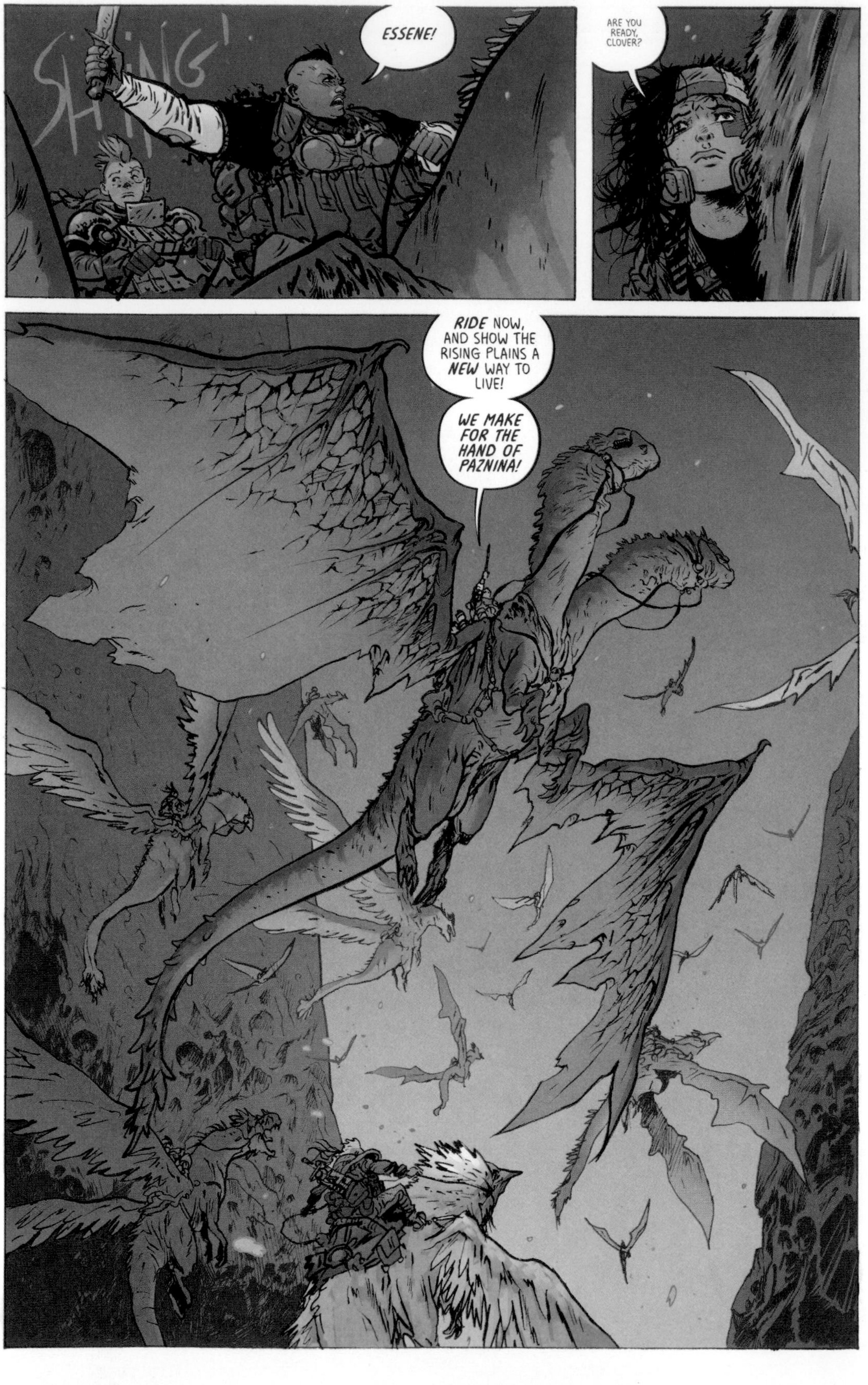
SHING!
ESSENE!
ARE YOU READY, CLOVER?
RIDE NOW, AND SHOW THE RISING PLAINS A NEW WAY TO LIVE!
WE MAKE FOR THE HAND OF PAZNINA!

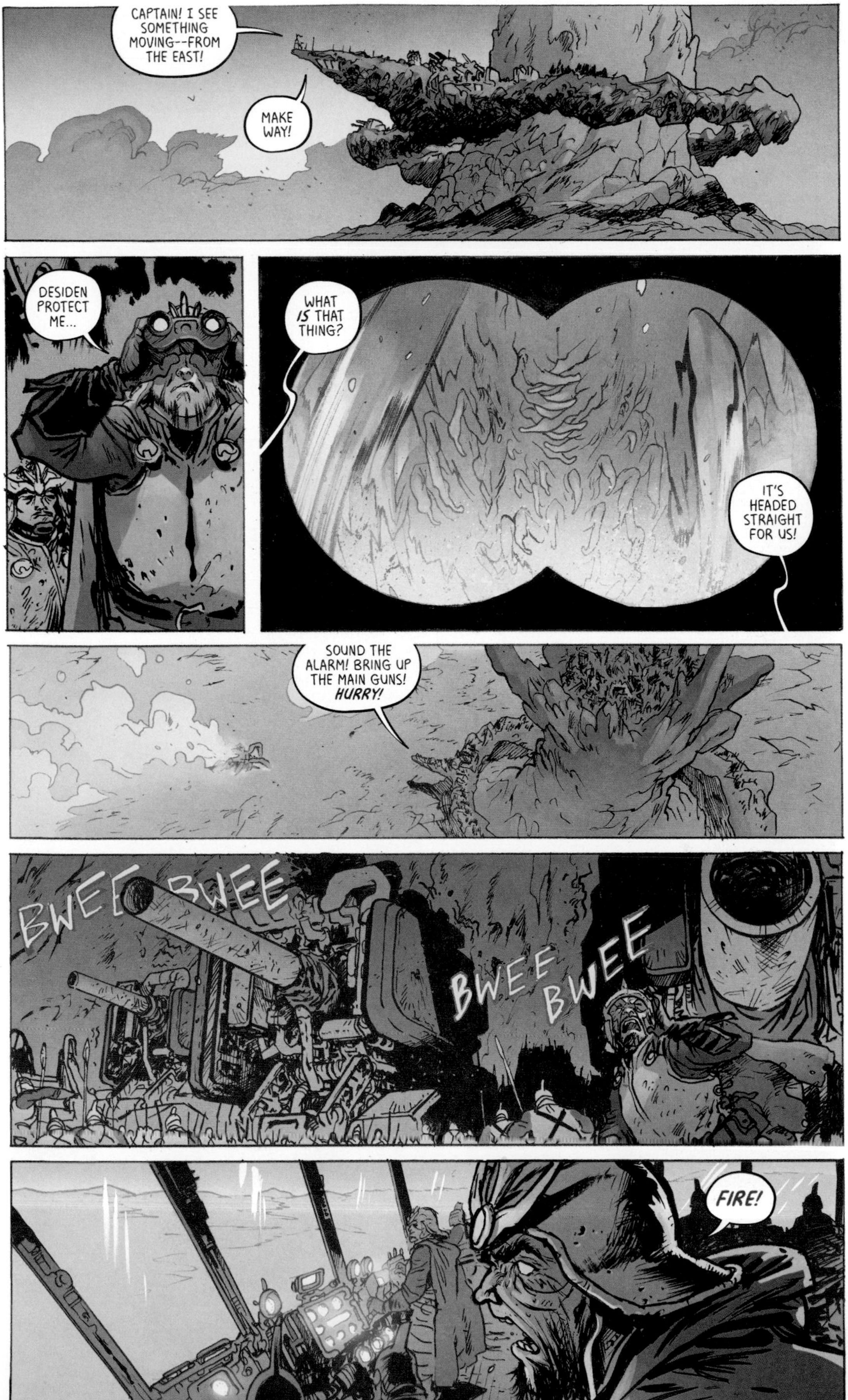
CAPTAIN! I SEE SOMETHING MOVING--FROM THE EAST!
MAKE WAY!
DESIDEN PROTECT ME...
WHAT *IS* THAT THING?
IT'S HEADED STRAIGHT FOR US!
SOUND THE ALARM! BRING UP THE MAIN GUNS! ***HURRY!***
BWEE BWEE
BWEE BWEE
FIRE!

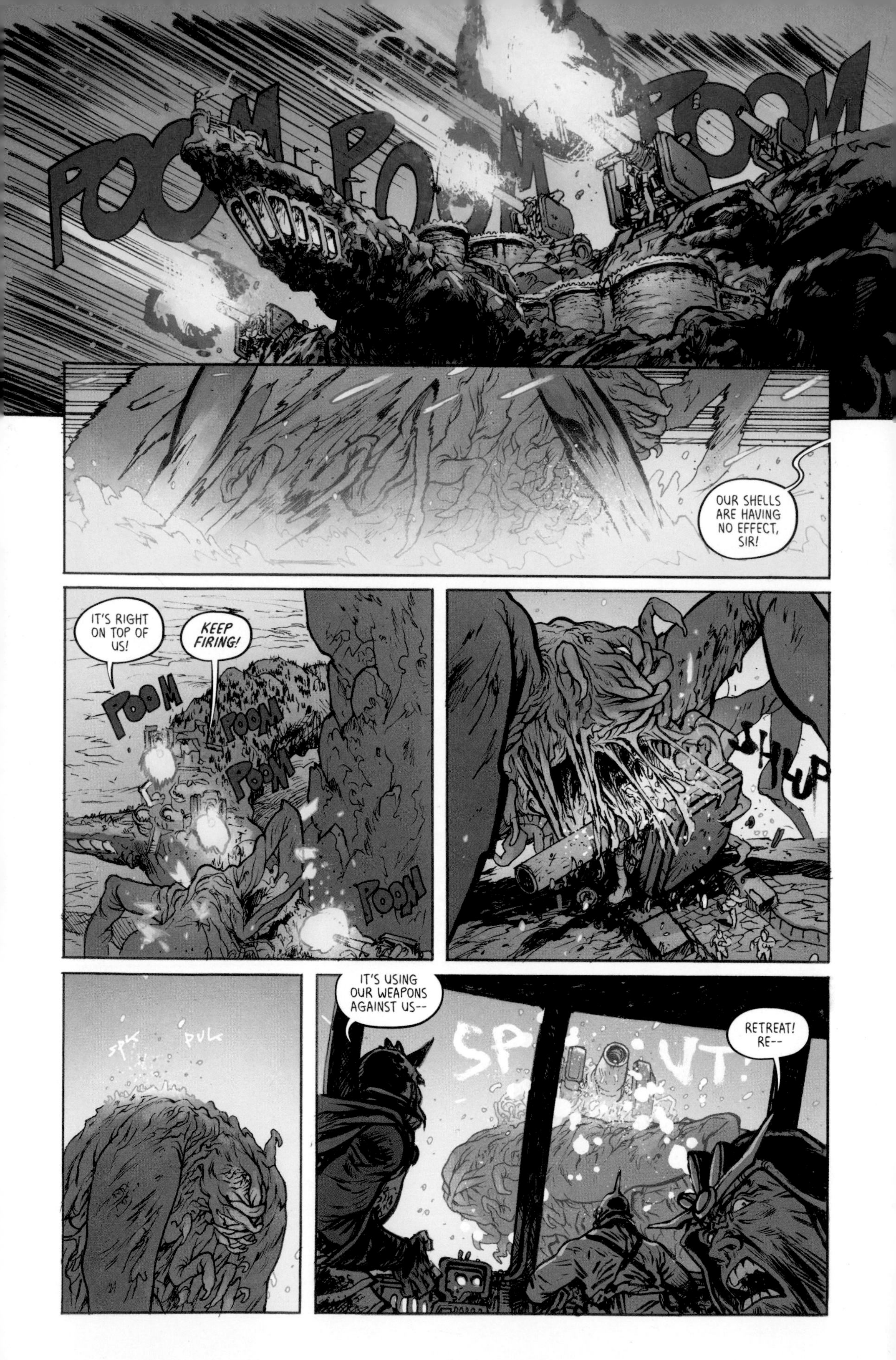
POOM
POOM
POOM
OUR SHELLS ARE HAVING NO EFFECT, SIR!
IT'S RIGHT ON TOP OF US!
KEEP FIRING!
POOM
POOM
POOM
POOM
SHLUP
SPK
PUK
IT'S USING OUR WEAPONS AGAINST US--
RETREAT! RE--

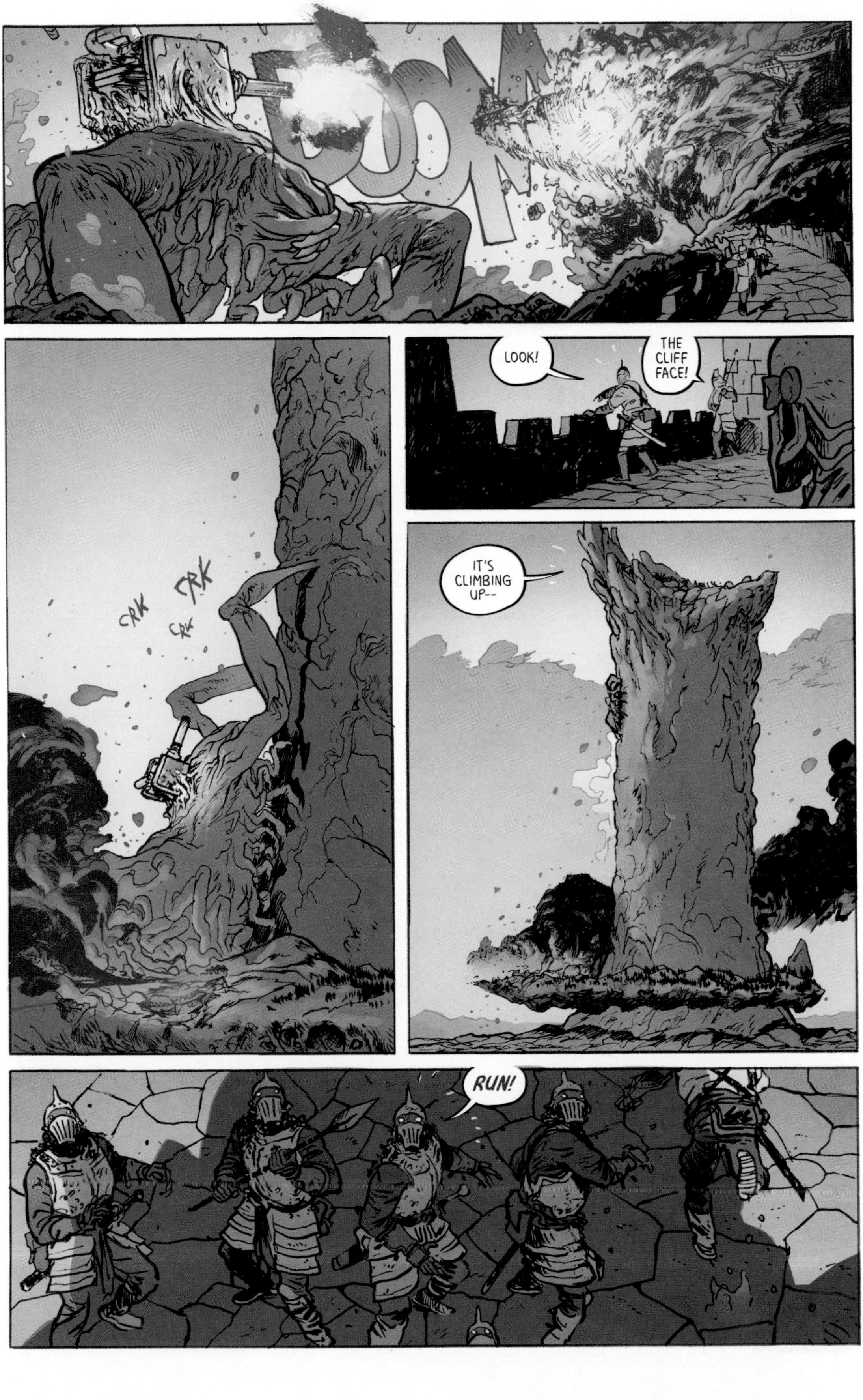
DOOM
CRK
CRK
CRK
LOOK!
THE CLIFF FACE!
IT'S CLIMBING UP--
RUN!

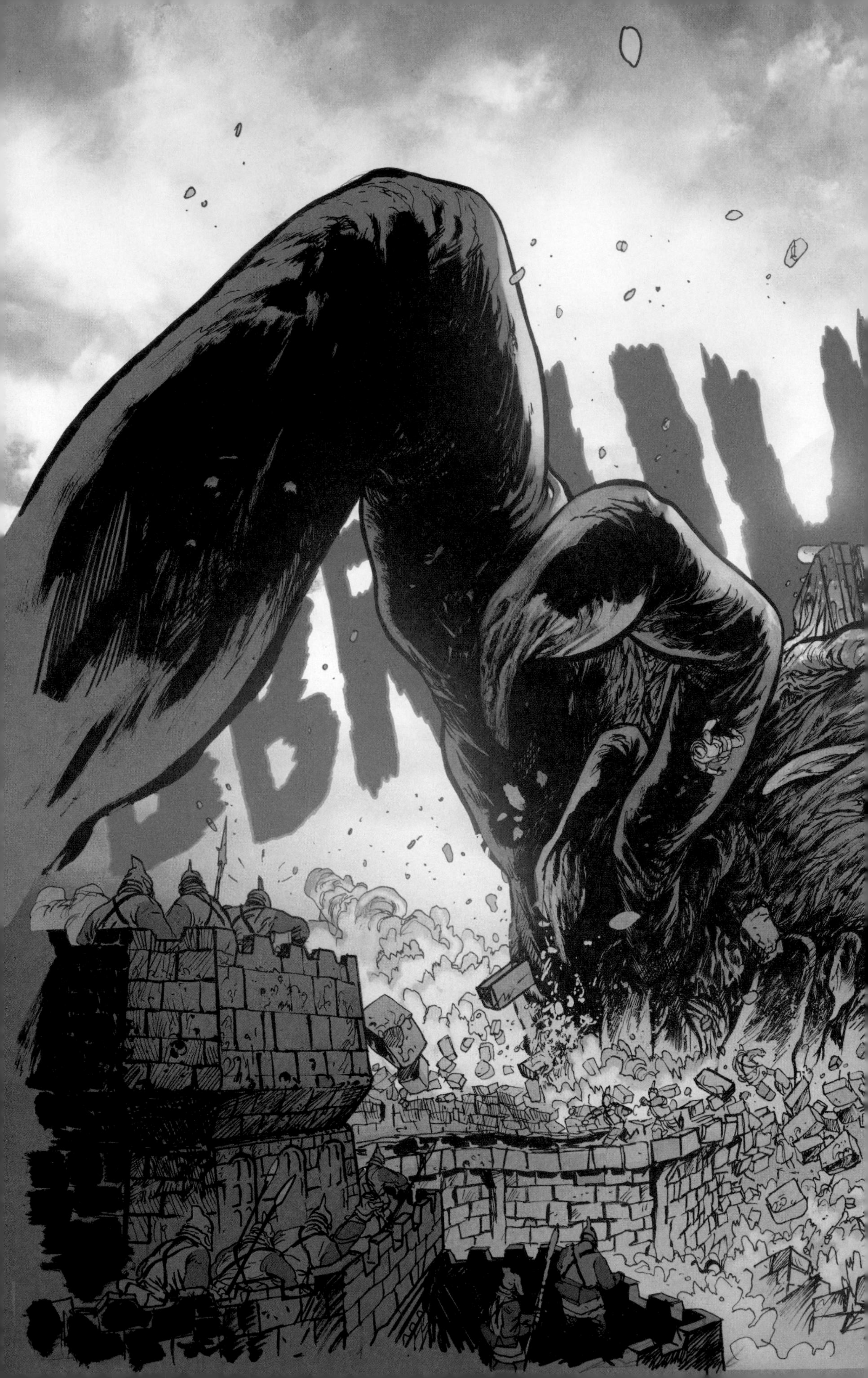

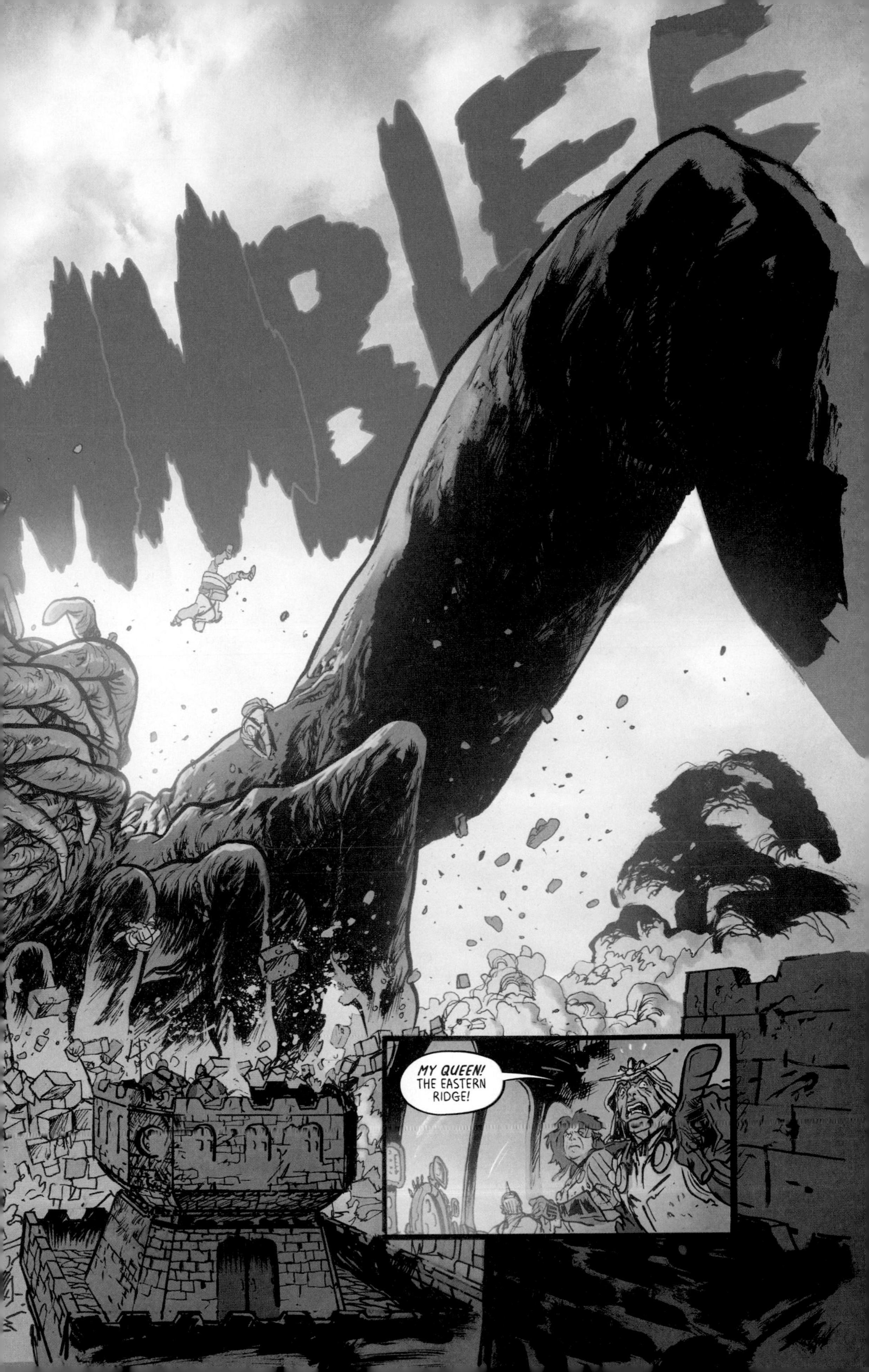

MY QUEEN! THE EASTERN RIDGE!

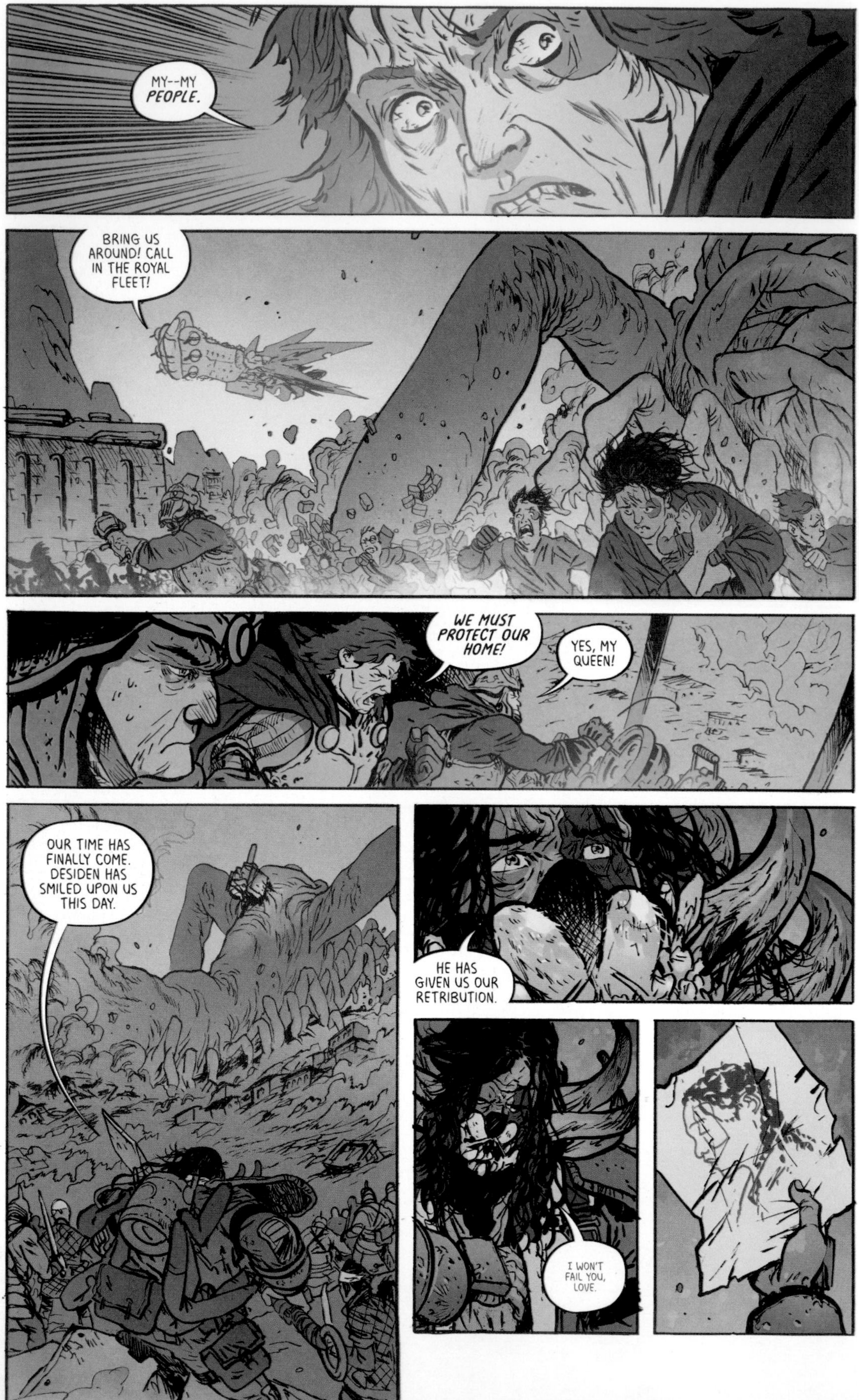
MY--MY *PEOPLE*.
BRING US AROUND! CALL IN THE ROYAL FLEET!
WE MUST PROTECT OUR HOME!
YES, MY QUEEN!
OUR TIME HAS FINALLY COME. DESIDEN HAS SMILED UPON US THIS DAY.
HE HAS GIVEN US OUR RETRIBUTION.
I WON'T FAIL YOU, LOVE.

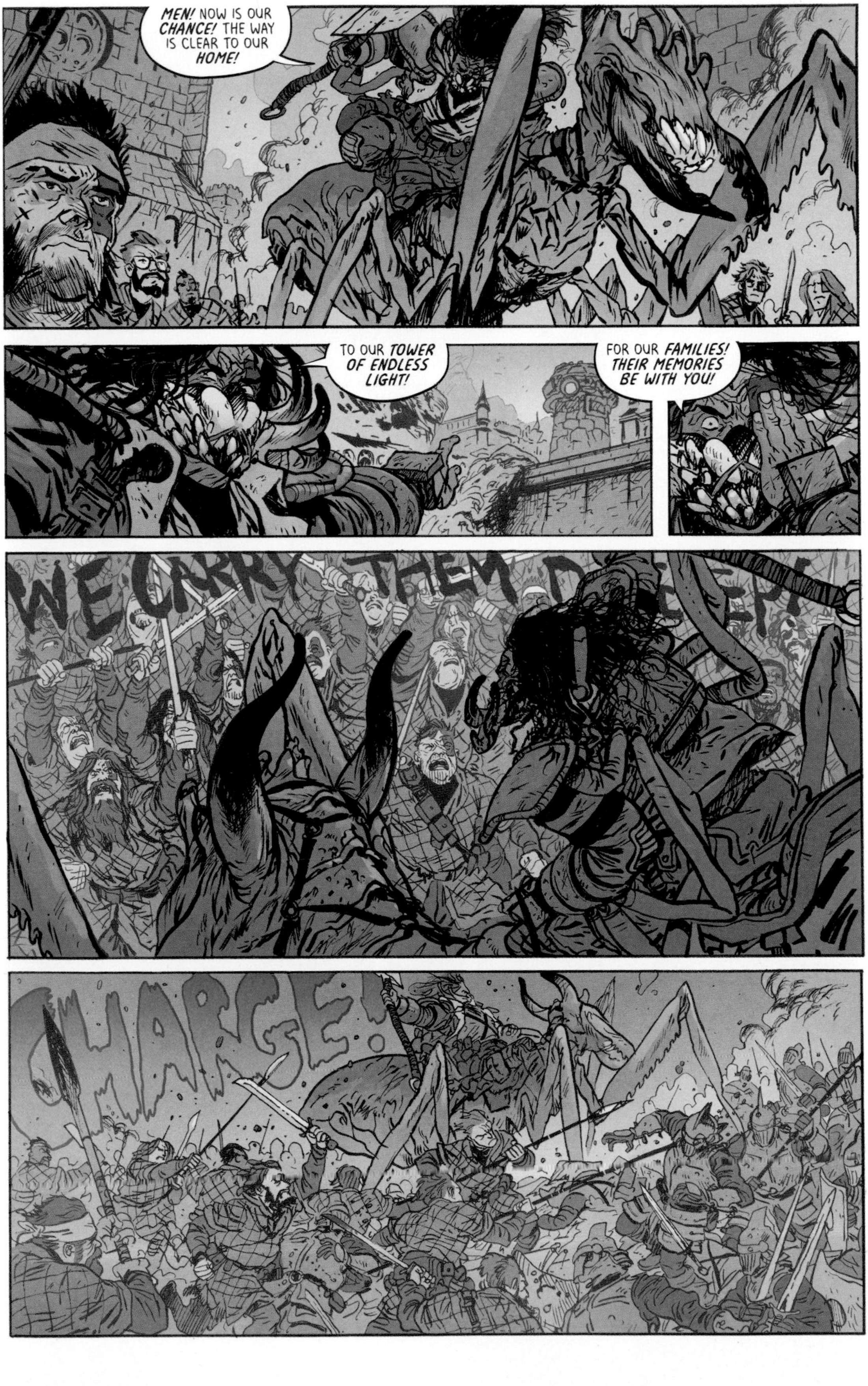
MEN! NOW IS OUR CHANCE! THE WAY IS CLEAR TO OUR HOME!
TO OUR TOWER OF ENDLESS LIGHT!
FOR OUR FAMILIES! THEIR MEMORIES BE WITH YOU!
WE CARRY THEM DEEP!
CHARGE!

CHOOM CHOOM BOOM!

OUR RIGHT CANNONS HAVE BEEN HIT!

KTOOM

KTOOM

BACKUP FAILURES ON DECKS 3, 27 AND 8!

BRING US ABOUT, TWENTY DEGREES! CONTINUE A STEADY RATE OF FIRE FROM OUR LEFT GUNS!

THOOM

AYE-AYE!

THE ROTO ARE APPROACHING THE WALL!

RAAAAHH!

ARROWS AT THE READY!

STRETCH!

LOOSE!

EAARRGHH!

SPNK

SPK

SHK

SPK

SPK

AUEEEE!

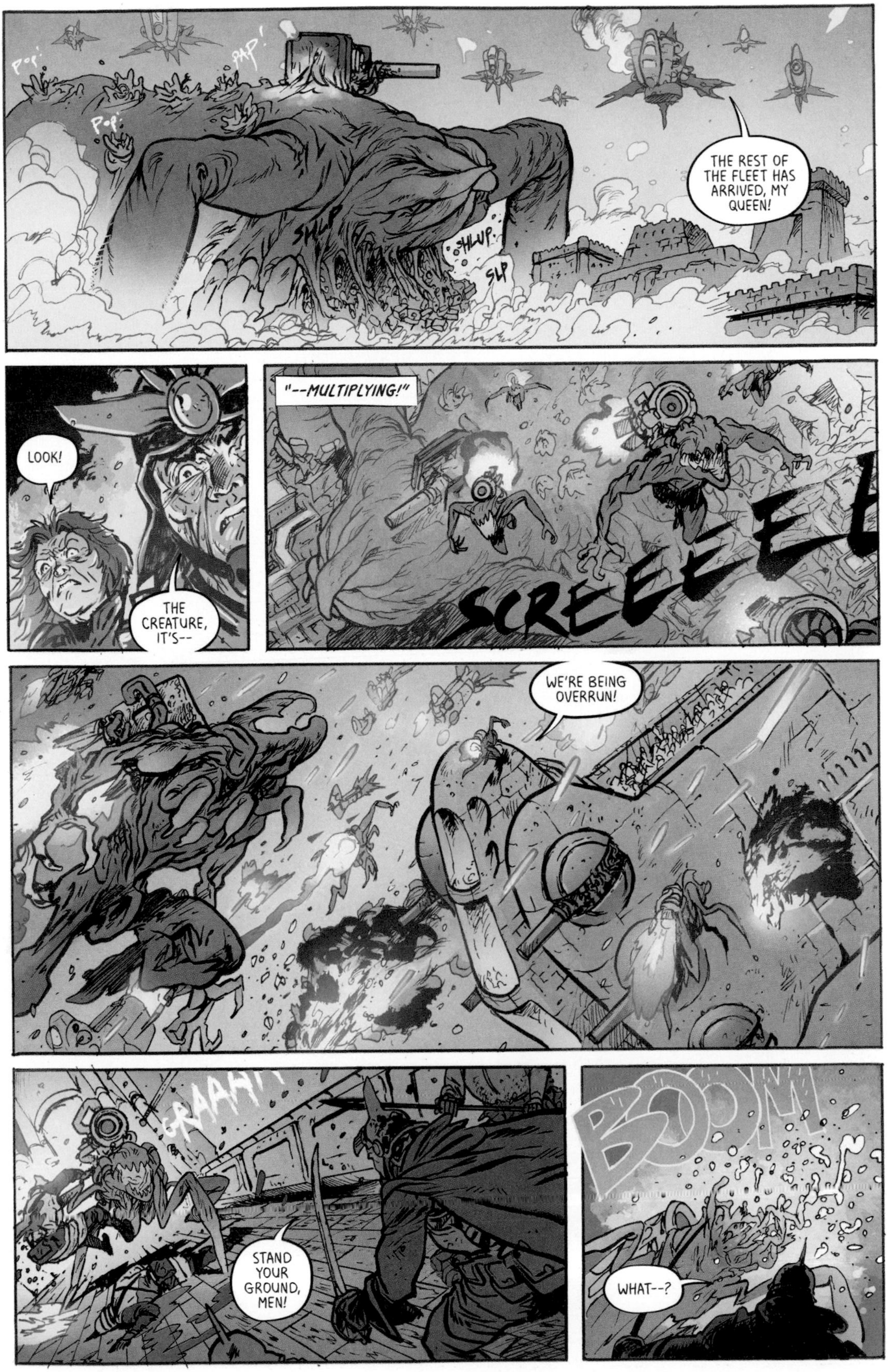
POP!
PAP!
POP!
SHLP
SHLUP
SLP
THE REST OF THE FLEET HAS ARRIVED, MY QUEEN!
LOOK!
THE CREATURE, IT'S--
"--MULTIPLYING!"
SCREEEE
WE'RE BEING OVERRUN!
GRAAAH
STAND YOUR GROUND, MEN!
BOOM
WHAT--?

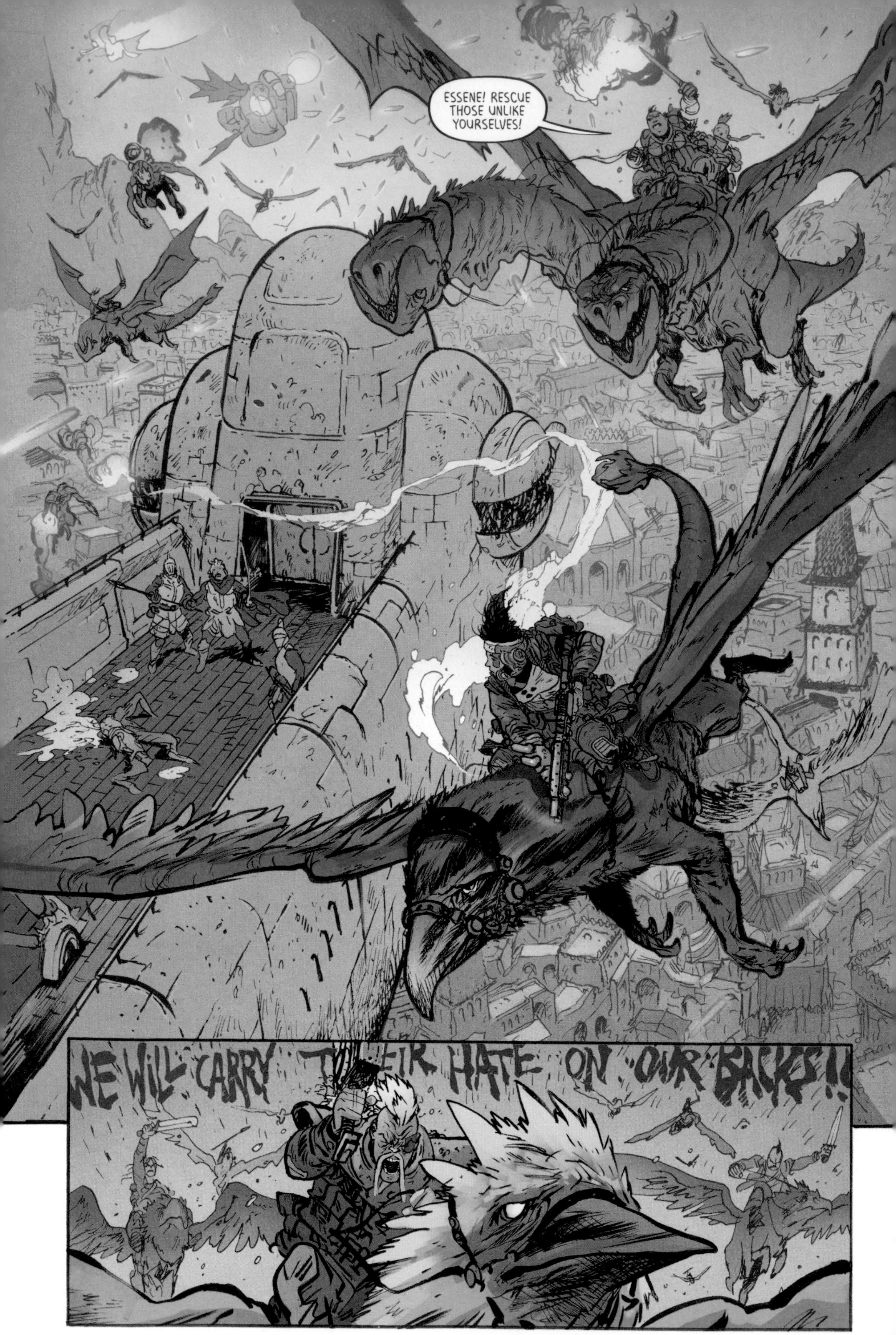
ESSENE! RESCUE THOSE UNLIKE YOURSELVES!
WE WILL CARRY THEIR HATE ON OUR BACKS!!

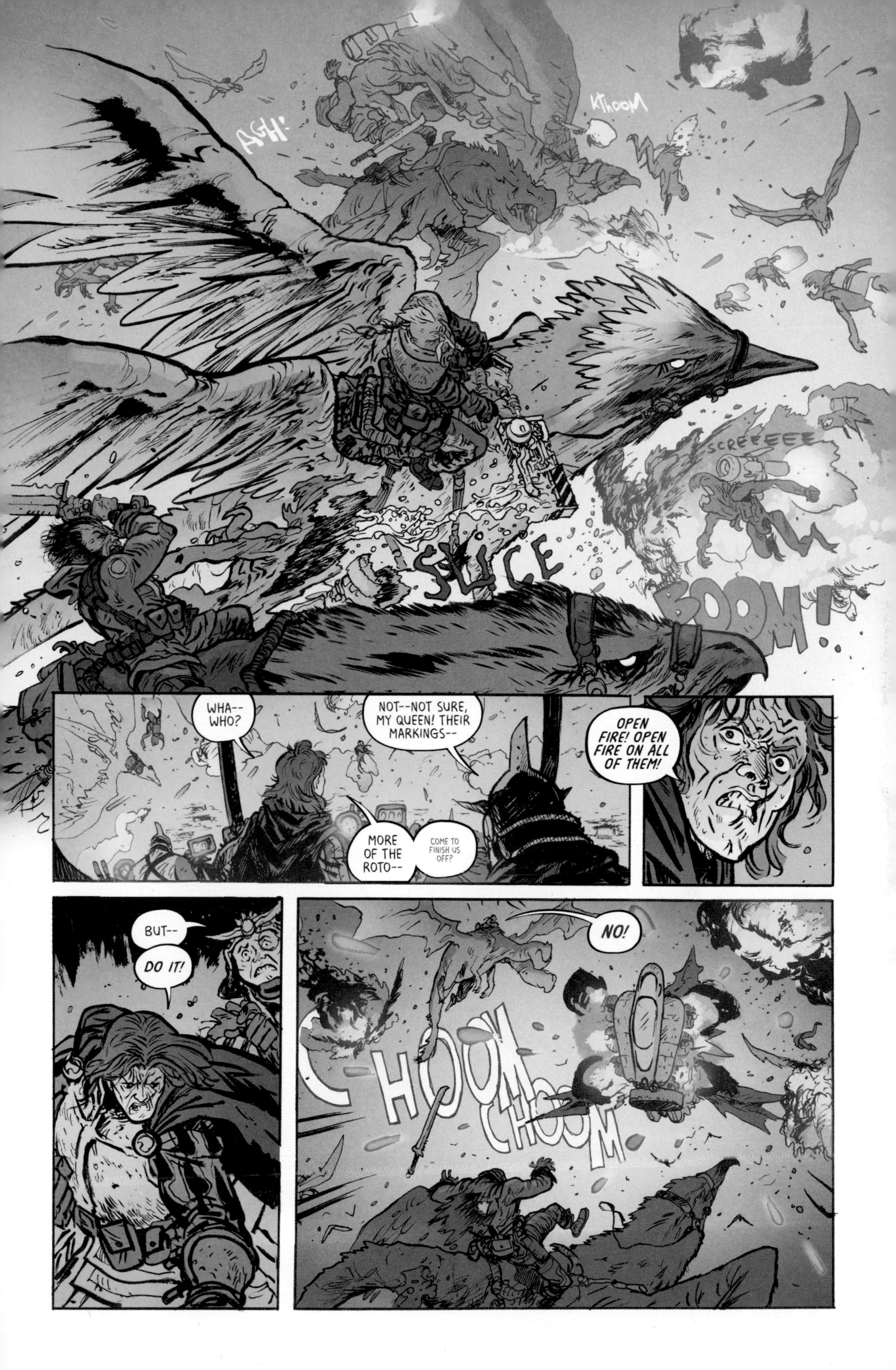
AGH!
KTHOOM
SCREEEEEE
SLICE
BOOM!
WHA--WHO?
NOT--NOT SURE, MY QUEEN! THEIR MARKINGS--
MORE OF THE ROTO--
COME TO FINISH US OFF?
OPEN FIRE! OPEN FIRE ON ALL OF THEM!
BUT--
DO IT!
NO!
CHOOM
CHOOM

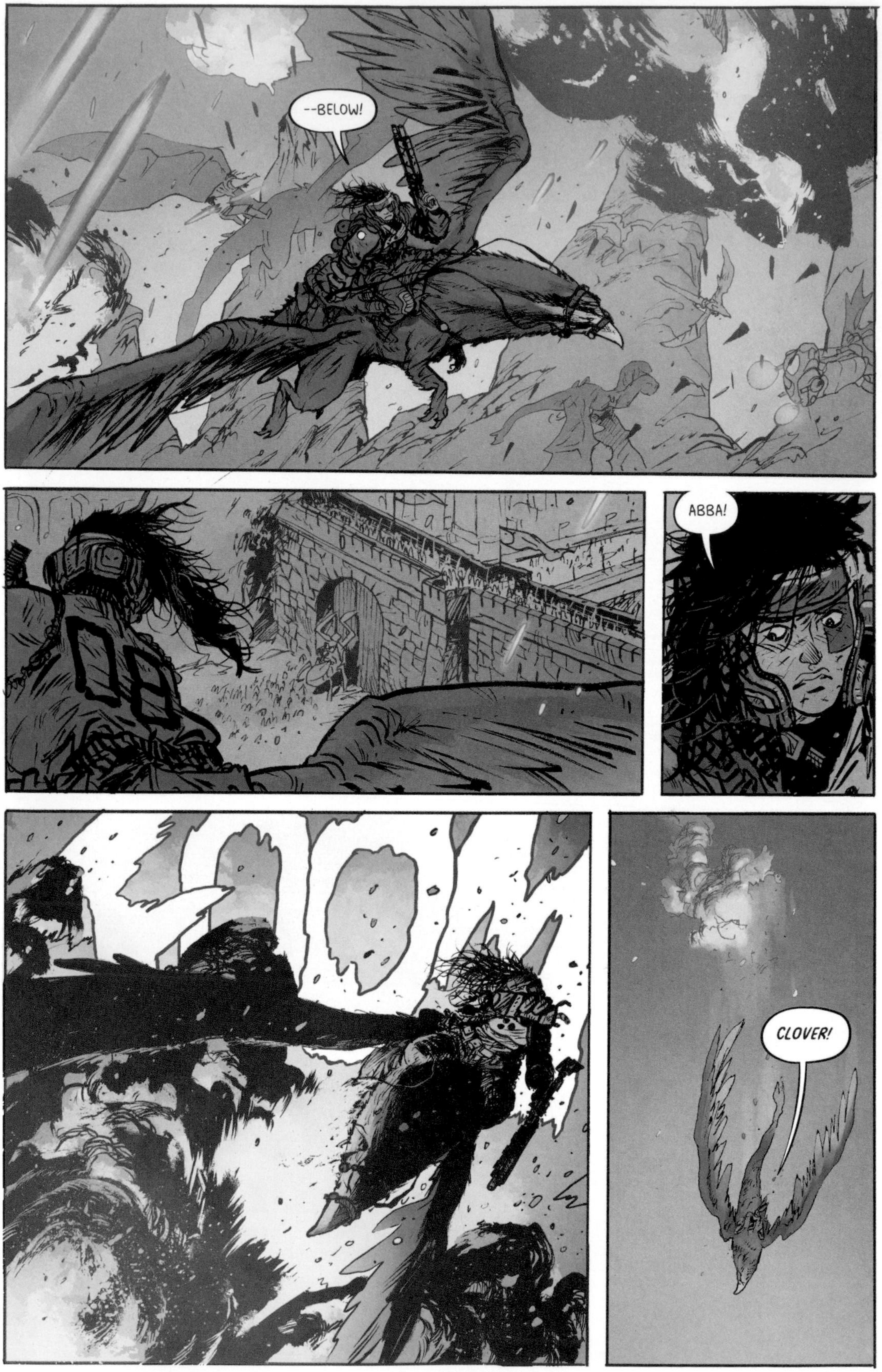
--BELOW!
ABBA!
CLOVER!

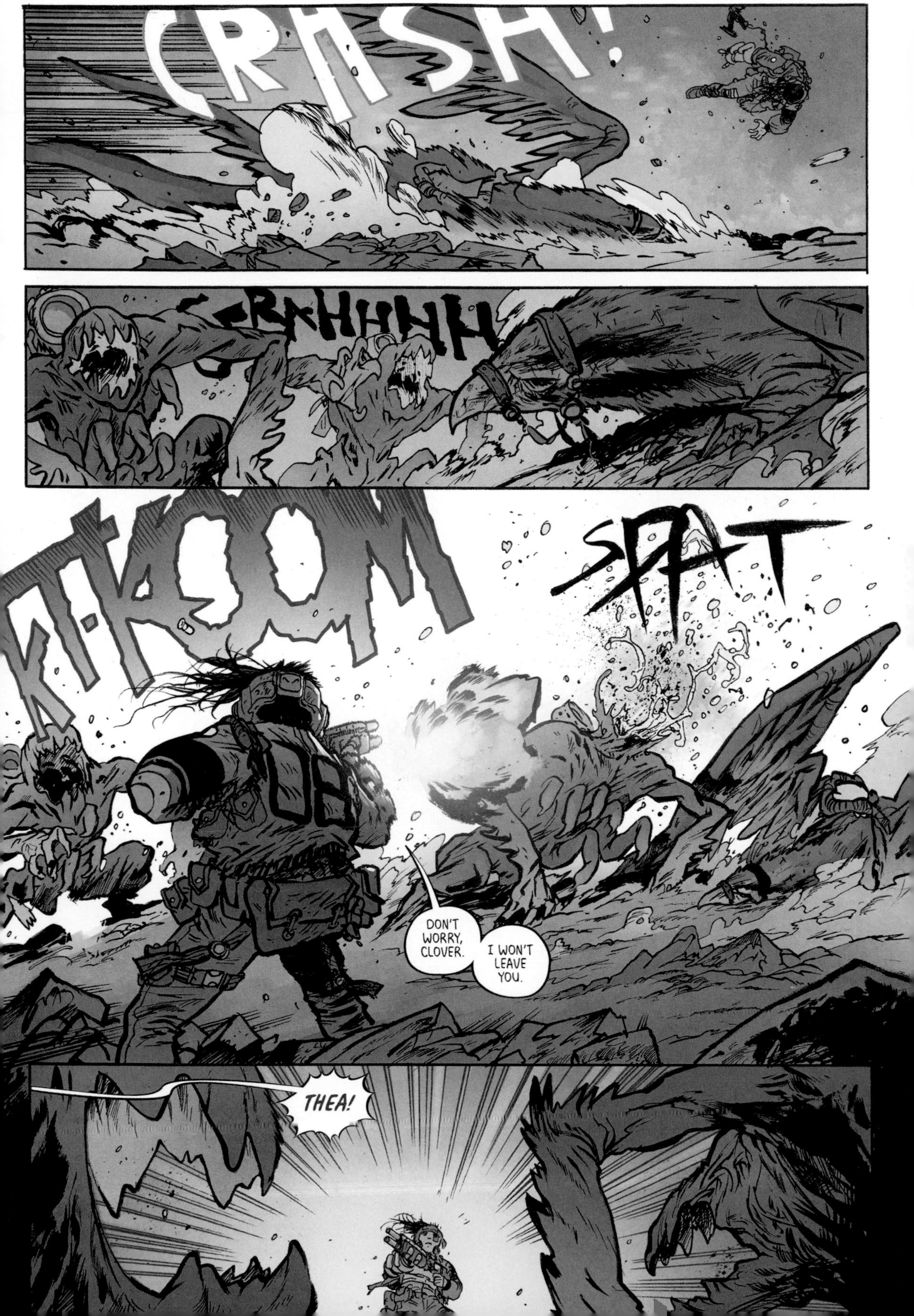
CRASH!
CRAHHHHH
KT-KOOM
SPAT
DON'T WORRY, CLOVER.
I WON'T LEAVE YOU.
THEA!

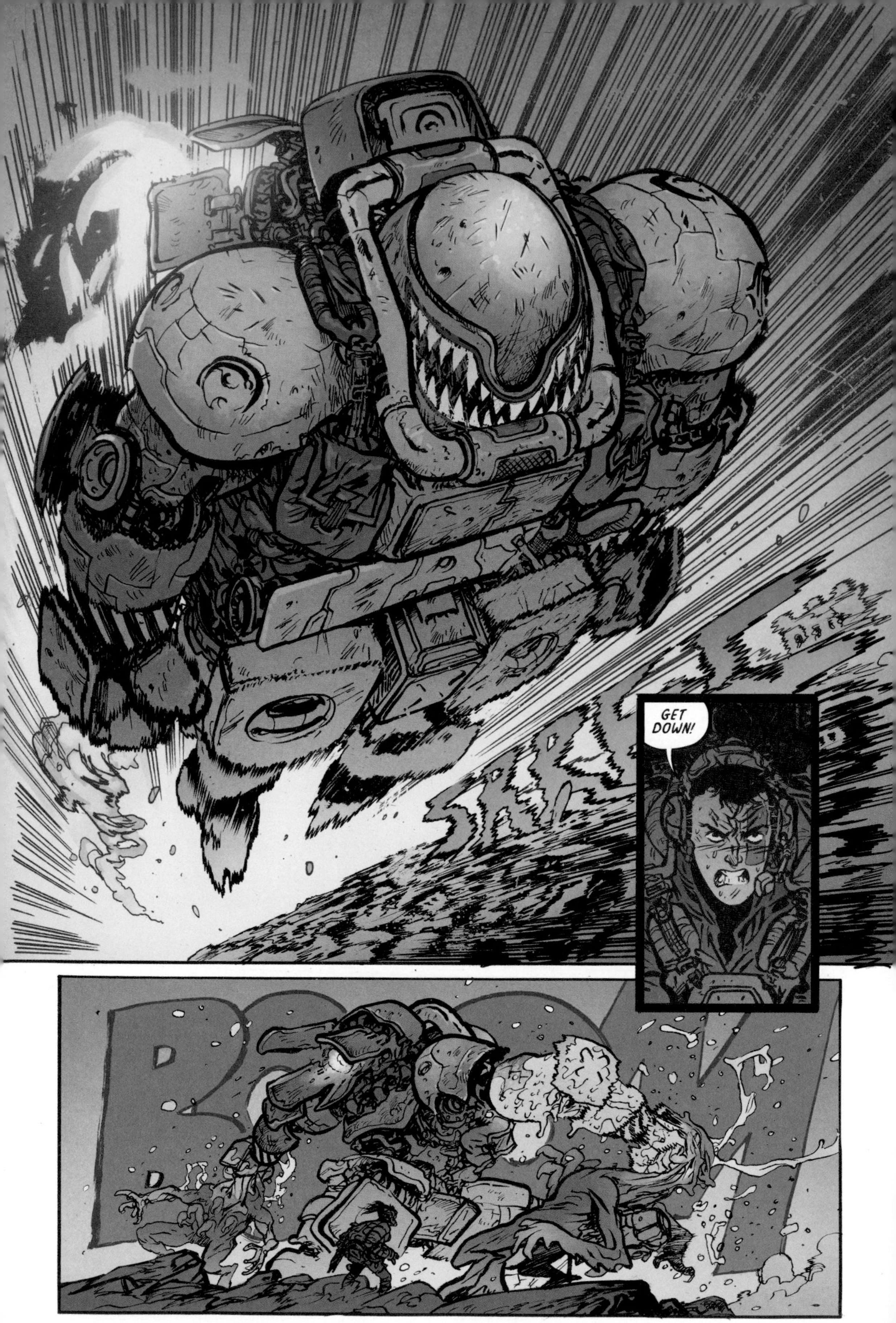
GET DOWN!

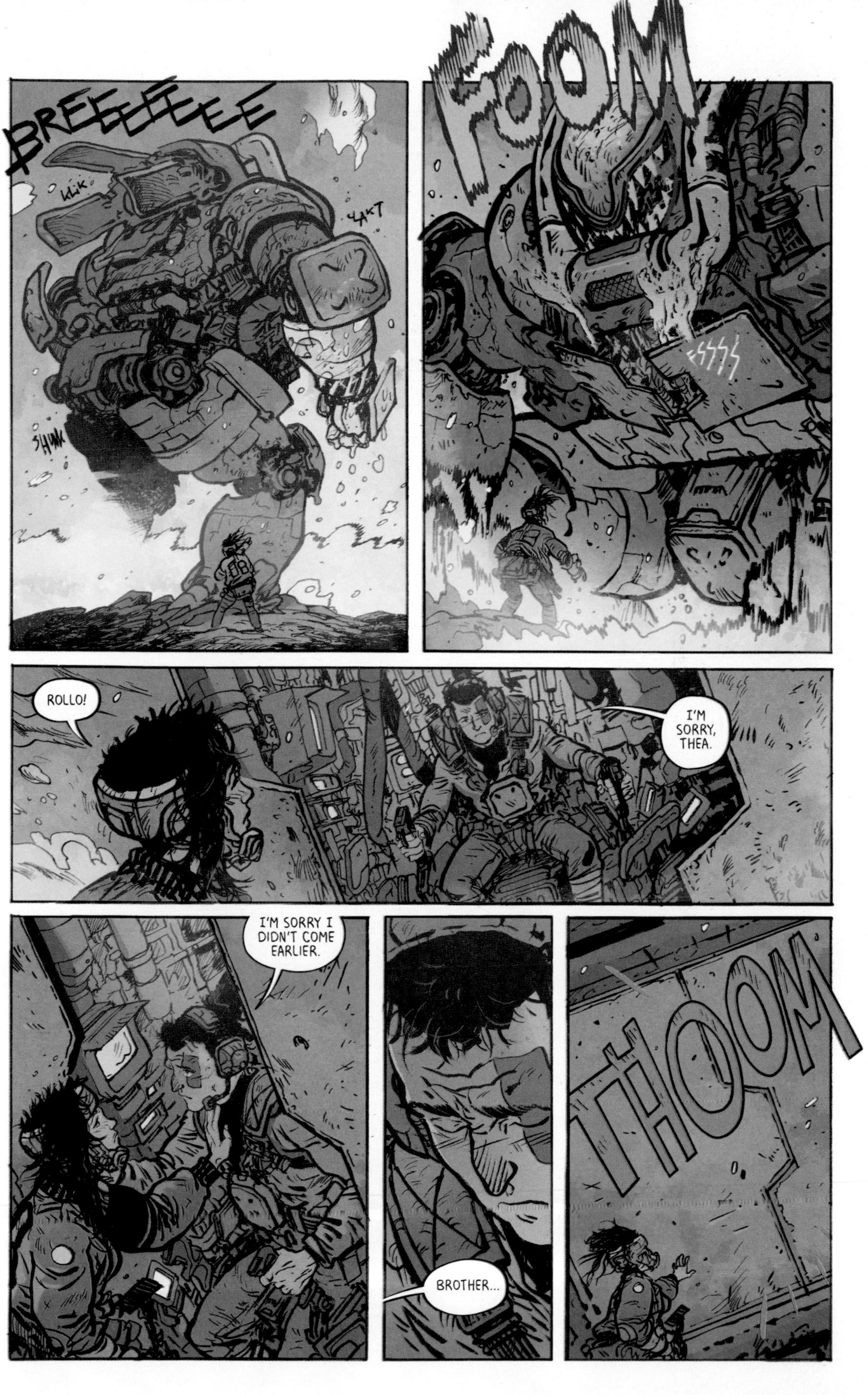
BREEEEEEE
KLIK
CHAKT
SHUNK
FOOM
FSSSS
ROLLO!
I'M SORRY, THEA.
I'M SORRY I DIDN'T COME EARLIER.
BROTHER...
THOOM

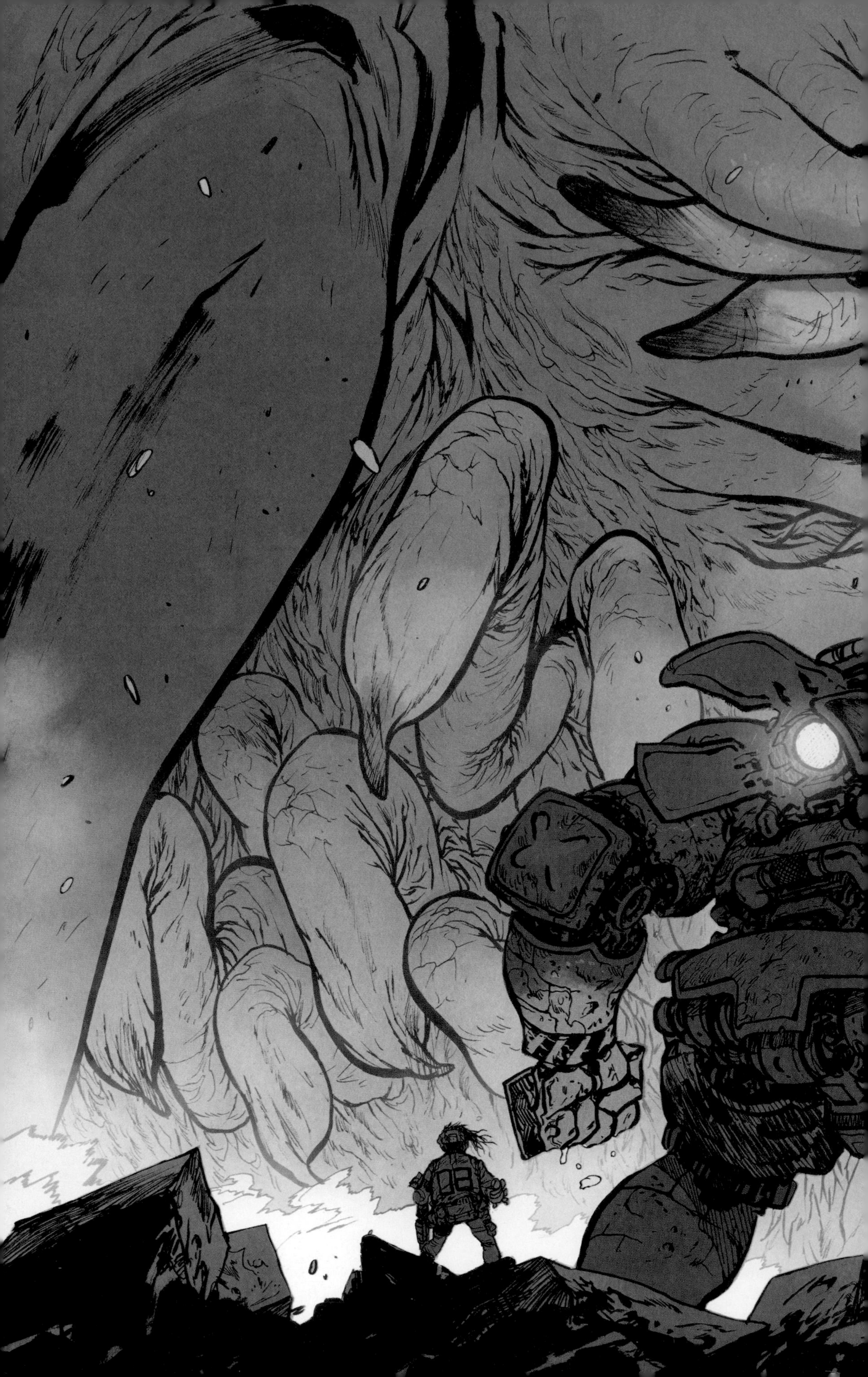

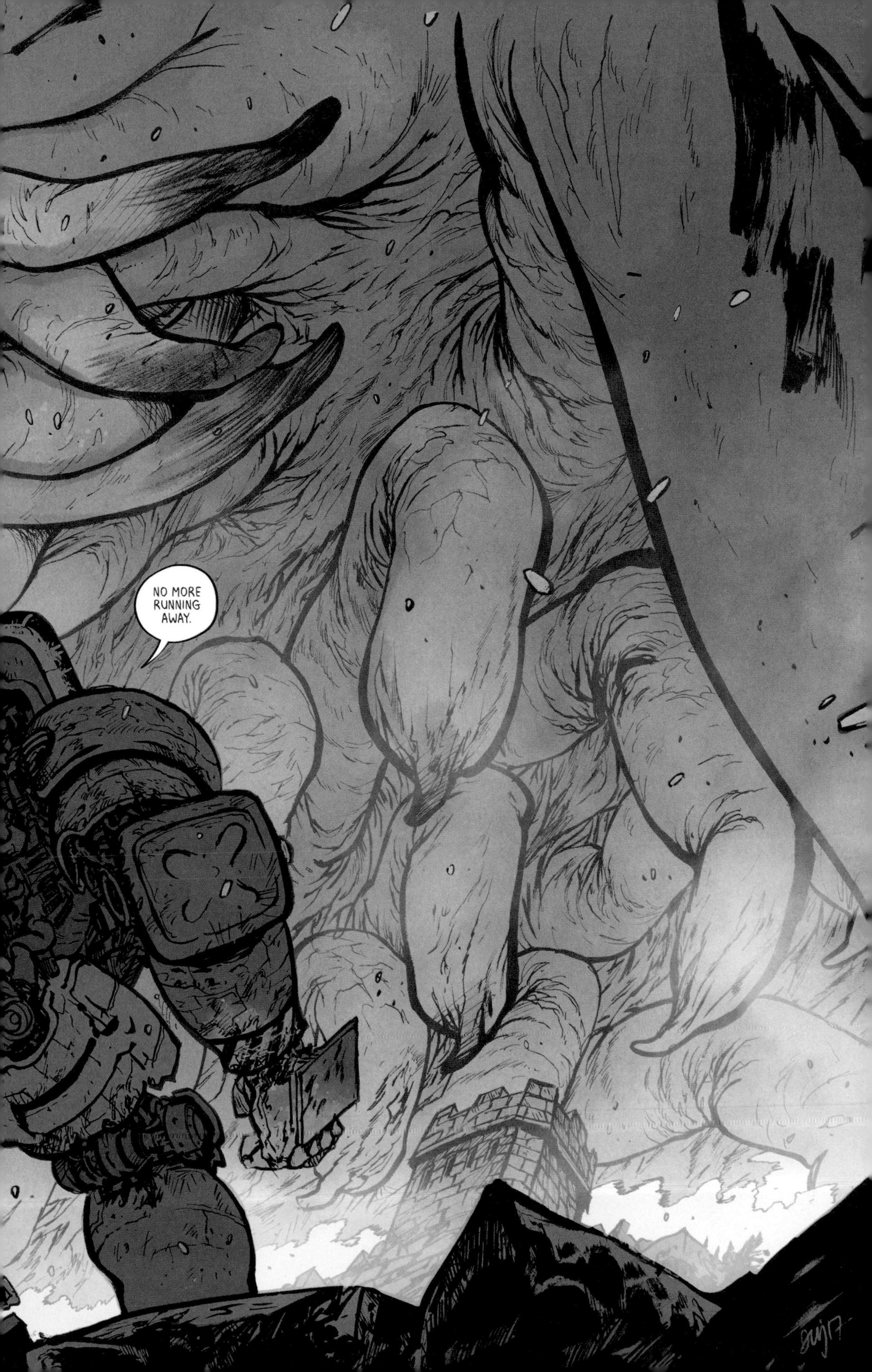
NO MORE RUNNING AWAY.

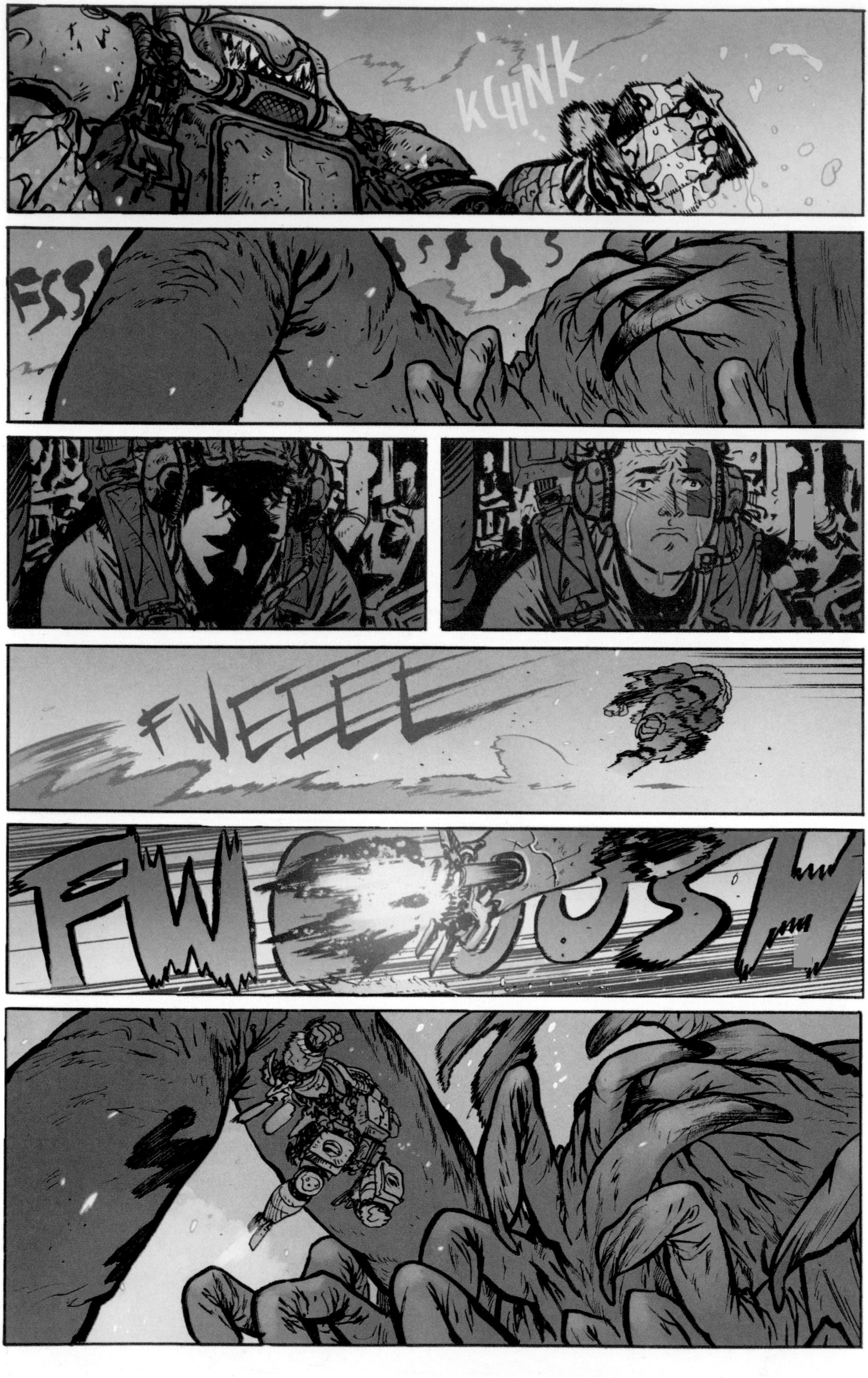
KCHNK
FSSS
FWEEEE
FWOOSH

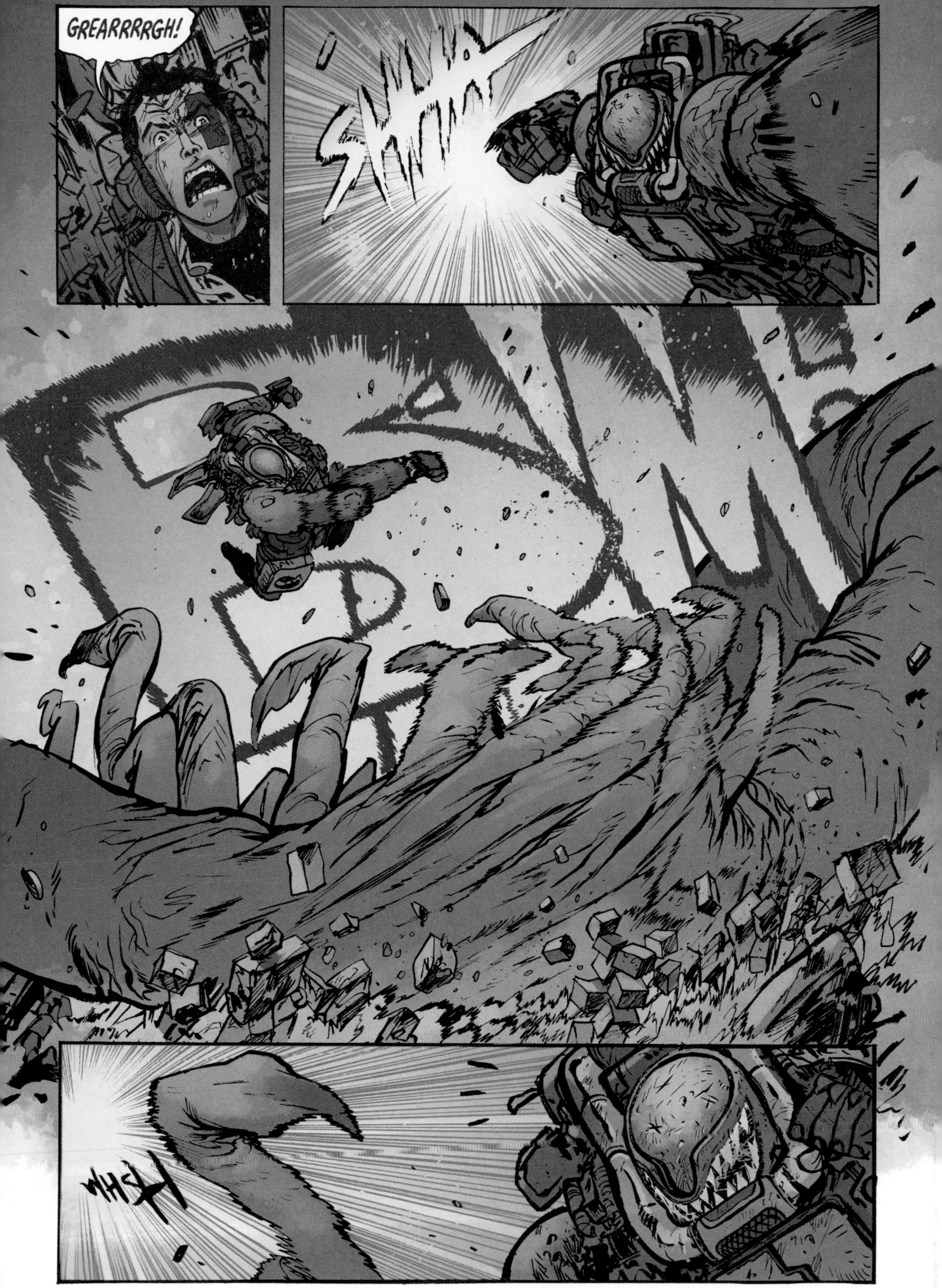
GREARRRRGH!

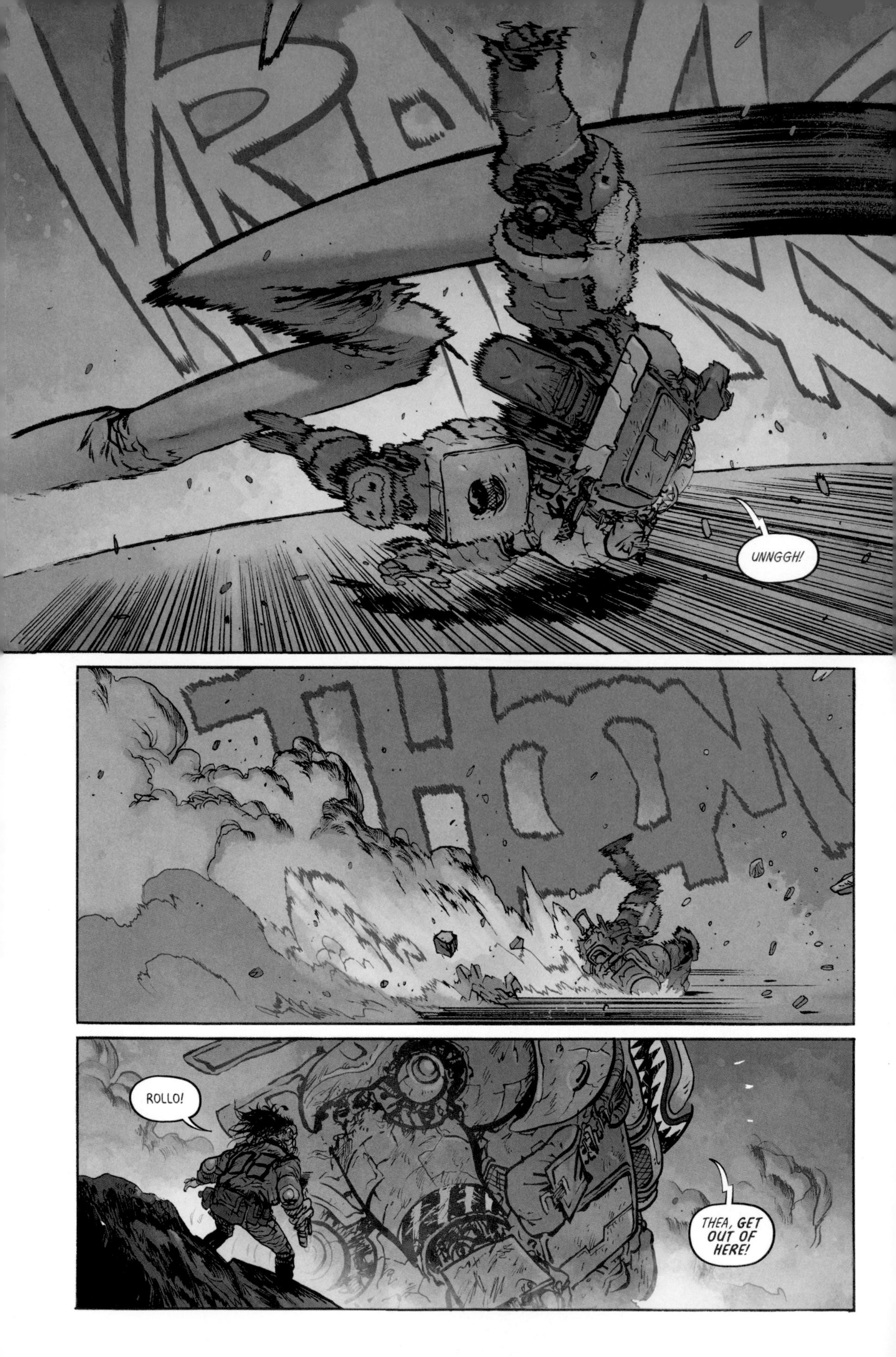
UNNGGH!
ROLLO!
THEA, GET OUT OF HERE!

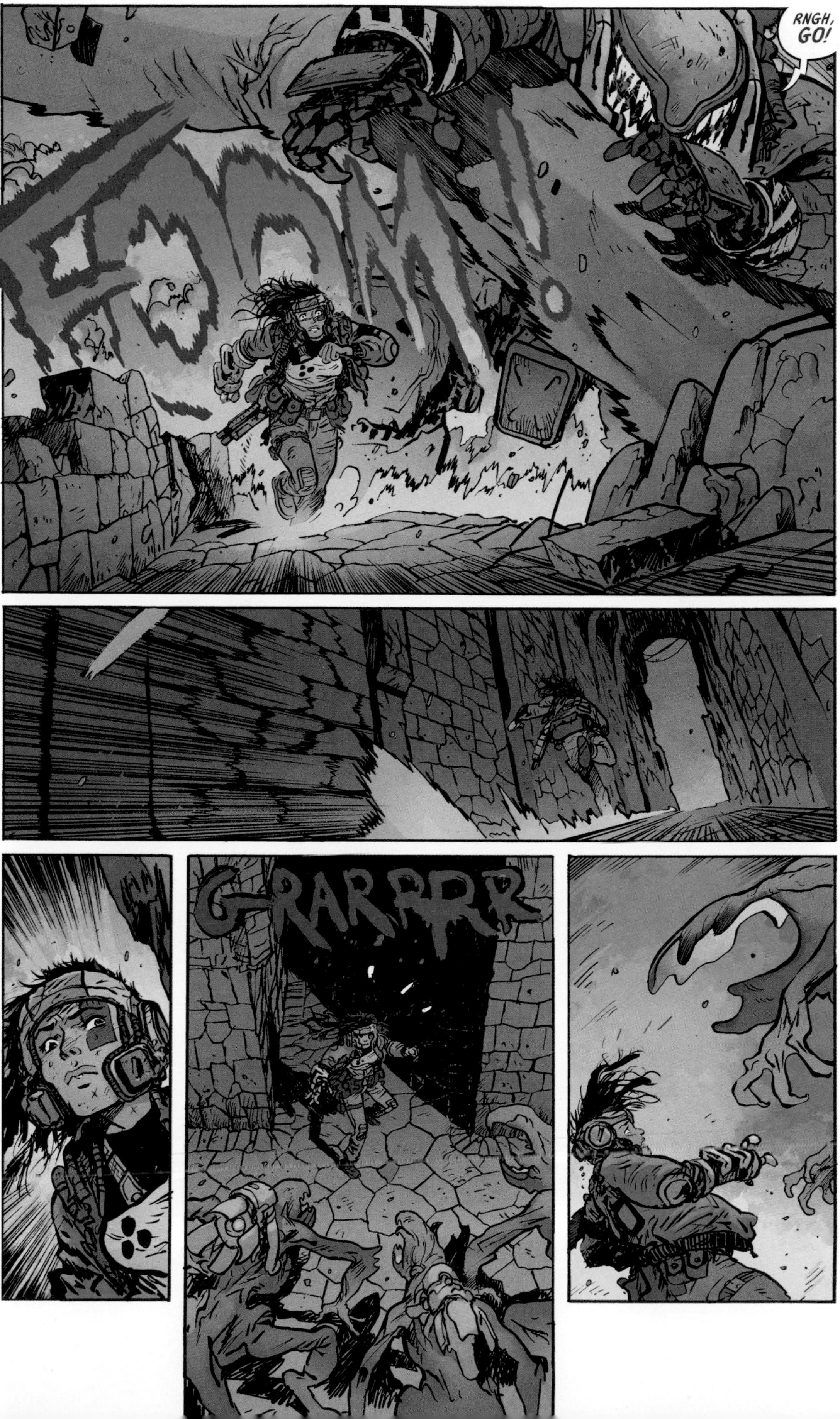
RNGH, GO!
FOOM!!
GRARRRR

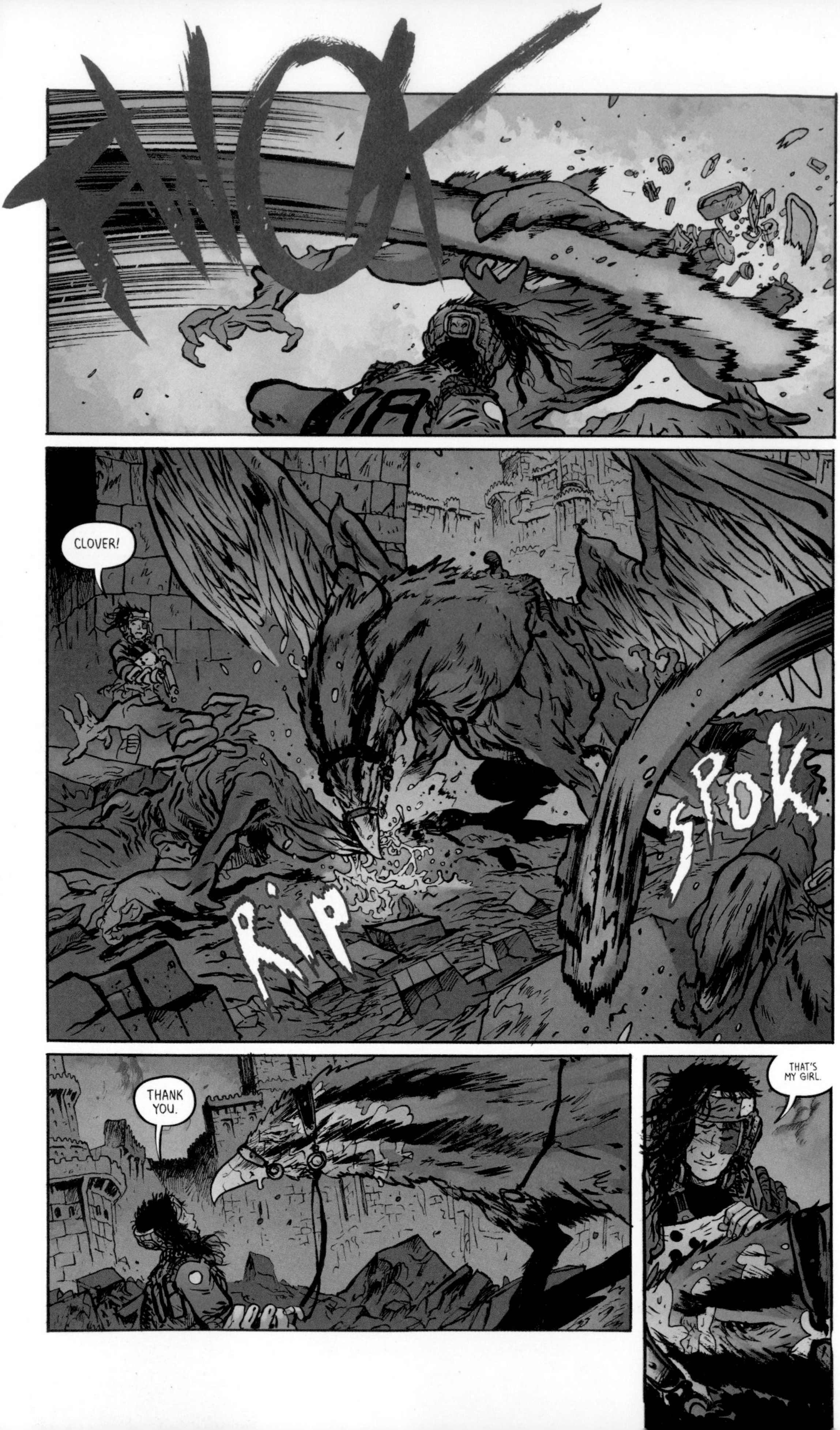
CLOVER!
RIP
SPOK
THANK YOU.
THAT'S MY GIRL.

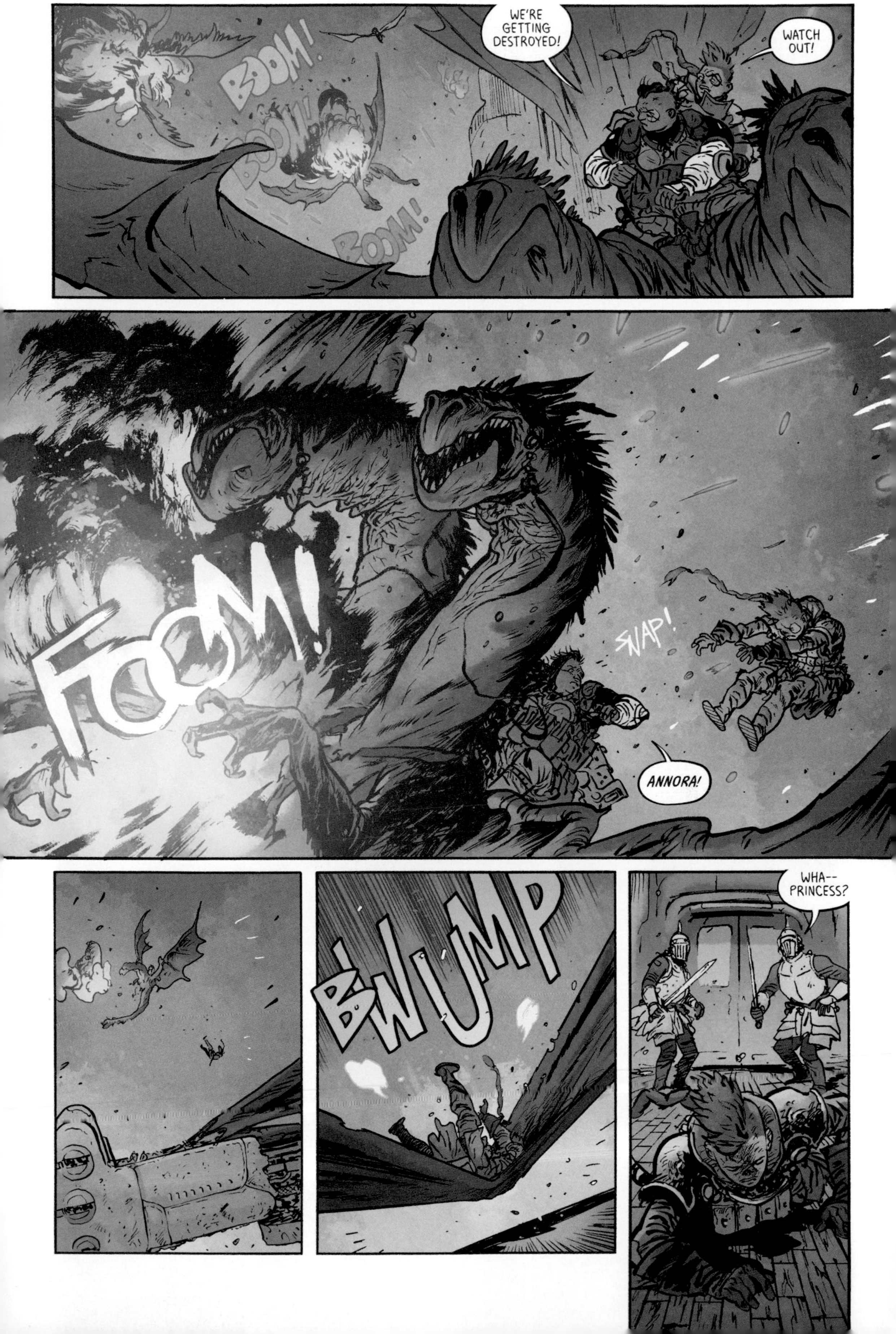
BOOM!
BOOM!
BOOM!
WE'RE GETTING DESTROYED!
WATCH OUT!
FOOM!
SNAP!
ANNORA!
BWUMP
WHA-- PRINCESS?

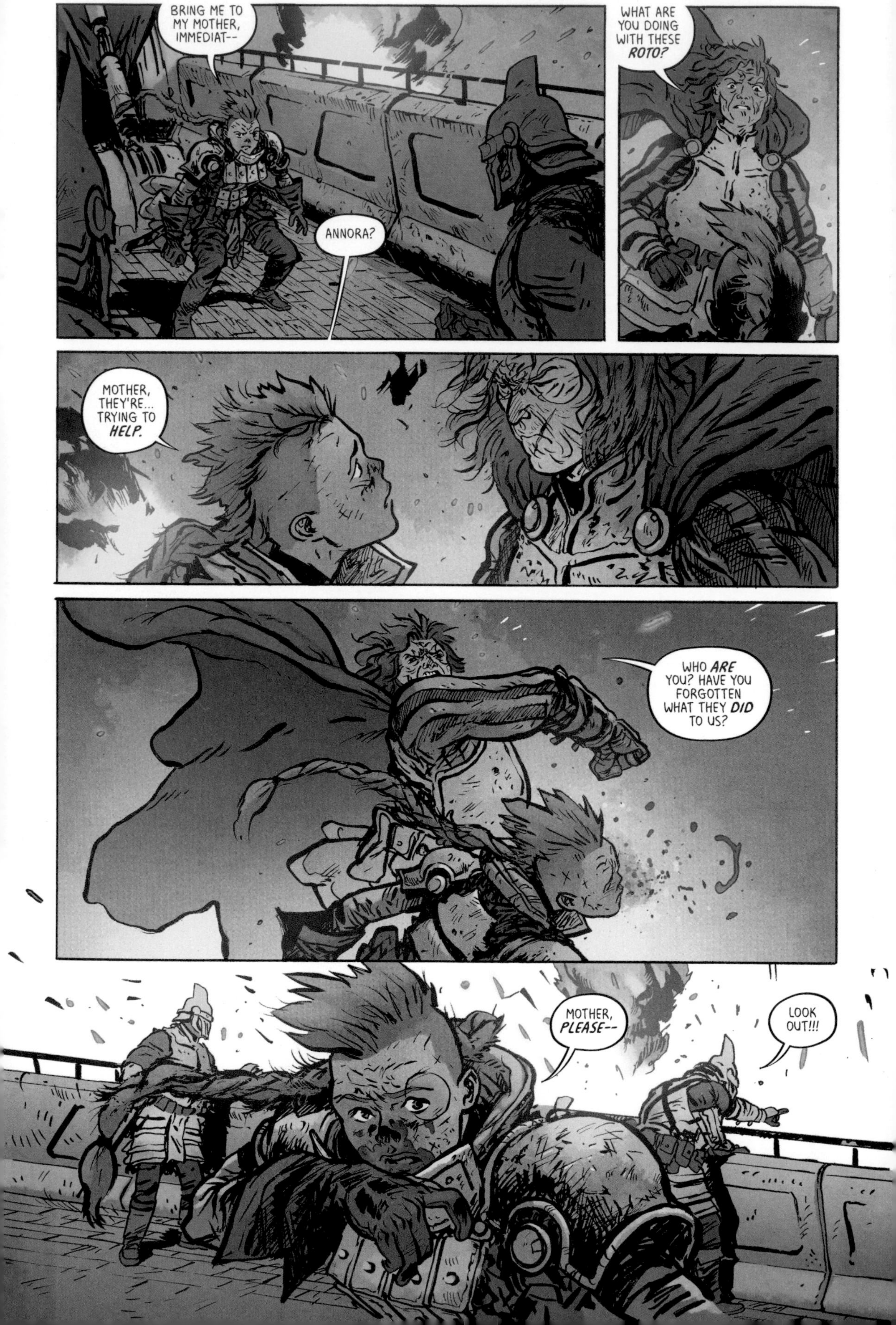
BRING ME TO MY MOTHER, IMMEDIAT--
ANNORA?
WHAT ARE YOU DOING WITH THESE *ROTO?*
MOTHER, THEY'RE... TRYING TO *HELP.*
WHO *ARE* YOU? HAVE YOU FORGOTTEN WHAT THEY *DID* TO US?
MOTHER, *PLEASE--*
LOOK OUT!!!

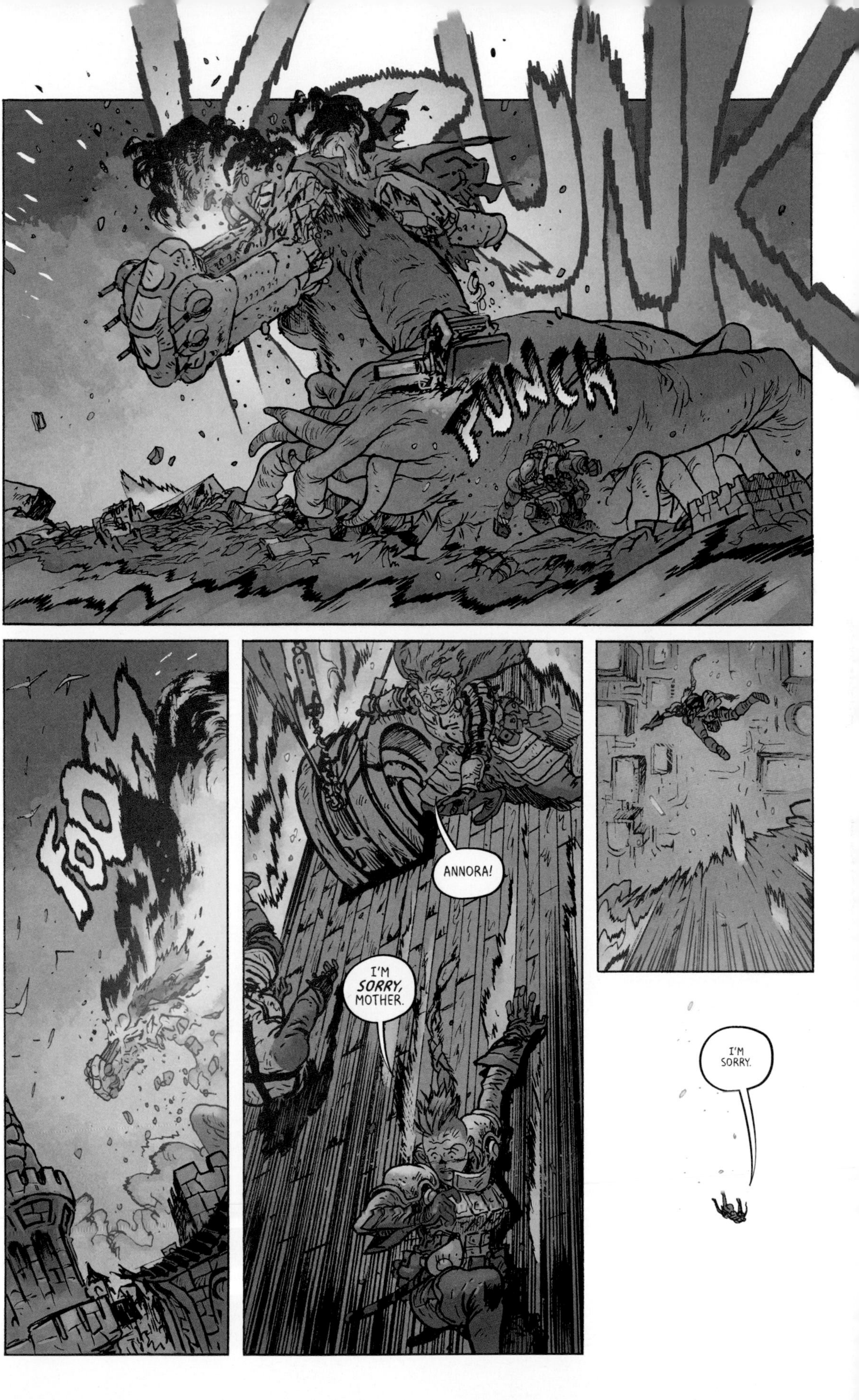
PUNCH
ANNORA!
I'M SORRY, MOTHER.
I'M SORRY.

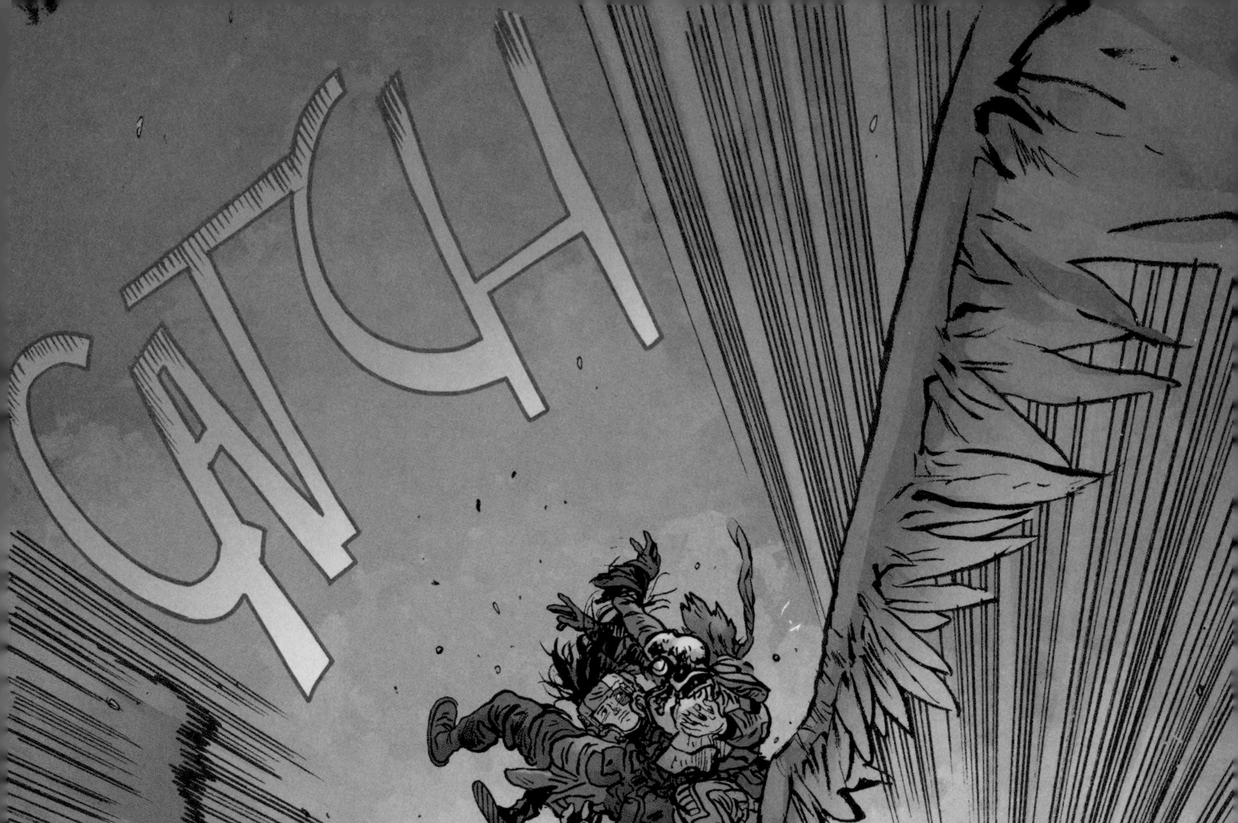
CATCH

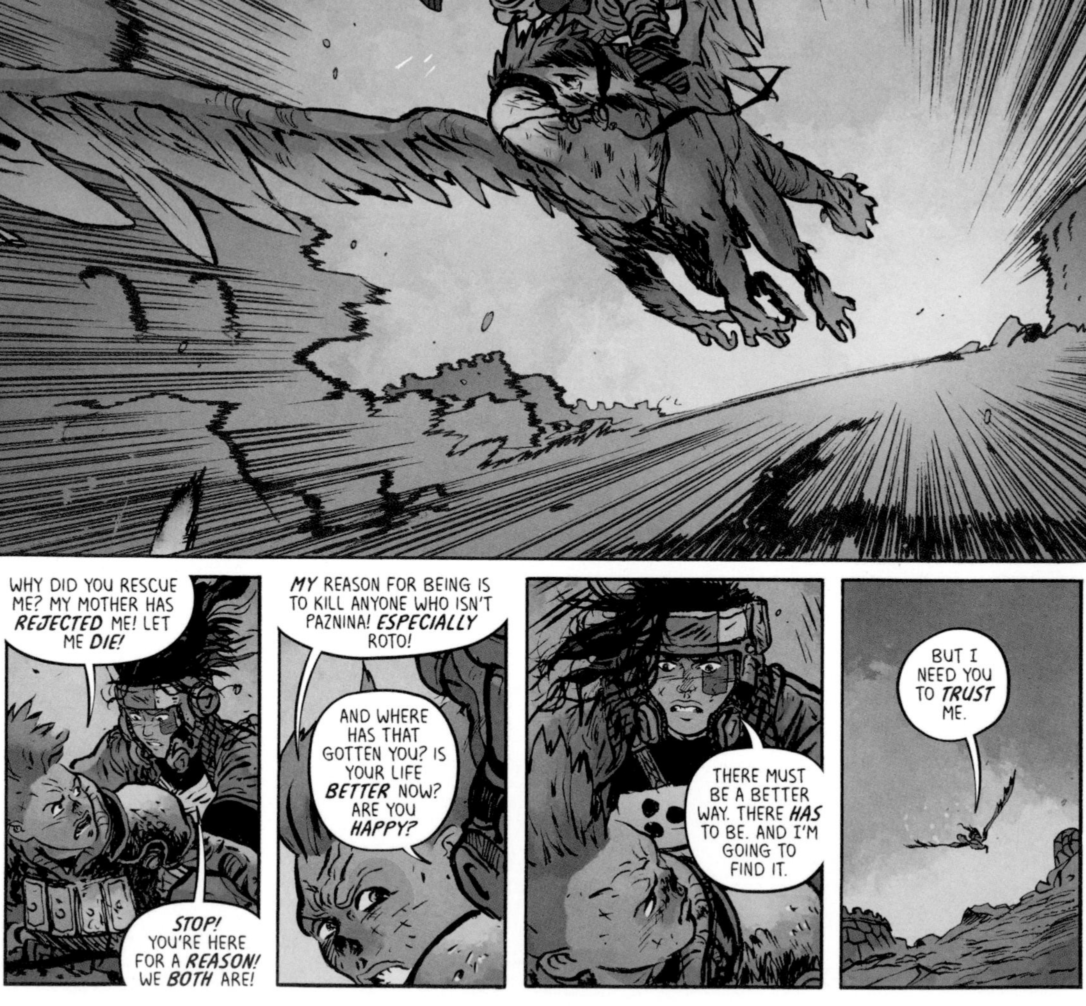
WHY DID YOU RESCUE ME? MY MOTHER HAS ***REJECTED*** ME! LET ME ***DIE!***
STOP! YOU'RE HERE FOR A ***REASON!*** WE ***BOTH*** ARE!
MY REASON FOR BEING IS TO KILL ANYONE WHO ISN'T PAZNINA! ***ESPECIALLY*** ROTO!
AND WHERE HAS THAT GOTTEN YOU? IS YOUR LIFE ***BETTER*** NOW? ARE YOU ***HAPPY?***
THERE MUST BE A BETTER WAY. THERE ***HAS*** TO BE. AND I'M GOING TO FIND IT.
BUT I NEED YOU TO ***TRUST*** ME.

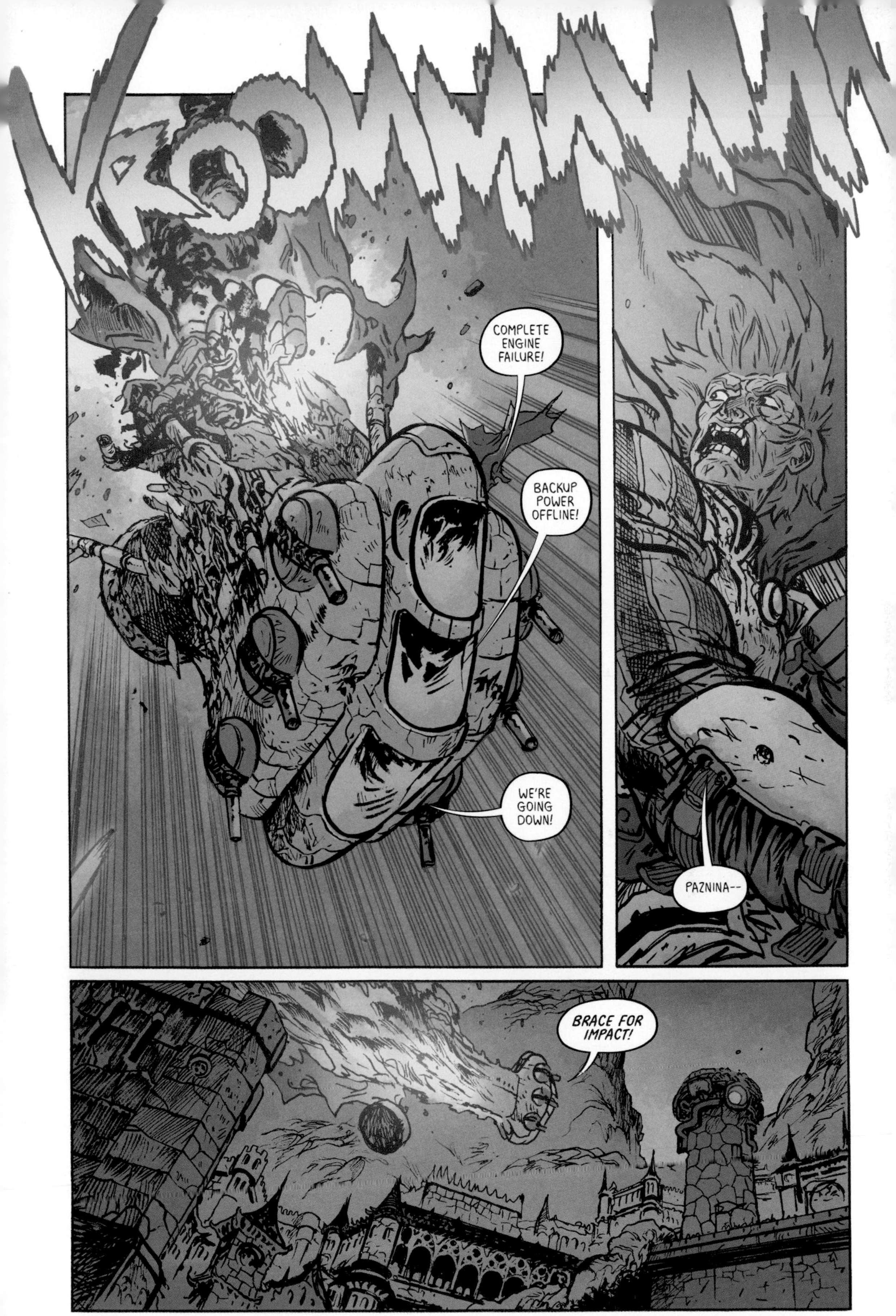
KROOMMMM
COMPLETE ENGINE FAILURE!
BACKUP POWER OFFLINE!
WE'RE GOING DOWN!
PAZNINA--
BRACE FOR IMPACT!

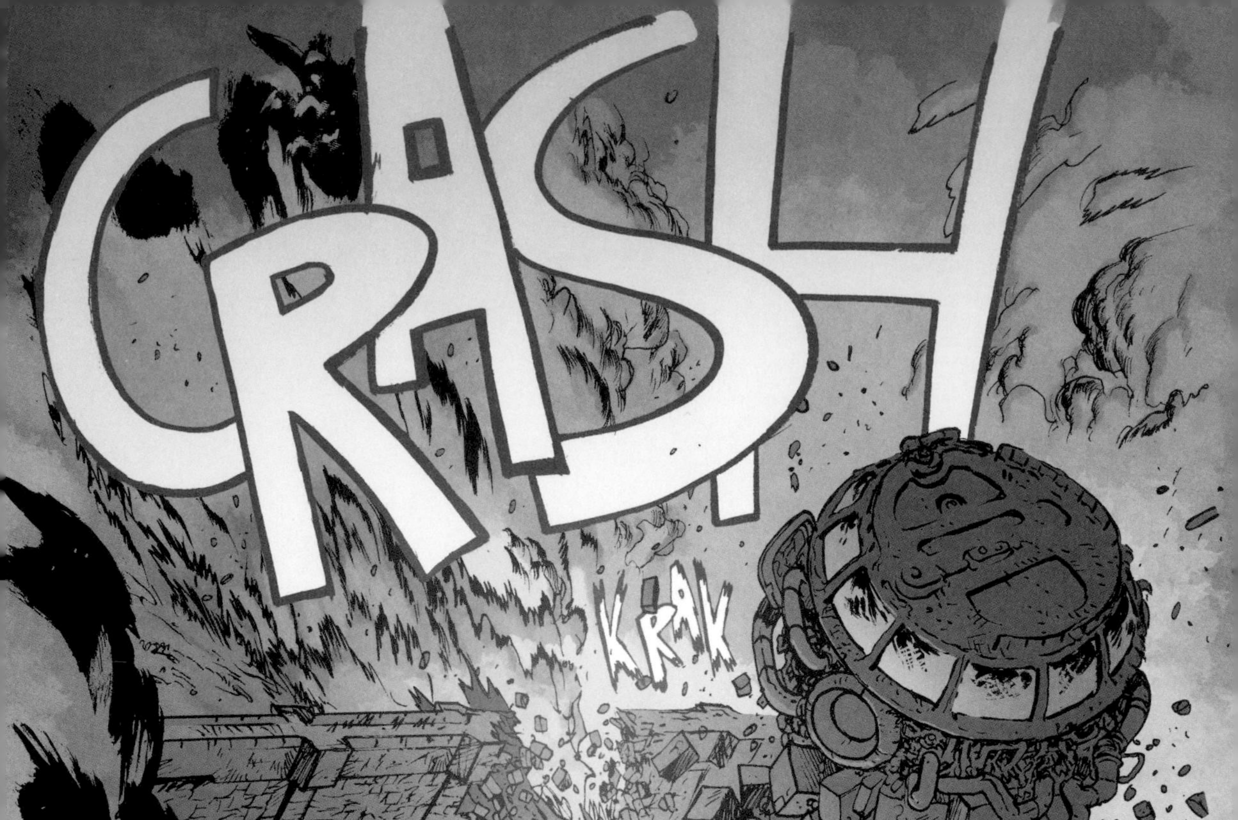
CRASH
KRAK

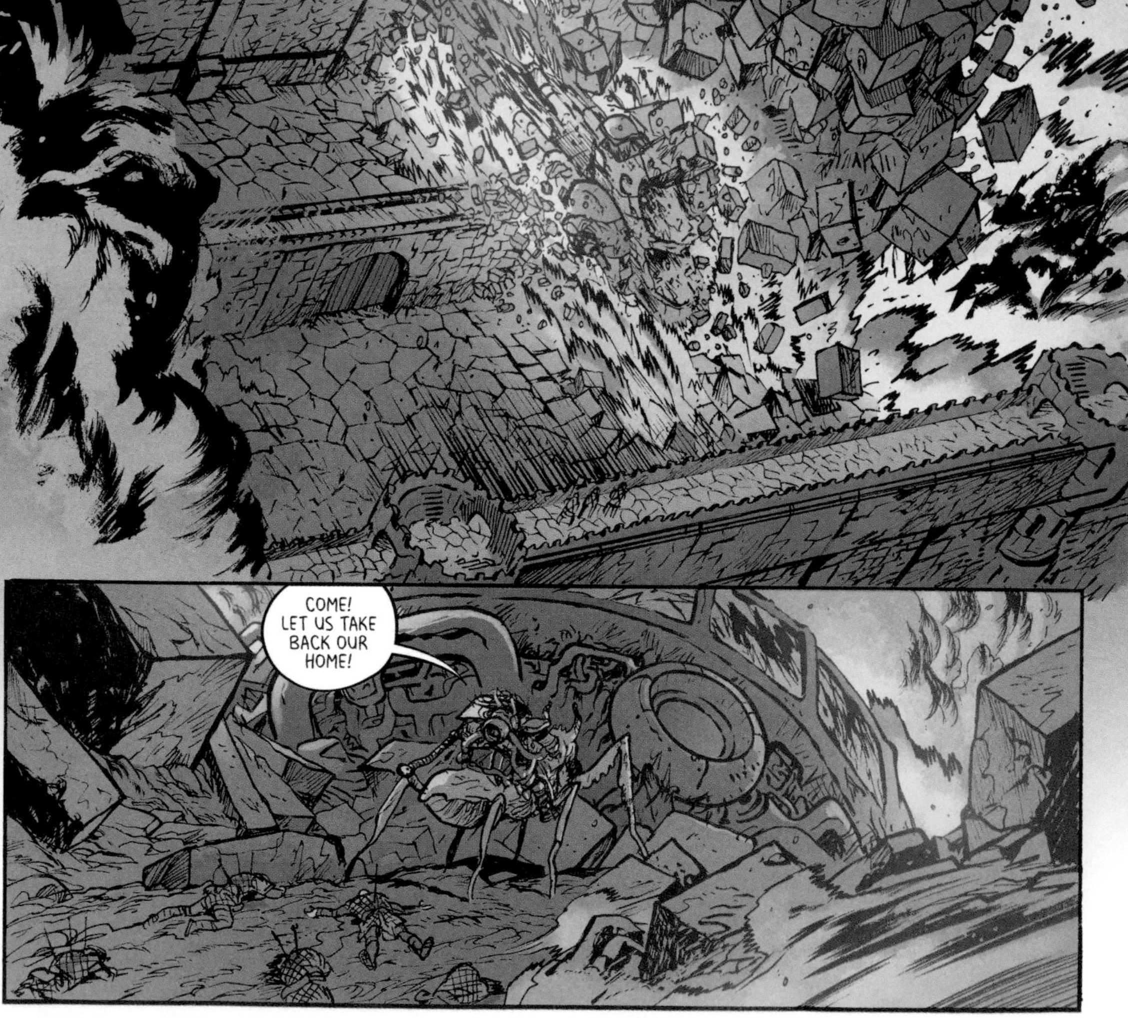
COME! LET US TAKE BACK OUR HOME!

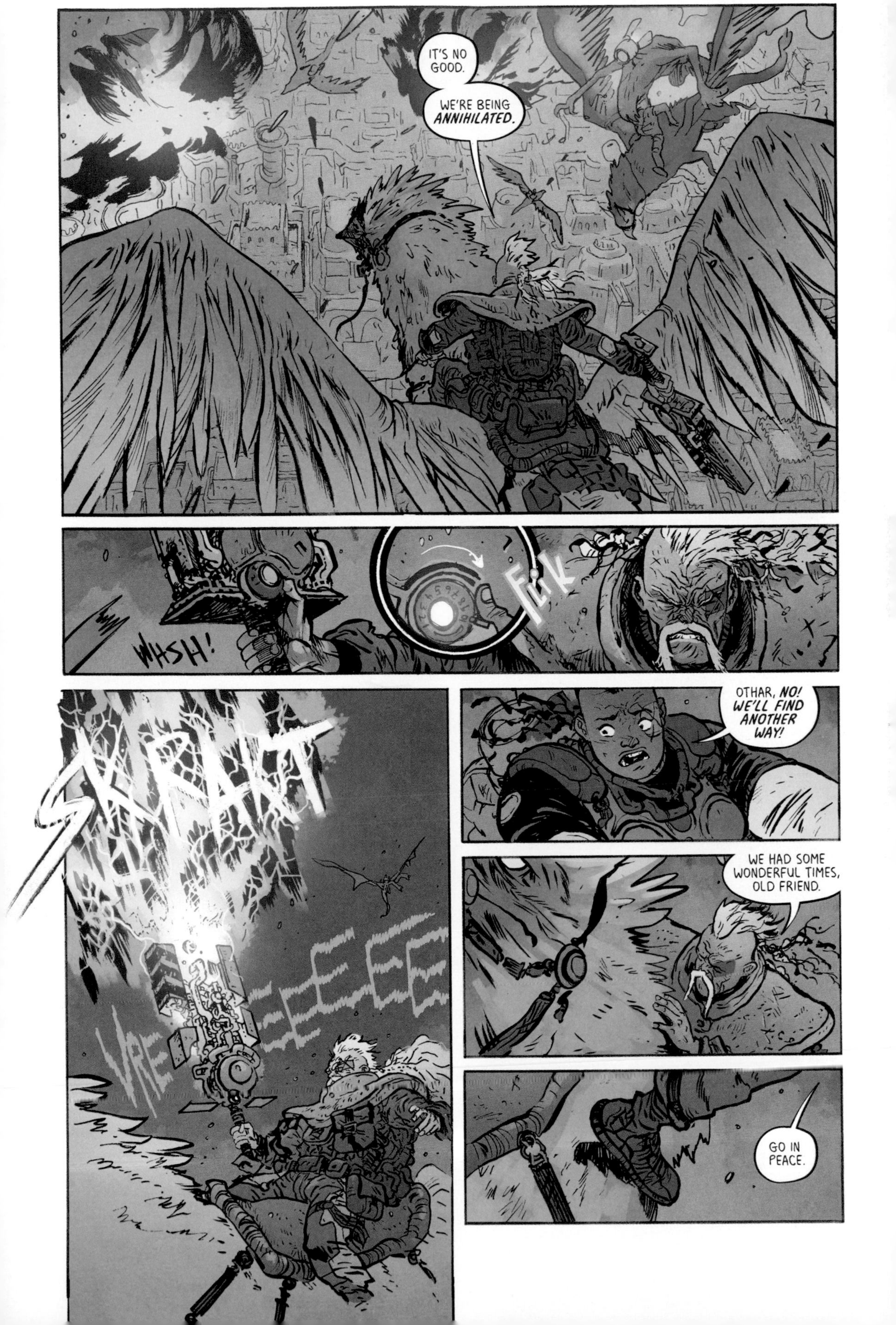

IT'S NO GOOD.
WE'RE BEING ANNIHILATED.
WHSH!
FLIK
SKRAKT
VREEEEEE
OTHAR, NO! WE'LL FIND ANOTHER WAY!
WE HAD SOME WONDERFUL TIMES, OLD FRIEND.
GO IN PEACE.

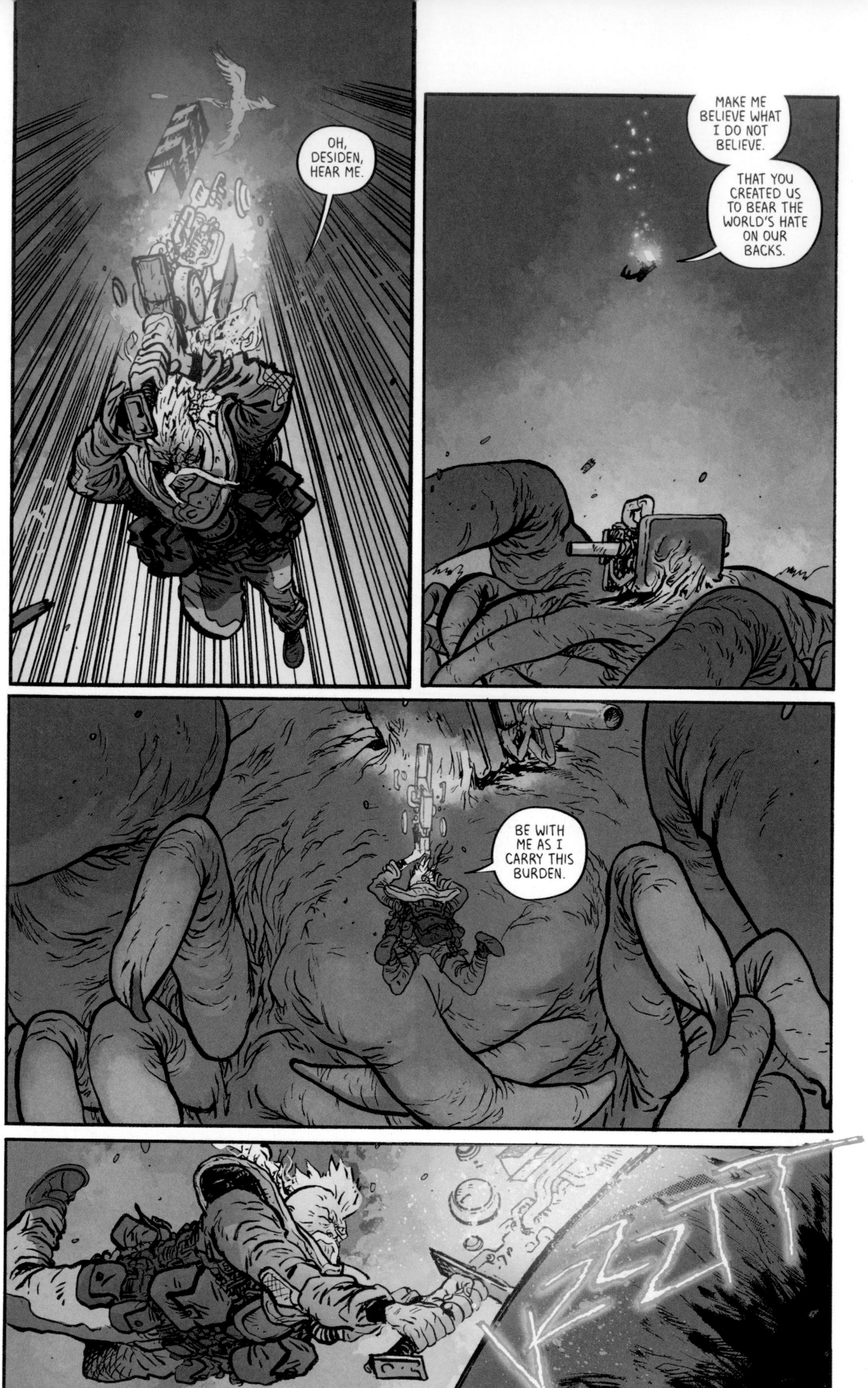
OH, DESIDEN, HEAR ME.
MAKE ME BELIEVE WHAT I DO NOT BELIEVE.
THAT YOU CREATED US TO BEAR THE WORLD'S HATE ON OUR BACKS.
BE WITH ME AS I CARRY THIS BURDEN.
KZZTT

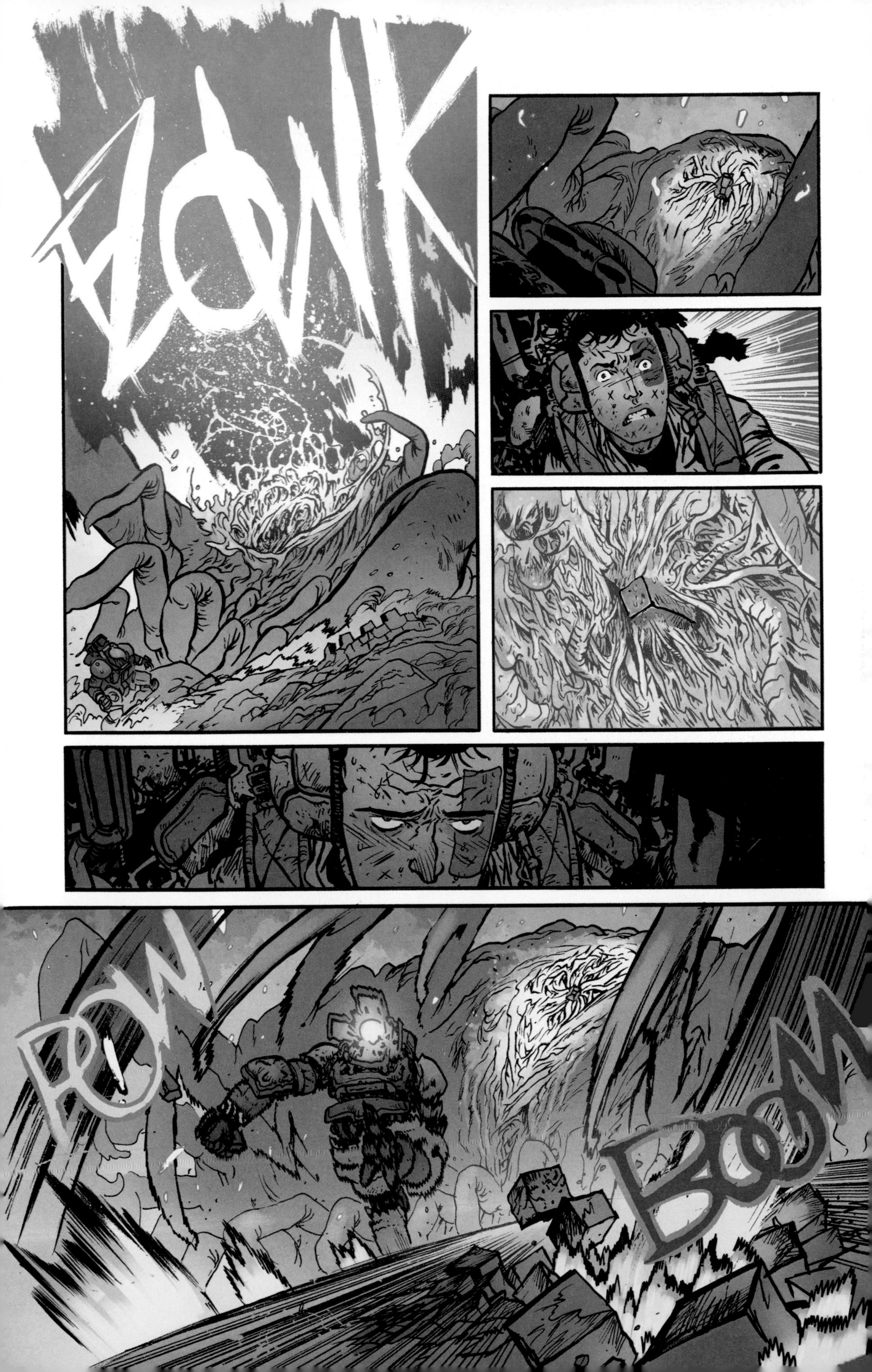
BONK
POW
BOOM

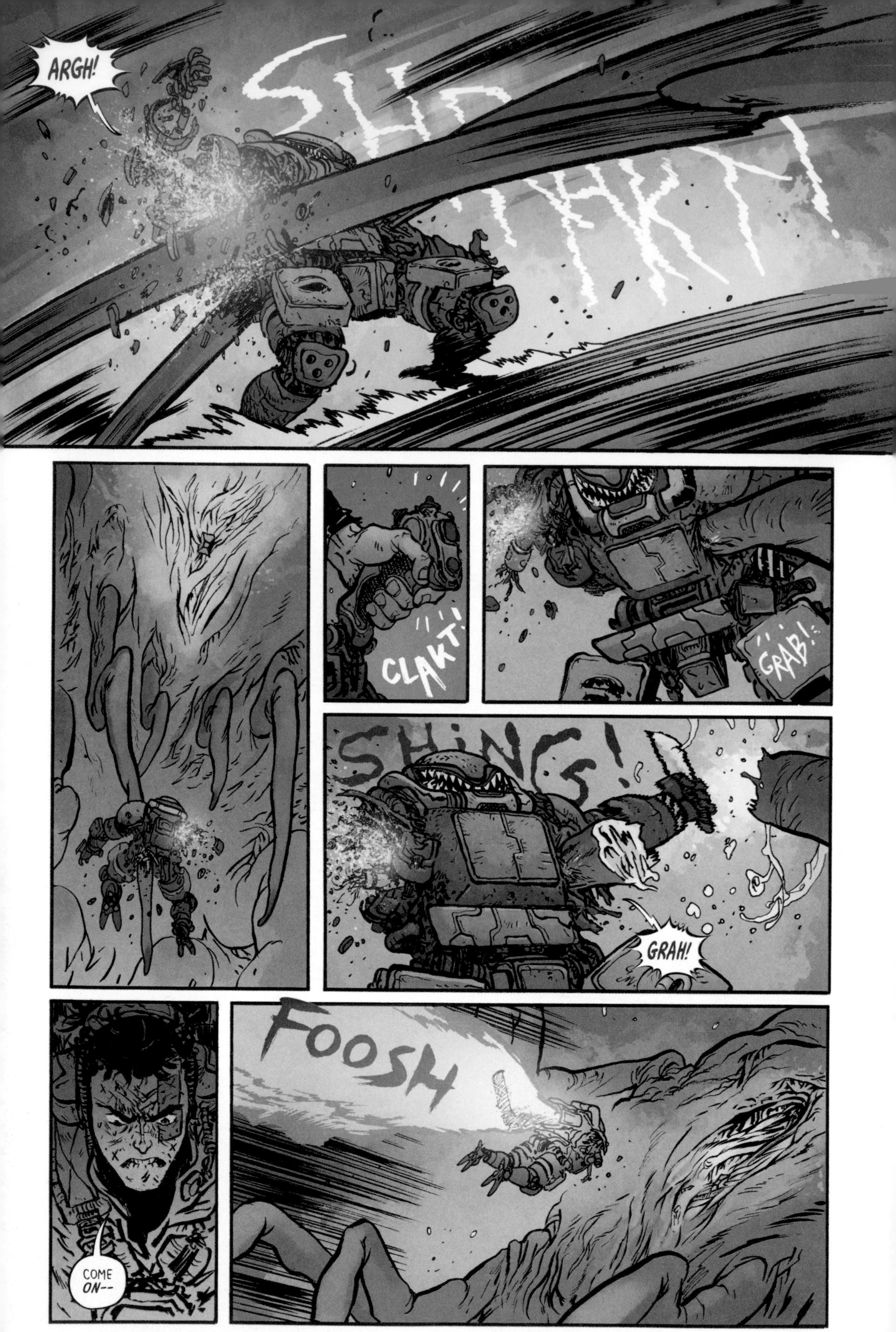
ARGH!
SHUNKT!
CLAKT!
GRAB!
SHING!
GRAH!
COME ON--
FOOSH

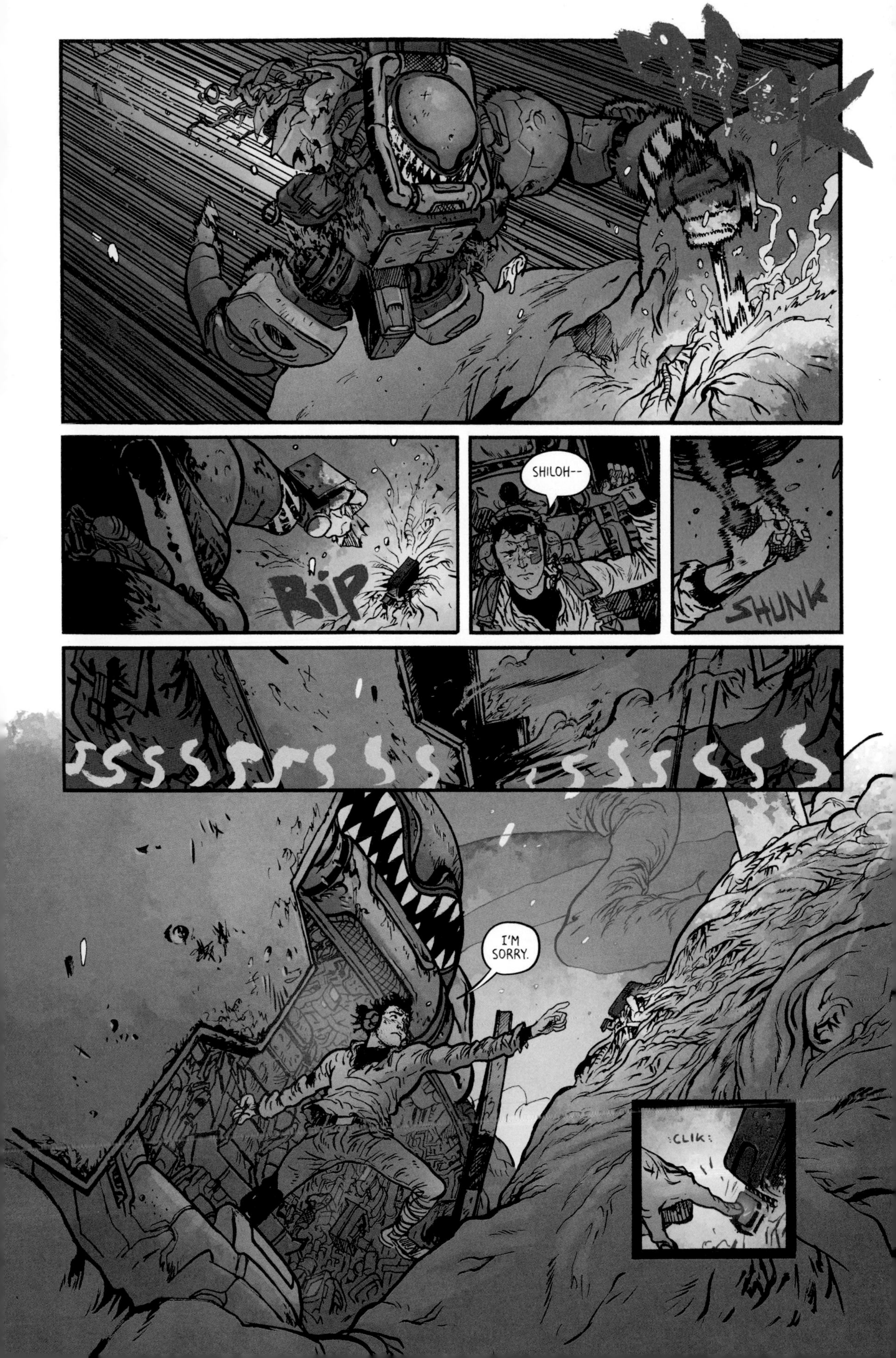
SHLOK
RIP
SHILOH--
SHUNK
SSSSSSSSSSSSSSSS
I'M SORRY.
CLIK

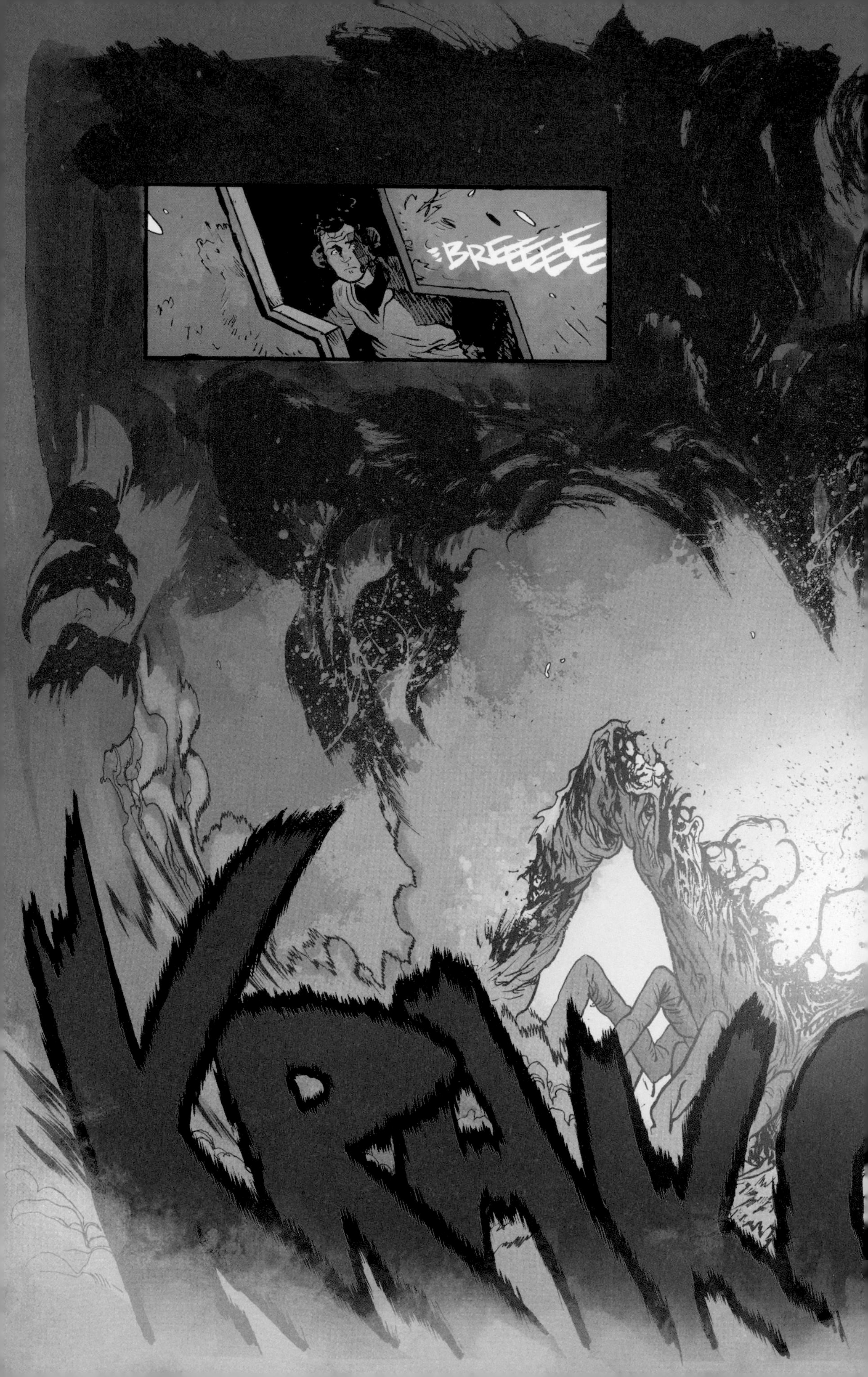
BREEEEEE

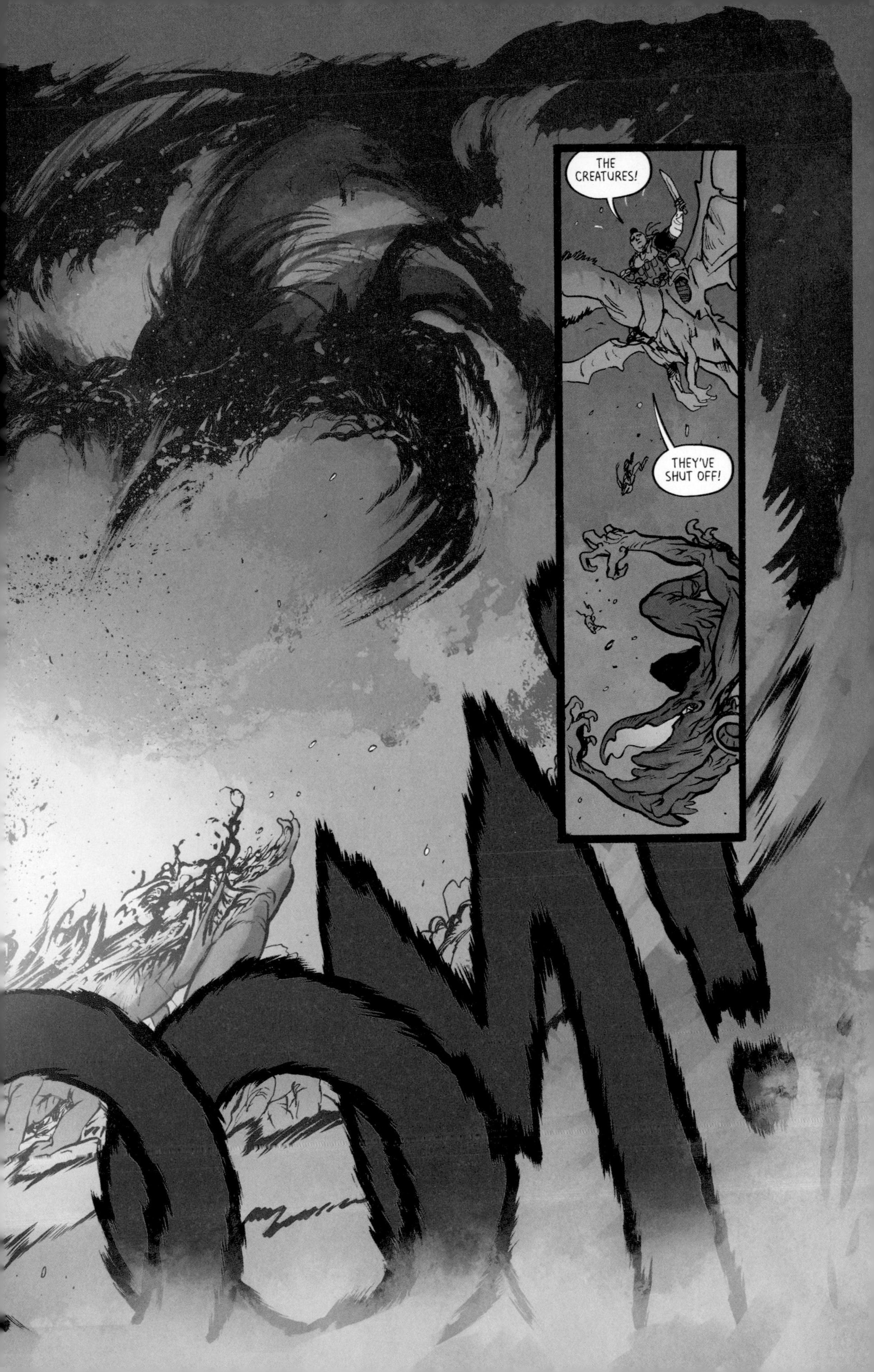
THE CREATURES!
THEY'VE SHUT OFF!

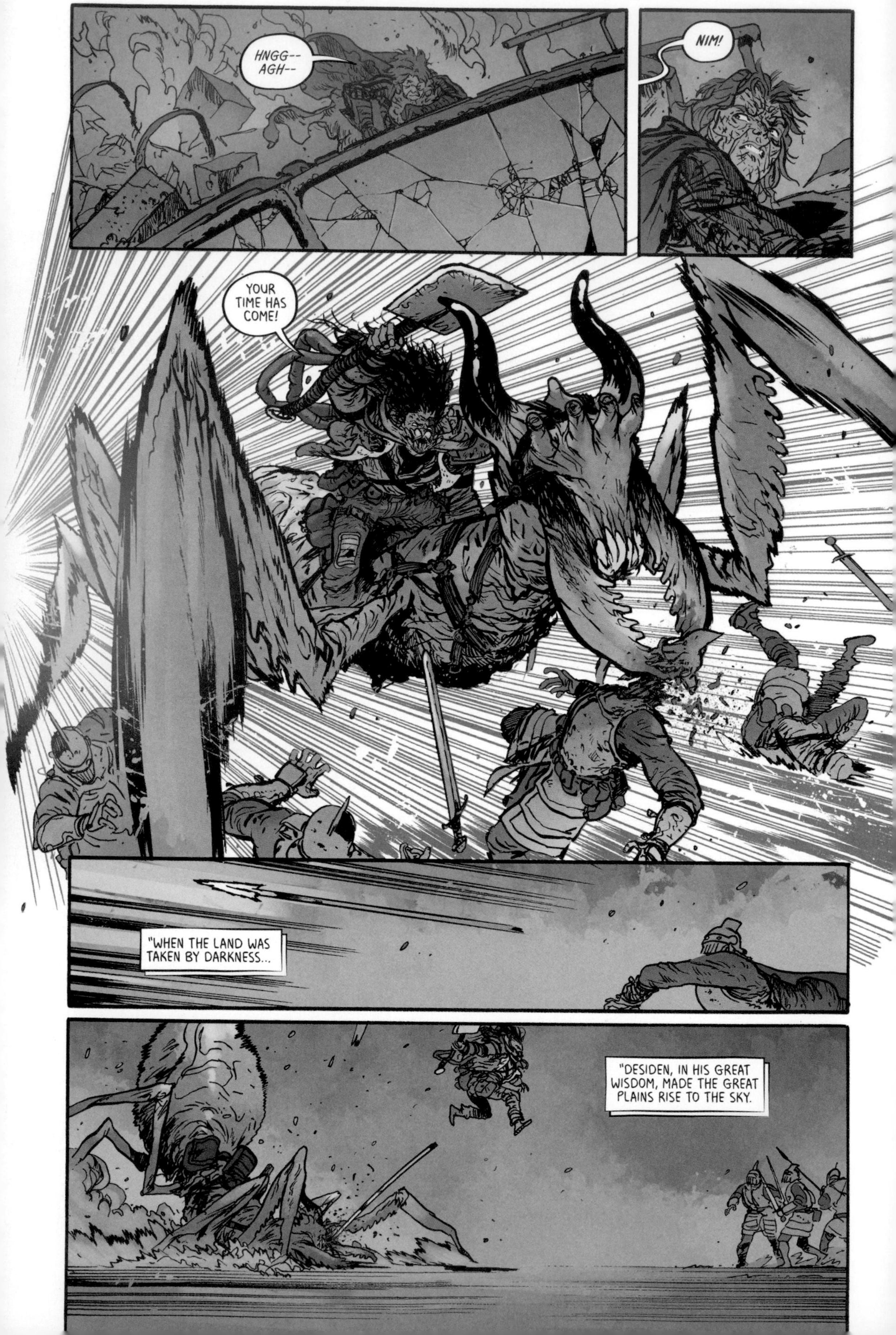
HNGG--
AGH--
NIM!
YOUR TIME HAS COME!
"WHEN THE LAND WAS TAKEN BY DARKNESS...
"DESIDEN, IN HIS GREAT WISDOM, MADE THE GREAT PLAINS RISE TO THE SKY.

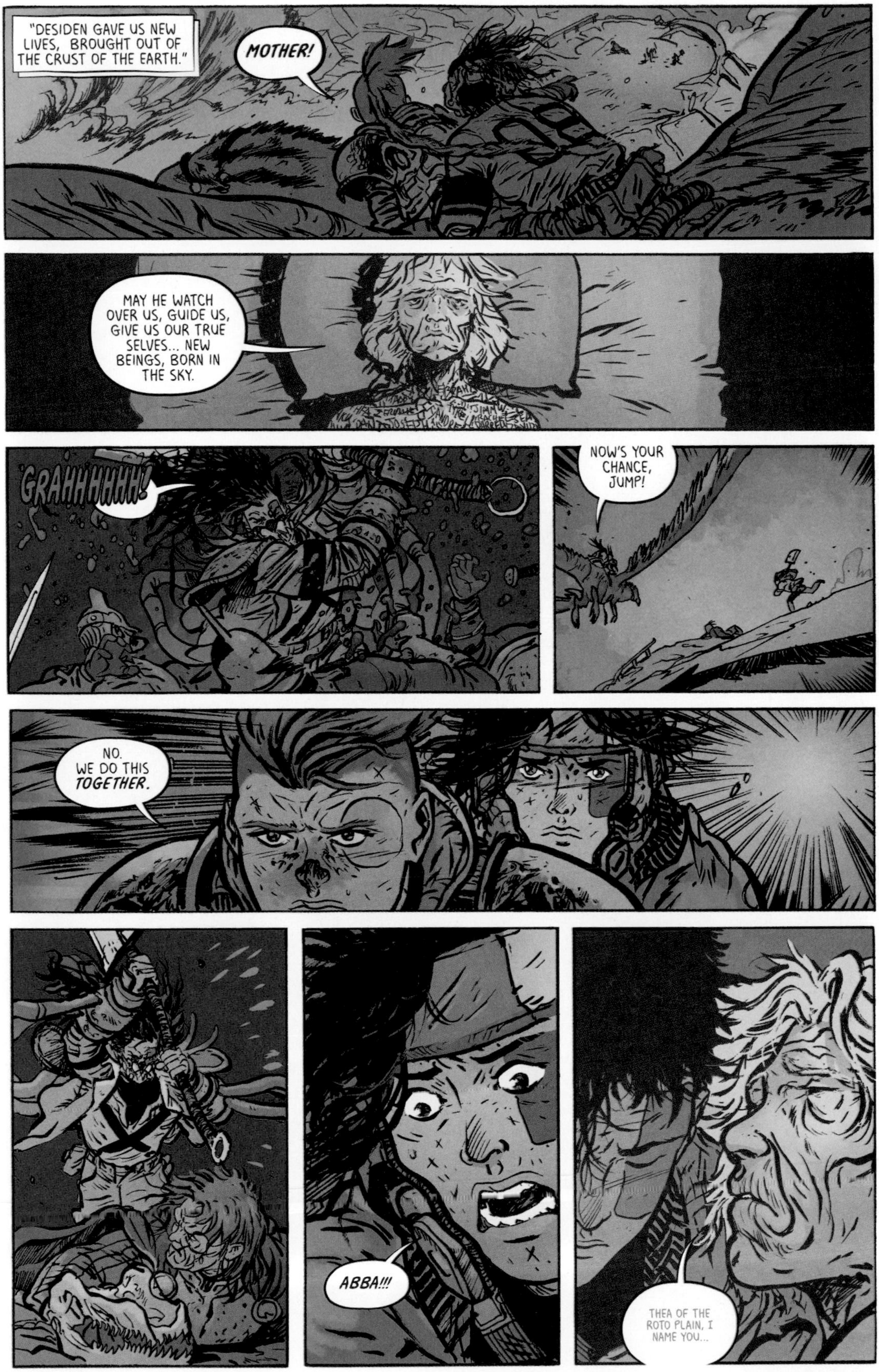
"DESIDEN GAVE US NEW LIVES, BROUGHT OUT OF THE CRUST OF THE EARTH."
MOTHER!
MAY HE WATCH OVER US, GUIDE US, GIVE US OUR TRUE SELVES... NEW BEINGS, BORN IN THE SKY.
GRAHHHHHH!
NOW'S YOUR CHANCE, JUMP!
NO. WE DO THIS TOGETHER.
ABBA!!!
THEA OF THE ROTO PLAIN, I NAME YOU...

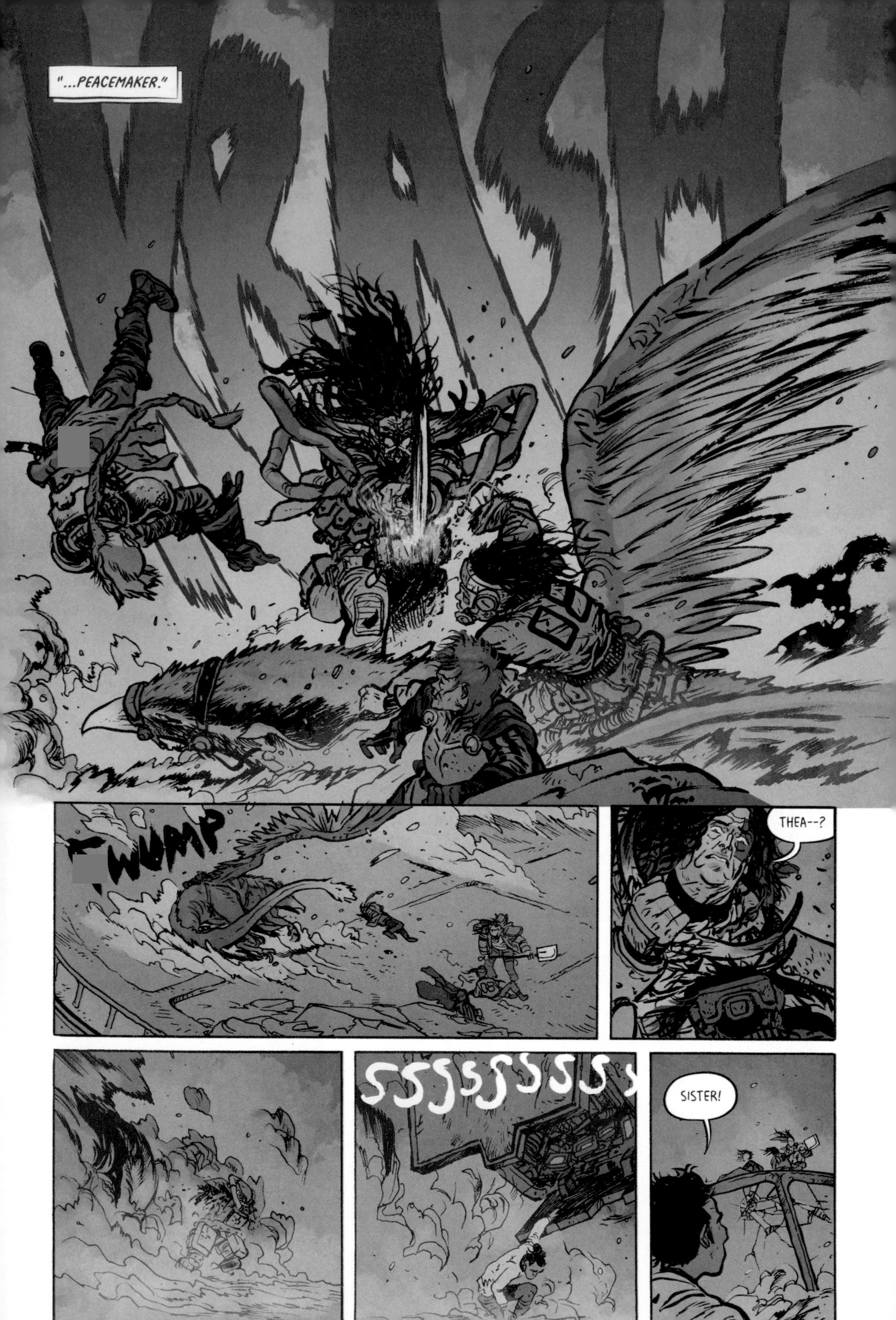
"...PEACEMAKER."
WUMP
THEA--?
SSSSSSSS
SISTER!

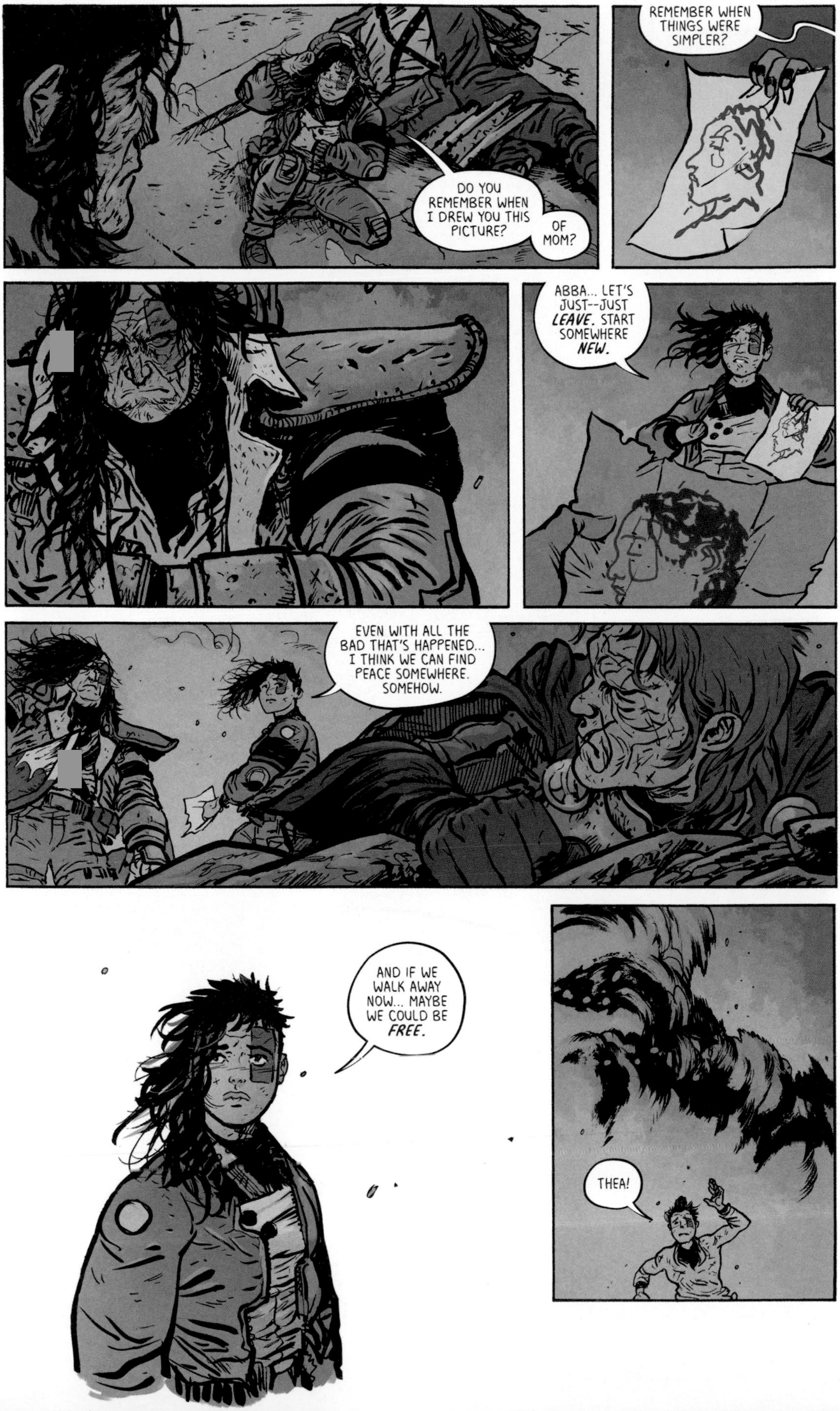
DO YOU REMEMBER WHEN I DREW YOU THIS PICTURE?
OF MOM?
REMEMBER WHEN THINGS WERE SIMPLER?
ABBA... LET'S JUST--JUST *LEAVE.* START SOMEWHERE *NEW.*
EVEN WITH ALL THE BAD THAT'S HAPPENED... I THINK WE CAN FIND PEACE SOMEWHERE. SOMEHOW.
AND IF WE WALK AWAY NOW... MAYBE WE COULD BE *FREE.*
THEA!

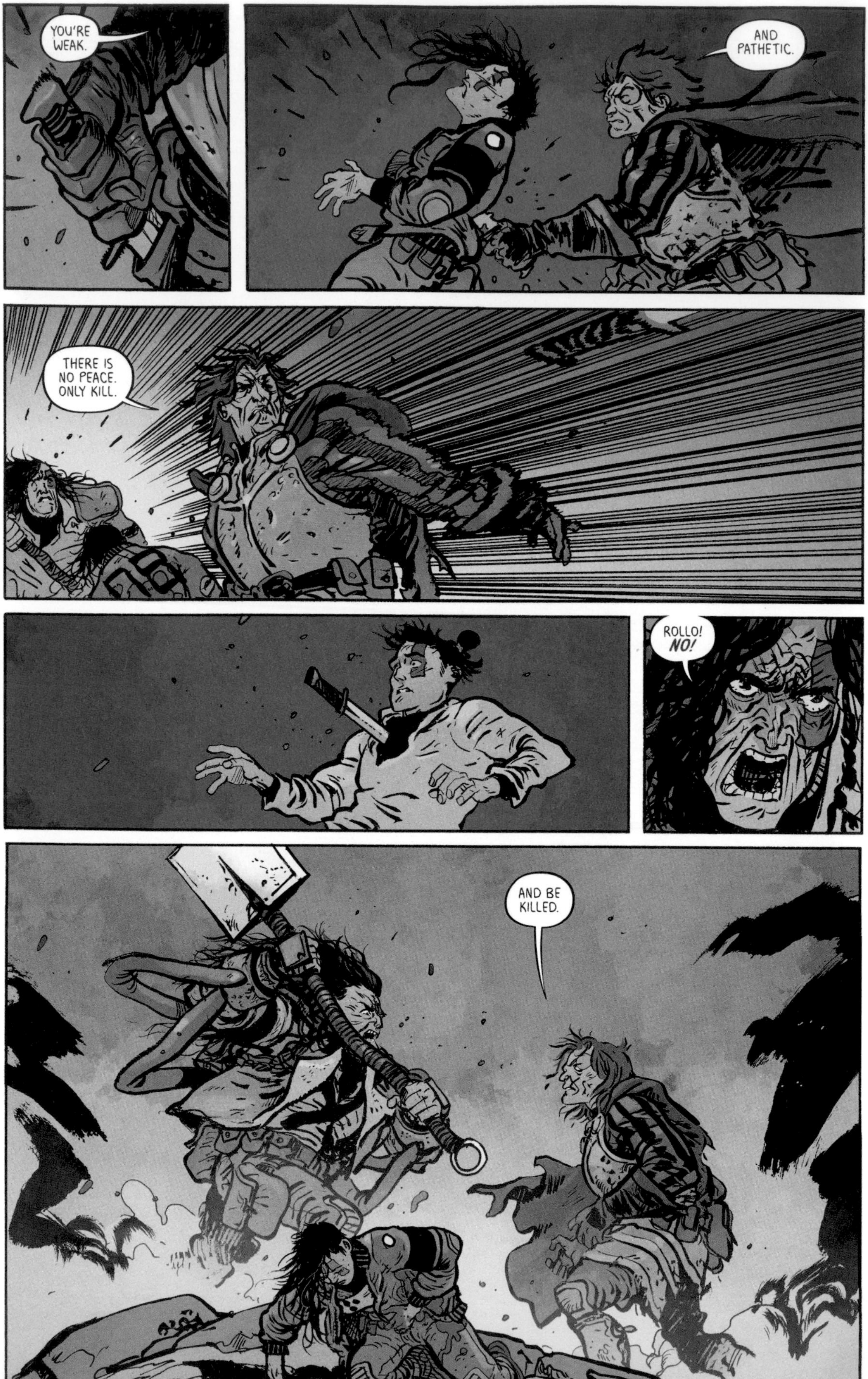
YOU'RE WEAK.
AND PATHETIC.
THERE IS NO PEACE. ONLY KILL.
ROLLO! NO!
AND BE KILLED.

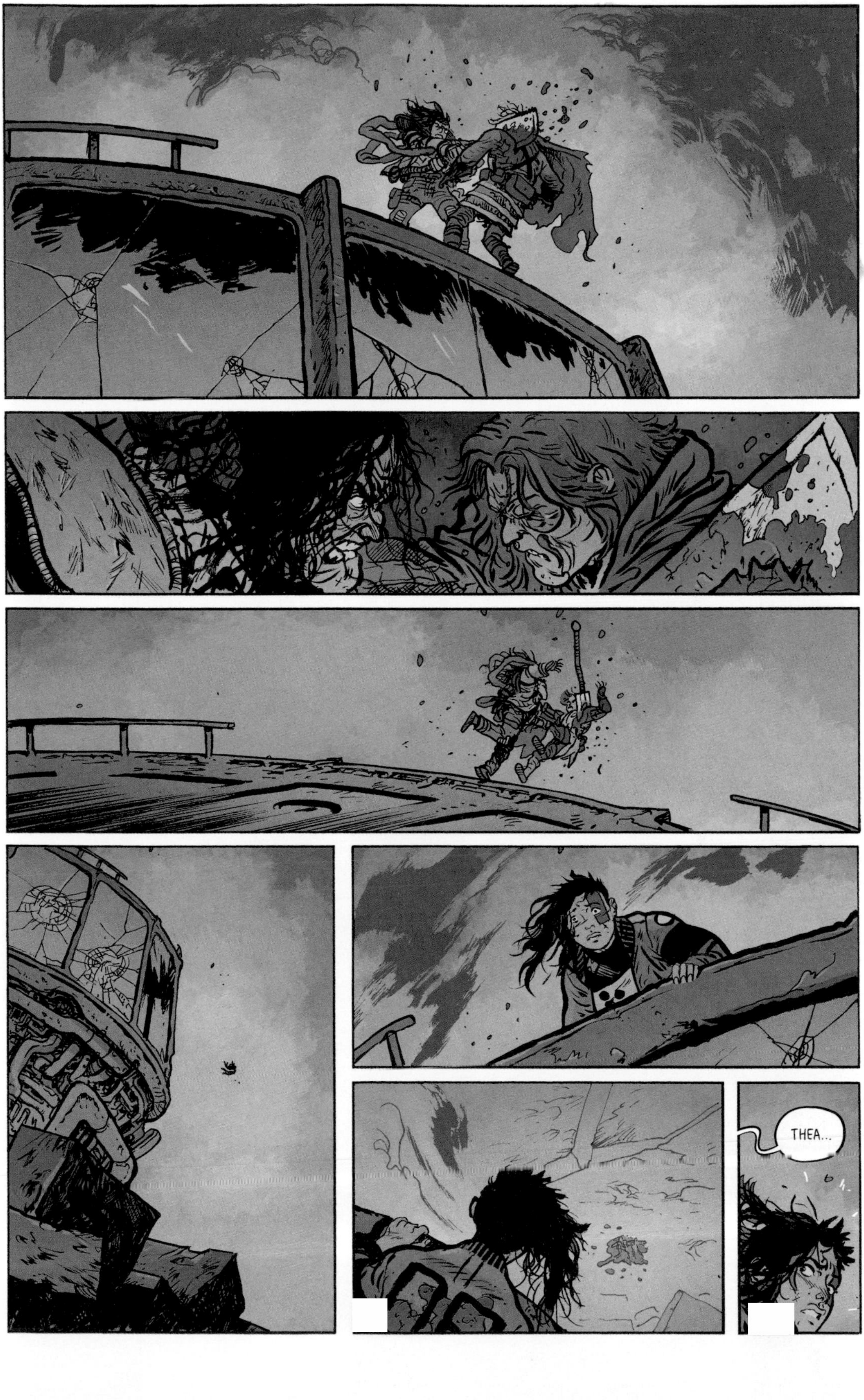
THEA...

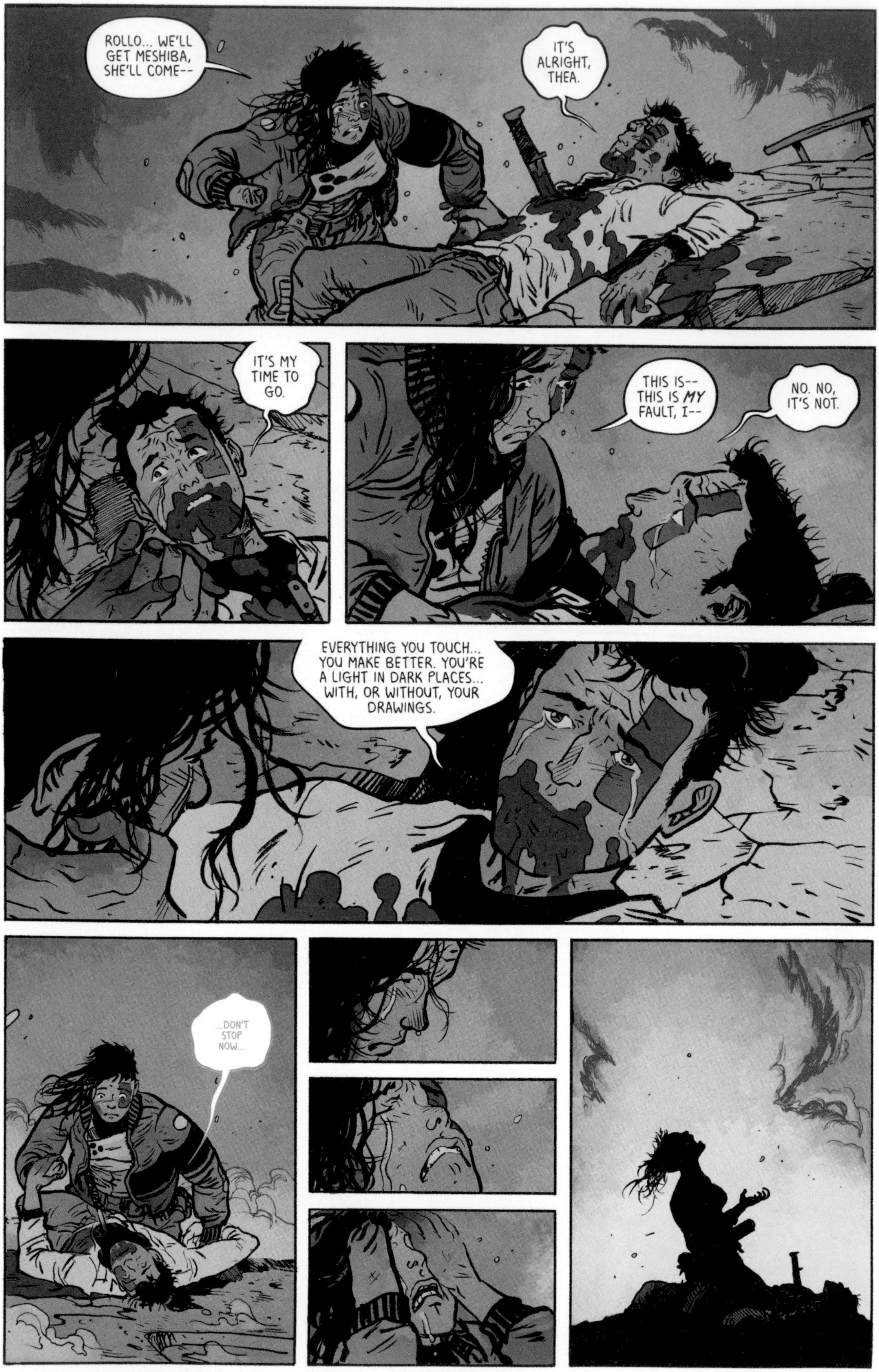
ROLLO... WE'LL GET MESHIBA, SHE'LL COME--
IT'S ALRIGHT, THEA.
IT'S MY TIME TO GO.
THIS IS-- THIS IS *MY* FAULT, I--
NO. NO, IT'S NOT.
EVERYTHING YOU TOUCH... YOU MAKE BETTER. YOU'RE A LIGHT IN DARK PLACES... WITH, OR WITHOUT, YOUR DRAWINGS.
...DON'T STOP NOW...

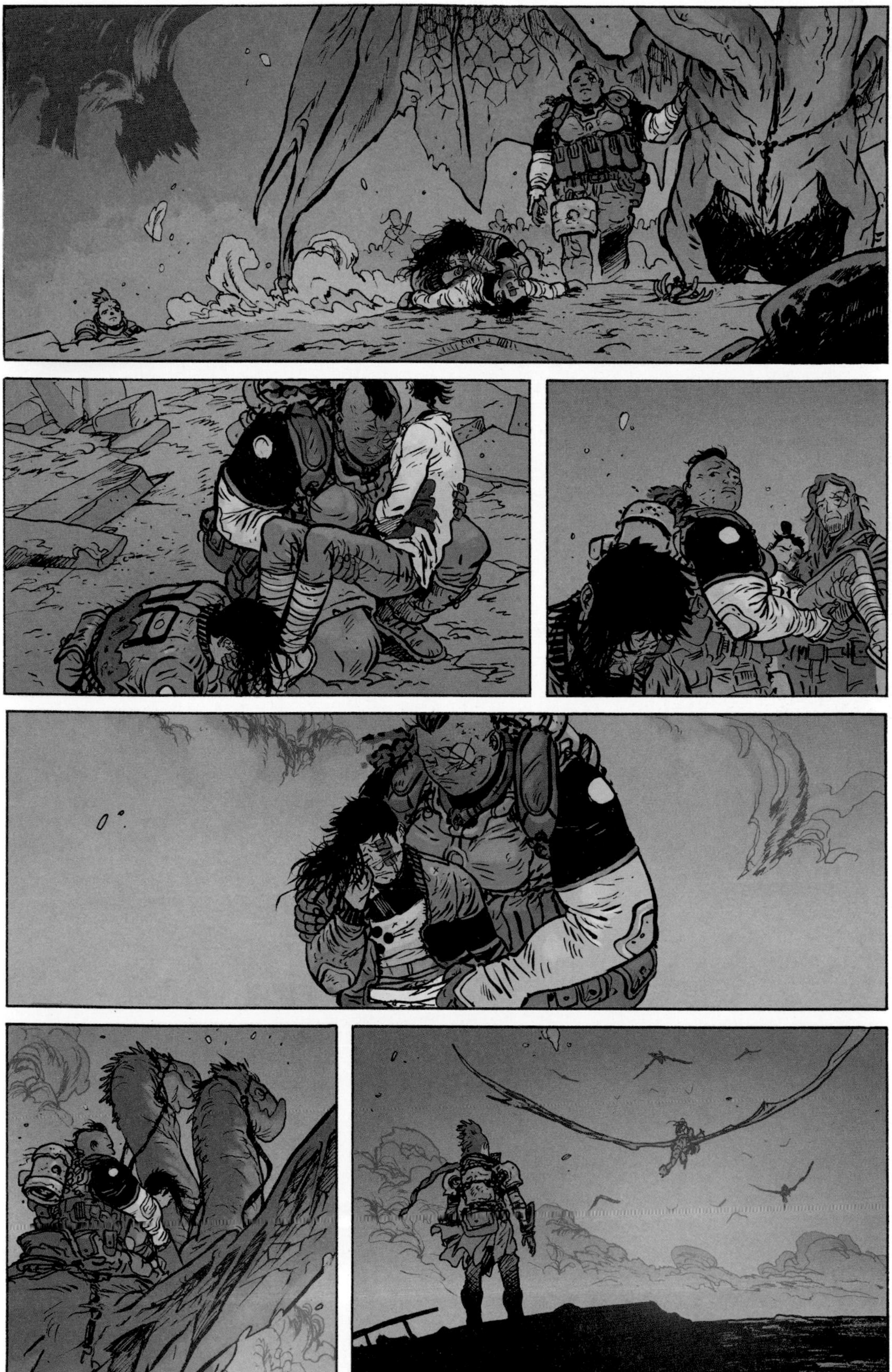

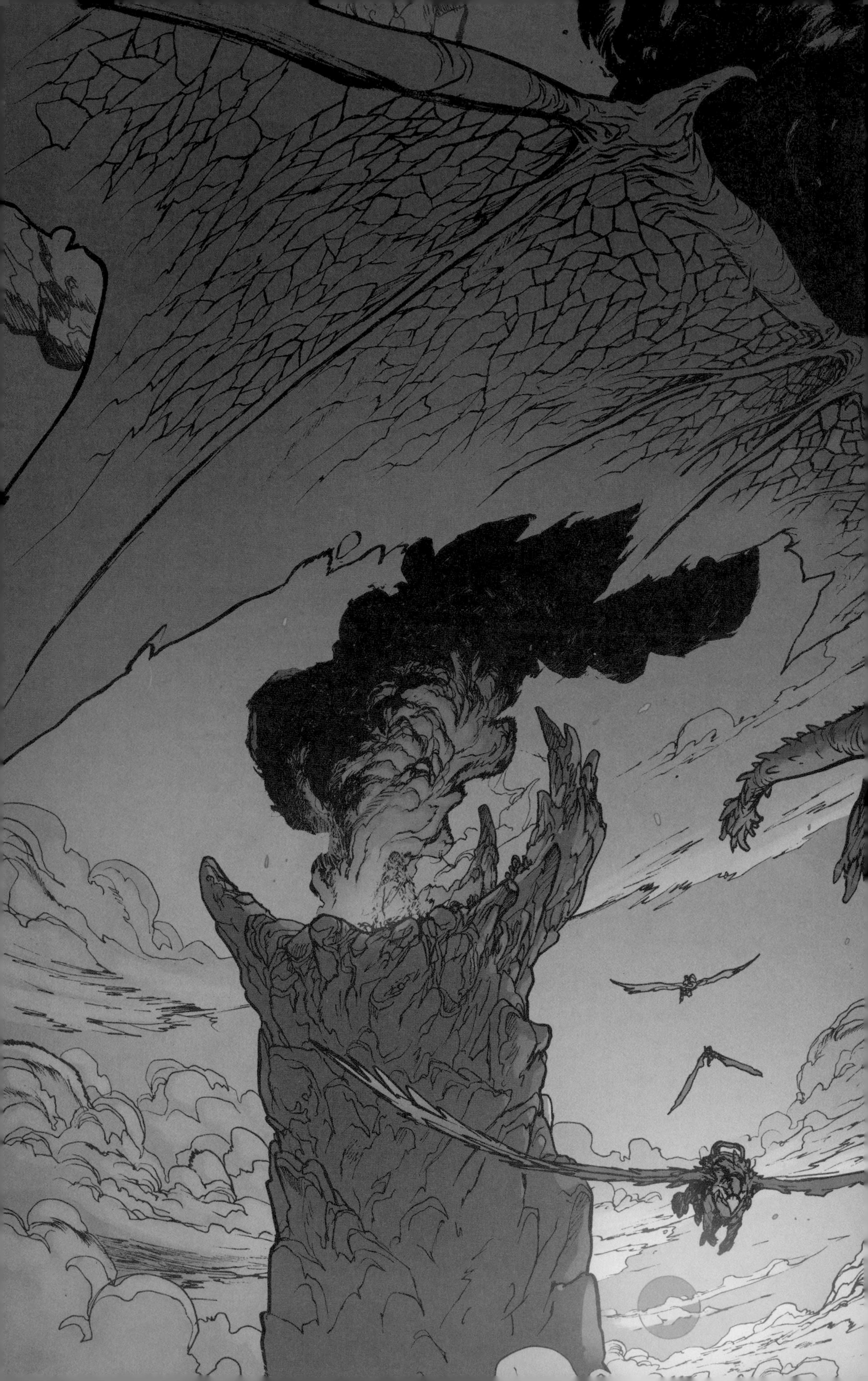

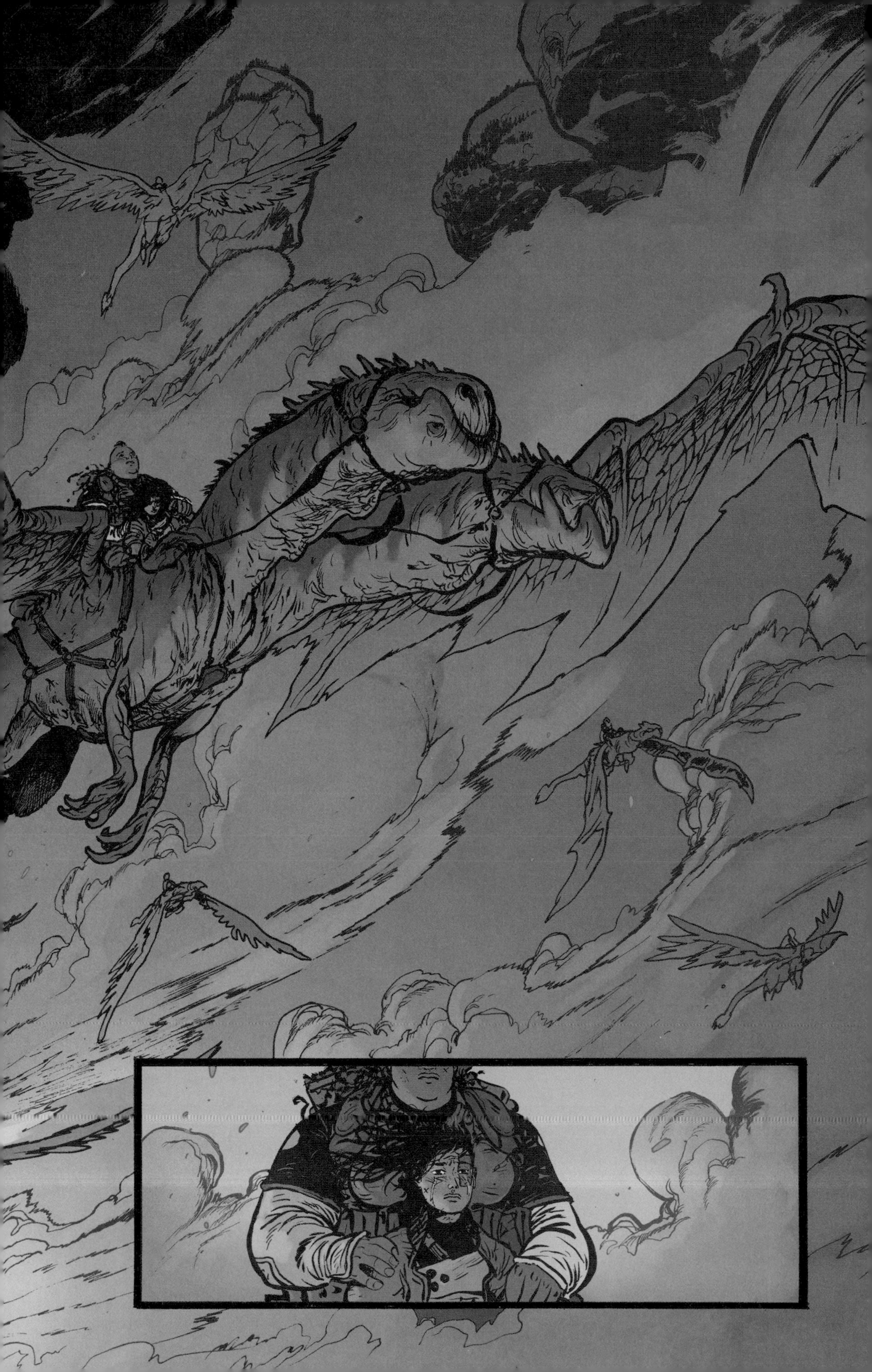

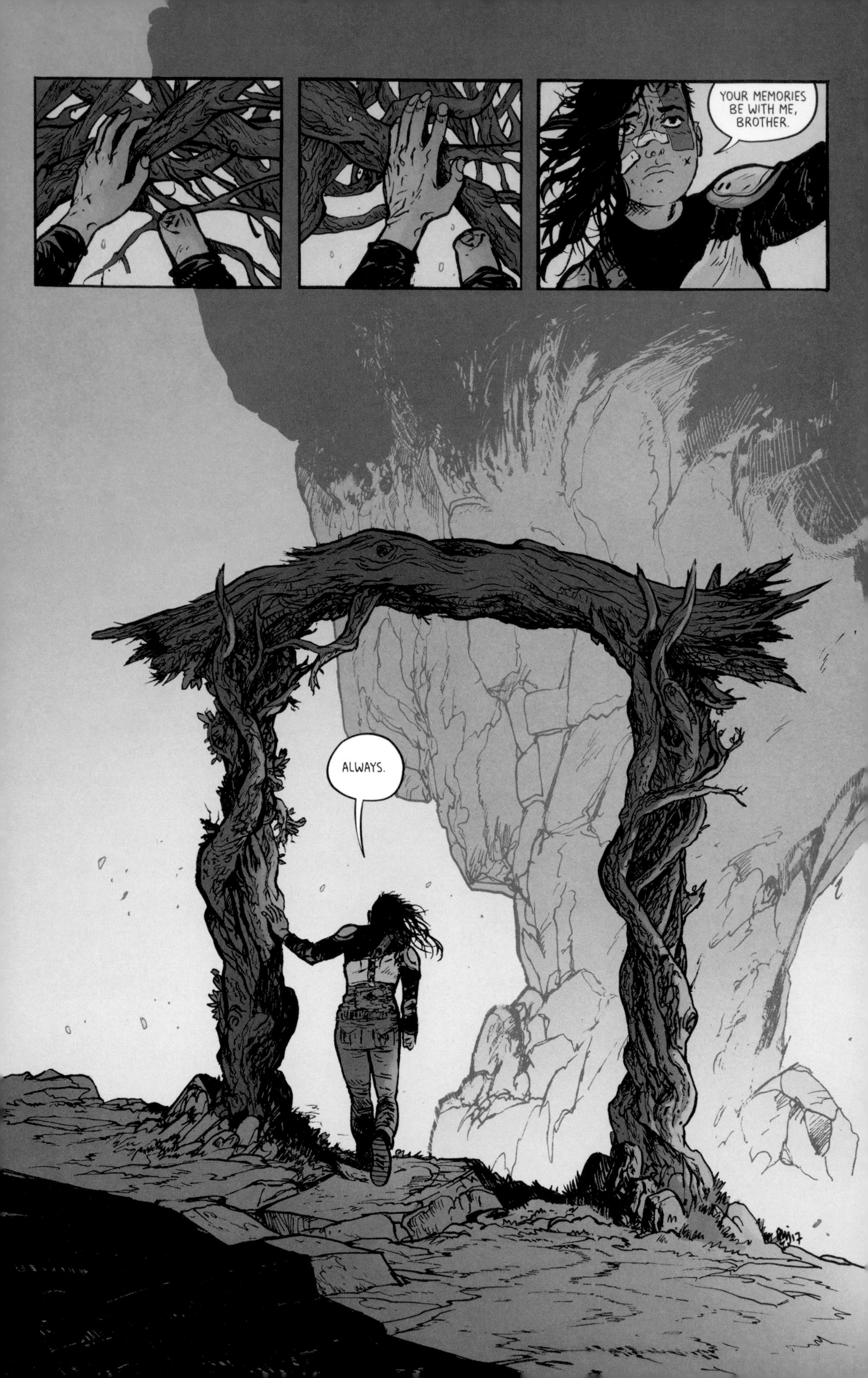
YOUR MEMORIES BE WITH ME, BROTHER.
ALWAYS.

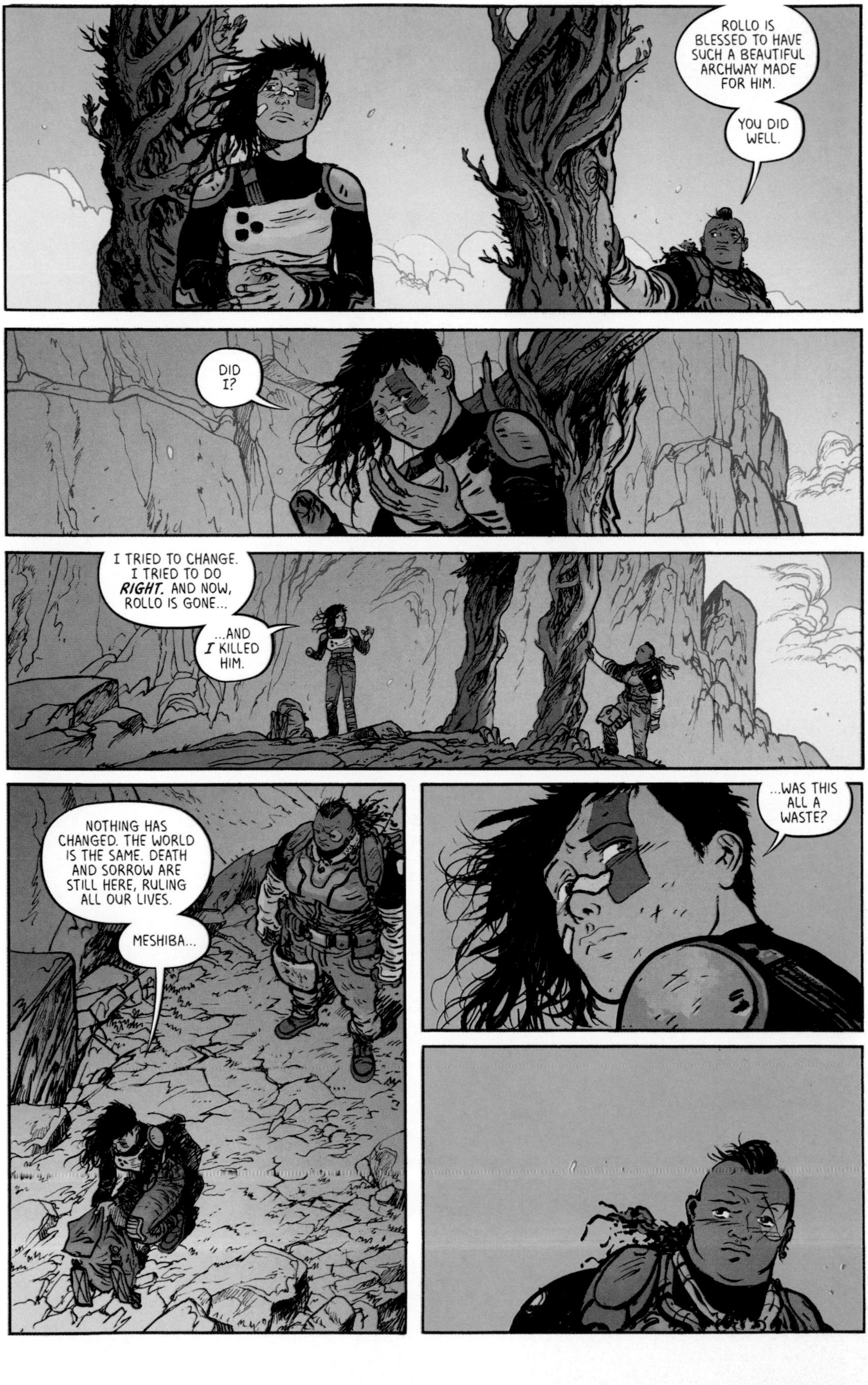
ROLLO IS BLESSED TO HAVE SUCH A BEAUTIFUL ARCHWAY MADE FOR HIM.
YOU DID WELL.
DID I?
I TRIED TO CHANGE. I TRIED TO DO *RIGHT.* AND NOW, ROLLO IS GONE...
...AND *I* KILLED HIM.
NOTHING HAS CHANGED. THE WORLD IS THE SAME. DEATH AND SORROW ARE STILL HERE, RULING ALL OUR LIVES.
MESHIBA...
...WAS THIS ALL A WASTE?

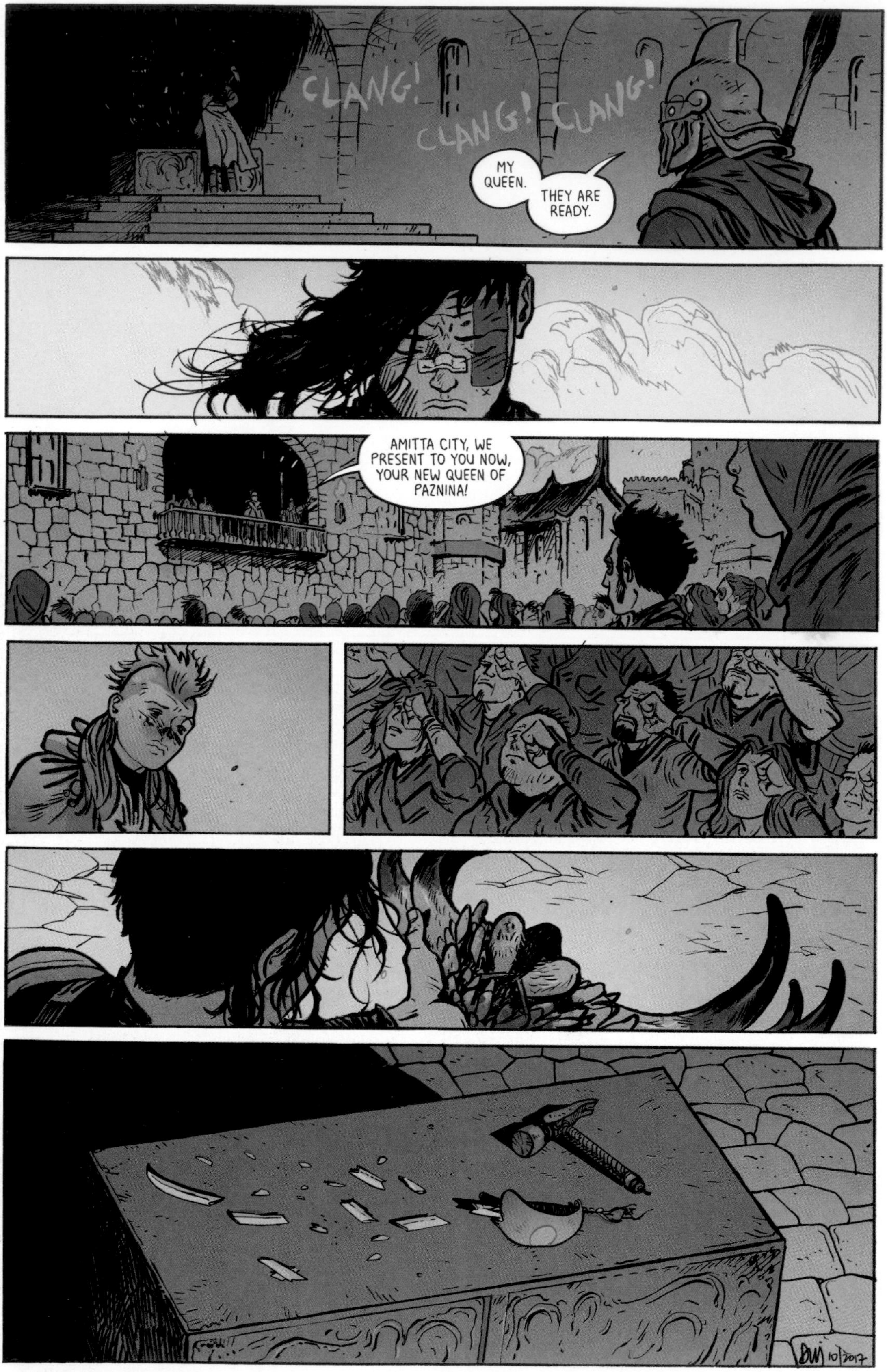
CLANG! CLANG! CLANG!
MY QUEEN.
THEY ARE READY.
AMITTA CITY, WE PRESENT TO YOU NOW, YOUR NEW QUEEN OF PAZNINA!
DM 10/2017

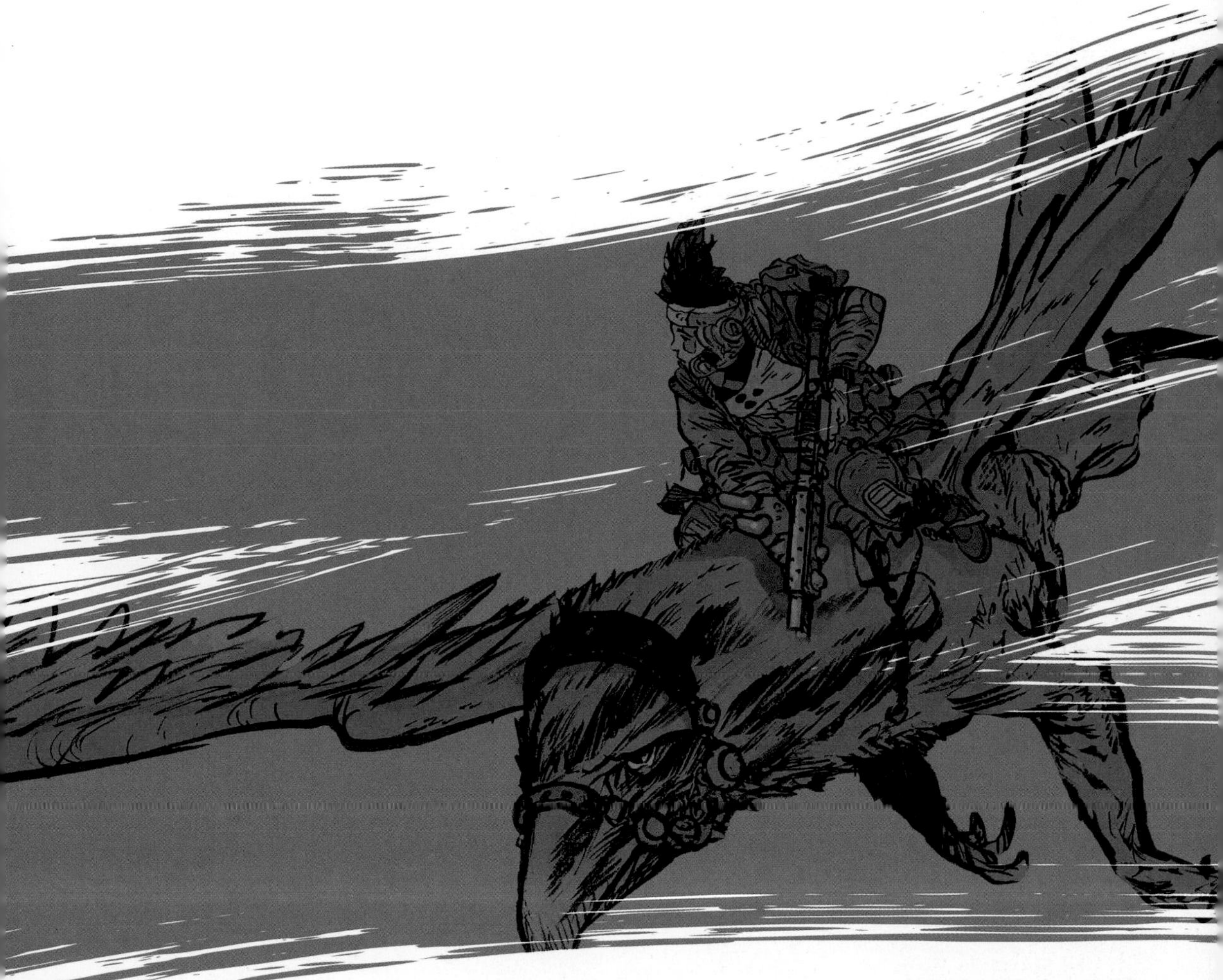

THE END

For more tales from ROBERT KIRKMAN and SKYBOUND

Sean Mackiewicz
Niko Walter
Mat Lopes
Gasolina
VOLUME 1: BIENVENIDO

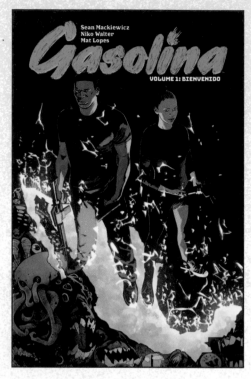

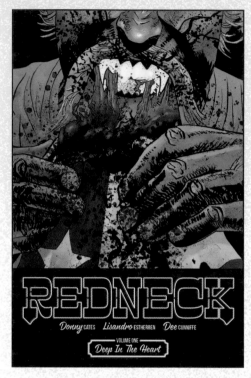

VOL. 1: BIENVENIDO TP
ISBN: 978-1-5343-0506-9
$16.99

REDNECK
Donny CATES Lisandro ESTHERREN Dee CUNNIFFE
VOLUME ONE
Deep In The Heart

VOL. 1: DEEP IN THE HEART TP
ISBN: 978-1-5343-0331-7
$16.99

BIRTHRIGHT
FATHERHOOD

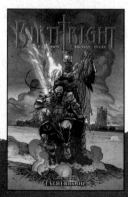

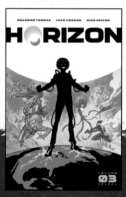

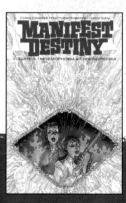

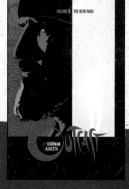

VOL. 1: HOMECOMING TP
ISBN: 978-1-63215-231-2
$9.99

VOL. 2: CALL TO ADVENTURE TP
ISBN: 978-1-63215-446-0
$12.99

VOL. 3: ALLIES AND ENEMIES TP
ISBN: 978-1-63215-683-9
$12.99

VOL. 4: FAMILY HISTORY TP
ISBN: 978-1-63215-871-0
$12.99

VOL. 5: BELLY OF THE BEAST TP
ISBN: 978-1-53430-218-1
$12.99

VOL. 6: FATHERHOOD TP
ISBN: 978-1-53430-498-7
$14.99

BRANDON THOMAS JUAN GEDEON MIKE SPICER
HORIZON
VOLUME
03
REVEAL

VOL. 1: REPRISAL TP
ISBN: 978-1-5343-0047-7
$9.99

VOL. 2: REMNANT TP
ISBN: 978-1-5343-0227-3
$12.99

VOL. 3: REVEAL TP
ISBN: 978-1-5343-0487-1
$16.99

CHRIS DINGESS • MATTHEW ROBERTS • OWEN GIENI
MANIFEST DESTINY
VOLUME 5 • MNEMOPHOBIA & CHRONOPHOBIA

VOL. 1: FLORA & FAUNA TP
ISBN: 978-1-60706-982-9
$9.99

VOL. 2: AMPHIBIA & INSECTA TP
ISBN: 978-1-63215-052-3
$14.99

VOL. 3: CHIROPTERA & CARNIFORMAVES TP
ISBN: 978-1-63215-397-5
$14.99

VOL. 4: SASQUATCH TP
ISBN: 978-1-63215-890-1
$14.99

VOL. 5: MNEMOPHOBIA & CHRONOPHOBIA TP
ISBN: 978-1-5343-0230-3
$16.99

VOLUME 5 THE NEW PATH
BY KIRKMAN AZACETA
OUTCAST

VOL. 1: A DARKNESS SURROUNDS HIM TP
ISBN: 978-1-63215-053-0
$9.99

VOL. 2: A VAST AND UNENDING RUIN TP
ISBN: 978-1-63215-448-4
$14.99

VOL. 3: THIS LITTLE LIGHT TP
ISBN: 978-1-63215-693-8
$14.99

VOL. 4: UNDER DEVIL'S WING TP
ISBN: 978-1-5343-0050-7
$14.99

VOL. 5: THE NEW PATH TP
ISBN: 978-1-5343-0249-5
$16.99